OWL

and the

CITY OF ANGELS

Kristi Charish

GALLERY BOOKS

New York   London   Toronto   Sydney   New Delhi

G

Gallery Books
An Imprint of Simon & Schuster, Inc.
1230 Avenue of the Americas
New York, NY 10020
www.SimonandSchuster.com

First Gallery Books trade paperback edition March 2016

GALLERY BOOKS and colophon are registered trademarks of Simon & Schuster, Inc.

The Simon & Schuster Speakers Bureau can bring authors to your live event. For more information or to book an event contact the Simon & Schuster Speakers Bureau at 1-866-248-3049 or visit our website at www.simonspeakers.com.

Interior design by Lewelin Polanco

Library and Archives Canada Cataloguing-in-Publication

Charish, Kristi, author
Owl and the City of Angels / Kristi Charish.
Issued in print and electronic formats.
I. Title.

PS8605.H3686O95 2016   C813'.6   C2015-905962-3
C2015-905963-1

ISBN 978-1-5011-2210-1
ISBN 978-1-4767-7988-1 (ebook)

For my cat, Captain Flash.
May you never run out of socks to terrorize.

OWL

and the
CITY OF ANGELS

1

Tomb Raiding Isn't All It's Cracked Up to Be

Noon, about two stories underneath Alexandria

I brushed another chunk of two-thousand-year-old dirt off the horse femur. It was lying in a shallow alcove in the Hall of Caracalla, part of the catacombs that ran underneath Alexandria. I readjusted my baseball cap and cleared the sweat off my forehead before glancing up at the man crouched on the other side of the mummified horse remains. Mike, the dig supervising postdoc I'd been saddled with, was a couple years older than me and suffered the poor posture and starters' beer gut rampant amongst grad students everywhere. Especially the ones who spend more time than wise hunched over a computer and/or things buried in the ground.

Annnddd Mike was still engrossed with the front end of the skeleton . . .

I swore silently. Great. Just fantastic. Out of all the dig sites on my list, leave it to me to pick the one in the middle of a heat wave with stifling stale air and the overattentive postdoc. I'd been stuck in Egypt for three days now on a job that should have taken hours. If Mike would just leave me alone for fifteen minutes even, I could find my way into the lower levels, grab my Medusa head, and get the hell out before anyone double-checked my paperwork.

"Shit." I dropped my brush and braced against the wall as the entire burial chamber shook; the catacombs ran under a main artery of the city, and every time a heavier-than-average truck passed overhead, the whole thing trembled. On the bright side, the truck meant it had to almost be lunchtime. Maybe I could convince Mike to take a long break . . .

Artifact or not, three days in this tomb with Mike—the one postdoc in the entire IAA who doesn't shunt his work on to grad students—and I was well past my breaking point . . .

Come on, Owl, keep in character: you're Serena, a young, impressionable grad student trying to wrangle a decent dig for her PhD, not an antiquities thief with personal space issues . . .

Mike shifted, leaning further over the horse's skeleton.

Curious, I glanced up and caught where he was looking—not at the horse skull.

Oh screw staying in character. Captain would be getting restless, and this job was taking too long anyways.

"I swear to God, you stare down my shirt one more time, I'm going to break your nose with my pickax," I said.

Mike sat up and feigned shock—or maybe it was shock at getting caught. "What? I swear, I wasn't—"

I glared. "Mike, I'm tired. My sinuses are filled with enough dust to last a week, and the only thing I want right now is a cold beer, which is now impossible because the beer fridge broke yesterday—meaning I'm stuck with warm beer, only half an excavated horse, and you staring down my shirt." I derived some satisfaction as the shock on his face faded to a resigned white pallor when he realized I wasn't buying his protest.

"I refuse to take my frustration out on the skeleton," I continued. "The horse can't help that it's caked in two thousand years' worth of dirt—and the beer is technically still drinkable. Guess which of the three things pissing me off right now that leaves? I'll give you a hint, Mike. It's the one acting like a dick."

He shifted and wiped the fresh sweat off his face with a dirt-covered palm. He gulped, "I'll—ah—how about I go grab us water and lunch?"

I glanced back down at my horse femur. "You do that," I said, and went back to brushing sediment off the bone until Mike's last footstep was followed by the gate clanging shut behind him.

Finally. I pulled my cell out of my pocket and dialed Nadya. From now on no more sneaking in as a grad student . . . For whatever reason, these days the IAA was upping security just about everywhere. Where normally I'd only worry about the dose of sedative needed to knock out an overly attentive postdoc like Mike, now I had to contend with security checking up on us at random intervals. Understandable, considering the boom in demand for antiquities, but that didn't mean it didn't still piss me the hell off . . .

The IAA, or International Archaeology Association, is the organization that governs every single university archaeology department on the planet. They're also the self-appointed authority responsible for keeping all supernatural elements under wraps, and they aren't shy about enforcing it. Creative bastards too. They'd not only tanked my career but also driven me half off the grid.

Which was another reason I needed to get a move on.

Come to think of it, if I'd just let postdocs like Mike stare down my shirt while I'd been in grad school, I'd probably have had my PhD and a cushy museum job by now . . . I'm sure there's a life lesson to be learned in there somewhere.

Nadya picked up after the second ring. "Alix? What is taking you so long?"

"Not now," I said, keeping my voice low on the off chance the echo carried. "I've got ten, maybe fifteen minutes until Mike gets back. Do we know where the hell the Medusa head is yet? And I don't mean 'it's in the crypt'; I mean exact location down to the room corner if you've got it. I really don't want to have to break in here at night."

The IAA guards were only half the problem; I was more worried about the vampires. Just because Alexander and the Paris boys hadn't crawled out of their hole in three months didn't mean they weren't skulking around looking for me. This was the third job back-to-back in North Africa. If Alexander had gotten word about the Morocco catacombs and my impromptu pit stop in Algeria, he'd have feelers out in every city along the Barbary Coast and right on through to Istanbul.

There was a pause on the other end. "Alix, we can abort the job and come back in a month—after things cool down," Nadya said.

I read between the lines. The Morocco catacombs hadn't been the problem. It'd been the Algerian private collection. Let's just say helping myself to a couple Pharaonic pieces hadn't gone well with the owner . . . or the Algerian police.

I shut down that train of thought. Out of principle I couldn't have bypassed Algeria—even if I'd wanted to, and provided Rynn, Mr. Kurosawa, and Lady Siyu never found out . . .

"Nadya, if you get me the exact location, I can grab the Medusa head and still be out of here before anyone's the wiser."

"I couldn't find the exact location—notes on the Russian archaeology server were spotty—but it should be somewhere under you."

"Under me? There's an entire flooded catacomb underneath me." The underground rooms and chambers spanned three floors, all decorated with images of the Greek Medusa, the protector, mixed in with the Egyptian pantheon. A spiral staircase connected the first two floors, winding its way from the burial dining hall past the carved Medusa heads to the second-level burial chambers, and then on to the flooded third. Since no one had figured out how to reroute the rainwater away from the dig site and drain the last level, the third level had been cemented off decades ago. Considering the state of Egyptian sewers after the recent string of revolutions, opening up excavations down there was a moot point.

"I am not a genie, Alix—I do not make maps appear out of thin air—and Alexandria was your stupid idea."

"Hey, not fair—"

"Mr. Kurosawa told you to get *either* the Moroccan death mask or the Caracalla Medusa head, not both," Nadya said.

I shut up. It had been my bright idea to hit both jobs . . . and stop in Algiers. And no, it's not greedy; it's good game planning and time management. Speaking of time management, I checked my watch. Two minutes had passed since Mike had left. Half an hour was his usual lunch break . . . Now all I needed was the map. Considering the upped IAA security at the catacombs—and everywhere, for that matter—I hadn't dared bring one on me. Hard to explain a treasure map stuffed in my backpack at a random spot search . . .

"Nadya, you've got my laptop ready?"

"Give me a minute." I heard Nadya fiddling with my laptop, followed by a stream of Russian curses a moment later. "Alix, I can't make head or tail of the login screen—call the elf and get him to do it for you."

By "elf," Nadya meant Carpe Diem, my World Quest buddy . . . and actual elf. The real deal, supernatural version. Yeah, I hadn't been too happy about finding that little fact out either. I had enough supernaturals to deal with in my life right now, including my boss, Mr. Kurosawa, and my on-again-off-again boyfriend, Rynn. Off again if he ever found out about Algiers . . .

There were a couple good reasons why I didn't want to call Carpe; near the top of my list was the fact that though he might be my World Quest teammate, deep down at the bottom of his sorcerer's black heart he was just another goddamn thief. Giving him access to my inventory was more temptation versus trust than I cared to test—I know I'd have a hard time not pilfering his game inventory. There was one other reason though, that topped that one. "Because every time I talk to Carpe he starts whining about that stupid book."

"I thought that was in Egypt," Nadya said.

"My point exactly—look, it's easy, log in to my World Quest game and pull up my maps inventory. The red one, top-right corner."

I heard more swearing on the other end as Nadya typed. "Found it. Egypt, no?"

I shifted the phone so I could rummage through my backpack for my GPS. "Yeah. Under that there should be a list of cities. Pull up Alexandria and go to the Caracalla's tomb. Left corner will have a legend shortcut search. Enter *Medusa head*." In fact, there were many Medusa heads in the Caracalla catacomb, but only one that would register as worth stealing in World Quest. I'd had the map in my inventory for a while now but had never really considered going after the World Quest version—not worth the time or effort lootwise. But, if I knew World Quest and the developers' penchant for historical accuracy bordering on obsession, the location would be dead-on.

And no, there is no ethical debate about using my video game to make my day job easier. Consider it an out-of-game exploit.

"I found it," Nadya said, and gave me the coordinates to plug into my GPS. Hunh, it really was right underneath me, give or take twenty feet.

"You're by the horse burial, yes?" Nadya said. "There should be another burial chamber directly below you—a circular chamber, about twice the size of the one you're in now. The map shows the Medusa head on the north side above a sarcophagus."

Sarcophagus? Out of reflex my heart sped up. I don't have the best track record with sarcophagi. To be honest, I was more worried about the highway caving in above us than any lingering supernatural residents. The IAA wouldn't have let Mike down here without a half-decent sweep, and up until a few decades ago the entire catacombs had been flooded. Any supernaturals should be long gone.

Still . . . "Any red dots on the map?" I asked. Red dots on World Quest maps denoted in-game monsters.

"No—nothing."

I let out my breath. No red dots, no monsters.

"OK, Medusa head, north side, chamber below me." I made certain my phone compass still worked underground and checked the time. Twenty-five minutes tops before Mike returned from lunch. I could explain away a five- or ten-minute absence, but I'd have to be fast. If things went as planned, we'd be back on a flight to Vegas by early evening.

Get to work, Owl, and get the hell out. I scribbled on a sticky note—*bathroom break*—and stuck it by the horse femur, then ducked through a narrow passage to a side burial chamber—one where I'd scouted out loose tiles the day before during one of Mike's washroom runs.

I kneeled down, pulled some heavier tools from my backpack, and set to work lifting the corner tile. Within a moment I pulled it free and shone my flashlight down. The light reflected off stagnant water and an exposed stone surface. I cracked the first light stick and dropped it down.

As it struck the water and sunk to the bottom, the tiles decorating the floor flared into existence. Greens and blues that hadn't seen sunlight in almost two thousand years depicted a mosaic of Medusa heads arranged in circles that wound their way in and out of the light stick's glare.

I gave a low whistle. Not every day you get to see something that untouched.

On a positive note, I gauged the water at only a few feet deep. The exposed stone surface I'd picked up with my flashlight, however, was a more disconcerting matter; a second sarcophagus . . .

Emperor Caracalla, the guy who built the catacomb, was the head of the Roman Pharaonic cult of Alexandria in the second century AD. His lifelong obsession was getting his hands on the Egyptian burial spells that would grant him a Pharaoh's ticket to the immortal afterlife. As part of his spirit quest, he massacred twenty thousand Alexandrians, slaughtered a perfectly good set of chariot horses—one of which I'd spent the last three days excavating—and assassinated his own brother. A real all-around, outstanding citizen . . . Shame he never did find the right Egyptian burial spells.

I wasn't sure I wanted to know what—or who—Caracalla stuck in the second sarcophagus.

I took another breath. The IAA cleared the place, and World Quest had no monsters listed in here . . . and Caracalla at least had the good taste to bury himself with a gold-and-emerald-encrusted Medusa head . . .

I set a climbing hook into the stone pillar above the hole and secured my rope, doing my best to think about the Medusa head and not the second sarcophagus.

I started lowering myself down the hole, when my phone started to buzz and chime in my pocket. I frowned. I was sure I'd turned the damn ringer off—in fact, I know I had . . . I glanced at the number. Son of a bitch . . .

"What the hell do you want?"

"You missed game time," came Carpe's voice, closer to feminine than masculine on the sliding gray scale of male vocal texture.

Goddamn it—he must have been monitoring my or Nadya's phone. "I'm working—" I started.

"You're in *Egypt*," he said, his voice thick with accusation.

I closed my eyes; I didn't have time for this. "Carpe, I don't know how many times I have to tell you, I'm not getting your goddamn book!"

"You're doing this out of spite because I didn't tell you I was an elf."

Ha. Far from it. In fact, I wished to hell he'd never told me. "No, I'm not refusing out of spite, I'm refusing on grounds of self-preservation."

"It's a quick trip past the pyramids, you could be back in a day—"

"I don't care! I'm more interested in my neck—specifically that at the end of the day it's still attached to both my head and body."

"Alix, it's a matter of life and death—"

Knowing Carpe, I doubted that very much. I started to lower myself through the hole. If I lost reception, all the better. "No, if you keep this up, I'm going to take out hits on you in World Quest—*then* it will be a matter of life and death."

I heard the rumble overhead before I felt the chamber shake around me. I swore.

"Owl? What's that noise?" Carpe said, his voice wary.

"Got to go," I said, and shoved the phone back in my pocket. I grabbed the edge of the floor with my free hand and held on to the rope with the other. I wasn't risking my neck going against a real mummy just for Carpe's stupid spell book . . .

As the growl of the truck above faded into the distance, the chamber didn't stop shaking. I felt the hook holding my rope give.

Shit. I threw my weight against the edge of the hole as the rope slipped through my fingers and disappeared into the shadows of the pool below. With a last look down at the pool I started to pull myself up. That had been way too close—

A snap echoed through the chamber as the stone tile I was holding onto cracked.

My legs were still suspended over the crypt. I held my breath and carefully pulled myself up. I could still climb out and get the hell out of this mess . . . I kept thinking that even as the tile snapped cleaned through.

"Son of a—" The rest of that sentence was distorted by my hitting the stone sarcophagus.

Pain shot up my side as the ornate lid of the stone sarcophagus broke my fall, knocking the wind out of me. I lay there for a moment, my ears ringing as I mentally checked that everything was working and still where it was supposed to be.

Well, look at the bright side: at least the sarcophagus stopped me from plunging into the stagnant water. It smelled so much worse down here . . .

Back still smarting, I pushed myself up to seated. By the weight, I knew my flashlight was still tucked inside my jacket, so I fished that out first and turned on the high beam to quickly survey the burial chamber and get my bearings. The entire room was roughly sixteen by sixteen feet, maybe bigger, and consisted of rounded, arched walls and a vaulted ceiling. All four walls were decorated with carved and painted Medusa heads, a common protection symbol Pharaonic Romans buried themselves and their goods with. For some strange reason, out of all the Greek and Roman gods out there, the Pharaonic Romans had focused on Medusa as a protector. Thank God Gorgons were isolated to the northern side of the Mediterranean—something about a deep-seated fear of water. They don't actually turn you into stone, in case you were wondering. That's a myth. They cover their victims with ash and a gluelike substance that cauterizes flesh on impact before solidifying—think Pompeii.

Still intact above the waterline were paintings of the usual Egyptian pantheon suspects: Horus, Isis, Anubis, Osiris. The entire chamber was overly elaborate for the time period and depth, even for an emperor.

As my flashlight illuminated the north wall directly across from me, I picked out the second sarcophagus sitting in a raised alcove, Latin words carved into the wall above it, and underscored with hieroglyphs.

Caracalla.

Pass go and collect two hundred dollars.

Next, I checked the hole in the ceiling I was partially responsible for. There was no way I'd reach it standing on the sarcophagus—too high. Climbing was out—the walls arched inwards towards the ceiling. I was trapped until Mike and the rest of the dig team came looking for me.

Well, at least with the collapsed floor I wouldn't have to explain what the hell I was doing down here.

I spotted my backpack a few feet away from where I'd landed on the sarcophagus. Flashlight in mouth, I made my way towards it. Get bag, get Medusa head, figure way out . . .

Unfortunately the sarcophagus had different plans. Years of dampness had covered the domed lid with a slick slime. A hand's reach away from my backpack, my knees shot out from under me. "Oh you've got to be kidding—damn it!" I said as I slid off and landed in knee-deep, stale water.

Soaked and smelling worse than I had any right to, I pushed myself up and noticed a hole in the side of the sarcophagus—a small one, but a crack nonetheless. I swallowed. Sarcophagi and tombs in general don't bother me—they come with the territory; it's when they're broken open in a sealed-in room that I start to worry.

OK, Owl—here goes the hard part . . . I edged my flashlight beam through the crack to see if there were any remains left inside . . .

I yelled as two rats shot out. One dove headfirst into the water, but the second leapt off the stone lid and landed on my head. I shouted again and tried to pull the rat off, but it held on to my hair for dear life. I shook my head in an attempt to dislodge it, but that only gave it the bright idea to dive down my cargo jacket. I batted my body until the rat fell into the water, squeaking once before swimming off after its friend. I shook my head; I'd seen a lot of rats on dig sites, but I'd never had one try to use me as a hiding spot. I chalked it up to rat cabin fever and turned my attention back on the sarcophagus.

Empty.

My calves steadied in the water. Empty was good.

I checked the submerged floor for uneven breaks or outright holes before wading through the knee-deep warm water towards Caracalla's sarcophagus. Halfway there the stale water deepened past my waist. The floor must have shifted over the past few thousand years. From the blue-white light cast by my submerged light stick, I got a better look at the green-and-blue Medusa-decorated floor, which was even more impressive up close. Days like this, what I wouldn't give for a few hours and a decent camera . . .

I also noticed there wasn't a passageway out in sight, with the exception of the one in the ceiling directly above me.

Caracalla had been sealed in. Couldn't blame whoever made that call. With the exception of an IAA fiber optics camera, I was probably the first evidence of humanity to set foot in this chamber in almost two thousand years. Two thirds of the way across, my flashlight beam caught gold, and a glint reflected off the lid.

Bingo.

The water shallowed out as I approached the platform. The sarcophagus was raised high enough off the floor that I'd have to climb on top to reach the Medusa head. The left corner of the stone pedestal was cracked where it met the water, but otherwise it looked sturdy enough.

It was by chance that I caught the submerged tiles switch from pictures depicting Medusa heads to a Roman numeral five inches from my foot. I checked the rest of the floor between me and the pedestal; laid out in a four-by-eight grid was a series of Roman numerals, each one different.

Shit. A Roman numeral code? But how many numbers, and what was the sequence? More importantly, what happened if I screwed it up?

Time to call Nadya.

"Alix, what the hell happened? The entire city shook."

Leave it to Nadya to bypass all pleasantries . . . "Just a minor cave-in—I'm fine, in fact it might have bought me some time."

"Where are you?"

"Let's just say the good news is I don't have to explain to anyone what the hell I'm doing down in Caracalla's tomb since the floor collapsed underneath me. You should see the artwork—"

"Alix, just the Medusa head!"

"All right, all right." I transferred the phone to my shoulder to get a better look at the layout with my flashlight. "Listen, off the top of your head, have you ever heard of a Roman numeral booby trap associated with Caracalla's tomb?"

"I don't see anything on this map, but the Romans were fond of math problems. Is there an equation nearby?"

I scanned the area, but nothing stood out. I also didn't see any major levers or plates—nothing that would indicate poison darts or giant rocks.

Oh hell, I was never good at math anyways . . . I tossed my bag onto the sarcophagus. "Never mind, Nadya—I've got it." I shoved my phone, which was still on, in my pocket, backed up to the edge of the shallows, took a running start, and leapt right before my foot touched the first Roman numeral.

I landed halfway on, halfway off the sarcophagus. I was ready for the slime this time and dragged myself up before I slid back into the water.

I pulled my phone back out of my pocket and balanced it between my ear and shoulder. "OK, I'm on the sarcophagus—"

I heard Nadya swear. She was not a fan of my run-and-jump method of avoiding traps. "Just be careful with the head piece. It's high carat."

The purer the gold, the easier to dent. That noted, I started to work on the surrounding rock with my chisel. I winced as the chisel hitting rock echoed around the room.

"Alix, quietly! I can hear you banging over the phone."

"I can't do it any quieter," I said as I hit it again. The sarcophagus stone chipped as I struck it, and I cringed at the damage. Normally I'd use something more elegant, like acid or some other solvent, but I was short on time.

"Come on, you stupid decoration—get out of the damn stone," I said, and wedged my chisel further into the groove. The gold Medusa head lifted a quarter of an inch.

Two or three more strikes and I'd be able to work it out . . .

Something larger than a rat scraped against the stone wall, and I got a whiff of something astringent and rotten at the same time.

A chill ran down my spine. I spun in the direction the noise had originated in, careful to watch my footing on the sarcophagus.

Nothing moved as my flashlight illuminated the shadows, and the noise didn't repeat. I chalked it up to my own personal brand of paranoia.

Still, I picked up the pace on the Medusa head. A minute later it popped free. I switched the phone to my mouth so I could use my chin to hold the head while I fetched the duct tape out of my bag. Trust me, duct-taping an artifact to your stomach sounds a little gutter trash as far as thieves go, but I'm a hell of a lot less likely to lose it that way than if it's stuffed in my bag or pocket—especially if I have to run.

Which, if things went as planned this time, wouldn't happen . . .

Oh God, I hope to hell I don't have to run this time. I had enough of that in Algiers . . .

"Alix, do you have it?" Nadya's voice came over the phone.

"Uh—ye-ah—" I finished securing the Medusa head to my stomach and retrieved the phone from my mouth. "Yeah, got it—" I scanned the ceiling and wall on this corner of the chamber, looking for a way out I might have missed. Nothing . . . Shit. "Look, I've got to find a way out of here—I'll call you back as soon as I'm out of the dig site," I said, then hung up the phone and stuffed it in my front cargo pocket before she could argue.

Maybe I could figure out a way to get back out that hole in the ceiling . . .

I grabbed my bag and, after one last pat on the duct tape, leapt off the sarcophagus past the Roman numerals. I swayed as I hit the water and overcompensated, stumbling forward to avoid falling back on the grid . . .

Something solid brushed up against my leg.

I swore, more from surprise than anything else—I hate running into things in the dark. I aimed my flashlight to remove the dark factor.

The front half of a fresh rat corpse brushed up against my khakis. *Son of a*— Out of reflex, I scrambled back.

I felt the tile sink under my foot.

"Oh shit." I stood perfectly still as the room grumbled, the sound of stone grating on stone. Now what the hell had I just triggered? No holes in the wall, no trapdoors underneath me . . . I glanced up and caught the stone slab sliding open above.

I dove out of the way before the first cannonball-shaped stone hit the water in front of me, making a loud clicking noise as it struck the tile floors beneath. I let out an involuntary yelp as the second cannonball hit my shoulder. I heard more slabs begin to slide open above.

So much for keeping my head dry. I took a deep breath and dove under the surface towards the broken sarcophagus on the other side of the room. The stones pelted the water around me, but soon I was in the deeper section and out of range.

As soon as I reached the shallow end I stood up and pushed wet hair out of my face before glancing back at the stone trap . . . Damn, that had been awful easy. On the one hand, I should be thanking my luck; on the other hand, as a general rule, my luck sucks in situations like this.

I heard another scrape along the far wall and aimed my flashlight, hoping to catch whatever had made the noise. I had a sinking suspicion it was whatever had bitten the dead rat in two. Like before, whatever it was clung to the shadowed recesses my flashlight couldn't penetrate.

The sooner I got out of here the better. I crawled back up on top of the cracked sarcophagus. The hole was only nine feet away, but high enough that I couldn't reach the edge. I angled my flashlight along the wall, searching for foot- and handholds, but I only found a carved depiction of Anubis, which wasn't recessed enough for me to get my toes in, or pronounced enough to hold my weight. I turned the flashlight as I heard the scraping noise for a third time, swearing I caught movement just outside my light stick's range . . .

I heard a door slam shut a few floors above me, followed by hurried footsteps. "Hey, Serena?" Mike called.

Five minutes early, but under the circumstances . . .

I shone the light back through the hole and waved the beam around for good measure. "Down here, Mike."

His face appeared over the hole.

"The floor gave way when the building shook," I yelled up. More or less the truth. "I need you to throw a rope or something down," I added, keeping the far side of the room in the corner of my eye.

"Just wait there, I'll go get help," Mike said, and disappeared from view.

The thing in the corner moved again, and this time I caught a glimpse of what looked like an arm. Yeah, not a chance in hell—

"No!" I yelled, maybe a little too desperately. When Mike's perplexed face returned, I added, "I don't think the room is stable—do you have your rope up there?"

"Found it," he said.

I hoped that either Mike didn't notice the climbing hook, or, if he did, I could talk myself out of it. "Tie it to something sturdy and lower it down."

I heard Mike moving in the cramped space above me.

The "thing" hiding in the corner grunted, and this time I was ready—I managed to hit it in the face with my flashlight beam.

An embalmed head, showing too much decay to be recognizable, looked up at me with empty eye sockets. What had to be the mummified remains of Caracalla snarled at me, displaying a rotting mess of sharpened black teeth.

"Make it faster, Mike," I yelled. Leave it to me to find the one IAA dig site with a mummy still in it . . . What the hell was the IAA doing nowadays? They were supposed to clear supernaturals out before hapless researchers like Serena and Mike showed up.

Caracalla said something . . . or I think it tried to say something; its vocal cords weren't exactly in the best shape. I mean it when I say the Romans messed up the Egyptian incantations. On top of that, I might be a genius at translating written languages—I can read and write ten, three of them dead—but I can't speak one of them to save my life.

Caracalla's mouth twisted up into something reminiscent of a smile, and he began to wade through the water towards me.

I scrambled as far back as I could until the carved Anubis idol dug into my back.

"Mike, I mean it, get me the hell out of here—*now*," I screamed. There had to be something around here to throw . . .

Caracalla reached the end of the shallows and stretched one of his black arms towards me before submerging under the water.

Son of a bitch, they could swim? Mummies weren't supposed to swim . . .

"Almost there," Mike said as the end of my rope slipped over the edge.

I searched the water for Caracalla as I waited for the rope . . .

Crack.

Above me, a fracture line appeared in the floor near the hole. Mike swore.

"Mike, out of the way—" Son of a bitch—I jumped back into the knee-deep water as a slab of stone, followed by a screaming Mike, crashed into the sarcophagus. The rope followed him down last, sliding off the slippery stone surface and disappearing underneath the water.

Damn it. I headed over to where Mike sat in the water. "Mike, are you OK?" I said, shaking his arm, hoping nothing had broken.

He shook his head. "Fine—yeah . . ." His voice trailed off, and his eyes widened as he stretched out his hand, still shaking from the fall, and screamed.

I glanced over my shoulder. Caracalla stood a few feet away. This close it really resembled a walking corpse rather than an Egyptian mummy. If it'd been a proper mummy, maybe I could have reasoned with it, but this? Not exactly the top of the supernatural food chain . . . though somehow fitting, considering how big an asshole he'd been.

Mike regained his voice. "Oh my God, it's a mummy—a real mummy—" In a surprising show of agility, he jumped out of the water and wedged himself up against the sarcophagus—*behind* me.

"Hey!" I grabbed his jacket and pulled him back out so he was standing beside me. "Not cool, Mike," I said, and slapped him hard on his injured shoulder. I didn't care if this was his first supernatural; hiding behind coworkers was not cool.

Mike ran his fingers through his hair as he attempted to regain something resembling composure. If anything, I was impressed with how well he kept his balance on the narrow ledge, reminding me of a beer-gutted, facial-hair-wearing ballerina.

Don't ask me why that visual came to mind; it's amazing what adrenaline does.

"The handbook . . . the handbook says something about this," Mike said.

I rolled my eyes. The IAA student handbook was next to useless when it came to supernaturals. One chapter on ghosts and a few phrases in ancient languages—most of which seemed to loosely translate to "please don't eat me."

I'm paraphrasing, but you get the picture.

"We're supposed to try and reason with him until the IAA gets here," Mike continued, turning panicked eyes on me. "Quick, Serena, offer him something."

I glared. "It's living in a pit full of water, eating *rats*. I don't think there's anything we can offer it that we'd be willing to part with." Though a small part of me was wondering whether I'd be willing to part with Mike. It was a very small part, but I'd be lying if I didn't admit it was there.

I have to give Mike credit; he didn't give up. "Greetings, Emperor Caracalla," he said, clearing his throat.

Oh this was going to be good . . .

From the growl Caracalla let out, my guess was he thought about the same. I kept searching for something I could use as a weapon.

"There are some nice people on their way to get you out," Mike continued, shaking in fear.

The mummy growled again, flashing his black teeth.

Mike stepped back into the sarcophagus. "They'll feed you all the rats you want—promise!"

Oh for crying out loud. "Grow a backbone, Mike."

Mike whirled on me. "I'm trying to negotiate," he said.

"You're making an idiot out of yourself. Now help me find something to skewer it with before that sorry excuse for a mummy decides we look better than the rats."

Mike snapped out of his fear-induced panic and focused on me.

"That's more like it—hey!" I said, as his eyes went wide with excitement and he gripped my arm with both clammy hands. He wrapped his arms around my waist and neck in a reverse bear hug, placing me directly between him and Caracalla.

"What the hell?!" I pried at Mike's arm wrapped around my throat, but it didn't budge. Stronger than he looked when terrified . . .

"Here! Emperor Caracalla. Let me go, and you can have her—"

"Are you out of your mind? Since when the hell is toss your dig mate to the mummy in the manual?"

"Extreme measures. I'm making it up as we go along right now," Mike told me. Louder and to the mummy he said, "Wave once if you are amenable to my terms, great Caracalla."

Oh you got to be fucking kidding me.

I could have sworn Caracalla laughed . . . then again, it was hard to tell. It could just as easily have been growling.

Time to stop playing Serena, the grad student. "Hey Mike, remember what I said about breaking your nose for looking down my shirt?"

"Shhh! Quiet. I read that Caracalla liked his women meek and docile." To the mummy he added, "She's a little rough around the edges, but not too bad once you clean the dirt off."

I shook my head and readied my foot. "Just wanted to let you know trying to trade me to a mummy deserved a hell of a lot worse than a broken nose, that's all."

Mike howled as my foot connected hard with his precious bits. He let go and doubled over, eyes wide in shock.

"And you also get a broken nose." I grabbed Mike's head—already conveniently doubled over—and connected his nose with my knee. Mike's eyes glassed over for a brief moment before he sunk to the floor and passed out against the sarcophagus. I turned back to Caracalla, still approaching through the water. As tempting as it was to offer the mummy Mike, I wasn't willing to cross that line. It was just safer for everyone involved, especially me, if Mike was left out of the negotiations from this point on.

Now, left with only the mummy to deal with, I had a chance to better scan the room for options. By some unknown miracle, Mike's rope had fallen near the sarcophagus in the shallows. I hopped down from the pedestal lip and felt under the surface for the rope, never letting the mummy out of my sight as he paced the edge of my side of the shallows. "You stay on your side, I'll stay on my side . . ." I said, more of a hope than a threat.

Caracalla glanced up toward the hole in the ceiling before spreading what was left of his lips in macabre mimicry of a smile.

Great, just fantastic. The mummy had the wherewithal to figure out there was a new exit.

My fingers brushed against the nylon rope. I wrapped it around my wrist and searched my bag for my grappling hook. In general, I stay the hell away from grappling hooks. You're more likely to eviscerate yourself or fall to your death than orchestrate a timely escape. Having said that, I was desperate.

I tied the rope end off fast and reeled the hook back for a throw. It bounced harmlessly off the ledge and fell back down in an arc. Right idea, wrong execution . . .

I shoulder-checked Caracalla in time to see him reach into the water. I got a good look at what he retrieved: a jagged, broken bone—femur was a good guess . . .

And human.

"Hello—anyone?" I yelled, hoping someone else had come back down to see what had happened to me and Mike. "Need some help down here, like right now." But all that came back was the echo of my own voice warped by the water in the tomb—that, and another truck running overhead.

The mummy made a grating, laughing noise that reminded me of a monster on a bad amusement park ride.

Come on, you stupid rope, come on. I threw it again and was rewarded with a catch.

Caracalla dove under the water.

Son of a bitch. Why the hell hadn't I ever read anything about swimming mummies? I might be able to shimmy up the rope, but not before I could pull Mike out. Maybe I should just leave him for Caracalla . . . but I dismissed that thought and repeated my newest mantra: I am better than Mr. Kurosawa and also the IAA.

I shone the flashlight over the surface but didn't spot Caracalla. Damn it, what the hell was I supposed to do with a swimming mummy?

I retrieved my phone and made the call I'd gone out of my way to avoid making since setting foot in Egypt.

I called Rynn.

To give him credit, he picked up on the first ring.

"Alix."

No detectable anger, no accusations . . . this was good. "Hey Rynn, listen, I'm in a bit of a jam—what do you know about Egyptian mummies from the Roman era? The ones who look more like rotting corpses."

There was a brief pause. "What the hell are you doing in Egypt?"

"Yeah, about that—I decided since I was already on the continent, I might as well hit both the Moroccan and Egyptian jobs. Last-minute decision, and I didn't have time to call." I winced at the white lie. I'd had the time to call, just not for the argument that would have followed.

"We agreed you'd tell me what jobs you were doing." Rynn tried to hide his frustration, but I'd gotten a lot better at picking up on it lately.

"And I'm telling you now—" I started.

"Before something tried to kill you!"

"Well, we also said you weren't supposed to become Mr. Kurosawa's new security."

"I told you that's temporary—"

"Well, so is Egypt!"

Rynn sighed. "Roman mummies don't do well with bright light. UV is best. Has to do with degeneration of the retina."

OK, that was useful. I patted my jacket until I found my UV flashlight. Never leave home without it. I aimed and shone it on the surface. "He's under the water—how do I find him?"

"Just keep the flashlight on the water. He shouldn't resurface."

I switched the setting to flood, illuminating the whole room. "Rynn, I know you hate the whole thieving thing, but man, if you saw half the stuff in here . . ."

"Keep me on the phone until you're out of whatever hole you've crawled into." Rynn kept his voice professional. He usually did on business, but there was genuine concern under the irritation.

I was guessing Rynn also needed me on the phone to get a signal on my whereabouts—considering the circumstances, I didn't think that was half as bad an idea as I normally would. "All right, what do you want to talk about?" I said, and began tying the loose end of the rope around Mike, making sure it would hold.

"I think the fact you're in Egypt is a good start."

"There's not much to tell. I saw an opportunity to get both pieces on Mr. Kurosawa's list, so I took it."

"We agreed to do it my way—"

I tested the rope one last time to make sure it would hold me as I climbed up. "Yeah, but your way means I end up aborting the job halfway through because it's too dangerous."

"No fucking offense, Alix, but considering the circumstances, I'm the only one in this conversation with a point. And this is the second time you've done this."

My first instinct was to tell him this conversation would end as soon as he quit Mr. Kurosawa's security job, but my thought process was interrupted as bony, clawlike fingers reached through the water and dug into my khakis.

Shit.

"Got to go. Work is rearing its half-rotting head," I said, and tossed my pack and phone onto the sarcophagus before Caracalla pulled me under.

Eyes closed, I kicked at Caracalla's face with my free boot as he towed me under and towards the deep end. I dragged my hands across the bottom on the off chance I'd come across something to use as a weapon.

My lungs were burning by the time my fingers grazed something that felt like a stick. I gave one last kick at Caracalla's head. I didn't dislodge his hand, but I did dislodge my boot. Good enough. I broke through the surface and swam for the safety of the sarcophagus in the shallows. I heard, rather than saw, Caracalla surface a few feet behind me.

I scrambled back up on top, finding my flashlight on the edge of the pedestal just short of the water. I reached for it just as Caracalla broke the surface.

He offered me another grin as I jumped back, tightening my grip on the bone.

"Well, you can't blame me for trying," he said, his voice raspy from vocal cords as dry and tight as sinew. "Why don't you leave me the large one and we'll call it even?"

I almost dropped the bone out of sheer shock. "Wait just a fucking minute. You speak *English*?" To think I'd spent the last ten minutes terrified I was dealing with some ancient, mindless monster . . .

Caracalla's smile widened. "Of course I speak English. I've been listening to you insects natter for over a century—your kind, and your superiors," he said, and I picked out the mix of British- and American-accented words, along with something else foreign to my ears. "And I see they've sent me—what is it your ilk calls it again?" I got a good look at just how many black teeth he had. "Takeout."

I eyed the flashlight, wondering if I could reach it in time. "They won't like you eating one of their archaeologists," I said.

I could have sworn his empty sockets glittered.

"You really think they'll care what I've done with your corpse?" he said. "Only a decade or so ago I had the pleasure of drowning a young man who swam through my lower catacombs. He thought your superiors might care what I did to him as well. Your very presence here disproves that theory spectacularly."

That made me pause. OK, the IAA was evil, but they weren't in the habit of feeding archaeologists to the odd supernatural . . . Were they? "I don't believe you. It had to be an accident." OK, even I can admit that sounded naïve.

Caracalla laughed and picked up what I thought at first was a rat. It was a black walkie-talkie, an old one. "Oh I think not. Not the way he screamed. I ate him very slowly, and all the while they listened on the other end. Chatted with me even, until the 'batteries' died." He pronounced the word *batteries* as if it were still strange and foreign to him.

The IAA was made up of a bunch of bureaucratic assholes, but I'd always assumed their particular brand of fuck-off only extended to throwing miscreants like me under the bus. Not actively sacrificing the ones who toed the lines . . .

"Why the hell would they do that?" I said.

Caracalla inclined his head at an unnatural angle, as if considering my question. "Hard to say, but I suppose they hope I'll one day tell them where my treasure is buried. Or maybe they hope I'll tell them the incantations for immortality." He leaned towards me. "I'll let you in on a little secret before I kill you. I won't tell them. Eating archaeologists like you is much too much fun."

Somehow I thought I should be a little more surprised, or angry. Then again, it was the IAA . . .

"Well, not that it hasn't been a nice chat," Caracalla said before disappearing under the surface. I launched myself at the flashlight, but he was faster underwater than I'd wagered. A desiccated arm covered in sinew and tattered linen wrappings shot out like a viper.

Before his hand could close around my neck, I grabbed his wrist and started tearing through the skin and what was left of his wrappings. He smiled and leaned in to smell my skin. "I haven't killed anyone in years. I eviscerated the last fellow. I wonder what I'll do to you? Shame you don't seem to have one of these," he said, shaking the old walkie-talkie. "I would have preferred an audience."

I grunted and kicked at his midsection. Something gave way, but it did nothing to dissuade him. *Come on, Owl, think. You studied the Pharaonic cults, for Christ's sake . . .*

"You could always start to scream, beg for your life?" Caracalla suggested. "The noise might make it more interesting."

I snorted. I had a better idea. I tightened my grip on my bone—it probably belonged to one of the archaeologists he ate.

"Or you could simply accept the end of your life and worthlessness to the IAA. Just another disposable archaeologist," Caracalla continued.

I may suck with supernaturals in general, but I'm an expert on mummification. Caracalla might be walking and talking, but there was one thing the Romans hadn't bothered to do.

"You're wrong," I said, now struggling to keep his hand at bay—there wasn't much left to peel off.

What was left of Caracalla's lip curled up.

"About the incantations," I said. "That's the last thing the IAA wants from you, on account of how much you screwed them up."

The muscles in his face contorted into a snarl. "And how would you know that?"

"Because if you'd gotten the incantations right, I wouldn't be able to do this," I said, and rammed the femur through one of his eye sockets.

Caracalla screamed and grasped at the bone protruding from his face.

The Roman Pharaonic cult hadn't bothered removing the organs.

He fell back into the shallow water, still batting at the bone. As he floated out, I heard the first high-pitched squeak. Rats, apparently flooding out of thin air and shadows, began swimming towards his body as it drifted towards the deep end.

Hunh, apparently humans aren't the only species who like a little revenge.

And time to get the hell out of here.

I made sure the gold Medusa head was still safely taped to my stomach, then rechecked the grappling hook to be sure it wasn't going to come loose and clock me in the face. Once that was done, I shimmied up the rope and climbed the hell out.

No one had come looking for us. The chamber was empty.

I glanced back down the hole. Caracalla wasn't going to be getting up anytime soon, and I could always send someone else in for Mike as soon as I reached the stairs . . .

I started for the main hall and stopped. Damn it, why can't I ever be the bad guy? Because then I'd be just like them, that's why . . .

I looped the rope through my hook and used a pillar as a lever to pull Mike out.

"That was amazing—" Mike called up when I started to pull on the rope I'd secured around his waist earlier.

Fantastic, he was conscious. Blood streamed from his nose as I helped him over the ledge, but his eyes were wide, almost manic.

"I can't believe you took out a mummy with a stick—"

Bone, actually, and one of Caracalla's victims at that. And I'd really been hoping on Mike being unconscious for that part. "Yeah—well—adrenaline does wondrous things." I reached into my backpack, wrapped my hand around the bottle of chloroform I kept for emergencies, and dunked it over the sleeve of my shirt. I hesitated, but only for a moment. I did not need Mike conscious so he could tell people how I took out a mummy single-handedly. For one, it was against IAA rules to engage supernaturals. Granted, there are no protocols for when they try to eat you—IAA mediated or not—but they still get in a bunch about breaking rules to save your own neck. More importantly though I was ready to blow this popsicle stand.

When I went to knock Mike out though, he grabbed my wrist. "*That wasn't from the IAA handbook*," he said. "You're not a grad student, you're the Owl."

You know, it's always when they're safe and sound that they remember I'm the bad guy. Why is that?

Well, at least I didn't feel bad about what I was about to do anymore. "You know what, Mike? After trying to trade me to the mummy, you should have quit while you were ahead." I elbowed him in his broken nose—no such thing as fair in a street brawl—and rammed my chloroform-soaked sleeve in his face.

His eyes went wide, but he passed out before he could make a half-assed attempt at swiping my arm away.

"Sleep tight," I said. And by that I meant he should have horrible nightmares filled with supernatural monsters for the rest of his archaeology career . . .

I ditched my one remaining boot and slipped on my runners, which were, miraculously, still dry in my bag. I weighed the pros of losing the jacket too but decided not to waste the time.

I thought about calling Rynn, but he'd only yell at me about Egypt some more, so I sent him a text instead. *Ditched mummy. Running for border.* He'd get the message. I called Nadya next. And yes, my phones are now heavy duty and waterproof. Another one of Rynn's changes as part of Mr. Kurosawa's security . . . God, I hated his new job . . .

"Alix?"

"I'm still in the catacombs. Mike tried to play supercop—don't worry, I knocked him out, but he made me when I shoved a chewed-off bone through Caracalla's eye socket. I'm leaving now—I'll tell them there was a cave-in and bolt for the hostel," I said, as I jogged down the narrow passage towards the spiral stairs. All I had to do was run to the guys at the front gate and tell them there was a cave-in. Nothing about Caracalla, nothing about Mike. They'd head in and find him on their own, and by then I'd hopefully be halfway across the city.

"Alix—you need to run!" Nadya said, a new level of panic in her voice. "Don't stop, and whatever you do, don't go through the gates! Go around back and hop over the wall, and *run!*"

I reached the door and peeked out. There wasn't even a guard on duty—probably on lunch break. "But I've got a clear path to the street. Jumping over the fence will only get me attention," I said, and almost opened the door and bolted for the road.

Except Nadya didn't get scared without a reason, and if there was one thing she could smell out, it was trouble.

"I'm already in the building across the road and just saw a van of IAA agents pull up."

Across the street from the dig site, the door to a nondescript white van slid open. Five suits exited, led by a woman with brown hair tied in a severe bun, dressed in a pencil skirt of the color I like to call "lawyer black," along with matching heels.

"It's a trap, Alix. I don't know how, I don't know why, but the IAA found you."

My heart rate spiked as the agents turned the corner and headed for the catacombs gate. Shit. "Nadya, running—*now*—" I said. I threw up my hood and bolted out the door, not bothering to see if the IAA agents saw me.

"I should have known that tip Mr. Kurosawa received on the Medusa head was too good to be true," I said to Nadya, then stopped. It hadn't been the Medusa head that had tipped them off; that lead had been fine. It had been Algiers . . . Son of a goddamn . . . they'd *known* I'd hit the Algiers job, and they'd known exactly what bait to use—the gold prisoner chains and cuffs Cleopatra II wore . . . my very first excavation . . .

And I'd been stupid enough to fall for it.

Damn it, why the hell hadn't I stopped at Morocco?

Because I have lousy decision-making skills at the best of times, that's why.

"We need somewhere to meet—" Nadya began.

I reached the stone wall that ran along the back of the dig site. Instead of replying to Nadya I dropped my phone in my pocket so I could scramble up. When I reached the top of the wall, and because I'm a sucker for morbid punishment, I shoulder-checked the approaching IAA. They were at the gates now, five in total, and I watched the lead as he raised his arm and pointed straight at me.

I dropped down on the other side and hit the ground running. I fished my phone back out of my pocket before I'd turned a corner. "Screw it, Nadya we've got bigger problems than a meeting place right now. The IAA agents just spotted me."

"Lose them in the crowd before you grab Captain—"

"I know that!" Still running, I slid out of my jacket and shoved it and my red baseball cap into my bag. I slowed to a jog and turned down the first crowded side street I came across that was still travelling in the general direction of my hostel.

My name is Alix Hiboux, archaeology grad school dropout and international antiquities thief for hire.

Have I mentioned I don't do supernatural jobs?

Welcome to my life.

2

Mummies, Monsters, and the IAA

Ah—12:45 p.m., maybe? Oh who cares what time it is, I'm running from the IAA.

I broke out the other side of a crowded alley onto a more or less empty street twenty feet from my hostel, the Queen of the Nile.

I thought it was a whorehouse too, but no; just catered to backpackers.

I might not have had the sense to stay out of Egypt mid-revolution, but at least I'd picked a nondescript hostel close to the dig site. I ducked back into the alley and scanned the street, ready to run at the first sign of IAA. There were none waiting outside.

Well, the universe didn't completely hate me today. Not that I'm dumb enough to trust my own judgment . . .

Breathing hard, I bolted for the hostel entrance.

"Excuse me—sorry—dumb tourist," I said as I pushed past a group of backpackers huddled around the front desk. No one paid me any mind—everyone's attention was glued to the TV. More protests, if the glimpse I caught of the newsreel was any indication. That had me worried. No matter how noble the cause, large aggregates of angry people are destined to leave hordes of dead and unconscious bodies in their wake. And millions of dollars' worth of property damage.

I threw a quick wave over my shoulder that no one paid attention to as I ran up the stairs. Relief flooded me as I unlocked and scanned my room. No sign of rifling through my things or tampering with the lock.

"Pssst, Captain," I said.

Captain, my vampire-hunting Mau, chirped and exited from under the bed. He gave me a big yawn and another whine before snorting and sitting on his haunches. "Trust me, you'd have hated the catacombs—full of water, no vampires."

I upended my dig backpack and took only the flashlights, cash, and Serena's fake ID. I ditched my dig backpack, cargo jacket, and tool kit out the window behind a balcony flowerpot, then stripped off my wet clothes and discarded them in the room's trash can. I made sure the Medusa head was still strapped to my stomach. No way in hell was I risking dropping this thing while I ran for my life.

I retrieved my red backpack from the closet and dumped my spare clothes on the bed. I grabbed a pair of clean jeans, T-shirt, and a white anorak—this one fitted with a drawstring hood. The next thing I ditched was Captain's food. I earned a meow for that.

"We're running, not vacationing. I'll buy you more when we get out of Egypt," I said, and opened the backpack compartment I'd modified into a cat carrier. "Now hurry the hell up and get in before the IAA has a stroke of genius and decides to search the hostels." Or the revolution moved in. The way Egypt's last few revolutions had gone, I figured the looters had to be wetting their lips while they waited in the wings.

I did one last sweep of the room to make sure I hadn't left anything incriminating, then double-checked to make sure my extra ID and more cash were in the red backpack before looking for IAA out the front window.

No sign of IAA suits, but an angry crowd was assembling a few blocks away. Damn it. I pulled out my phone and called Nadya.

"Alix, where are you?" There was a slight panic to her voice, and she was keeping the volume down on purpose.

"Gee, Nadya, I'm in my hostel with a revolution brewing outside. What the hell happened? You were supposed to be looking out for protests while I was two stories under the city stealing our Medusa head."

"I was—something is very wrong. One minute everything was peaceful, the next—" Nadya broke off. I heard angry shouting in the background, half of it from Nadya in broken Arabic. I thought I picked out the distinctive crash of a TV breaking, followed by more swearing in both Russian and Arabic.

"Nadya! Vent your anger later—*at me*—not Egyptian protestors who might decide they're better off shooting first."

She lowered her voice. "It's fine. I'm in a bar not far from the cruise docks. We just had a differing opinion of what constituted closing time."

I rolled my eyes. I'll just bet. "Where did they come from? It was peaceful last week—hell, it was peaceful this morning." In fact, there'd been no riots or violence on anyone's forecasted horizons. Protests, sure, but not riots. Granted, it'd be naïve to pretend I understood the nuances of the current Egyptian political environment . . .

"Unless the IAA trucked in rioters this morning," Nadya continued. "Even you have to admit it was a powder keg waiting to happen. It wouldn't have taken much."

It struck me as a little too convenient as well, though starting a citywide riot to chase down a thief was outside even their normal operating standards . . .

The IAA supernatural rules were why I'd been thrown out of grad school. I'd accidently uncovered a supernatural artifact during my PhD research. No one—including my supervisors—had caught on until after the paper had come out. They'd convinced naïve and impressionable me to retract everything with the promise they'd fix any and all fallout. Technically they'd followed through on that . . . for them, not me . . . by throwing me under the bus and ruining any negligible chance of a career I'd had left. Apparently that had been easier. Or more fun, take your pick.

But this? Granted, the IAA had made some passing and laughable attempts to flush me out over the last two years, but baiting me in Algiers and orchestrating this complex a sting operation? I always figured they were more pissed off about the damage to a couple dig sites early on in my thieving career than anything I'd taken.

All right, they might have been pissed about me using what was left of my fine-excavating tool kit to pick the lock of the livestock freight container they threw me in while they arranged to disappear me somewhere in Siberia, but still . . .

Time to leave while the going was still marginally possible. I went to grab my backpack and swore. Captain was still sitting on the bed. When he caught me looking, he meowed.

"Get in the carrier *now*," I said, and pointed to my backpack less subtly.

Captain only meowed louder.

Of all the spoiled . . . "Look, I don't have time to give you a cat treat. Now get in the carrier—unless you want to test the whole Egyptian cat reverence thing." Talking to my cat is probably the first sign of madness, but I figure the more I say, the better chance I have of getting my intentions, if not message, across.

Captain chirped but this time complied.

Finally . . .

"Any sign of the IAA where you are, Nadya?" I asked.

"Just a moment"—I heard scuffling—"no, none where I'm at. What about you?"

Sliding my backpack/Captain carrier on, I checked out the window one last time. The crowd down the street was getting closer, but still no sign of IAA black suits or vans. "Coast is still clear. I'm getting while the going is good, where do you want to—"

Angry shouting carried down the hall. "Just a sec, Nadya," I said. I flattened up against the dry and peeling wallpaper so I could edge the door open a crack—just enough to see what the commotion was down the hall.

Two suits were forcing open the doors to all of the rooms, one by one, regardless of what the current inhabitants thought about it.

I shut the door—quietly. "They're here. Must have shown up on foot," I whispered to Nadya. I grabbed the desk chair and wedged it underneath the door handle, then checked outside the balcony facing the back of the hostel. Two IAA agents—these in street clothes—were waiting below, and I only spotted them because I knew to look for the headsets. I went to the front window and hazarded a glance down. Still no agents milling around there. That meant these two pairs had to be an exploratory team, probably canvassing every hostel and budget hotel in the city.

"Damn, someone at the IAA got up on the right side of the bed this morning," I said under my breath. Must have been real early too, in order to organize all this.

"Don't you dare do anything stupid."

I always figured "stupid" was a matter of circumstance and opinion. There was a bang and someone shouted in English-accented Arabic for me to open the door.

Now or never . . .

"Got to run. Call you when I'm clear." I stuffed the cell phone inside my jacket and hopped up onto the ledge. I was on the top floor, and an awning forked out over my window a foot or so above me. I stood up, balancing between the ledge and frame, and reached for it. It was an inch outside my grasp. I glanced down . . . three stories . . . that wouldn't necessarily kill me on impact, would it?

There was another bang at my door, followed by someone trying to turn the handle and force it open. Thank God the chair held. I reached for the awning again, standing as far on the tips of my toes as I dared. Goddamn it, why the hell couldn't I be an inch taller? I'd have to jump it.

As if knowing what I planned, Captain let out a shrill whimper. "We're not jumping, we're climbing," I said, putting more confidence into the words than I felt, as if saying it convincingly enough made it true.

Just don't look down, Owl. And with a silent Hail Mary, I jumped for the awning.

My fingers gripped the wood rail, and I pulled myself up. I heard the door inside my room crack while my feet still dangled outside the window.

Adrenaline coursed through me. I edged my feet to the side of the building and out of view as the door gave, then I scrambled up onto the roof.

Like most median-income buildings in Alexandria, the hostel roof was made of red mud brick and exposed rebar protruding at various intervals—part property-tax shelter, part keeping your building expansion options open. I ran to the side that bordered a narrow alley. On the neighboring building there was a fire escape ladder within reach.

The IAA suits' voices carried to the roof.

"—potential suspect on foot, may be headed your way, team five—"

They'd found my open window. I didn't wait around to hear more. Not one to look a minor miracle in the mouth, I threw myself at the ladder and straddled between the two buildings. The metal groaned against its mud-brick-buried hinges . . . *Don't look down, Alix, you don't need to see how high up you are . . .*

I looked down. The street was a lot farther away than I thought it'd be. Damn it, I hate heights. There's a video game involving a lot of leaping between high buildings I avoid for that very reason. Captain mreowled in his carrier.

"Yeah, I think this is a stupid idea, too, but it's the only one we have right now." I was about to start climbing down when I heard the door crash open in the room directly below me. A few feet down was another window, albeit smaller, but still easy to spot me through.

I changed direction as fast as my feet would take me and threw myself onto the roof as I heard an agent fumble with the window catch. I pulled my feet over the edge and peeked back down in time to see an agent stick his head out.

"No sign of her out here. Head up to the roof, I'll stay here—"

Praise be to Egypt's loose building codes, I was able to jump two more roofs and one balcony before I ran out of leaping-distance options.

I searched for a way down and found an alleyside balcony about six feet below me with a clothesline strung between it and the next building that I guessed would hold me for the remaining two-story drop to the ground . . . or break as soon as I put any weight on it.

At this point I'd take whatever the hell I could get. Besides, from the increased volume of screaming and breaking glass, the protest-turned-riot was close on my heels. It was get on the ground now, or get trapped on the roof between the IAA and the mob.

I lowered myself over the edge and braced for the six-foot drop to the balcony . . .

I heard the distinct chime of my phone. I swore, wishing I'd had the brains to turn the damn ringer off. Captain mewed, loud and baleful.

"You adding to the noise isn't helping," I told him as I dropped down and checked my cell—in part to silence it, but also to see who the hell it was.

Rynn.

Damn it, not the time for an update. At least that was a good indication we were still on versus off . . . despite Egypt . . . and provided he never found out about Algeria . . .

"I'm out—" I started.

"What the hell did you just do?"

I paused. Answering questions like that with Rynn was tricky. "OK, I thought we'd come to an agreement about you asking me things you really don't want to know the answer to—"

"Knock it off, Alix. I'm serious."

Yeah, he said that now . . . funny how sentiments changed when details emerge . . .

"Apparently the IAA is more pissed about me knocking off a mummy than usual," I said.

"There has to be more to it. The Egyptian cell phone and military lines are so plugged I can't make head or tails of anything going on in Alexandria. There are reports of explosions and gunfire from your end of the city—"

Somehow I doubted that was entirely the IAA's fault. Even if they'd hacked every cell phone in the city trying to flush me out, it wouldn't get messy this fast. "I think that has less to do with the IAA and everything to do with the riot—speaking of which, the masses are heading my way, so if you don't mind—" I swore as I caught sight of an IAA suit on the neighboring building's roof. My cover behind the worn patio set wasn't foolproof, and he spotted me in a matter of seconds, pointing to his friend.

Wait a minute, what was in his hand . . . "Oh hell no, when did the IAA start carrying guns?" I said. They wouldn't shoot though, would they? Not in a crowded city . . . In answer, a bullet struck the mud brick not too far from my head.

Damn, they meant business this time.

"Alix?" Rynn said.

"Got to go."

He swore. "Run—call back when you can, I'll try to keep tabs on the IAA."

I hung up and glanced down at the alley, then up. On the roof across the street stood another three IAA agents. If I climbed down to the street now, I'd be a sitting duck.

Lucky for me the balcony door was ajar. There was a lull in the bullets, so I threw Captain inside and dove in after him.

The apartment was modest; a couch and TV took up the bulk of the living space, accompanied by a small kitchen. I spotted a family of three—maybe four—hiding behind the couch, staring at me, their eyes wide.

Never underestimate the value of pure, unadulterated shock. It means people don't react.

I jerked my thumb back at the destruction outside their balcony. "One hell of a protest," I said in broken Arabic.

The man nodded, slowly, but didn't say anything. "Door?" I asked, or hoped that's what I asked. I've said it before, and I'll say it again: languages are not my forte.

The woman, huddled around a kid and wearing a bright green head-scarf, nodded and pointed through the kitchen.

With no intention of wearing out my shock value, I grabbed Captain and bolted out the front door and down four flights of stairs. When I hit the street, I was met by a sea of people in a mix of traditional white robes and typical Western wear of jeans and T-shirts. I wedged myself against the doorway, hoping they'd pass. They didn't, endless and thick enough to crowd the narrow street. A woman screamed farther back, and I heard glass breaking.

The riot had caught up.

I shoved my hair inside my hood and tied it tight. Somehow I doubted there were many blond tourists fitting my description racing through the city now. "Hold on tight, Captain. The ride's about to get rocky," I said, and only after making damn sure my backpack was well strapped to my front did I dive into the crowd.

The thing you have to remember about mobs is that they're their own entity. The only way to navigate one is in a Zen-like state of calm—go with the flow . . .

Well, that and throw a punch at anyone who tries to trample you and hope to hell no one decides this is the day to mug a tourist . . . or has the bright idea to throw something flammable.

I kept my eyes peeled for the IAA as I rode the sea of people down a narrow side street, one that would take me to the docks.

It's always a pain to navigate a mob—especially if you're short; the landmarks and road signs just, well, vanish. I caught sight of mosque spires I recognized five or six blocks to my right as the mob came up to a fork, and I rode the section that broke to the right. Turn left at the mosque, and I'd almost be home free.

I heard screaming behind me, pitched enough to indicate fights breaking out. A quick glance over my shoulder told me exactly what the problem was; more people were flooding into the street and causing a traffic jam. That didn't bode well.

Someone fell into my back, catapulting me over a man who'd

tripped ahead of me. Captain shrieked—out of fear or indignation, I couldn't tell. I was too busy getting my feet to land under me and ducking a bottle as it soared overhead—striking a woman a few feet ahead wearing a bright blue scarf. She disappeared, whether trampled or escaping to the side I couldn't be sure as two more bottles shot overhead.

So much for riding the mob in a Zen state . . .

I dove under a picked-over and abandoned date cart. The wood of the cart creaked as people climbed over it, but it didn't upend.

I realized my pocket was buzzing. I answered to a tirade of Russian cursing from the other end.

"Nadya?" I said, plugging my ear.

"Yes, Alix, I'm here—" I heard something crash on Nadya's end, followed by more Russian cursing.

"Nadya?" The crowd was thinning now, so I watched for a good spot to make an exit.

Through the crowd of feet I picked out the black pants and leather shoes of two IAA agents. Damn it . . . I placed the phone back to my ear and heard more screaming in Russian. "Nadya, what the hell is happening on your end?" I whispered as loud as I dared. "And where the hell are you?" I asked when the yelling didn't stop.

"I'm hiding in a bar, and me and the management have come to an agreement." I didn't miss the threat heavy in Nadya's voice. Now I knew what the shouting had been about.

"How the hell did I end up in the riot and you in the bar?" I said, keeping track of the IAA's feet.

"Because unlike you, I'm capable of planning ahead," Nadya replied.

"Oh come on! I could hardly have predicted a riot *and* IAA—"

"Alix, *move* or you won't make it. I have an out, but it is time sensitive—a half hour only. Call me when you reach the docks—I'll keep my eye out for you," she said, and hung up.

Damn it, barely any time at all. I set my stopwatch for thirty minutes and hoped I didn't screw it up.

I picked out a third pair of black IAA-issue shoes on the other side of the cart. The only way he could have gotten in was through the other end of the alley . . . Son of a bitch, I *hate* playing cat and mouse—especially when I'm the mouse. On top of the IAA closing in, the crowd was filling back in again fast. I needed to move now, or I'd be boxed in. And I had no illusions about my chances up against three agents.

Well, there's one advantage to me being shorter than most people: I'm harder to shoot in a crowd.

The cart I was hiding under had been picked over, but it still carried dates. Let's hope enough to cause a commotion in an already volatile environment. "Time to change the game the IAA's playing, Captain," I said, and checked that he was still secure in my backpack. I grabbed the handles and pushed the cart up and over, spilling the dates into the crowd.

There were a few indignant yells—some for the dates, but mostly for the fact that the wooden cart had pushed an already volatile crowd into a nonexistent corner. Already short tempers flared at the loss of even more personal space, and one by one they turned on each other—including the IAA agents.

While someone threw a punch at large agent number one, I shot out from behind the cart and vaulted over it. I kept Captain closely clutched to my stomach—though I'm the first to admit there's comedic value to the idea of some hapless Egyptian lifting my backpack and being rewarded with a face full of claws.

I pushed past two more mob goers/protestors and climbed over another food cart, toppling it over to get myself more than an arm's length away from the fray.

I checked for the IAA agents as I aimed for an alley—one that was too narrow by far for the mob's purposes. The IAA agents were still standing, but too far back in the crowd to reach me anytime soon. Ducking a wild punch aimed at anyone dumb enough to get in the owner's way, I climbed over a fallen pair of brawlers and bugged down the alley as fast as my feet would carry me.

I was breathing hard now—my cardio had gotten better since Bali, but I was still a long way off from marathon material. I checked over my shoulder for the IAA again. They'd reached the alley and were moving faster now . . .

There was a window a few feet ahead that had been opened a crack—not enough to tempt looters, but large enough I could wedge myself through. I vaulted up and crawled through.

I'd landed in a restaurant kitchen, where half the staff was madly trying to shut everything down while the remainder tried to chase out customers still left up front. An angry cook glared and shouted something derogatory before reaching for a cricket bat.

No time for niceties. "Sorry," I offered in Arabic as I darted past him into the dining area. Another man behind the bar shouted, and I noticed a gun. These guys were ready to shoot looters. I pushed past a customer and opened the front door.

Two IAA agents were standing in the doorway, mid-conversation on their communicators and about ready to open the door.

"Oh you got to be kidding me," I said.

For a moment none of us moved, including the men in the bar.

Who says there isn't a common international signal for we're all about to get screwed?

I recovered first—years of practice and paranoia—and managed to stumble back and put a booth between me and the IAA.

The IAA does not recruit slow. Both agents reached into their jackets, though neither was willing to pull out a gun—yet.

"Alix Hiboux, aka Owl, we're detaining you on IAA authority for breaches against regulation," the one closest to me said, a midforties agent sporting a crew cut. I rolled my eyes. Where did they get these people? Probably poached from some military department, maybe even CIA. The IAA was funny that way. They might be the Grand Poobah of clandestine operations, but *clandestine* was the operative word. Officially they didn't exist, so recruiting practices consisted of cloak-and-dagger-style poaching from various military and government spy departments. The mix of agents that resulted was eclectic, and more often than not a little crazy. Have to be to believe half the supernatural stuff that's out there . . .

Stall, Alix, stall . . . I raised both my hands over the booth's ledge. "OK, seriously, guys, this is overkill for a minor dig site. Don't you have anything better to deal with? Like hiding supernaturals or something?"

Blond crew cut sneered. "You *are* our top supernatural threat."

"Seriously? Caracalla's catacomb barely rates petty theft on the antiquities scale, let alone supernatural. And the only supernatural in there is Caracalla—and I didn't steal him, I shoved a femur in his face. Hard distinction for you guys to make, I know—"

"Put your hands on your head and drop to your knees," crew cut yelled, interrupting me.

Yeah, not happening . . . "This isn't about Algiers, is it? Seriously guys, traps don't count, and those aren't supernatural either. Hell, you guys practically owed me the Cleopatra cuffs in damages and back pay," I yelled back.

"You've got to the count of five, Hiboux."

There must be some universal rule about the kind of people who want to become IAA agents . . . something along the lines of "assholes only need apply" . . .

"OK, we might not like each other very much, but everyone in the IAA knows I don't deal with dangerous artifacts or digs." To be fair, the IAA might be dicks, but I figured that was why they'd never mounted a serious manhunt for me before. On their sliding scale of threats, I rate somewhere between a mosquito and a pigeon—mildly annoying, swat it if you can, but otherwise ignore it.

I glanced around the bar and noticed patrons and staff were filing out through the kitchen—had to be another exit.

"Just hit her with the tranquilizer so we can get the hell out of here," IAA agent number two said, a contrast to crew cut, with dark skin, no hair, and falling somewhere in his midtwenties.

Tranquilizer? Yeah, I did not plan on sticking around for that. Besides, number one looked like he'd rather spend a few rounds beating me up first—you know the type— to teach me a lesson for not following the sting operation script.

Don't think about the IAA logic too much—I know I try not to.

I licked the sweat off my lip and checked the bar out of the corner of my eye. I noted a jar of what looked like boiled eggs and garlic sitting on the bar within reach.

"All right, the hard way it is," I said. I grabbed the jar and launched it at crew cut's head.

You know what's better than seeing an IAA agent slip and fall on a pile of dates? Watching one start an international incident.

Crew cut's gun came up, and Arabic-voiced madness ensued. Everyone in concert seemed to dive for cover as a loaded-gun standoff ensued.

As bullets flew in both directions, I dropped to the floor and crawled after everyone who *didn't* have a gun—the minority, in this case.

The route led through the kitchen, and I happened to pass what had to be the cooks' tip jar. I stuffed twenty bucks inside. I know, it barely scratched the surface, but I wouldn't have felt right not leaving anything.

Out of all the people who spilled out of the restaurant into the alley, no one gave me a second glance as they ran for their lives. I could relate. I was in a different alley—a little off course for the docks, but the hell away from the IAA—I hoped. My bigger problem was that I'd fallen behind the mob. I checked my phone timer. Twenty minutes left. I wouldn't make it past them in time. I needed another route.

Behind the mob. Need another route to the docks, I texted Nadya.

The nice thing about text was Nadya couldn't yell.

The dig site, came Nadya's text.

Oh screw that. I dialed. "Nadya, no! I'm stupid, not suicidal—and they have guns that they're shooting . . . at *me.*"

"They're still searching for you in the riot, and Rynn says the mob is giving them logistic problems as well. They never expected you to beat them out of the dig site, and they won't expect you to double back," she said calmly.

I pulled up a mental picture of Alexandria as best I could. If I doubled back, I'd shave maybe ten minutes off my run . . . still, I didn't buy the IAA leaving the catacombs unmanned.

I peeked out the alley again to gauge the mob, the bulk of which was now a few streets over, leaving only the stragglers, looters, and injured behind. "Oh you got to be fucking kidding me."

"Alix?"

"Dig site it is," I said as I watched three new suits moving amongst the mob stragglers. They were zeroing in on me again. One of them glanced my way. I ducked back out of his line of sight and swore as glass shattered above my head.

On the bright side, all I had to do was run like hell a few blocks past the catacombs and I should end up at the docks. "Keep me on the line and I'll be able walk you through it," Nadya said.

I fished the Bluetooth piece out of my pocket. "Just make sure you keep the directions coming. I've got no bearings over here."

"There should be an alley coming up on your left; take that one."

"Fine, great, awesome, alley on my left—" I turned left as instructed and skidded to a halt a few feet in. There was a collapsed wall blocking the way in the form of a pile of rubble . . . guarded by two chickens and a goat. The chickens ran for cover, but the goat just dropped the T-shirt it was eating and bleated at me. "Nadya, it's a fucking pile of rubble with farm animals!"

"Then find a fucking way over it—and hurry! I can't hold our ride out forever."

"I didn't avoid the open sewer so I could run through a flock of livestock," I mumbled. With the revolutions, garbage and other city services had gone to the wayside, and the open canals that ran through Alexandria had taken the brunt of it. The ones that hadn't already been filled in with concrete to stem waterborne diseases were swimming with discarded livestock and other assorted garbage.

"Alix! Do it!"

I swore, switched Captain to my back, and started to climb.

At least the goat got out of my way.

Halfway up, Captain let out a baleful howl.

"Yeah, I hate livestock too," I said, and continued to climb.

It was followed by a second, louder cry.

I glanced back over my shoulder to see what had riled him up.

"Shit . . ."

A trio of Egyptians stood at the bottom of the rubble pile, watching me, grinning. Two of them were a good foot taller than the third, and all three were wearing traditional robes and headdresses. I wasn't sure if it was the difference in size or the smaller man's years, but he appeared to be the most intelligent. That, and his eyes never left me.

"That is her, boss?" one of the larger men said to the shorter one in Arabic.

The smaller man smiled, displaying a set of teeth a few baskets shy of a picnic, and nodded. "Same as in the picture—more or less." He switched from Arabic to halted English. "This isn't your lucky day," he said to me.

"Got to go, Nadya," I said.

"Don't you dare hang up—I need you online so I can reroute you."

Two larger goons started towards the pile. "Extenuating circumstances," I said, and hung up.

I climbed faster, wracking my brain for anything big I'd stolen of late, but it wasn't like Mr. Kurosawa had me lifting artifacts of note. Damn, the IAA needed to come up with better things to do with their spare time.

"Why don't you come down so these men don't have to hurt you?" the shorter man yelled.

Screw that.

I made it two-thirds of the way up before I felt the tug at my foot and face-planted in rubble. Hands gripped my backpack like a handle and dragged me down. Captain howled; might not be vampires, but that doesn't mean my cat can't tell trouble when he sees it.

One of the men cursed my cat as teeth hit their mark through the nylon.

My stomach turned. I'd stuck Captain in there so we wouldn't get separated—not to hand him over gift-wrapped to a thug residing in a country whose current dietary selections were suspect. Not a slight to the Egyptians, just that supermarkets are the first casualty in a revolution.

Captain howled, and I heard nylon tear. It was followed by more Arabic cursing as my cat dug his teeth in again.

Teach them to manhandle my cat . . .

I saw a baseball-sized piece of rubble within reach and edged my hand towards it as Captain fought.

A swift kick was delivered to my gut, followed by one to my leg.

I winced but wrapped my hand around the brick. Too bad for them I'd gotten a lot of experience having the shit kicked out of me this last year.

"Hey asshole," I said.

There was a grunt followed close by another yell and a high-pitched cat screech. I felt claws dig into my back as one of the goons tried to wrench Captain away. I clenched my teeth; if they so much as tore a tuft of hair off my cat . . .

"I'll come down, but you got to do one thing for me," I yelled. I'd only have one chance to take them by surprise.

There was a grunt of acknowledgment—as much of an encouragement as I was going to get from these guys.

I tightened my grip on the rock and flipped over. Only one of the goons had made it up the rubble pile—the other was having difficulty scrambling up, and the leader hadn't bothered trying. Between Captain's teeth and my sudden movement, the backpack was wrenched out of the goon's hand.

I slammed the rock into the goon's head. "Leave my cat the hell alone!"

The goon's footing had been tentative at best. The rock only stunned him, but it was enough to set him reeling . . . well, that and Captain had managed to tear a hole in the backpack large enough for his head to fit through. There was a blur of white and brown fur as he tore deeper into the thug's hand, which was met with shrieks. Captain had drawn blood in three different spots, and it mixed freely with grime, making a reddish-brown mess.

"Serves you right trying to steal a girl's backpack—never know what's in there," I said, but I doubt the man was listening even if he did speak English.

Now if my damn cat would just let go so we could get the hell out of here.

The man reeled back precariously, but Captain wasn't having any of it. No way in hell was he letting go now that he figured he had the upper hand.

"Let—go—you—stupid—cat," I said, and wrenched the bag with both hands, trying to get Captain to let go so the man would fall already. Captain only growled and the thug's shrieks pitched an octave higher as Captain did more damage. The other two were scrambling at the bottom of the pile, yelling at him and each other.

The bag gave an inch as a strap sheared under pressure, and I almost stumbled back over the other side of the rubble pile. Out of shock more than anything else, Captain lost his grip.

I wrapped both arms around a half-bagged, indignant Mau cat and ran—or rolled—down the other side of the rubble, leaving three angry Egyptians screaming in my wake.

I landed in a shallow, stagnant puddle. Great, all that effort to avoid the sewers . . .

I turned back to grab my backpack. Captain was sitting beside it . . . on the ground . . . glaring at me.

I held up the backpack—well, between the struggle with the Egyptians and Captain's handiwork, what was left of it. "Come on. I don't have time for this. Back inside."

Captain just glared at the backpack, back at me, and let out a drawn-out meow.

"Look—I get it. Locked in backpack bad. I'll make a note of it and put a head hole in, OK? Now just get the hell back in and stay there before they figure a way over or around."

Captain snorted but hopped back in. To show I was keeping my end of the deal, I made sure he had enough room to stick his head out.

Time for me to do what I did best: run like hell.

I got Nadya back on the line and set off at a jog, doing my best not to try to think of the waterborne diseases I'd just soaked my shoes in. Instead, I wondered what the hell I'd stolen over the past few months that had the IAA this riled up.

3

Old Enemies, New Friends

1:30 p.m., still running in circles around Alexandria

I peeked over the top of the stone fence and swore.

Past the gate and across the street was my route to the docks, but the dig guards and Mike were still milling around the site. At least there was no sign of IAA suits, but that in itself didn't exclude them from being somewhere out of sight.

I dropped back down to the ground. Well, I could jump over and make a run for it—if I was fast enough, they might not react before I was out . . .

"What the hell did I ever do to you, Egypt?" I said.

"Besides stealing priceless artifacts?" came a familiar male voice.

I frowned. I'd recognize that voice anywhere.

I spun on my heels and came face-to-face with a man not much taller than me, with a suntanned face and wearing the more traditional Egyptian garb you see at the dig sites. Except this wasn't an Egyptian.

"Benji," I said, and unceremoniously pulled off his headscarf. "I should have known they roped you into this." Benji was an old colleague of mine, one I'd gone out of my way to help when he'd stumbled onto Chilean mummies. Except he wasn't happy about owing me some help navigating the odd dig, so he'd backstabbed me in Bali a few months back.

We weren't on good terms.

He held his hands up and started to back up. "Alix, it's not what it looks like. Let me explain—"

He didn't get much further than that, on account of me punching him in the face. Benji yelped and grabbed his nose. "Son of a bitch! Oh my God, I think you broke it!" Or at least that's what I thought he said, on account of him clasping his bleeding nose between his hands.

I shook my hand out. Rynn's self-defense lessons were coming in handy, though I didn't know if my bar of entry into violent conflict resolution needed lowering. My God, hitting someone in the face hurt . . . I'd have to remember to use my knees next time. Didn't stop me from pinning Benji against the wall. "You sold me out to a bunch of vampire junkies!"

Benji winced, but whether from the accusation or my arm across his throat, I wasn't sure. "Jesus—I know, all right! But I didn't know they were junkies, I thought you were the junkie—that's what they told me. My *God* that hurts!"

I raised my fist, and Benji's eyes widened. "OK, look, I can explain. I came to help."

"How stupid do I look?"

He shrugged and nodded towards the dig site. "Considering you walked right into an IAA trap?" Benji frowned. "Come on, Owl, Algiers? Even I guessed that one—"

Shit. "Yeah, well, never mind," I said, and let Benji off the wall. "And what the hell is with the IAA manhunt anyways? And you've got five seconds to make it good."

He managed a glare. "Or what? You'll hit me again?"

"No." I turned so Benji could get a good look at Captain, who obliged with a hiss. "I'll let him at you. I'll warn you, he's a little wild. Found him slinking around the pyramids—"

"OK, OK. Jesus, when the hell did you get so violent?"

I crossed my arms.

Benji rushed to continue. "All right, all right—I'm not exactly in the IAA security know, but I picked up a couple things because I've had my ears open. They've been looking for you the last couple months, but it wasn't until a couple weeks ago that they got real serious—don't ask me why. All I know is it's got something to do with a theft."

I shook my head. "That's impossible—" I would have explained I'd been in Vegas two weeks ago, and the week before that, but Benji stopped me.

"I'm just telling you what I know. A theft five days ago in Morocco tipped them off, so they set up Algiers. You beat them to it, but then yesterday someone somewhere flagged Serena. The lines went nuts after that."

I closed my eyes for a second. The IAA had known exactly what bait to set out and where to look for me . . . I was getting as predictable as Captain was with vampires. "What was the theft?" I went over the last few things I'd lifted: Not the Moroccan burial mask, too soon; Norwegian burial jewelry, no; Easter Island idol . . . that might have done it. They don't like major monuments going missing, though still.

Benji shook his head. "No, they were looking for you before that. All I know is it's this side of the globe and the theft had your signature all over it—"

Six weeks ago I'd lifted a Dionysus idol outside Athens, but with the economy collapsing, it was open season in Greece. Who wasn't lifting stuff there? Besides, none of it rated supernatural, except for the Easter Island idol, and even that was minor. The IAA wouldn't go to these lengths over that, not unless they'd eaten a really great batch of mushrooms . . .

Then again, when supernatural shit is involved, I suppose anything is possible.

I snorted. "They've probably got another ruined temple to pin on me and are trying to track down my signature for insurance purposes."

Benji frowned. "OK, that's not completely unreasonable. Might I add you did trash the temple in Bali—just like I said you would?"

I clenched my fist. "Not on purpose—and no offense, but the Naga did way more damage than me—and I haven't trashed any dig sites since then."

He ran his hand through his hair, accidently knocking his black-rimmed glasses to the side. "And there you go again with the excuses. Why can't you—for once, that's all I'm asking here—admit you might be partially responsible?"

See, now this is the problem I have with the IAA. No allowances for the supernatural . . . Put your neck out to save the world and what happens? A temple was partially destroyed—which, for the record, I wasn't happy about. If the resident Naga hadn't taken issue . . . Oh why the hell do I even bother. "Fine. I was somewhat responsible for ruining a temple. But you intentionally sold me to a pack of goddamn vampires!"

Benji glared. "OK, like I said, it was an honest mistake—*which* I'm trying to make right—and you did strong-arm me into getting you into the dig site in the first place."

"Strong-arm?"

"Yeah! *Strong-arm.* You know, holding something over a person's head *indefinitely.*"

"No, I mean what were you? Born in the 1950s? And what the hell do you expect? The entire batch of you treat me like I'm some kind of goddamn leper!"

I expected an argument. I've been in the game long enough to know how to deal with reluctant archaeology accomplices like Benji. I didn't expect the color to drain from his face. I think that was worse—like validation.

All of a sudden I really didn't feel like talking to Benji.

He did though. "Look, I would have warned you ahead, but after Bali they started watching everyone's communications—and not just because of you—"

I lowered my head and glanced at Benji from under my eyebrows.

"OK, well, partly because of you, but mostly because of Bindi. No one saw that coming. Including her and Mark, they're down, like, seven archaeologists in one year."

I heard voices coming from the catacomb entrance, so I dragged Benji farther into the shadows. "That still doesn't come close to explaining how the hell you ended up here."

"It wasn't out of my way. I was transferred to Cairo a few months back, and when the IAA chatter about Serena started, I figured it might be you and got myself attached to the dig. It wasn't hard," Benji added, pushing my arm off and standing up straight. "You have a lousy habit of trashing places. They were more than happy for another set of hands—"

"Do not."

Benji snorted. "Did you see what those stones did to the floor? Did you plan on setting off a few traps, or did that just happen while you were ramming—"

I motioned for him to keep his voice down. "I had to improvise—and the psychopathic mummy came after me."

"Look, I'd have tried warning you earlier, but they've been tight-lipped about things." He looked more tired as he said it. I got the sinking suspicion the IAA was tight-lipped on everything after Bindi and Red. Losing archaeologists because they get eaten is one thing, but having them jump physiological sides with IAA secrets?

"You won't break their perimeter on your own, but my partner is indisposed this morning, and they'll let me by," he said as he handed me a plastic bag containing the same robes and scarf he wore.

I stared at them, then back at him. To say Benji didn't exactly look friendly was putting it mildly. If he thought for one second I believed he was going to help me slip the IAA out of the goodness of his heart . . .

"You know, I've got a fantastic bag of magic beans in my pocket I can sell you, they'll grow a beanstalk and everything—"

"Oh will you knock it off! I'm trying to help you—"

"Why?"

"Because I've got a fucking conscience and I'm having trouble sleeping, all right!"

"So, just so we're totally straight here—I'm helping you feel better about yourself?"

He shoved the bag back at me. "Just put it on before one of the guards grows a work ethic and actually patrols the back of the building."

I grabbed Benji's plastic bag. Selfishness was reasoning I could understand.

Besides, if it was like Benji said and the IAA had the city cordoned off—and considering the ensuing riot and abundance of agents, there was no reason not to believe him—I didn't really have a choice. Not unless Captain and I wanted to try and hide out in the desert for the next two weeks while they combed the city.

"I need to get down to the cruise docks," I said.

Benji thought about it, then nodded. "We should be able to head straight there. We just need to get past the gate and one of the lines."

"How did you even know I'd be back this way?" I said, throwing the robe over my head, keeping my backpack and Captain in front.

"Easy—with the way they roped off the city, I figured there was a chance you'd be back this way—last place they'd look for you."

Yeah—for the last place I should have run, again it was damn predictable. . . .

Benji checked his watch. "Come on," he said, once I'd approximated him in outfit and appearance. He shoved a set of papers in my hands: Kelly Black—probably his partner. "If anyone stops us, let me do the talking, and just say yes," he said.

"I think I know protocol."

Benji snorted. "Not since they've tightened ranks, you don't. Just follow my lead."

"Isn't that how the Chinchorro mummies woke up?"

"You're never going to let that go, are you?"

I would have given him a snappy comeback, but we were in earshot of the two guards.

I felt Captain stir in my backpack, and he let out a muffled mew.

"Captain," I whispered. "I know we've had our differences these last few days, but please, for the love of God, stay quiet."

I recognized the guards from my time as Serena, but I'd never picked up their names. Both of them would have preferred to be somewhere else in this heat, but whereas the first was happy to ignore us and imagine he was somewhere else, the second wanted to make damn sure everyone at the dig knew exactly how pissed he was to be here.

He gave us a second once-over. "Papers?"

I handed him mine along with Benji's as the guard examined my face, his mouth drawn in a tight line.

A bead of sweat collected on my upper lip.

His eyes passed over me, though as he focused back in on Benji, his frown deepened. "Why do you need to leave the site? Dig break's not supposed to be for another hour and we've got rioters heading this way."

Why were we leaving the site? Because we wanted a goddamn soda or beer, or we just felt like taking a goddamn nap—in other words, none of your goddamn business and get back to pretending you're doing something and leave the smart people alone!

"Had another batch of stone fall—we need medical supplies and clean water," Benji said.

I kept my mouth shut, out of shock over Benji's polite justification more than anything else. I'd been so busy trying to get a few minutes away from postdoc Mike over the past three days that I'd had minimal contact with the guards and missed the jump in scrutiny... and my major concern had been getting into the site, not out for snacks.

The guard glanced from Benji to me, then shrugged. "Just try to be more careful in there."

If I'd had control of my voice again, I'd have told the guy exactly where he could take his careful and go. Benji, however, only nodded. "Sure thing," he said, and the two of us kept walking through the gate before I could shoot my mouth off.

Knowing my track record, there was probably a benefit to that.

Captain, picking up on my nerves, continued to squirm under the robes. "Knock it off," I hissed as we waited for the intersection to clear. *Come on, lights, come on, lights . . .*

"Hey!" one of the guards yelled.

Both of us froze on the edge of the sidewalk and turned around, slowly; me trying desperately to keep imminent panic off my face.

"Be back in fifteen," the guard said. "We've got a shift change, and I don't want to miss my break."

My panic evaporated. Seriously?

Benji raised a hand and gave them a meek wave and smile.

"And watch for the rioters—I don't want to have to come out and find you."

Seriously? What were we, two?

"Jesus, Benji. When did security get like this?"

"They've been upping security for the last year, but it wasn't until Bali that they pulled private contractors in," he said as we crossed the street and lost ourselves in the crowd. "That's who those guys are— they're responsible for accounting where archaeologists are at all times and making certain we're *safe*." If there was any question about what Benji thought about the contracted security, the way he spat out *safe* cleared up any misconceptions.

"So basically you're prisoners now. Great," I said.

Benji didn't dignify that with an answer, but he didn't deny it either as we continued down the road. He checked over his shoulder before shoving me inside a convenience store, then glanced out the front again.

"There's a pair of agents coming," Benji said. "They'll swing back around and loop the other street."

I got the meaning. If they were looping back along the main streets and I used the alley, I had a short window of opportunity in which to slip by them. I had to marvel how good these guys had gotten since I'd left . . .

Come to think of it, I wonder if I'd have ever gotten out in the first place if things had been like this . . . I pushed that thought to the back of my mind. Archaeologists like Benji were more than happy to treat me like I had the plague, and I don't have a martyring bone in my body. As far as I was concerned, they could get buried in the bed they'd all made for themselves.

Funny how much easier it is to tell the world to fuck off in my head . . . why is that?

Having guessed we probably weren't in the store to buy anything, the man behind the counter glanced warily between Benji and me. With the threat of rioters looming, I didn't blame him. His fear I knew how to deal with. I passed the equivalent of twenty dollars across the counter, nodding to the back exit. He took the money, glanced again at me and Benji, shrugged, and went back to reading his magazine. I saw the two agents pass by. "Those two out front means the one in the street over will walk by soon, right?"

Benji nodded.

Time to use the ever-diminishing window of exit. "Come on," I said, and shoved Benji towards the back door. He didn't say anything as I continued shoving him into the street, across the road, and into the next alley. We were almost at the next street crossing—three blocks from the docks—when Benji dug his feet in. He swore under his breath and pushed me into the shadow of a structurally unsound escape stairwell.

"Hey!"

"Shhh, will you? They changed their pattern."

For a second I thought it might be a setup—that Benji was leading me into a trap. One look at his panic-stricken face erased that though. Benji didn't do well under pressure.

It dawned on me just how many sleepless nights he must have had to stick himself in this situation.

"We'll wait until they go by and dodge through?"

Benji shook his head. "No, you don't understand, the pattern will be off. They've been running it to prevent exactly what we're doing. I picked it up while I was keeping an eye out for you—it wasn't hard, they coordinate it across the radio channel. The point is there's at least two agents for the next three streets."

OK, that did throw a slight wrench into our plans. *All right, Owl, you're supposed to be the pro here. Think fast.*

A wise rule of thumb says the best lies are steeped in truth. Time to challenge that theory.

"Here's what we're going to do. You'll head them off and run interference while I run for it."

Benji frowned. "Not a chance in hell. I'm not letting you throw me under the bus. I don't have that guilty of a conscience over Bali."

Yup, back to the Benji I knew and exploited. "Relax. I'm not throwing you under the bus. In fact, I'm probably doing you a favor."

He stopped wringing his hair. "How the hell do you figure that?"

"Easy. You're going to lie like hell," I said, and steered him back into the alley to give him the short rundown of my plan.

—ᴍ—

I slapped him on the back to send him in the direction of the street we'd passed through a minute before. He got a few steps away from me, shaking his head before stopping in his tracks. He turned to face me with a look of determination, the kind that usually leads to a disagreement over ethics or some misplaced need to do the right thing—I should know, I used to wear the same expression.

"Benji," I started.

"Look, I know you took the Medusa head. You did a lousy job excavating it out of the sarcophagus, by the way."

Yeah, well, I'd been in a rush. And not the time to get brave, Benji.

"Benji—" I began, adding a warning to my voice.

He held up his hands, and I saw a tinge of contempt cross his face—just for a moment, but it was there. "Save it. I don't expect you to give it back. I just wanted to say now we're really even."

"Fine," I said, maybe a little more aggressively than I needed to, but this was the Benji I remembered. It wasn't like I expected the goodwill to last past the clearing of his conscience.

There was something else though. He ran his hand through his hair again, deciding whether to say anything. "Look, I don't know what you stole, and I seriously do not fucking care—it's way too high above my pay grade, but whatever it is, these guys really want you. *Bad.* Just . . . I don't know . . . try to be careful . . . or something." And with a shake of his head, he jogged out of the alley towards the street.

That left me with more foreboding than I wanted to think about . . . and there went Benji breaking the mold again.

I didn't have to wait long for his diversion.

"Hey! Help! You guys—IAA—Owl snatched me from the dig site!" he screamed at the top of his lungs. He gave them one hell of a performance as he stumbled down the alley and waved towards the agents; with the broken, swollen nose, he not only sounded convincing but he also looked the part. I ducked farther under the haphazard stairwell and pulled down my headscarf as the two agents patrolling the street ran past. I heard one of them yelling into his headset—hopefully calling for backup from the rest of the agents nearby.

That was my cue. Captain summed it up with a meow.

"You said it. Let's get the hell out of Dodge."

I hazarded one last glance at Benji distracting the agents before bolting into the street. I made it to the next alley without incident. Two more blocks to go.

I hustled through the next street and into the adjoining alley before skidding to a stop at the end. I could see the water now and smell the heavy fuel mixed with sewage that Alexandria's harbor is notorious for. Only one more block to go. Almost home free. I don't think I really believed Benji would pull through until that moment—not that I had any time to ponder the greater meaning of that in relation to my on-and-off friendship with the universe . . .

But, yeah, we were square after this.

Now to find Nadya without attracting undue attention . . . I pulled out my phone to text her while I kept one eye on the docks, watching for IAA.

I felt the hand on my shoulder and the muzzle of a gun as it pressed into my back.

I swear to God there hadn't been even a footstep. I started to raise my hands.

"Stop right there," I heard a woman say, and the gun jammed further into my lower back. Captain growled, but the woman didn't seem to notice, and for once Captain had the wherewithal to stay hidden. I shushed him and hoped the agent didn't notice. First, Captain doesn't stand a chance against guns, and second, the IAA has been blissfully oblivious to the existence of my vampire-attacking cat. Them knowing would be bad for both of us.

The agent spun me around, and I came face-to-face with a six-foot-tall woman in her late thirties, dressed in the requisite black suit, her gray hair pulled back in a ponytail. The gun was now aimed at my chest.

The best way I've found to deal with abusive authoritative figures is to show ambivalence in the face of threats. Chances are good I'll get hurt, but it pisses them off enough that they start making mistakes. I glanced down at the gun, then up at the agent's face, arching an eyebrow. "I thought you guys were supposed to capture me alive," I said.

She shrugged, keeping her temper in check, and leveled the revolver down at my leg. "Alive and shot are two very different things," she said.

"Madam?" I heard a second, younger, less-jaded-sounding voice ask over the communications.

"I've apprehended Owl. Let Director Brook know and send backup to my location—"

I inched my foot away from the wall, hoping the audio distraction might give me a chance to run.

A knee connected with my midsection faster than I could have dodged, and I doubled over in pain. The agent continued with her conversation as if nothing had happened. With minimal wincing, I pushed myself back up to standing and bit back the first smart-mouthed response that came to mind. This one wanted an excuse to beat me up; worse, she knew what she was doing.

Finished with her check-in, she stood in front of me. I didn't like the smile that spread across her face. "You know, come to think of it, you do have a reputation for running," she said, taking the collar of my jacket and forcing me to face the wall. "No reason you can't be shot in the process, considering the trouble you've caused."

I winced as she shoved me hard into the wall. "OK, I don't care how many of you the IAA overstaffed, there's no way a Medusa head and Moroccan death mask warrant this level of make-work—"

I didn't have a chance to finish as she hit the back of my head. God, do I hate IAA muscle. Impossible to have a civil conversation . . .

If I ran, she'd just beat me up more before shooting me. Wincing, I stood still and braced myself for another smack to the head or the sound of a gunshot.

Crack—

Funny . . . that didn't sound like a gun. Smack to the head? No, I'd feel pain by now.

I opened my eyes. The agent was lying on her side in a heap. Nadya stood in the doorway, holding a cricket bat over her shoulder.

"You wouldn't believe what the kids down the street charged me for this thing," she said as she discarded it back inside. "Come on, help me move her." Together the two of us dragged her none too gently inside the doorway. We both heard the female voice over the comm.

"Roger that. Team three, two, and five, head off to main entrances while we attempt to establish visual. Please respond, team four."

Damn it, I hate organization. They'd know in a matter of seconds I was back on the run. Nadya swore. "Come on, we need to get to the docks."

"Wait." I crouched down and rifled through the woman's pockets. Now, if I was an evil agent, where would I keep a covert walkie-talkie?

"Alix! I agree with principle, but we don't have time to rob her right now—come on."

"Just a second. Trust me, this'll be worth it." My fingers brushed against something. "Found it," I said, and held up my prize as a woman

repeated her request for team four to respond. Catching on, Nadya nodded. A heads-up might help us.

By chance the agent's wallet was in the same pocket, so I lifted that as
well. Not for cash, though; out of principle, I'd put any I found towards
beer and cat food, but it was also useful for tracking. There were wonders
you could do with someone's name and credit card if you knew the right
people in low places.

Nadya glanced at her watch and swore in Russian. "Now, Alix!"

I jumped back up, closed the door on the unconscious agent, and
raced after Nadya towards the docks.

It wasn't until we reached the street across from the cruise terminal
that she came to a halt. We were so close I could taste the oil in the air. . . .

But Nadya just kept watching the road. Over the radio, the IAA was
reorganizing. It wouldn't be long before they drifted this way. "Let's get
going while the going is good—"

"Shhh." She covered my mouth and pointed towards the docks. "Be
quiet, they're watching for you."

"I don't see anything except vendors and tourists . . ." I trailed off
as I picked out two vendors who weren't quite belligerent or desperate
enough as they hounded the stream of tourists filtering by. I watched as
one of them answered a cell phone, then nodded to the other.

Son of a bitch. Plainclothes agents.

A cold pit formed in my stomach as I realized the cruise-ship dock
wasn't completely off course of my escape-plan repertoire. Hostels,
crowded train and subway stations, even blending in with the other
grad students on digs—hiding in plain sight was one of my talents. God
knows that's how I've made my way around more cities and dig sites than
I care to count. They'd guessed correctly that once I was this close to a
crowded escape route, I'd be inclined to bolt for it. If it hadn't been for
Nadya, I would have. In fact, come to think of the whole sting operation,
they'd bet a lot that I'd play to my strengths to get lost in the crowd.

Meaning someone in the IAA had bothered to do their homework.
Worse, they apparently knew my habits better than I did.

"Nadya, someone at the IAA is changing the game," I said, and related to her my guess on how they were tracking me, including what Benji had related about changed protocols, particularly since Bali. Nadya cursed under her breath.

"What?"

"Maybe nothing, Alix. I just heard something about changes from people I used to know in Russia—new security clamping down on students and PIs, but I thought it was just chatter, complaining about regulations like they always do."

"Yeah, well, we can worry about it once we're the hell out of here." I nodded at the plainclothesmen. "We've got those two to worry about, and we can assume they're looking for me trying to blend in."

Nadya chewed her lip in thought, then shook her head. "Maybe not. I have an idea that will make my plan work. They are looking for you to blend in, no?"

I nodded.

A slow smile spread across Nadya's face as she pulled out her pocket laptop and began to type. "I came up with a backup plan in Algiers in case you got caught. It's risky, but I think it will help us and throw them off."

"How?"

Nadya's smile spread. "Easy. We do what any good Tokyo hostess would do. Give the client exactly what they want."

We watched as six tour busses pulled up to the terminal and a couple hundred people piled out and milled around the vendors.

Instead of making a run to slip in, we waited until Nadya's phone chimed with a new message. "Now," she said, and under the cover of a seventh tour bus we bolted across the road and into the throng of tourists.

I swore as I lost my footing on a badly tended pothole; I was more concerned with watching out for IAA than where I was going. "What about the plainclothesmen?"

"Not a problem. My backup plan is taking care of them," she said as we reached the now crowded cruise terminal courtyard, with more

tourists than common sense dictated packed into a tight space; probably because of the riots. The cruise companies didn't want to risk losing
passengers out in the wild city.

No one paid us any mind as we raced for the customs house—
hopefully that went for the plainclothesmen too. But instead of getting in
line, Nadya veered us to a service door. She kicked open the door to what
had to be a janitor's closet and shoved me inside. There was a duffel bag
tucked in the corner, hidden behind the floor bucket. Nadya had it open
in two seconds, revealing two smaller, brown-paper-wrapped packages.

"Here, put these on," she said, handing me one and taking the other
for herself.

Inside I found a long-sleeved white shirt, bright blue tank top, oversized sunglasses, designer jeans, and a pair of sandals—all overtly designer, and not in a subtle, well-put-together-look way but more like an
"Oh my God, who exploded the label gun over your outfit" kind of way.

Nadya was already out of her own khaki jacket and halfway into a
pair of shorts covered in CC letters . . . well, everywhere.

I held my cruisewear up. "OK, I suck at fashion on a good day, but
even I know these are over the top—"

Nadya glanced at me as she slid on one of a pair of stiletto sandals.
I'd gotten flats instead. At least some practical thought went into this . . .

"Just put them on—now! We don't have much time."

Great, my ass was about to turn into a walking advertisement for
Chanel. Fantastic, just what I always wanted . . . I changed into the clothes.

"And here, put Captain in this," Nadya said, and held out the last
item in the duffel—a designer leather pet carrier, complete with logos.
I had to hand it to her; when she picked a theme, she saw it through. I
opened the new carrier and held it open for Captain. After a careful sniff,
he chirped at me.

"You heard Nadya," I told him. "It's this or face her." Captain decided
the new bag would be just fine.

No sooner was he inside than Nadya threw the closet door back
open.

The nearest cruise ship, the one with brightly colored lettering and ribbons everywhere, had begun loading.

I lowered my dark sunglasses to get a better look. Two IAA agents in suits were waiting beside the customs booth.

Shit. "It's a no go," I said, "they're already there."

But she only grabbed my hand and dragged me behind her. "I swear to God, if you don't keep walking and pretend like you belong in first class . . . Put those sunglasses back on and stand up straight," she scolded as she continued straight on past the line and up the stairs. I glanced at the agents. They were looking at us now . . . along with everyone else at the cruise terminal, and not just because of the spectacle Nadya had dressed us in. We'd completely bypassed the line.

"They're looking straight at us—"

"Just keep *walking*! And smile," Nadya hissed out of the corner of her mouth, her smile fixed as we climbed the stairs.

Two Egyptian officials were waiting at the top, accompanied by a cruise ship official holding a sign with KUROSAWA HOLDINGS scrawled across the side in red and gold letters.

Nadya saw her too. Nadya jumped and began waving her hat, revealing her natural brown hair—normally she wore a neon red wig. That was beside the point—if people hadn't been looking at our spectacle before, they sure as hell were now . . . even the IAA agents were tracking us visually if not physically.

There went my comfort zone. "All right, I'm all for hiding in plain sight, but there's supposed to be a goddamned element of *hide* in there— oomph!"

Nadya jabbed me in the side with a well-placed elbow. "If you mess this up, so help me."

"This is the worst plan ever." I noted a fishing boat off to the side. If we ran now, pushed a few people over, we might make it . . .

"For God's sake, *smile*—and let me do the talking," Nadya said.

"Mrs. Voldynova?" the cruise woman said, fidgeting with what looked like passports in her hand.

Nadya extended her hand and turned her full-wattage hostess smile on the Egyptian customs officers.

"We're so sorry to be late. We got caught behind the crowd while walking the museum," Nadya said, laying her Russian accent on thicker than usual.

Relieved, the woman handed the Egyptian officials the two passports. Passports with our photos inside.

"I would love to know how the hell you pulled that off," I whispered.

Nadya didn't even glance at me, a pleasant but bored expression fixed on her face.

The cruise ship woman spoke in a hushed voice to the Egyptians, but I made out the important point. VIP.

How the hell had Nadya accomplished this in such a short frame of time?

As Egyptian customs checked our faked passports, Nadya whispered, "I picked up spare passports after you almost lost yours last month. I had Lady Siyu arrange the cruise ship in case things went poorly." Brilliant, really; passports were always kept on cruise ships. I'd have to remember that one for later.

"That's not even the best part. Wait until you see the finale," she said.

I tilted my sunglasses down and stole a sideways glance back at the IAA agents. They were already pushing people aside on their way up the steps. "Well, whatever else you have cooked up, it'd better be fast."

"Relax and watch the show."

Shouting erupted just outside the customs line, attracting just about everyone's collective attention.

A figure emerged from inside the building, racing ahead of Egyptian security in a spectacular show of disorganized chaos. It was a woman of about five three or so, wearing a hooded, loose khaki jacket—the kind I was fond of—and a canvas dig bag over her shoulder.

More Egyptian customs mobilized, pushing their way into the crowd after the woman. The crowd was working in her favor though—she was agile enough to weave in and out, knocking fewer people over than the guards following them. She was headed straight for the boarding cruise ship.

The hood fell back, and a dirty-blond ponytail trailed out the back of a red flames baseball cap.

"Oh you've got to be kidding me," I said.

I caught Nadya smile. "Like I said, they wanted an Owl to chase after, and there she is. Authentic looking, isn't she?"

I watched my decoy double turn and swear in Arabic at the customs agents chasing after her before flashing them the finger and leaping onto the cruise ship platform, pushing past the cruise employees, who were shocked into inaction.

"OK, I do *not* act like that," I said.

Nadya arched her eyebrow.

Regardless of what I thought of the show, the agents coming up the stairs decided she fit the part better than I did. They doubled back through the crowd to join the chase on the ship. My double was now on the deck, and I watched as she grabbed something off a table and launched it at the pair of suited IAA.

It missed them and shattered on the pavement below.

A beer bottle.

I swore. "OK, that's just mean," I said to Nadya. I had no doubt the weaponized beer bottle was an illusion to a Corona I'd launched at Rynn a few months back. I'd had my reasons, and they'd involved finding out he was an incubus . . . through a third party, after I'd already slept with him . . .

Not my proudest moment, a bit of an overreaction, but you got to admit I'd had a point.

"Like I said. Authentic," Nadya replied.

I was fixated on the decoy to see what the hell else Nadya had told her to do, so I missed customs handing back our passports and waving us through. Apparently we didn't look like a threat, and the commotion on the cruise ship was incentive to get everyone boarding faster. The cruise representative steered us past security. Craning my neck, I caught the IAA plainclothesmen push their way up the plank in pursuit of the decoy.

"Nadya, it's not an escape plan if we all end up on the same boat. These guys aren't like regular suits. They're smart."

Nadya shook her head as we speed-walked to keep up with our cruise hostess. "Not them, whoever is pulling the strings. Besides, we're not getting on that cruise ship."

"It's the only one in the harbor."

"That's because the one we're on has already left," she said.

For not having a goddamn ship to walk onto, Nadya didn't seem nearly as perplexed as she should have been. Screw appearances. I spun her around. "I think we should be a hell of a lot more concerned about not having a ship."

She pursed her lips and grabbed my hand again, pulling me after her before the hostess noticed we'd stopped. "We're VIP-class passengers. We don't worry about silly things like departure times. We have helicopters. So look like you care a hell of a lot less before you screw this up. I plan on spending tonight on a six-star luxury cruise ship, not in an Egyptian jail!"

We turned the corner, and sure enough, there was a helicopter with the cruise ship logo waiting for us.

I readjusted my sunglasses as the two of us settled in. "Have I mentioned lately how frighteningly good you are at espionage?"

"No, but I'll take it as a compliment. And thank Rynn, he gave me the idea of using a decoy a while back."

Yeah . . . thank Rynn, for going behind my back and discussing my work strategies with Nadya. I had a sinking suspicion Rynn and I were headed for "off" again at warp speed.

It wasn't until we touched down on the cruise ship deck that I gave my nerves a break. The ship was already well out of port, so I doubted the IAA would search for me on the open seas when they eventually clued in to the fact that the decoy wasn't me.

Something occurred to me that a better person would have asked much earlier. "What happens if the IAA gets hold of her?"

"They won't," she said, and glanced over at the cruise hostess leading us towards our cabin. "She is *Rynn's* contact."

So she was supernatural. Yeah, if the IAA did get close enough, they were in for a treat. Shame it hadn't been the agent who'd threatened to shoot me in the leg . . .

Our hostess came to a stop partway down the hall and, with a flourish, opened a door made of polished teak.

I let out a whistle. Man, I thought first-class planes were cushy . . .

There was a full kitchenette and bar, accompanied by a plush living room done in a classier version of a nautical theme, with couches, drapes, and linens in coordinating blue, tan, and white. The furniture, like the door, was teak, and the balcony was . . . damn, I wish my balcony in Seattle was that nice.

Nadya had the sense to thank and tip the woman, while I just stood there, drooling at the decor.

"Don't get used to it," she said after the hostess left. "The next port of call is Greece, where we'll be transferring off first thing in the morning. We'll fly out of wherever they aren't looking."

Nadya gave me a pointed stare and picked up Captain's carrier, cooing through the screen at him before picking the larger of the two bedrooms. "In the meantime, I'm taking a nap."

I ran my hand through my hair. After the run through Egypt I just had? Less nap, more drown my shot nerves in alcohol. "I'm going to go find the bar," I said.

Nadya frowned from the doorway. "You should probably call your boyfriend first. I did not tell him about our side trip to Algiers, but you should."

I winced. Yeah, I think that's what I needed the drink for.

As Mr. Kurosawa's interim security, Rynn was somewhat responsible for knowing what happened during my retrieval jobs, as well as assessing risk. That's where the problems had started. I'm not exactly one for well-drawn-out plans—I have plans, they just tend to be more "let's see what happens when we get there" over drawn-out steps. What can I say? I like flexibility.

He was going to be pissed about Egypt and Algiers. As much as I hated to admit it to myself, I couldn't blame him. This job had turned into a three-ring circus.

I nodded to Nadya and headed for the fridge . . . God, I hoped the room was stocked. It was, in the form of a six-pack of Corona. Small miracles . . .

Beer in hand, I grabbed my phone and headed onto the balcony. I leaned up against the rail and watched Alexandria get smaller and smaller in the distance.

I couldn't shake the feeling I was watching it burn, even though from all reports the protests were mostly contained now. A flash of chaos in the frying pan. Or maybe that was just the lingering smell of oil.

The IAA. Out of all the specters from my past, they'd been low on my radar, well behind the vampires. The Algiers bait, the elaborate Egyptian sting . . . someone in the IAA knew what I was going to do before I did. The question was who?

Benji's words came back to me. Whatever I'd stolen this time had pissed them the hell off. Again, it'd be real nice if they bothered to tell me what it was, preferably before the shooting began. It wasn't like I'd stolen anything earth shattering. The only contact I had in the archaeology community was Benji, and he was a reluctant contact at that.

Speaking of Benji, there was another black strike for the IAA to throw against Owl; kidnapping and holding hostage poor unsuspecting graduate students. Damned if I do . . .

Here's hoping Mr. Kurosawa had a way to intercept them as well. My God, I was becoming more and more dependent on my evil boss to clean up my messes. Here's to slippery slopes.

Well, no sense putting off the inevitable. I took a deep breath and opened my phone. There were already two text messages waiting for me.

The first one was simple. *Next time, call. Preferably before someone is shooting at/trying to eat you.*

OK. Safe, no accusations or told you so . . . It was the second, most recent note that worried me though. *Will route travel info to Nadya. Think someone is spying on you—explain when you land in Vegas.*

I almost put the phone away and bailed on calling. That's my first instinct—ignore the problem and pretend everything is fine ... or avoid it until it magically disappears, not that it ever does. Kind of the same logic Captain uses when he begs for people food and about the same success rate—zero—but hey, there's always a chance.

All right, I felt I owed him an apology too. That's the worst thing about cultivating meaningful connections and relationships with people ... well, not human, in Rynn's case ... I'm still wrapping my head around that small detail too. The point is, as soon as you start trusting people, no matter how much you fight it, at some point along the way you start caring what the hell they think of you.

Damn it, I hate self-reflection.

I dialed and waited for him to pick up. It only took two rings.

"Alix?"

In spite of all the lies I'd told myself over the past two years—hell, in the last hour running through Alexandria—there was another reason I needed to talk to Rynn. One I didn't even want to admit to myself ...

"Rynn, things went really bad—and it's my fault."

I was scared as hell of the IAA, and I desperately needed someone besides Nadya to talk to.

And with that, beer well in hand, I began to explain just how badly things had gone over the past two days, including how the hell Alexandria had happened in the first place. Algiers.

There's only so much you can lie to yourself before reality crashes in.

4

Enter the Dragon and Let the Circus Begin

Three days later, 2:00 p.m., Mr. Kurosawa's private casino

I leaned against Mr. Kurosawa's white marble bar. It was cold, and right now his private casino within the much larger Japanese Circus compound had to be a hundred degrees. I eyed the tray of champagne flutes sitting just a hand's reach away. I was tempted—they'd be cold too. Unfortunately I needed to keep a clear head, since Lady Siyu was hell-bent on blaming everything that had gone wrong these past two weeks on me.

This was exactly why I never used to meet my clients in person.

"Look, the problem wasn't me being there. The problem was they were looking for me before I even stepped on the plane for Morocco," I said, and checked the front door again. Still no Rynn. Damn it, he was supposed to be at these debriefings . . .

Lady Siyu hissed softly and strode across the private casino floor towards me, her heels clicking against the gold-flecked black marble tiles; they were part of the redesign, since the previous wooden floors had burned to a crisp. If I hadn't known any better, I'd never have guessed that this place had been a broiling inferno three months ago. Even the slot machines looked as good as they had before the fire. Not a trace of soot or smoke, not even singed wood. It was as if nothing had happened. Every piece back in its place, every last damned soul . . .

Lady Siyu carried a heavy manila folder between her red lacquered fingernails. Today she looked less the geisha and more the business-woman, dressed in a black pencil skirt, matching jacket, white shirt, and a simple gold pendant in the shape of a twined serpent. She also wore a pair of darkened sunglasses even though the light in the room was already candlelight dim.

Not surprising though. Lady Siyu was a Naga, a half snake, half . . . well, not human . . . let's go with really mean female version of the species. The brown eyes she wore, part of her human façade, tended to slide back to yellow snake slits when her temper got the better of her . . . which was most of the time she had to deal with me; hence the dark sunglasses.

Before Oricho, the previous head of Mr. Kurosawa's security, had tried to kill his boss and take any and every supernatural in a hundred-mile radius with him, he'd hinted that Lady Siyu's hatred of me had to do with her dislike of conversations containing anything more than the bare minimum of necessary syllables. I also figured it had something to do with me trying to blame Oricho's coup on her . . . and harpooning her tail probably hadn't helped.

Mostly though, Lady Siyu just didn't like humans.

The feeling was mutual—about Nagas, I mean, not other humans.

In fact, I'm pretty sure most human resource divisions on the planet had rules in place to ensure employees like me and Lady Siyu never stood in the same room together.

I sighed. Of course Oricho, the one half-decent supernatural under Mr. Kurosawa's employ, had to be a murderous supernatural sociopath. Figured.

Lady Siyu halted in front of me and lifted a corner of her red lac-quered lip, exposing a fang as she removed a photograph from the folder. "You were instructed to maintain a low profile," she said.

"I was maintaining a low profile," I replied. "What you're referring to is what we humans call running for our lives."

She arched a black eyebrow over the top of her sunglasses and slid the photograph across the bar. "Then how do you explain *this*?"

I glanced over at Mr. Kurosawa. He was still sitting on his white leather couch with his back to me.

I took the photo. It was time-stamped three days ago and showed me in an Egyptian bar, a jar of pickled eggs held over my head, ready to launch.

I held the photo up. "Oh come on. They were already after me when they took this."

Lady Siyu's expression darkened. "That is still no excuse to give the International Archaeology Association a photo opportunity." She tossed the rest of the folder on the table for me.

"Where's Rynn? Isn't he supposed to be at these debriefings?"

"The incubus is indisposed."

Fucking fantastic. Leave me to navigate these two on my own, because that never led to disaster. Only the casino almost burning to the ground.

I flipped open the cover.

Reports on my whereabouts the last month, plane tickets under my aliases . . . there was even a list of artifacts I'd potentially stolen. A few of them were dead-on, a few were absent, and the rest were damn good guesses.

Creepy? Definitely, but even I had to admit a part of me was impressed. "Where the hell did these come from?" I asked.

Lady Siyu arched one of her perfect eyebrows. "I find it interesting that only when something threatens to impede your thieving habits you rear your self-absorbed mind from whatever ditch it lies in."

I looked up from the papers and photographs. "Dear God, that was multiple syllables."

Lady Siyu looked like she was about to throttle me. "Necessary to convey your complete lack of judgment."

"Hey, it's not my fault the IAA decided this was the month to re-member they had a rogue archaeologist!" I held up the catalogued thefts. "You want someone to blame? Try all these jobs you've had me doing—"

Mr. Kurosawa let out a sharp breath, calling me and Lady Siyu to silence. I froze and did my best not to make a sound. The last time I'd managed to piss off Mr. Kurosawa, I'd ended up almost dead; I would have been if not for Oricho. Rynn might be head of security—albeit temporarily—but he wasn't here to help me if I screwed things up.

Considering the way Lady Siyu was eyeing me, I wondered if that was on purpose.

Mr. Kurosawa stood and straightened his suit before turning around.

In human form he was average height, medium build, and not par-ticularly memorable—except for the telltale waxy red tinge to his skin. Dragons in general take a lot of concentration to hold other forms well, even more so when they were pissed or irritated. The red skin was a tell, if you like, and a far sight better than destroying a suit worth more than most of his employees' annual salaries. Myths and legends get a lot of things wrong when it comes to supernatural monsters, but the one about dragons hoarding their treasure is true.

Mr. Kurosawa nodded to Lady Siyu and said something in the lan-guage I'd come to call "supernatural common"—though it has been strongly suggested by Rynn that I never repeat that term ever again on pain of death by said insulted supernaturals.

Whatever Mr. Kurosawa told her, Lady Siyu spun on her heels and beat a hasty retreat through the maze of slot machines. I noted he hadn't bothered to hide his black, whiteless eyes. That didn't bode well.

Mr. Kurosawa regarded me before retrieving two glasses of cham-pagne and handing me one. I took it; you don't refuse a dragon.

He raised his glass and said, "I believe two successful acquisitions in a row deserve some praise." I followed suit, remembered that poisoning me was a waste of time. Like Rynn said, if Mr. Kurosawa or Lady Siyu wanted to kill me, they'd do it themselves. I downed the glass in one shot to calm my nerves, glad I hadn't taken one earlier.

"The IAA has always had a passing interest in you, if I recall our research before approaching you with my offer," Mr. Kurosawa said.

I shook my head and placed the empty champagne flute back on the bar. "*Passing* is the operative word. Oh I'm sure they'd love to make an example out of me, but—and no offense to the things you've had me fetching—compared to the supernatural stuff they're trying to shove under the rug, I barely merit a memo."

Mr. Kurosawa nodded, in thought. "What kind of contact did you have with the IAA while in Egypt?"

"Besides them shooting and me running?" I shrugged. "We didn't exactly have time for small talk."

The black eyes focused back on me, and the start of a frown touched Mr. Kurosawa's face. "I see. Please, humor me. Start at the beginning and relate the events in Egypt to me."

I shrugged. "Well, they were ready for me in Alexandria," I said, and related the chase, the riots. Mr. Kurosawa ignored me until I got to the part about the theft. "Between trading insults and running into Benji, I got the impression they were pretty pissed about one of my recent acquisitions."

"Which piece?"

I shook my head. "The IAA wouldn't tell me, and Benji didn't know."

"Are you certain of this, Owl?" Mr. Kurosawa said.

I shrugged again. "As sure as I can be without knocking on their front door and asking."

His upper lip twitched, but whether in amusement or irritation I couldn't be sure. "Perhaps," he said.

Perhaps? What kind of statement was that?

Before I could probe further, Mr. Kurosawa snapped his fingers, and I heard the click of heels somewhere back behind the recesses of the slot machine maze.

"You have the Medusa head?" Mr. Kurosawa asked.

I nodded and wrapped my fingers around the gold-and-emerald figurehead in my pocket. I'd spent some time examining the Medusa head on the plane ride back. Out of all the things to go after in Egypt, why the hell this had piqued Mr. Kurosawa's interest escaped me. There was equivalent stuff to be found on the black market, worth more money and easier to get hold of. Maybe Mr. Kurosawa would actually tell me what he wanted with this round of artifacts. I didn't hold my breath on that though.

"Two acquisitions in one trip, both the Medusa head and the Moroccan death mask. I am impressed."

Yeah, he'd said that already . . . this time I felt the "but" sliding in there.

"The incubus reports he was not happy with your alteration of plans."

There it was. "He usually isn't," I said.

Mr. Kurosawa gave me a measured stare before retrieving a tablet from the mirrored coffee table I hadn't seen before. "In this case, I agree with his assessment. As much as I appreciate your independence as a contractor, you will notify him from now on with any changes to your plans."

Great, Rynn had looped Mr. Kurosawa into this. Fantastic . . .

I opened my mouth to argue, but before I could say anything, Mr. Kurosawa glanced back up from the coffee table, his black eyes carrying a warning. "Consider this a protection of assets, not meddling in your affairs. You ending up dead from your own recklessness is bad for business."

I bit my tongue. He might look human, but he wasn't. Dragons were volatile, powerful supernatural entities prone to eating people who pissed them off—especially thieves. This was not the battle to draw my lines over, even though this felt less like a security concern and more like a land grab for my autonomy. And, as Rynn demonstrated, my friends were getting in on it too.

The click of Lady Siyu's heels filled the room as she rounded the row of slot machines, balancing a silver tray, which she extended towards me.

Mr. Kurosawa arched an eyebrow at me, his black eyes lending the gesture an ominous effect. "I believe you have Caracalla's Medusa head for me."

One minute I was being chastised for going to Alexandria, the next I was being asked to hand over the treasure . . .

Sometimes there's only one way to make a client happy: give them whatever the hell they want.

I stuffed my pride and handed over the gold Medusa head to Lady Siyu on a silver platter. Assholes . . .

"Not a scratch," I said, dropping it onto the silver tray so it made a soft clank.

Lady Siyu arched an eyebrow, and the corner of her mouth twitched before she turned on her heels and disappeared back into the casino's dark recesses.

"In answer to your question about the photographs," Mr. Kurosawa said, pulling me back from fantasizing about Lady Siyu tripping head-long over her stiletto heels and swallowing the damn gold head. "We intercepted a third party working on behalf of the IAA."

That didn't sound right. The IAA was a clandestine network with its very own spy ring. I'd never heard of them hiring third-party clandestine organizations to do their work for them. "Who?" I said.

"That is a very good question. Lady Siyu is still investigating. They are very adept at covering their tracks. We only intercepted these through the IAA communication lines."

"As you can imagine, this raises concern for us. Mr. Kurosawa's job offer made allowances for the vampires, not the IAA," Lady Siyu said, slinking back out of the shadows. The silver tray was gone, but this time she held a larger, thicker folder between her red lacquered nails, which she handed to Mr. Kurosawa with a light bow before taking up station back by the bar.

I felt a chill run down my spine. If they terminated our contract because I was a fuckup, my protection from Alexander and the Paris boys was over. Lady Siyu would probably give Alexander a heads-up too.

Mr. Kurosawa held out the file and nodded for me to take it. "I believe the IAA's renewed interest in you has something to do with this. Please take a look and tell me if any of it looks familiar," he said, and I noted his skin had turned a deep shade of red, and smoke now rolled off his skin and poured out through his nose.

I opened the file. The first page was an aerial photograph of a mountainous desert region, with a single location outlined in red, accompanied by a series of numbers and letters etched along the side in handwriting. Satellite pictures . . . I wondered whether Mr. Kurosawa's casino empire branched into media and communications. I flipped to the next page and found the legend to the letters and numbers. Coordinates for burial sites and time-line references. A second photograph was clipped to that, showing a pixelated close-up of the region circled in red.

"Wait a minute," I said. It was a little out of focus, but the structure and cave-spotted cliff were familiar—there were only a handful of places with settlements like that on the planet. I glanced up at Mr. Kurosawa and tapped the stone buildings jutting out of the side of the cliff like some forlorn ruined castle. "This is Deir Mar Musa, the Monastery of Saint Moses the Abyssinian, outside Damascus in Syria. It's named after an Ethiopian prince who ran away from home to become a monk during the sixth century."

Lady Siyu snorted. "He was sainted for running away?"

"No, you don't get sainted for running away from your problems—otherwise everybody'd be a saint. You get sainted for getting *killed* running away from your problems. Slight distinction, I know, but it's the Catholics' way of appreciating real commitment. In this case, it was the Byzantines who helped martyr him, and even that changes depending on which legend you buy into. Half of them say Moses was Ethiopian royalty and the other half claim he was an escaped Egyptian slave turned thief. Depends who's telling and which version suits their moral agenda."

Mr. Kurosawa cleared his voice. I took that as a hint to get back on track.

I flipped a few more pages to see what the hell else had been jammed in there. Dig site records going back to the early 1950s, when the site had been discovered, printouts of reports, inventory of the murals . . . Jesus, these were the original IAA records, stamp and all. IAA archives were notorious to get into—like a Fort Knox for dig site files. Nadya and I stuck to the outer university department databases if we needed records, and even that came with pretty significant risks.

"Where and how did you get your hands on their archives—" I started to ask, then shook my head. "Scratch that, I don't want to know the answer, do I?"

Following the photographs of the Syria dig site were lists of IAA inventory, mostly photographs of the medieval murals dating back to the eleventh and twelfth centuries. Interesting stuff, but not worth the time of most real collectors . . . unless they were after the actual murals.

Difficult but doable.

I came across the most recent set of dig notes and photographs. Their dates indicated they'd been taken in the last few months.

I glanced up. Mr. Kurosawa was watching me impassively. "This can't be right. The IAA pulled out of the monastery two years ago when the Syrian civil war sparked." Supernatural entities were one thing—that went with the territory—but wars and politics were things the IAA avoided. Better to leave supernatural things buried so they didn't get caught in the crossfire.

Mr. Kurosawa's black eyes regarded me, and his mouth set in an unreadable expression. "I assure you, those are accurate. We are not in the habit of acquiring false documentation."

What the hell had brought them back to the monastery in the middle of the Syrian civil war? Besides a few frescoes painted by Christian priests, there wasn't anything of value. Hell, if it was frescoes you wanted, I had a line on some of Michelangelo's submerged under Venice, buried when they filled up all the wells during World War II.

There had to be something more to reopening the dig than a couple of twelfth-century Catholic frescoes . . .

The next set of photographs wasn't of the monastery, though. They were close-ups of the surrounding hillside, with hollows and rock formations highlighted in color-coded ink, probably for cross-checking in someone's legend. I found a collection of recent sketches of the surrounding hills, indicating a collection of stone circles that hadn't been visible in earlier photos. Tombs or burial sites maybe.

The next few pages read like an IAA handbook example on how to document a site, mapping the tunnels and caves that ran underneath the monastery. Items had been pulled out of the tunnels recently and were catalogued—stone tools, flint pieces, stone bowls, even a carved fertility idol or two. My throat went dry as I noted the carbon dating on the stone tools and rock structures ... 10,000 BC. Neolithic. They'd uncovered another Neolithic site—an advanced one. If the flint tools and bowls were any indication, very advanced, considering the initial carbon dating.

"Son of a bitch, the bastards found something." I held out the dig diagram and photos for Mr. Kurosawa. He glanced at them, then back up at me, awaiting an explanation.

"They aren't interested in the monastery," I said. "Those tunnels and stone structures? That's what they're really after. They're Neolithic, over ten thousand years old. That region of the Levant would make them the Qaraoun, an advanced culture of the late Stone Age. Think after we figured out farming, but before we traded in the chipped stone tools for bronze weapons." Though for all I knew about the life span of dragons, Mr. Kurosawa might have been around for that.

No wonder the IAA had wandered back into a war zone to excavate. They weren't looking at the stone circles either; they were excavating the tombs. And from the sketches and photos, there had to be hundreds of them....

A pit formed in the bottom of my stomach. Something I'd read about the monastery being abandoned in the mid-nineteenth century, and details over the deaths of a 1950s archaeology expedition reared its ugly head from the recesses of my buried grad school memories ...

I started flipping through the pages at a faster rate. It had to be in here somewhere. Part of me hoped it was just my imagination and lack of sleep playing tricks on me.

There it was, buried halfway through the bulky folder, little more than a footnote copied from a textbook. A brief history of the dig site and a nickname taken from a piece of Arabic graffiti carved into the stone over one of the archways back in the 1950s, when it'd first been discovered: City of the Dead.

Shit.

Both Mr. Kurosawa and Lady Siyu were still regarding me, as if I were a rat in a maze. "Look, if they found what I think they've found, this is bad." As in stay the hell away from the Middle East for a while bad. "They shouldn't even be there. Even if they've uncovered Neolithic remains, every tenured professor in the IAA knows the Syrian monastery is off-limits for extensive digs."

"And why exactly is that, *thief*?" Lady Siyu said, taking a step closer. It wasn't my imagination; both Lady Siyu and Mr. Kurosawa were studying me a little too closely. I brushed the observation off—*one thing at a time, Owl.*

"Because it's too dangerous." I spread some sheets out across the bar. "What's missing from all these files is the recent history of the monastery. Either whoever you had steal these files missed them, or some idiot in the IAA misplaced them. In 1850, the monastery was suddenly abandoned by all its inhabitants. Every monk, every person in the neighboring village, vanished."

"The area has been war torn for many centuries. Abandoning a remote location is nothing of value," Mr. Kurosawa said.

"Except that people didn't leave because of war. Every last one died of an unknown plague that wasted its victims until they were little more than breathless, sweating husks. Which, if whoever got you these files had bothered to do their homework, you'd know from the church records."

Mr. Kurosawa inclined his head and exchanged a glance with Lady Siyu before nodding for me to continue.

"The disease started in the monastery and spread to the surrounding village. The monks tried to flee at first, but out of fear villagers forced them back, locking them inside, never to reopen. A hundred years later, when visiting archaeologists heard the story, they started to poke around and went looking for the tunnels the dying priests raved about on their deathbeds. Every last one of them died as well."

"The imaginations and ravings of madmen are not proof. People die all the time. It's one of the many weaknesses of your species—the most exploitable, in my opinion," Mr. Kurosawa said.

Was I ever glad I paid attention in history class. Thank a morbid fascination with ancient things that can kill me so I can stay away from them.

"Well, you'll be happy to know the next team who came along in the early eighties agreed with you. Until they fell sick and the researcher in charge had time to make one very delirious phone call about temples and sacrilege before they all died. *Right* after coming into contact with the Neolithic pieces brought up from the tunnels by the monks and left by the altar." I rifled through the photographs until I found what I was looking for. "The City of the Dead was one of the first documented cases of a modern-day supernatural plague." I held up the photograph showing the pieces the 1980 team had come into contact with. "The place is cursed."

Lady Siyu stopped me with a sharp hiss and strode over. I noticed she was carrying a digital tablet. "We do not care about the site or what the IAA cares to waste its archaeologists' lives on. What we do care about is why pieces from the city are turning up in private collections."

"That's . . . impossible," I said. My issues with the IAA could fill a book, but they knew how to keep a lid on dangerous artifacts.

She handed me the tablet. "See for yourself," she said.

Two images were already open on the screen. The first was a head shot of an attractive redheaded woman whom I recognized as Daphne Sylph, an actress from the early '80s who was more famous for looking like she hadn't aged a day than for any of her forgettable films; the second was a clip from an article covering an L.A. charity party Daphne held for helping communities in the developing worlds, and which featured her own private collection of artifacts.

There were photographs of three artifacts sitting in a case. I scrolled down to a series of close-ups: a stone chisel described as "mega-Neolithic chipped flint," followed by a piece of a very well-preserved carved stone bowl and a bronze sword.

"Shit." I switched back to the folder and pulled out the inventory from the latest IAA dig. The pieces were uncannily close to the ones catalogued ... so close that if I had to bet on the pieces being the same ...

"OK, you may be on to something—" I started, then stopped mid-sentence when I caught sight of Mr. Kurosawa's red face and Lady Siyu's hint of fang.

"Now I ask you once again, Owl, why do you suppose the IAA has orchestrated this manhunt?"

"*Thief*," Lady Siyu added.

Oh hell no ... Despite the heat in the room, my skin chilled. They'd both moved in closer, as if I'd somehow turned into prey in the last five seconds.

"Woah, now wait just a minute," I said. "You think it was me?"

"It would explain why the IAA was so persistent in Egypt." Mr. Kurosawa smiled, and I caught sight of black serrated teeth. Shit, this was not good. Now I knew why Rynn hadn't been invited to the party.

I took a step back, but I was already at the bar. "OK, just because the IAA thinks I stole something doesn't mean I did. You couldn't pay me enough to go into that city—it's cursed." I hopped up onto the bar and swung my legs over. I didn't think I could make it to any of the doors, but at least it gave me time to shoot my mouth off.

"That is your specialty, is it not? Sneaking into their dig sites and taking things from right under their noses?" Lady Siyu said.

"OK, yes—" In fact, the theft did have my signature all over it, and so did the others Benji had pointed out ... "But this is someone else."

Lady Siyu hissed and dragged a claw across the stone bar as she walked around, effectively cutting off any hope of exit.

Appealing to my innocence was only pushing the conversation in the wrong direction. *Think, Owl, there has to be something that shows you didn't do it.* Unfortunately, the time line was no damn good. The fact that I'd been in Morocco, Algiers, and Egypt only made me look more guilty—which was why the IAA had figured it had to have been me, and falling for the Algiers bait had only confirmed I'd been in the area. All right, what about the job itself?

Lady Siyu hissed and flashed her fangs, as if about to strike.

Something to hold her off . . . matches? No, that'd just piss her off . . . I spotted the soda gun in the well—what was it Rynn had said about Nagas being more like salamanders than snakes? Something about their skin and scales being sensitive to acid rain . . . Worth a shot. I grabbed the soda gun and held it out towards her. She snorted. Not exactly spectacular self-defense on my part, but she did narrow her eyes at the soda gun.

OK, think. If I *were* the thief—and, for the record, I'm *not*—how the hell would I do it, assuming getting into the dig was the least of my worries? From what I could tell, the real thief hadn't had any trouble in that department, otherwise the IAA would never have suspected me. Moving the artifacts across two continents would be where I'd get twitchy. I wouldn't risk a flight out of Syria, not even chartered. With the site open the IAA would be on high alert for anything that could release a supernatural plague.

A boat would work, but not through the Mediterranean—too obvious. Maybe by the Red Sea or Persian Gulf—or just head south, then fly out of Africa . . .

The point is it'd take me a minimum of two weeks to get it to the continental US.

Lady Siyu lunged at me, spitting venom. I yelled and fired. Club soda shot out, drenching the front of her suit. The skin around the neck of her shirt and below her cuffs began to turn a slow shade of red. She shrieked, but jumped back. After the shock vanished, the look she gave me was pure death.

Talk fast, Alix, before she strikes again. "Wait! I can prove I didn't do it!" I said. Lady Siyu wasn't interested in hearing. She hissed and strode towards me, knocking the soda gun out of my hands. I backed into the corner and braced myself. Oh hell, this was going to hurt.

But before Lady Siyu reached me, Mr. Kurosawa barked out a

command—or that's what I assumed it was, considering I don't understand a goddamn word of supernatural common. Lady Siyu froze less than a foot away from me, close enough that I could smell the perfume trailing off her skin and feel her breath on my face. Everything went very still. Especially me.

"Explain, Owl," Mr. Kurosawa said.

I took a deep breath and tried to steady my heart. "OK, first, the time line doesn't match up with me being in North Africa. Yes, I was there, but I would have to have already been at the Syrian dig site two weeks ago, minimum. I was in Vegas," I said, and explained my logic of how the theft was pulled off using a route through Africa.

Mr. Kurosawa seemed to consider it, which raised Lady Siyu's skepticism.

"You expect us to believe the thief would have to circumvent the IAA after stealing artifacts from their midst?" she said.

God, I wish I could wipe that sneer off her face. If it wasn't for the fangs . . .

I held up a hand. "Despite what you two would like to think, the IAA actually knows what they're doing when it comes to covering up the supernatural. They'll be looking for these—" I pointed to the objects on the tablet. "And if they haven't found them already, they will soon, courtesy of Daphne Sylph."

Mr. Kurosawa spoke to Lady Siyu in supernatural. Normally the routine is Lady Siyu nods and slithers off into some dark hole—and yes, I'm proud of myself for that one. This time she spat back.

Only when Mr. Kurosawa turned a deeper shade of red and barked out another command did Lady Siyu back down, though if I was any judge, she wasn't too fucking happy about it.

Mr. Kurosawa focused his attention back on me. He indicated the couch opposite the mirrored coffee table. I took the seat—and promptly downed a second glass of champagne as he settled back. Thin line between calm and buzzed be damned.

"Lady Siyu thinks I should let her kill you," he said, smoke billowing out of his nose. "Though I will admit, your current argument is compelling, if not convincing."

"No offense, but I think she'll take any excuse she can get to kill me."

A slow smile spread across his face, and I noted his teeth had shifted back to the white, human-looking version. "It is as you say. So, tell me, if I entertain the notion that you are not the thief, who is?"

I wracked my head for any other antiquities thieves who could have pulled it off. Unfortunately, none of the good ones that came to mind were stupid enough to touch the city. They all valued their skins too much. "Whoever did this is very good," I said tentatively.

"Better than you?"

I weighed that one carefully. Whoever had pulled it off had managed to convince both the IAA and Lady Siyu it was me. Even if it wasn't on purpose, that meant they had to be as good as me, maybe better, since I was the only thief in anyone's crosshairs.

"Let's just say they'd have to be good enough to get by the IAA, and dumb enough to go after the city."

Mr. Kurosawa reached for a glass containing a deep red liquid, wine maybe—or something else dragons ate. Vampires weren't the only supernaturals fond of blood. "Lady Siyu's contacts insist that very thief could only be you."

I shook my head. "I'm not that stupid."

His smile widened as he took another sip. "That, as you might say, is a matter of opinion. One that is currently divided in my house. I do not like a divided house."

God, I hate supernatural logic. The equation here was simple; they were supernatural, I was human. My existence was currently presenting both a benefit and a problem. Things don't stand in tandem for long. I either helped make the problem go away, or before long the inconvenience would start to outbalance the benefit.

And I doubted very much Lady Siyu really thought I was the thief: she just wanted an excuse to kill me, and this was the first chance—lately—to fall in her lap.

"Since we are divided," Mr. Kurosawa continued, "here is my compromise. First, you will go to Los Angeles and retrieve every piece from this collector."

OK, B&Es were not exactly my specialty, but I could handle it if it meant Lady Siyu didn't get to eviscerate me.

"Second, since someone did remove those artifacts from the city, and you are currently our only suspect, I require you to find the real thief."

"If such a human exists," Lady Siyu added.

OK... a little more difficult. Like I said, whoever this thief was, they were good enough that I had no leads. "And if I can't find out who it is?"

"Then I will have no choice but to revisit Lady Siyu's evidence."

I stopped myself just short of swearing. Great. Just what I fucking needed. If I couldn't find out who did take the artifacts, I'd be back up on the plate for slaughter.

Mr. Kurosawa stood and straightened his suit. "Since Lady Siyu is occupied, I will lead you to the entrance myself."

I figured that was more so Lady Siyu didn't accidently kill me. I didn't see Mr. Kurosawa leading many mice out of the mousetrap.

I followed close on his heels. Getting lost amongst the slot machines was a bad idea. It looked straightforward enough, but when I glanced back over my shoulder, I could have sworn the machines changed their arrangement. Some kind of magic-induced maze. Contrary to popular belief, I do in fact learn from my mistakes. I wouldn't make a very good enslaved soul. Especially not one trapped in a slot machine.

I'd probably just start hoarding treasure behind his back . . .

We reached the heavy black doors painted with red Japanese characters. "Lady Siyu will forward you documentation we've collected on the thefts, and the incubus will accompany you to Los Angeles," Mr. Kurosawa said as the doors swung open as if of their own volition.

Yup, I'd seen that one coming too.

"Things will not go well if you do not find me the thief. We supernaturals agree with the IAA in that we do not wish to be exposed to the human population at large."

Mostly because I didn't dare turn my back on Mr. Kurosawa, I bowed to him and watched as he retreated back into the casino.

Before he stepped into the slot machine maze, he stopped.

Reflex kicked in, and I started to gauge how fast I could get to the elevators . . .

But Mr. Kurosawa didn't attack. Instead, he said, "You are correct in your assessment of the City of the Dead. Keep in mind that even we supernaturals sometimes lose places for a reason."

And with that, he was gone, and the black doors slammed shut behind me. I headed to the elevators and called Nadya.

"Alix, I'm relaxing. I don't want to hear about any more disasters for the next three hours, preferably after I've convinced the attractive Japanese bartender Rynn hired to come over and say hello."

"Seriously?"

She sighed. "Just tell me what is so important you are interrupting my quiet afternoon."

"What do you know about the Syrian City of the Dead?"

There was a pause on the other end. "Enough to know if you're the one asking it counts as an imminent disaster."

"Yeah, well the good news is it wasn't me."

"Bad news?"

"Someone beat me to it and everyone thinks it's me."

Nadya swore. "Meet me down by the pool."

I hung up and rode the elevator down. I really hoped Nadya had some candidates for the theft, because I had no plans of letting Lady Siyu gut me.

5

The Devil's in the Details

2:30 p.m., the Garden Café. Where the hell is Nadya . . . ?

It took me a minute of scanning the casino's greenhouse-themed restaurant to spot Nadya, who was sitting outside at a table by the pool. I headed through the giant glass doors decorated with what looked like gold cherry blossoms—or maybe they were lotus flowers. I was never one for plants in the first place, and recent events with vampires had turned me off lilies forever. Now Lady Siyu took perverse pleasure in filling the Japanese Circus with lily of the valley arrangements whenever I returned.

I slid into the seat across from Nadya. "Here, see what you can make of these," I said, passing her the stack of files Lady Siyu and Mr. Kurosawa had left for me at the front desk. "I'm officially the one and only suspect on the IAA's shit list for one City of the Dead theft."

For her part, Nadya only glanced at the folder before turning her attention back to the bar. She was busy trying to make eye contact with the new bartender, an attractive Asian man with hair bleached within an inch of its life, and re-dyed in a color scheme I could only call tequila sunrise; red at the ends, shifting to orange, then white-yellow at the roots.

"What number cosmo are you on?"

"Two." She angled her sunglasses down to glare at me, then waited until she caught the bartender's eye. She winked, raising her empty martini glass and flashing a smile.

Not that I'm an expert in relationships, but to me, the bartender looked more interested in mixing drinks than sneaking a glance at Nadya. Wonder of wonders, Rynn hired bartenders who actually worked . . .

"How many cosmos before you throw in the towel?" I asked.

"As many as it takes, Alix. I'm a professional hostess. Trust me, I can hold my alcohol. Besides, I haven't had a fix in a month, and the bartender isn't the only view out here."

I followed her gaze. Nadya had a good view of the nymph pool boys Mr. Kurosawa employed to take care of the pools and various stray bodies that seemed to accumulate around supernaturals in general. They were close enough that you could enjoy the show, but not so close that their plastic faces unnerved you.

Nadya didn't have my inherent fear of supernaturals. Then again, Nadya didn't have my experience—probably since she was a sight better at spotting them, and I . . . well . . . let's just say I have a blind spot, one that had led to a number of problems over the years.

I watched as a pale man sporting a tuft of white hair carried a glass rack across the pool area, walking with a wide, lumbering gait to the outdoor bar. After stopping to chat with Nadya's bartender, he unloaded the fresh glasses.

Fish demon? No, not pale enough and shouldn't have hair. Turnip demon then?

"Hunh?" I said, as Nadya broke my train of thought.

Nadya had started perusing the files, both the dig and the surveillance package. "What the hell is this?" she said, holding up the photos taken of me out on various recent jobs.

"The IAA tracking me for the last two to three weeks?" I said.

Nadya gave out a low whistle, followed by something in Russian as she flipped through.

"Told you they'd gotten more organized," I said, and glanced back up at the bar. The man with the tuft of white hair was still there. Was it me, or were his arms too long?

Nadya shook her head. "No—I mean, yes, this is much more extensive than I'd expect from them, but I was referring to the theft. This? Infiltrating dig sites, lifting artifacts right under the IAA's nose? It's got your signature all over it." She held up the list of recent heists the IAA had attributed to me, some of which were mine, and others that weren't but could have been. "If I didn't know better, I'd swear these were all you."

"Apparently the IAA agrees with you. Though I'm starting to think I was just in the wrong place at the wrong time . . ."

Nadya frowned. "Perhaps," she said, picking up one of the photographs of the dig itself, then switching to the notes. She had a knack for cross-referencing research and would pick up anything I'd missed. "But regardless, I think someone is trying to make it look like you did it."

The same thought had occurred to me too, though it didn't sit well that someone in the underground antiquities community would purposefully try to throw me under the bus.

Yes, there is such a thing as honor amongst thieves.

"That reminds me—" I pulled out my phone and typed out a quick message to Hermes. Hermes was a courier who specialized in delivering stolen goods under the radar of customs and other authorities. He was one of the best working in the continental US, and the only one who specialized in antiquities. If he hadn't delivered the items himself, he'd have a good idea who had.

Hermes—info on Daphne Sylph L.A. purchase? Some asshole's setting me up.

I attached the article and accompanying video footage from an entertainment channel showing the three stolen items at the charity party to the email. No sense giving Hermes more than needed. He might take the whole honor amongst thieves thing seriously, but that didn't mean I wanted to let the fox into the chicken coop. The pictures would generate enough questions as it was.

The busboy had finished at the bar and was heading back through the service door. "Daikon demon?" I asked Nadya, nodding at the busboy.

Nadya glanced up from the folder, frowned, and shook her head. "No. Frog. Good guess though," she added.

It was not, but Nadya was encouraging me to get better at picking them out. You know the kind of people you've surrounded yourself with by the lies they tell. Good friends lie about the little stuff and tell you the truth when it's important—regardless of what you want to hear. Bad friends either always tell the truth or always lie. Either way, it ends up being pointless noise.

I've come to terms with the fact that some supernaturals, like Carpe and Rynn, are OK, but those are extreme exceptions, not the rule. Most supernaturals hate humans. The majority of humans don't know super-naturals exist, so they have no opinion one way or the other . . . except about vampires. They still don't believe in them, but somehow everyone's convinced they're romantic, immortal creatures who have nothing better to do than spend their days trolling high schools for teenagers in need of rescuing from a boring, uneventful life and parents who just don't understand them. . . . Well, vampires do troll for high school kids, but trust me, it's not romantic, it's convenient. Like fast food.

"Alix," Nadya said, still leafing through the pages, "I think this is more serious than you realize."

"Because the IAA finally got their shit together?" I said it as cava-lierly as I could, but in all honestly just the thought of my near brush in Alexandria still sent my heart racing.

"No, because I think there is more to this than Mr. Kurosawa is let-ting on."

There was that slow set of chills riding down my spine. Nadya was good when it came to archives and data pushing—better than me. Where I saw a collection of papers and data on a site depicting sporadically connected events, Nadya saw patterns. Again, that's why Nadya avoids trouble, and I stumble in headfirst . . . "I got the impression they were being pretty damn transparent when Lady Siyu suggested I be lunch."

Nadya shook her head. "Something smells very wrong with all this, and I think it begins with the IAA, not the thief."

Nadya began arranging the data into piles. "Start going through these and find me everything you can on the dig teams—take notes on each one, what they worked on, which notes were theirs . . ." She handed me the set of notes from 1950 and took the more recent ones for herself, opening up her laptop at the same time. "And Alix?"

I looked up from my pile.

"Do a bar run first. We're both going to need more than one drink."

The pool had gotten crowded as people settled in around us for post-gambling sun and alcohol, mostly for drowning their sorrows, though a few looked celebratory. I pinched the bridge of my nose and tried to drown out the background noise as I crossed off another set of dig notes on Dr. Caitlin, one of the first 1950 grad students to fall ill. They'd sent her farthest into the tunnels, either because she'd presumably been smaller, or they'd figured the least senior grad student got to play canary. Fifty-fifty on those odds.

Over the last two hours, Nadya and I had pored over the three IAA excursions and, for the most part, had accounted for all the dig team members. The only one we couldn't find any information on was the current dig team, including the postdoc who would be running it.

I glanced over at the bartender, wondering what my chances were of wrangling another Corona as a bachelorette party, led by a trio of girls with a gradient of blond shades of hair sidled up to the bar. Unfortunately, Rynn was still hiring, so the bar was short staffed.

Speaking of Rynn, there'd still been no sign of him . . . I couldn't decide if that was a good or bad thing.

"More than I expected, less than I hoped for," Nadya said, putting down her folder. "The good news or bad news first?"

"Bad news please. I refuse to delude myself with false hope."

"The Syrian City of the Dead is a cursed place, one of the few real ones."

I frowned. "We knew that already."

"Yes, but you're not seeing the bigger picture." She picked up the most recent dig approval forms for reopening the Neolithic dig. "In order to open up a class-five restricted site, which supernatural plagues fall under, you need the entire IAA Board of Directors' approval."

"Which is right there on the bottom of the form," I said.

"The stamp is there, but I can't find any signatures."

"I've never seen a signature on one of these. They're kept under some clandestine fortress, aren't they?"

She nodded and pulled out what looked like another form. The paperwork was something I sure as hell didn't miss about the IAA. They might rival the Illuminati and Masons for most clandestine, but they were sticklers for a paper trail.

"But in order for the board to approve even a class-three restricted site—which, by the way, because of skin walkers and genies includes every site in Russia, so I am very familiar with the paperwork, especially since my professors couldn't be bothered to pull themselves out of their vodka bottles long enough to fill out a form when there was a sober graduate student hanging around—they require every individual on the dig to be listed with the stamp."

"It's to make sure if a skin walker gets out, they know who the possible victims are, right?"

Nadya nodded gravely and handed me back the copy of the permit. "No names means this is either forged or the IAA doesn't want a record of them having been there. Alix, I know restricted sites—we had enough trouble with our class threes. The director would never approve this project. It's too dangerous."

On that hand, Nadya was right. Every IAA dig on the planet went through an approval committee, whose sole purpose was to make sure nothing was crawling around the site that they couldn't hide from the general public. The word *curse* should have been enough to put a stop to the whole thing.

"Maybe the treasure is just that damned good," I said.

She shook her head. "The IAA is a lot of things, but treasure hunters they are not. Either they were leveraged to approve it, or someone managed to bypass their approval completely." She paused. "The professor who is funding the dig is absent from the dig site itself. You saw who it was?"

I shrugged, determined not to make a big deal out of it. My old supervisor, Dr. Orel Sanders, was the one who'd signed off on the grant and was funding supplies. Unfortunately it didn't mean a hell of a lot. "That's not unusual for him. He never works on site. He doesn't even run the research, just hands it off to the next postdocs in line. Honestly, I'm not sure he even proofreads the papers and grants anymore. I only ever met the man twice; once for my interview, and then when I was kicked out." Though I wasn't in the mood to rehash getting screwed over by my supervisor and research committee, I still remember the exact conversation word for word, as if someone seared it into my mind . . .

"Don't worry, Alix," Dr. Sanders had said after I'd reported my run-in with the mummy. "Happens all the time. Just sign off on the retraction and we'll get you to a dig. No mummies this time, promise." He'd even had the nerve to smile and pat me on the back. Made me furious just thinking about it . . . my God, have I ever really been that stupid and naïve?

Sensing my mood change, Nadya switched tactics. "He might not be involved or even know about the dig, but his signature didn't get on the paper by itself. It's a lead. All we have to do is determine where all his postdocs are, and we should be able to figure out which one is running the dig."

"Except there's no guarantee the thief is using an IAA contact."

Nadya shook her head. "They have to have some connection with the IAA, otherwise they'd never have kept the theft this quiet. We just have to find it—"

"And hope to hell they're not as good at burying their past as I am." Still, a needle in a haystack was better than no lead at all. And Sanders's postdocs wouldn't be hard to find—all the university websites listed them.

"I will do my best from my end and see what more I can find out—both from these files and ones that might not be so obvious."

"I'll see what I can dig up about the sale from Hermes before I go to L.A.," I said. Needles in haystacks, but you work with what you have.

Nadya gathered up the papers—none of the maps or diagrams, mostly notes and references about the researchers involved. "There were some prominent Russian professors who wrote on the city and the plague. They should still be on the server—I'll see if I can dig them up."

The Russian university servers were notoriously unsecure due to staffing. They didn't have a budget to wipe old access codes, a fact Nadya exploited every chance she got.

"They're going to plug that hole eventually, Nadya."

"You don't know Russian academics. The loophole will be fixed, just not soon. My nose will tell me when to stop."

She might have an uncanny ability to sniff out trouble, but I doubted it would warn her about the servers. Then again, it had warned her to get out of archaeology six months ahead of me when it'd still been a smart idea.

"I also have some contacts in Japan still who might be able to help. They keep their eyes out for new digs like this—for their clients. I'll see if anyone has been trying to offload pieces in their networks."

Speaking of offloading other artifacts . . . I rifled through the folder and pulled out the list of thefts the IAA had attributed to me. If Hermes turned up nothing on Daphne Sylph's purchases, I'd shoot these by his way too.

I handed it to Nadya. "See if any of your Japanese contacts know anything about these thefts—the ones I didn't do," I said, and gathered up the remaining files.

I don't know whether it was the way she glanced back at her computer screen or how she fidgeted with the stem of her cosmo—both uncharacteristic for Nadya, who was a tyrant of etiquette—but there was something she wasn't saying.

"Spit it out, Nadya."

"Why are they sending you?"

I shrugged. "Because I'm their resident thief and they expect bang for their buck?" I'd been running over my meeting with the two of them. The more I thought about it, the less I was convinced Lady Siyu really believed I was the thief. This was just her sick and twisted way to get around the fact that Mr. Kurosawa wouldn't let her kill me.

Nadya shook her head. "That just proves my point. All they need to do—all you need to do, for that matter—is send those files to the IAA, find out who is in charge of the dig, and forward the tip to them. They could have an agent walk in five minutes later and confiscate her entire collection. That would be the simplest solution to the problem. Why send you?"

"Because they want the items for their own collection? For Mr. Kurosawa's section on 'rending, gutting, and other assorted ways to torture your human?' I didn't ask, Nadya, I was too busy worrying about my neck. Maybe they just like to see the IAA with their panties in a bunch as much as I do."

"Then why do they need you to find the real thief?"

"They said they don't want more pieces coming out of the city—and for the record, I agree with that one. Whatever that curse does, it's not fun."

Nadya pursed her lips. "I'm sorry, but it looks more like Mr. Kurosawa and Lady Siyu are placing chess pieces on a board."

"If they are, they sure didn't bother to explain the rules."

Nadya arched an eyebrow over the rim of her sunglasses. "You assume there are rules. There is something bigger going on here, and let's face it, you are not exactly one for looking at the big picture."

"I *am* looking at the big picture. Cursed City of the Dead artifacts, bad. Find thief raiding the place, good."

"More like flashing the big picture the finger before throwing a paint bomb at it."

"Paintballs, Nadya. And glad to see the faith from my friends—really, it's touching." I gathered up my stuff and turned to go.

"Alix?" Nadya said as I reached the door. "Just be careful. Things are not what they seem with this one."

My first inclination was to argue, but stupid and reckless is the one who ignores Nadya's instincts. And yes, I've been guilty on more than one occasion. I nodded and pushed the door open.

"And you should really talk to Rynn!"

I winced. Yeah, Rynn. Following the theme of my complete and utter failure to avoid the supernatural despite my best efforts, I also happen to be dating an incubus. On and off. But he was like the ultimate, extreme exception to the rule ... and we'd been friends before I'd discovered what he was ... and as far as supernaturals were concerned, incubi and succubi were on the less malicious side of the scale.

You know, sometimes I think the universe sits around waiting for me to say I'll never do something, then comes up with fun and interesting ways to throw me in that exact situation. You suck sometimes, universe. Seriously.

Anyway, it wasn't like he excreted a pheromone that was a more addictive and potent narcotic than heroin and smelled like rotting lily of the valley—which vampires do, in case you were wondering.

I gave a noncommittal wave to Nadya and headed back inside. As I exited the casino side of the Garden Café, I chanced a quick look at the neon-lit bar just past the entrance. Besides serving as temporary security, Rynn had also taken over Mr. Kurosawa's bar, and one of the renovations was a replica of the neon bar at the Gaijin Cloud, a host bar Rynn used to run in Tokyo that catered to foreigners.

I glanced back down as I saw him making small talk with a customer—or thought I saw him. I glanced away too quickly to be sure.

What am I, five? Damn it, come on, bravery, grow a pair. I couldn't duck around the nearest corner every time I thought I saw him. Besides, it wouldn't work; he knew where my room was and had a key.

Get it together, it's a goddamn conversation ...

I took another look.

It wasn't Rynn, just another blond, who, from a distance, bore a passing resemblance to him. Probably another one of his new hires . . .

Have I mentioned yet I'm not good with people? That's kind of been an underlying theme in my life.

I made it to the elevators. The mirrored glass on the inside was decorated with replicas of ancient Japanese artwork that reminded me of the painted tunnels beneath the Circus garage, the ones Oricho had kept over the centuries.

God, I hoped Lady Siyu and Mr. Kurosawa had at least had the decency not to completely trash them after Oricho's betrayal. Then again, I was dealing with supernaturals.

Right before the doors slid shut, someone shoved their hand inside, holding them open.

Rynn.

"You know, by the way you're acting, one would think you were trying to avoid them," he said, and slipped inside the elevator, leaning against the opposite wall of painted glass.

My brain froze for something useful to say. I'm not kidding when I say I don't do well with people. If there is a way to stick my foot in my mouth, I'll find it.

The whole on/off thing wasn't helping either . . .

Rynn stood there watching me as the elevator started to count through the floors. "Well?" he said, not making any move to close the distance. "That's normally the cue for the other person to continue the conversation."

I picked up Rynn's sandalwood-scented cologne. I wouldn't be able to forgive myself if I screwed things up without trying. I'm guilty of a lot of things—self-sabotage, recklessness, not giving people a chance. I was trying not to add tanking a perfectly good relationship.

"You've got about ten floors left," Rynn added.

I looked up at his face and his gray eyes and blurted out the first thing that came to mind. "I missed you." I'd actually planned on starting with *Sorry I may have gone off the grid for a few days*, since under the circumstances that seemed the most appropriate, but I could go with my brain's spontaneity if not its complete lack of tact.

Rynn arched a blond eyebrow, somewhat surprised. Apparently I wasn't the only one who thought I'd have gone with something else.

The question was, had it been the right thing? Something else I'm guilty of is a deep routed fear of rejection. Ever since I'd first met Rynn, my reluctance to put myself out there emotionally—even when I'd still thought he was human—had been an underlying theme.

Rynn still didn't make any move to close the distance.

I breathed again. OK, five floors left. *Come on, Owl, grow a backbone and make an attempt here. Brain, don't fail me now . . .*

"On a scale from one to ten, exactly how mad are you at me right now?" Again, I blurted it out before my filter kicked in, not that it exercises much judgment on a good day.

Rynn hit the emergency stop. "On a scale from one to ten?" he said, repeating each word carefully.

"Are you supposed to do that?" I asked, nodding at the red light.

That threw him off, and he gave the light a brief, quizzical look. "I'm head of security. I can do whatever the hell I want, and are you certain you don't want to add a few more numbers on there?"

I winced. *You had one job, brain, one goddamn job . . .* No more relying on my subconscious to do the right thing. "OK, what I meant to say is I'm sorry about Egypt. I should have brought you into the loop. *But* in my defense, I had no idea the IAA was looking for me—"

"Tell me, Alix, when did you finally call? Was that before or after they started shooting at you?" he said, the dark expression back.

"Actually, it was when the mummy tried to eat me—"

He snorted, then ran a hand through his cropped blond hair. From where I stood, it looked like he counted silently to three.

"I'm disappointed in you, but I missed you too, and I'm relieved you're still alive. From a professional standpoint I'm furious, because *everything* you've done in the last three months seems solely directed at making my job a living hell. Do you have any idea how hard it is to account for someone who goes off the grid? You try telling Mr. Kurosawa and Lady Siyu 'Sorry, she took off' when they ask for a progress report." He closed his eyes. "We said you weren't going to do this again."

He was right. That was exactly what I'd said. I just hadn't thought it would be so hard to follow through on . . .

"Technically I told Nadya, so . . ." I winced as soon as I said it. *Brain, please quit trying to make decisions for me while I'm ahead.*

Rynn narrowed his eyes at me before turning to face the elevator console. He punched in a code, and the elevator resumed its climb. "In fact, I'm so furious at you—for that Algiers stunt especially—I'm doing everything I can to keep it outside our relationship." He glanced up at me, and for a moment I thought I caught a flash of blue, something incubi did when they were either using their innate abilities or trying to rein them in. "You aren't making it easy."

The elevator chimed and the door opened onto the penthouse floor. Rynn stepped out first and set a fast pace for my room.

"Look, I can explain," I called after him. I wasn't trying to make his job impossible on purpose. I don't do well with authority figures on a good day, and having Rynn trying to tag me wasn't helping.

He reached my room ahead of me, the one I kept while I was at the Japanese Circus on business, and opened the door. It was more an apartment than a hotel room, with an office/living space, dining room, half kitchen, bedroom, and luxury bathroom. Whereas most of the high-end rooms at the Circus were fitted with antiques carefully selected and curated by Lady Siyu, it had not escaped my notice that they were completely absent from my room. Not surprising, since I'd trashed a Louis XIV dinner set on the first supernatural job I'd done for Mr. Kurosawa. Trust me, I'd had my reasons.

At least Lady Siyu had fitted it with cat supplies, including a tree, which Captain emerged from chirping. He took one look between me and Rynn and, instead of begging for food, disappeared into the bedroom.

Great, Captain would rather forgo dinner than stick around for this conversation. I followed Rynn in and dropped my folder on the table before leaning against it.

"Good, you can start with Algiers and explaining these," he said, and retrieved a set of heavy gold chains from a box by the desk, dropping them on the kitchen table. The chains held both a collar and matching cuffs the right size for a child. They were engraved in Latin with the name *Cleopatra Selene*.

I'd almost forgotten about Algiers . . . damn Hermes and his efficiency.

My eyes drifted from the cuffs back up to Rynn, who stood close to the door. Not a great sign. "I can explain," I said.

"I'm waiting."

I swallowed and stared at the cuffs. *Honesty, Owl, honesty.* "Those are the chains that Cleopatra the Eighth, the daughter of Cleopatra the Seventh and Mark Antony, was dragged through the streets of Rome in by Octavian after Cleopatra and Antony were defeated."

"And what, you just couldn't help yourself?"

I cleared my throat. "No, they were the first thing I ever excavated and were supposed to stay in a museum, not end up in someone's private collection. They hold sentimental value," I added.

Rynn's mouth dropped open a little, as if not quite believing what I'd just said. "Sentimental value?"

I nodded and held my chin up a little higher as I crossed my arms. "Yes. Sentimental value."

Rynn stared at me, frowning before shaking his head. "That . . . is so completely uncharacteristic for you, I think I believe it." He lowered his head, reminding me of a predator stalking prey—not far off. "That still doesn't explain why you didn't tell me."

"Honest answer? I didn't tell you about Algiers or Alexandria because I knew you'd try to talk me out of it."

"So you knew it was dangerous?"

"My job involves calculated risks. Unfortunately, most of the calculated risks I take fail whatever bar you've set."

"So let me get this straight, just so we're both on the same page here—the risks that I consider too high to take from a professional standpoint, you're arguing are in fact your job?"

"Actually, that's pretty damn accurate," I said.

"I'm not being unreasonable, Alix!"

"Oh come on. You almost wrote off Morocco, and you'd have written off Egypt if I'd told you—and don't try to tell me your feelings don't spill into it!"

Rynn looked back up at me, even more the predator with a flash of blue; brief, but it was there.

I wasn't completely immune to it. In fact, a number of things crossed my mind that I'd like to do with Rynn, and fighting wasn't one of them . . . well, probably not the kind of fighting you have in mind.

"Alix, if I let my personal feelings spill into my work, I wouldn't approve any of your projects."

Another thing we had yet to resolve. My profession. And just for the record, I'm not exactly a thief. I steal artifacts from the IAA . . . considering how much they screwed me over, I figure it's my own personal brand of grievances and pay retrieval. Besides, Serena and Charity always work for free. It's like I'm volunteering.

Yeah, Rynn hadn't gone for that either.

"Just be glad you didn't make the meeting this afternoon with Lady Snakebite and Mr. Kurosawa."

He frowned. "What meeting?"

"The meeting that was supposed to be a debrief and turned into 'try to get Owl to cop to a major theft she didn't actually didn't do'? Don't tell me you didn't get the memo. And, for the record, I know we're trying to keep the whole work/personal relationship separate, but you could at least have said, 'Hey Alix, can't make it but Lady Siyu might try to kill you.' And you think I'm bad with going off the grid—"

"Wait—back up for a second and start from the beginning."

I gave Rynn the brief rundown—omitting only just how close Lady Siyu had come to killing me. Rynn's expression transitioned from moderate surprise all the way back to predatory anger, except this time I wasn't the focus of it.

"The worst part is I have no idea who the hell the thief is. Anyone good enough isn't that stupid." I shook my head. "I'm still not sure what I'm going to do about L.A. either. I'm hoping Hermes is able to find out about the seller. He's got his ear to the ground when it comes to this stuff. By the way, you're supposed to be coming with me—hope you like L.A., maybe we won't kill each other over a weekend, professionally speaking ... hey, where are you going?" I said as Rynn headed for the door.

"To give Mr. Kurosawa and Lady Siyu a piece of my mind."

"Woah, did you not hear anything I just said? They think I'm a thief, and if I don't find out who is, or come up with better evidence clearing me, Lady Siyu is hell-bent on eating me—"

"Nagas don't eat people, they poison them and watch them die slowly."

"Either way it involves sharp teeth!"

"Trust me, they'll be expecting me. They broke an agreement with me, and you'll quickly learn supernatural species don't tolerate broken agreements. It's about the only thing holding our tentative society together."

Wow. Shame Rynn didn't lose his temper more often, because I'd gotten more on how their society even worked in the last five minutes than I had in three months.

"I'll be back after I deal with the mess those two have gotten themselves into," he said, then added something under his breath in supernatural, or that's what I figured it was. "Lady Siyu can make whatever case she wants. They know it wasn't you, otherwise you'd be dead already. Nadya is right about one thing, Owl. There's something else going on here besides the theft. I'll try to get us out of this L.A. fiasco."

"Why do I get the impression there's something important you're not telling me?"

He glanced back over his shoulder. "Because there is."

Great. More supernatural bullshit.

Rynn turned towards the door, and I thought he was going to leave—but he didn't. Instead, he stopped short of opening the door, and almost as an afterthought he managed to close the distance between us in less than two steps.

I let out a yelp as Rynn pushed me up against the wall. He traced the side of my neck with his breath, though his lips never touched my skin. Adrenaline coursed through me as he chased his breath with the tip of his finger, tracing a path from my ear to my shoulder. I gave a small gasp as Rynn's knee slipped between my legs and pushed up, forcing me to stand on my toes. His lips hovered a hairsbreadth from mine.

Oh this was new—more aggressive than I was used to from Rynn, but that didn't mean bad.

You can forget most of what you think you know about incubi. They feed off attraction, all the better if it's directed at them, but their power's passive, like breathing. It was one of the reasons Rynn used to work in a bar. Incubi are also very attractive. Rynn had light blond hair he kept short, and high cheekbones and light gold skin tone that had convinced me he was Slavic. And then there were his gray eyes, which shifted to a bright cobalt blue every now and then. That's where an incubi's real trick comes in; they can manipulate human minds and emotions. Point in case, I didn't notice Rynn's blue eyes until he stopped tweaking my head to forget. That was a deal breaker.

Rynn turned my face to the side, further exposing my neck, then this time trailed his lips all the way up to the corner of my mouth.

I drew in another breath as Rynn found my mouth and kissed me.

Yeah, this I could get used to . . .

Before anything really got going, it was over. Rynn broke off the kiss and pulled his body away from mine, including his hand, which a moment ago had been doing something really nice to the spot between my chin and neck.

I waited for Rynn to pick up where he'd left off. Nothing happened. I opened my eyes. Rynn was staring at me intently, his hands braced on either side of the wall as he loomed over me.

Just like that. Staring at me, his face betraying nothing.

I think every nerve in my body revolted at once. "Ah . . . no offense, but you think you might want to keep going, with, you know—?"

He closed his eyes and drew in a deep breath, drinking in the attraction pouring off me.

OK, I was done with the whole anticipation thing. Patience is not my virtue. I leaned forward and reached for Rynn's face.

Drawing in one last breath, he stepped away from the wall and crossed his arms. "Now you have an idea how I feel when you *don't fucking tell me where you're going*," he said.

Oh you have got to be kidding me. I leaned my head against the wall and ran my fingers through my hair. "Seriously? OK, there is no way that's playing fair," I said.

He leaned in again, so close his lips almost brushed up against mine. "You're right. It's not. And think about this, Alix. It would have been easier to make you feel what I've felt for the last three days, but I didn't. I respect your boundaries. The least you could do is consider mine. See you in a couple hours." Then he shut the door behind him.

You know, I think I hate it when he has a point.

I closed my eyes and attempted to reign in the thoughts that were still revolting and frolicking in a Rynn-populated fantasyland . . .

Oh this blew. Mark my words, at some point in the future I was going to get even.

Well, I had a few hours at least to check my email and do some reconnaissance on Daphne Sylph. But first a shower—a very cold shower—then coffee, then the one thing that would settle my nerves while I did my best not to think about the fact I was being blamed for the one theft I didn't actually do: World Quest.

I swore as I almost tripped headfirst on my way to the computer desk.

Captain let out a long, drawn-out meow from under my feet. Then he swished his tail before jumping up and heading for the kitchenette.

"The vet said no. You're on a diet."

He yowled, letting me know what he thought of my diet.

"No. No more food."

Captain trotted back out of the kitchen, his tail up in the air, and meowed again, louder and longer than before.

Oh for . . . Our begging sessions had become a nightly occurrence; Captain begging me to feed him, me begging him to shut up, usually with a pair of moccasin slippers thrown across the room.

According to Captain, clearly the problem was I didn't grasp just how hungry he was. I'd woken to half a pair of slippers—the front halves. Apparently it was harder to shred the fronts.

I didn't have time or patience for this. I sighed and followed him into the kitchen.

—⁂—

Hair still wet and with a fresh cup of coffee, I logged into World Quest and pinged Carpe. I'd been avoiding him in what I like to call TOFC, or Time Off From Carpe. It also stood for Turn Off the Fucking Computer, which was also an accurate description. See? Multiple and related contexts.

Hey. Asshole. Ready to play, or do you want to whine about your book some more? Got an easy quest to do.

Carpe's answer appeared in the dialogue box a few moments later. *I'm not talking to you, Byzantine.*

Yeah, like he hadn't said that before. *You know, I'm sure some things don't translate fantastically into elvishness, or whatever the hell it is you guys speak—but you realize by writing that you've already proven that you are in fact speaking to me, albeit passive aggressively.*

A few moments passed with no answer.

Seriously Carpe, I haven't been ignoring you. I've been playing online when you're offline. There's a difference—again, one of those subtle elf/human differences. Kind of like how you call cyber stalking being a friend.

Another few moments passed before his response appeared in the window.

Fuck you.

Great. Now grow a pair and either actually start to shun me or open the goddamn map I just sent you.

I didn't wait for Carpe's next response. Instead, I logged into World Quest and used a transport scroll to get myself to the treasure map I'd just sent Carpe, something from my collection of potentially interesting in-game locations—the Syrian monastery, to be exact.

I needed a better idea of what the Syrian City of the Dead actually looked like on the inside—the real one, not the incomplete diagrams Mr. Kurosawa provided me.

And that meant World Quest.

I snorted, remembering what Nadya said about not using the game to pillage dig sites. I paid my monthly membership—I'd do what I damn well liked.

While I waited for Carpe to stuff his nonexistent pride and show up, I started to look around the ancient site—Byzantine, to be exact. The game designers had done a nice job.

While I scoped out the area and waited for Carpe, my phone buzzed.

It was a message from Rynn.

See? Not one word about the damned elf before I left. Compromise and change are attainable goals for you too, Alix.

I snorted. I don't know what it was, but Rynn had serious issues with Carpe—

Incubi weren't jealous—not a species trait. No, it was more of a deep-routed hatred of elves. *He's an elf,* as if that explained it. I was deciding on something less than elegant to write back when Rynn beat me to it.

Train wreck appeared in my phone's text window.

Before I could think twice, I typed *whore* and pressed Send. Some things between us might change, but hopefully not everything. Maybe some change would be good for me.

Provided Rynn and Nadya weren't asking for a whole Owl makeover, I could possibly, maybe, give it a shot.

6

Karma's a Bitch

12:00 a.m., getting my World Quest fix

I sat up with a start and looked around my desk. I could have sworn something hit me in the face.

Captain chirped in my ear from his perch behind my shoulder. He readjusted himself, fixated with something on my lap.

I glanced down; there was a cork mouse floating in my coffee, the one I'd balanced in my lap before nodding off.

I held the mouse up. "Did you seriously just throw a mouse in my coffee?"

Captain chirped again in response.

I pulled the mouse out and launched it across the room. Captain took off, his hind legs skidding out as he tried to make a turn.

He'd have better coordination if he ate less . . .

I checked the clock. Midnight. I'd fallen asleep for twenty minutes. Why hadn't Carpe woken me? I swore as I saw my headphones and mic were on the desk. Must have taken them off. I slid them back on and woke up my screen. There were, like, five blinking messages from Carpe.

"Hey, still there?" I asked.

"Hey, snoring beauty. Want to do me a favor and move your fucking avatar?"

Shit. "Sorry, dozed off." My character, the Byzantine Thief, was standing wide-eyed in a cave with a team of dead goblins around me.

"No worries. In fact, I'm thinking you might have discovered an awesome game plan for the future. You fall asleep, monsters come out to attack your undefended avatar, and I smoke them and get all the XP. Win-win, Byzantine."

"Yeah, yeah—I said I was sorry already. What do you want from me? And don't say that fucking book." Coffee. That was what I needed, more coffee . . .

I set my avatar on autopilot and, headphones still on, headed to the kitchen. "Yell if something attacks us," I said as I turned the water on and filled the pot.

My guess was Carpe heard the running water, which was why he didn't add any other snarky comments.

Ever since my early days in grad school, I've played World Quest. It's a fantasy MMO based on real archaeological sites and monsters, and it's damn accurate. It's also one of the most punishing games out there, which is probably why there are only a hundred thousand or so players worldwide. You die without a resurrection scroll or someone willing to use one on you, and your character is done—game over. And trust me, resurrection scrolls were a bitch to come by. My character, the Byzantine Thief, has two. That's it. Two. I'd almost had to use one a few months back when our previous teammate, Paul the Battle Monk, had tried to off us and steal all our in-game shit. You know, since he's too busy driving his kids to soccer practice to grind, and since Carpe and I have nothing better to do with our time . . .

Asshole.

I hadn't seen Paul in game lately, probably because Carpe had posted a hit on him at one of the most-frequented in-game pubs, the Dead Orc. I'll let you guess the secret ingredient in their soup. Having said that, the Dead Orc provided gamers an interesting, albeit unorthodox, way of grinding for in-game gold . . .

Point being "Where's Paul" had become a form of jackpot grinding for thousands of new gamers. Have fun running, Paul. World Quest is a cruel, vindictive mistress.

"So, Byzantine, want to explain what the hell we're doing under this mountain?" Carpe asked.

The spot I'd transported us to was a series of tunnels running underneath the mountain range that bordered modern-day Lebanon and Syria. The version we were under, however, was set in the early Byzantine Empire, when they'd ruled the greater part of the Mediterranean.

"I told you, there's a ruin on the other side." And an army which I hadn't realized was there before I teleported over. Live and learn.

"You didn't add treasure onto the end of that phrase," Carpe said.

"It's World Quest, it's implied."

"Kind of like you implied you were going to get my book—"

"Enough! Knock it off about your damn book and kill some goblins already."

For the past two years Carpe Diem and I have played on the same team with a roster of revolving third and fourth parties. We originally agreed to only meet online in World Quest—and I'd planned on keeping it that way, an anonymous haven from my real life of running away from the IAA and vampires.

Until Carpe had broken our no contact rule. At the time I'd been pretty pissed, but I'd more or less gotten over it. That and I needed someone to play World Quest with.

Did I mention Carpe is also a world-famous hacker called Sojourn? And an elf? Though what the hell *elf* meant was up to interpretation. There was next to nothing on them in the IAA literature, and Carpe wasn't any goddamn help either.

Yeah, it hadn't escaped my notice that out of my three friends, two were supernatural. Again, the theme of the universe throwing what I won't do at me doesn't escape my notice.

"Come on, you were right there!" Carpe said.

I sighed. Oh yeah. Then there was that damn book. I was officially adding stubborn to the whole elf thing. The spell book he wanted was still in use by a mummy, and somehow I didn't think the mummy would part with it willingly. "No, Carpe. What I said was that I might be able to swing by Cairo if I had time. See what I did there? It's called a qualifier. In this case I added two of them. In human terms I was actually telling you hell would freeze over first—*which* you would have picked up on if you'd damn well bothered to listen."

"Well, why didn't you just say no?"

"I did. You wouldn't stop pestering me about it. Just like now."

"It's a matter of life and death—"

"So is me working for a dragon, and you don't see me whining about it."

"Who's to blame for that? If you'd have let them eat the onryo—"

"OK, that's wrong on so many levels—hey, chest!" I noticed the small chest tucked into a tunnel alcove. I equipped the dragon eye goggles in Byzantine's inventory, lending my avatar a steampunk vibe and the ability to see in-game magic. Crucial for not ending up dead. As soon as they were on, I looked at the chest. There was a symbol of glowing red flames. Fire trap. Definitely didn't want that sprung.

"Hey Carpe, you're wearing a fire cloak, right? How bout you come stand here between me and the booby-trapped box?" Whereas I played a human thief in World Quest, Carpe Diem played an elven sorcerer. I wasn't sure if he was just meta or unimaginative. Hadn't wanted to broach that one.

"Piece of cake," he said, and his avatar started casting. "So tell me, was it you who decided not to get my book, or the incubus? And how's that going, by the way? Got to admit he's lasted longer than I thought. I figured he'd have bailed out of the shit storm known as Owl by now—"

And of course elves liked incubi about as much as incubi liked them . . . "Never made it to Rynn, that one was all me. But hey, thanks for the vote of confidence in my ability to navigate adult relationships. Appreciate it, really."

"I mean, you can tell me, Byzantine, we're all friends here."

"Can we please just finish robbing the goblins blind and get to the temple?"

"Fine—sheesh, try to help a friend out . . . That's the one thing I will never understand about humans. You guys would rather lie to yourselves than take a few moments of uncomfortable self-reflection. I mean, if that's not the pinnacle of procrastination—"

"The game, Carpe?"

From what I'd managed to get out of Rynn, elves weren't evil—or not on purpose—and trust me, there was a pretty severe bias I had to weigh in there.

Rynn said elves tried to make everything fair for everyone—humans, supernaturals, you name it, like Zen Buddhism of the supernatural world. And therein lay the problem. Details were sparse, but what I'd gleaned from Rynn had been peppered with: "get everyone killed," "idiots couldn't design a battle plan if they tried," and "how would they like to be cannon fodder."

"In my opinion, Byzantine, you're totally letting the incubus dictate the relationship."

"Wow—wait, no—that's not what's happening here. And what the hell did I say about staying out of my love life?"

"Whatever. Makes no nevermind to me what you let the incubus tell you to do. Ahhh . . . you might want to step back. I'll be OK if this trap goes, but you?"

I moved Byzantine back out of range, but the thought worm Carpe had thrown at me wheeled its way around my brain. Was I letting Rynn dictate the relationship? Maybe I was—not like I'd had a lot of experience in relationships, unless you counted pissing off vampires . . .

I forced the mind worm out. I played World Quest to get away from real life, not discuss it with Carpe, whose motives were suspect at best. Speaking of motives, Carpe was disarming a treasure chest. Normally I'd be concerned about Carpe pocketing items, but for the most part we were relatively honest with our hauls; besides, I knew his pack was full from the goblins and I was the one with the bag of holding—a pocket dimension in a bag. Every good thief's best friend to haul every bit of loot.

"Like a real friend, Byzantine, I don't mind taking the odd spell in the face, kind of like a real friend wouldn't mind getting me *my goddamn spell book!*"

The coffee was done brewing, so I grabbed a cup before starting in again. "Is it you who wants the damn spell book, or your Grand Poobah?" The biggest bitch about being in the dark about most supernatural goings-on was having to invent my own phrases.

"Oh for—we don't have a 'Grand Poobah.'"

"Same difference. Some elf has to be in charge of the rest of you elves—hence, Grand Poobah elf—unless you'd like to fill me in with the proper name."

I smiled, took another sip of coffee as Carpe made a derisive noise, and continued, "You know, Alexander got pissed I called the head vampire a Grand Poobah too. Is Grand Poobah hate a supernatural thing?"

"Vampires? OK, you can't compare me to Alexander, he was trying to kill you."

"Yet you want me to go kick a mummy in the balls and, what? Take the book while he's clutching his knees? You do realize that strategy barely works in World Quest?"

"I never said kick the mummy in the balls—"

"Let me guess. Kick, then run really fast? Or maybe open a discussion on why he should give me the book?" I snorted.

"You deal with monsters all the time, just look at your boyfriend—"

"For the last time, no! No goblins, no Egyptian mummy sorcerers, no helping the elves in their reign of chaos."

"Now you're just name calling."

"Whatever floats your boat. Now open the damn treasure chest!"

Carpe didn't offer a comeback—or move his avatar to open the chest.

Oh for the love of— "Come on. You deserved that for the last dig about Rynn."

Nothing. Wait a minute, why was my screen flickering? I zoomed in on my game window. Sure enough, Carpe's character was giving me the finger.

"You goddamn son of a bitch—" And where the hell had he learned that? Damn it, I needed that hack. World Quest profanity filters were notorious. I got blacklisted at least once a month—mostly auditory, but every now and then written. Obscene gestures, on the other hand . . .

The World Quest censorship light flared orange on the right-hand corner of my screen. I sat straight up.

"Oh you've got to be fucking kidding me! How the hell is he supposed to be able to give me the goddamn finger and I'm the one getting the fucking sensor light? You're really raising the bastard standard, World Quest, you know that—*Shit*." The server flashed two more warning lights and logged me out of the game.

I sat back in my chair. "You asshole, that got me kicked off."

"Alix, this is our private chat line—I loop it out of the server. They can't hear you swearing like a sailor, promise."

"No, they kicked me off for your avatar giving me the finger."

"No way, they haven't got the build for the gesture filter patched in yet—"

The fact that that was even an emerging problem on their radar . . . "So what the hell gives?"

A series of pink and orange vertical lines flickered into existence across my black screen. "Carpe? You seeing this?"

"Already on it. It's not a hacker, it's the game."

An unsettling feeling formed in my stomach as I remembered something Nadya had said about not using World Quest to plan heists . . . But there was no way the game could know about my recent string of jobs.

Even so, the unsettling feeling remained.

The lines solidified into a solid orange screen with a black dialogue window in the center. Across the dialogue box in retro DOS green letters scrolled one word.

Probation.

I swore. *Probation? What the hell for?* I typed.

The green words flickered out, and new text scrolled across. *We designed World Quest for entertainment. Not so you could loot the ancient world.*

Oh come on! Like you can prove anything.

"Owl," Carpe said. "You should maybe leave this one alone. Seriously, I've never heard of the creators actually banning someone before."

Against Carpe's judgment, I kept typing.

"Owl, will you shut up and just apologize!" Carpe said.

I ignored him. *Ban me from World Quest? Look, if you don't want me using your maps to steal artifacts, maybe you should have put a disclaimer on the damn terms of use page. I pay my monthly membership, and I haven't broken any rules. You want to change them? Be my fucking guest, but you bastards don't get to ban my ass for breaking a rule that didn't exist!*

Hence, probation. No more thefts based on our blueprints. We mean it. And have a nice day.

And with that the screen returned to my game home screen.

I couldn't believe it. "What the fuck just happened?"

There was a pause on Carpe's end as I fumed.

"Please tell me you haven't been using World Quest to plan your heists," Carpe said.

"Uh, OK, but I'd be lying. What is it with everyone thinking that's a bad idea? It's an awesome idea. Bonus, they're accurate."

"Uhhhh . . . OK, resourceful? Yes. Ethical? No. Do you have any idea how much scrutiny World Quest would fall under if anyone else links your thefts to the game? Not just the IAA, I mean the supernatural community too."

I hadn't thought of it from that perspective . . . at all. I felt the beginnings of a pang of guilt. It's not a feeling I'm comfortable with—I try to avoid doing things that might make me feel guilty.

"Look, Carpe, I'm out for . . ." I checked the bottom of my login screen where a twelve-hour countdown clock blinked orange. "The next twelve."

He sighed. "You sure know how to ruin a game. See you online in twelve."

I shut down my login window and stared at the screen. Numb, that was the only way to describe it. Not being able to do anything about the game in the interim, I refilled my coffee cup and pulled up the theft files.

——⚋——

I closed out the last black market page on my list. Those had been a bust. The only Neolithic artifact for sale had been a piece of flint arrow three months back, originating from France—not even in the same geographic ballpark.

I next searched the entertainment magazine articles and video coverage, and stopped at the description in one of the captions.

"This isn't right," I said to Captain, who was perched behind my computer. The legend for the piece had to be wrong. The flint piece had been called early to proto-Neolithic, and the stone bowl had been labeled as late—about a five-thousand-year separation. The sword? The sword was labeled as Bronze Age. None of the three pieces were identified correctly.

I pulled up the video on the tablet and cranked the volume, to see how the entertainment personality explained the pieces.

"All three pieces were found in northern Israel at the Eynan dig site, a Neolithic city settled by the Natufians, a culture famous for the burial of their family members underneath their homes," the host said. She went on to ooh and aah over the idea of burying family members in one's house, and that fast devolved into cracking jokes about in-laws and exes. Funny how humor is how we cope with things that make us uncomfortable.

I stopped the video after it moved on to a collection of Greek and Roman statues. The mistakes were understandable, just not the kind Nadya or I would ever make—not to mention any other archaeology grad worth their salt. The sword could never have come from Eynan;

there was no overlaying Bronze Age. The city was decimated by droughts, as well as excessive farming and hunting, well before the Bronze Age reached the Levant. And they were wrong about the culture—the flint size was too large, for starters; they were Qaraoun, not Natufian.

Either the thief who'd sold the items or Daphne's collection curator hadn't known what they were doing. These just weren't the kind of mistakes I expected from the thief who'd pulled off this job. Unless I was dealing with another archaeology dropout—one who'd missed the "by the way, there be monsters" speech.

Not enough information to know what they were doing, just enough to be dangerous. Especially if they didn't know about the curse.

Before I could email my new theory to Nadya, my laptop pinged. A message from Hermes.

Dear Owl. We need to talk—Cheers, Hermes

That was . . . unexpected. One of the things I liked about Hermes was his ability to conduct business online without all the bells and whistles associated with meeting in person. I know it's counterintuitive, but there's a level of trust that comes with knowing you couldn't pick someone's voice or face out of a lineup and vice versa.

I'd really prefer not to . . . Kind of like our current working relationship. No offense, I responded, then fired off my email to Nadya.

A few minutes later I heard the ping of another email. *Dear Owl, None taken. Meeting in person nonnegotiable—Cheers, Hermes.*

"What do you think, Captain?" I said as he leapt onto my lap.

In answer, he let out an inquisitive meow, waited—probably to see if I was about to stand up—then settled.

Expecting wisdom from a house cat. Yet another illustration of my descent into madness.

Not like I had any other real leads jumping out at me.

All right. But this better be good. And hopefully not a trap. *Where and when?*

Dear Owl, Will let you know tomorrow—Thanks for accommodating, Hermes.

I shook my head and went back to the videos to see if there was anything else I'd missed. I was interrupted by a knock on my door.

1:00 a.m., maybe Rynn got off early.

Captain howled as I stood on my toes and checked through the eyehole.

What the . . . ?

Lady Siyu stood in the hallway, black sunglasses and all, tapping her foot. Should I open the door, or pretend I wasn't there?

Her nose twitched as she sniffed the air. She then tilted her head up and looked into the eyehole. She curled her lip, exposing a single, extended fang. "I can smell you," she said, "and if you do not cease to waste my time—"

I threw the door open. There was no point in delaying the inevitable. She'd only get meaner.

"What do you want?" I'd also learned from experience that conversational niceties were a waste of time in Lady Siyu's opinion. Not having to pretend I liked her was kind of liberating. If it hadn't been for her new life goal of figuring out a way to kill me without interfering with her boss's business, I might not even have minded working with her so much. There's something to be said for efficiency bordering on uncivil.

Lady Siyu pursed her lips. "I have new information to offer."

I crossed my arms while Captain wound around my legs, his hackles up. I made no move to let Lady Siyu past the doorway.

She looked relieved rather than slighted. "I have reason to believe the artifacts themselves are cursed. You are not to touch them."

That got my attention. Lady Siyu rarely offered me any relevant information.

"They are safe for most supernaturals to handle, such as myself or Mr. Kurosawa—even the incubus could handle them without much fault," she continued.

I didn't miss the way she pronounced *incubus,* as if it were something distasteful. Even having him as interim security hadn't elevated him past the whole harpoon-through-her-abdomen thing . . .

It was my turn to narrow my eyes. "I knew that already. Why else are you here?"

"The stone bowl is particularly problematic. If one of your kind were to drink from that vessel, I believe the results would be undesirable." Her eyes narrowed and she tilted her head to the side, reminding me of Captain when he was studying a toy. "If this casino is any indication, your species frequently drinks from vessels of unknown origin."

Great, thanks for the vote of confidence . . . Part of me wanted to roll my eyes, but technically she was right. First off, most people didn't know magic or supernaturals existed. Second, get a large enough group of people together, and someone is bound to do something stupid.

"There's more to it. You wouldn't be this concerned over a bunch of poisoned humans. In fact, I would have bet you'd do everything in your power to let the artifacts wipe out a few humans before going to retrieve them." I crossed my arms, looking a hell of a lot braver than I felt. "What the hell else gives?"

Lady Siyu hissed and turned on her heels back towards the elevators. "I do not find your attitude about this predicament amusing."

I hate being dismissed. "Trust me, I'm about the only one in this pony show with the right attitude towards the city and those artifacts."

She'd only taken a few steps when she stopped and glanced back.

Maybe she wasn't as dense as I thought . . . or maybe she was coming to terms with the fact that I knew what the hell I was talking about when it came to antiquities. Faster than I thought possible, the sunglasses were off and Lady Siyu's face was back in front of me. Before I could get out of the way, her fangs—each an inch long and dripping with yellow venom—were a hairsbreadth away from my face. She was still in human form. Barely.

Nope. Scratch that, no change. Absolutely as dense as I thought.

"You would be wise to remember the only reason I permit your continued existence is that you are more useful alive than dead to Mr. Kurosawa. Do not think that status is an unlimited one. It will ebb when the tide changes, and then?"

A drop of yellow venom fell, landing on my shirt. I stumbled back, tripping over the carpet and falling hard on my ass.

Lady Siyu didn't bother pursuing me. She swayed back and forth on her heels as gracefully as a cobra about to strike.

"Then, I think I might kill you myself," she said.

The elevator door slid open. Rynn stepped out, and he frowned as soon as he saw Lady Siyu.

She strode towards the open elevator, saying something to Rynn— *seereet,* or *sieret*; whatever it was, it was in supernatural—before she stepped inside.

There was a tense exchange between them before the doors slid shut, but this time I couldn't pick out the individual words. The problem with supernatural common is that the words are strung together in something that's akin to singing, making the individual words hard to tell apart.

I stood back up, brushing my hands against my jeans to cover the fact that I was shaking. "Well, all things considered, I think that went well."

"She didn't hurt you?"

I shook my head. "No, just had information for me, nothing I couldn't handle." There was very little I hated more than implying to Rynn I couldn't handle Lady Siyu or Mr. Kurosawa—unless they turned into monsters and actually tried to eat me. Then all bets to save my pride were off. Besides, I didn't need him trying to babysit me.

Rynn just stood there, and I realized he was waiting for me to let him in. I obliged.

Almost immediately his eyes fell on the open computer screen.

"You were talking to the elf again." It wasn't a question or accusation. Just a statement.

I nodded. "World Quest game time."

He glanced over at me. "Did the elf contact you in Egypt?"

It seemed an innocent-enough question, but sometimes I had a hard time reading Rynn's expressions. I was getting better, but some of his quieter moods caught me off guard. It sounds strange, but every now and then it was like there was another layer—almost human but not quite.

"Well, stalked me by cell phone is more accurate. He wants me to steal a spell book from a sorcerer's mummy who is still using it. I told him no," I added when Rynn's lip twitched. For a second I thought he was going to say something else about Carpe or his general dislike of elves. Instead, he nodded back at my login screen—my now defunct login screen for the next twelve hours.

"Why do you play?" he asked.

The question and his quiet mood caught me off guard. I thought about it. Really thought about it. I'd learned the hard way: making light of Rynn's questions when he was in a serious mood led to off-again relationship status.

It hurt his feelings. Yes, I care about Rynn's feelings.

"Because for a couple hours I get to forget who I am, my problems, and I get to be somebody who for once in my life has the upper hand. Is that good enough?"

He nodded but looked thoughtfully at the computer. "You're not a prisoner here, Alix."

Another comment that caught me completely off guard. "Yeah, Rynn, that's exactly what I am. I leave, I end up exactly where I was three months ago."

He focused his gray eyes back on me. "But you could choose to leave."

Funny . . . Oricho had said almost the exact same thing three months ago: *"You're free to die."*

"Yeah, but I prefer to stay breathing. Besides, getting chased by Alexander and his vampires was marginally worse than where I am now. Lady Siyu only threatens to kill me; she can't exactly follow through." Yet.

Rynn nodded, but he was focusing on a point behind me, distracted. I got the distinct impression I hadn't said whatever he'd wanted me to.

"What does *seereet* or *sieret* mean?" I asked.

Rynn focused back on me. "Where did you hear that?"

"Lady Siyu in the hall."

He frowned but shook his head and headed into my kitchen. "Nothing of any consequence. I wouldn't concern yourself with anything she says. Much of it is show. But don't go repeating it."

"Yeah—not reassuring in the least." I wondered what happened at Rynn's meeting earlier with Lady Siyu and Mr. Kurosawa, but before I could ask, he nodded to the case files beside my computer. "How goes finding the thief?"

"Well, the more I look, the less faith I have this guy or girl knows what the hell they're actually doing." I filled Rynn in on my theory that the thief in question might have only an undergraduate archaeology background. Rynn listened as I showed him the write-up on the artifacts and explained the discrepancy in the descriptions. "It could also be an elaborate cover-up to throw off the IAA from finding them. Hide in plain sight. Or just a simple clerical error," I added.

"Something you're an expert at," he said, then glanced up at me. "Hiding in plain sight, not the theft part—not that you aren't an expert . . ." He shook his head and went back to the computer screen before he could dig himself in any further.

"I like your theory about the thief being an undergrad," he said. "It explains the knowledge base and the disregard for the supernatural. It's smart."

"I think you need to check your head. You just complimented me professionally." Usually he and Nadya just yelled that I didn't know what the hell I was doing.

OK, that's kind of sad, and another argument for working alone . . .

Rynn faced me with an intensity that hadn't been there a moment before. "I've never questioned how good you are at your job. I question your risk assessment and political acumen."

One thing you get used to when hanging around an incubus: they pick up on emotions besides attraction.

"Any line on how the artifacts ended up in L.A.?" he asked.

I shook my head. "Not yet. I don't have many contacts there. Not enough serious collectors to be interesting, and the ones that are buy overseas anyways."

Rynn nodded. "I may be able to help with that."

"How?"

"My cousin. Someone I should really check up on and who owes me more than a few favors."

He refocused back on me with the unspoken question on his face: did I want him to stay or go tonight?

"Why do you put up with my job?" I blurted out.

He was silent and seemed to be studying the items on the tablet. Then he said, "Well, on the one hand, I'm still optimistic I'll wear you down."

The familiar pit formed in my stomach. Me walking away from my job wasn't likely to happen anytime soon . . .

He shrugged. "Mostly though, I figure it's a rather inconsequential flaw in an otherwise beautiful person."

He said it without looking at me, which was probably a good thing, because to be honest—emotionally I wasn't there yet. Let's face it, it's me. I don't know if I'd ever get there.

Or maybe my subconscious was hell-bent on sabotaging the only thing close to a meaningful romantic relationship I'd ever had. Wouldn't fucking surprise me.

As if sensing we were verging into dangerous territory, Rynn gave me a half smile. "Mostly I think I'll wear you down eventually on the thieving, Alix." He took another step closer. "So on a scale from one to ten, what are my chances of staying tonight?"

"One to ten? You sure you don't want to add a few numbers onto that?"

Rynn seemed to think about it, then shrugged. "Not really—I'm confident my odds lie on the one-to-ten scale."

I glanced up at him.

"Train wreck," he added, arching one blond eyebrow.

I closed the computer and turned my full attention on Rynn. I noted Captain had disappeared to one of his hiding spots. Carpe, World Quest, and the damned thief could wait until tomorrow.

My hair had fallen out of its tie and was hanging in a curtain over my face. I brushed it out of the way. "Whore," I said.

7

The Rock Star of L.A.

8:00 p.m., Hollywood Hills, Los Angeles

As soon as I stepped out of the damn car, I knew I was in trouble. The heels Nadya had given me were higher than I was comfortable in, and the dress ... well, the dress was very shiny ... and short.

I'd asked her three times if this was my only option. Apparently I was dressed conservatively.

I swore as the back of my stiletto sunk in the grass. No grace, but enough balance that I didn't fall on my ass. "Remind me again why I don't just take these damn things off and walk barefoot?"

"Because they won't let you through the front door. And you wouldn't have near so much trouble if you didn't keep cinching the dress down."

I did my best to catch up to Rynn and not maim myself stabbing the grass. He waited for me and held out a hand. I took it. I didn't have so much pride that I wouldn't take the extra support.

"You try walking in these heels," I said.

"Who says I can't? Though those might be a bit small."

I stumbled again at the image of Rynn in full drag back in Japan.

Considering some of the theme parties Gaijin Cloud had thrown, it wasn't that far-fetched.

"I feel ridiculous, and I'm dreading bending over," I told him.

"You look beautiful. Try to enjoy it," he said. I frowned, studying his face to see if he was making a joke. He wasn't. Which surprised me, since he hadn't said a damn thing when I'd stepped out of the bathroom back at the hotel.

"Easy for you to say—you're not worried about flashing the world."

Rynn snorted, but the tight set to his jaw softened, which was a minor win; something was bugging Rynn about visiting his cousin, but he'd been uncharacteristically tight-lipped about it.

"So, just so I completely understand here, your cousin is an incubus."

He sighed. "That would make the most biological sense."

All right, so I kept asking the same question, but this one damn well deserved re-clarification. "OK, but your cousin is *him*?"

Rynn stopped, looked up at the black sky drowned out by street and house lights, and swore under his breath. "Yes, he is my cousin. A damn lot of good that does me," he said, adding the last bit under his breath as we continued towards the mansion.

Yeah, not likely. I stopped him. "Oh you cannot leave it at that."

He frowned and narrowed his eyes. Son of a bitch, the great Rynn, host extraordinaire, visibly uncomfortable . . .

"You can find most of what you want to know online," he said.

"Those are called tabloids."

"In my cousin's case, the majority of it is accurate—probably on the tame side."

I held up my hands in surrender. "I'm just trying to understand how you failed to mention your cousin is Artemis Bast, lead singer of Kaliope—just putting that out there— Hey!"

Rynn dodged around me before I could continue my interrogation, and then we were out of the dark and into the lawn floodlights near the entrance, where there were more statues and fountains than could possibly be in good taste.

Kaliope was a pop/rock band that rose to infamy in the mid-1980s. Fifty-fifty whether they were more famous for their music or antics— my money was on the antics. The '80s were a brightly colored and debauched era. The band might have changed its roster over the years, but Artemis Bast had been a mainstay.

We'd barely reached the front door when Rynn glanced both ways, then pulled me behind a statue of a woman holding her breasts . . . no, wait, my bad. It was someone standing behind her holding her breasts.

"I haven't bothered mentioning Artemis because we don't get along." He glanced at the door, as if listening for something. "Suffice it to say my cousin is not a spectacular example of my species. Just be direct; he won't know what to make of you."

"Why do you say that?"

"Because most of the time I don't know what to make of you. Please stay close and watch yourself. Artemis isn't dangerous, but he's hard to predict at the best of times."

Rynn steered me towards the two massive front doors complete with antique brass knockers.

"So let me get this straight. Supernaturals have just as much trouble getting along with their relatives as humans do?"

Rynn paused before knocking on the door with one of the ornate handles. "Artemis is a complex individual who likes to push his boundaries. Inevitably he causes some sort of trouble and I have to clean up his mess, hence the favor I'm calling in."

That . . . surprised me. Everything Rynn had told me up until this point had painted succubi and incubi as more or less benign, preferring to tread the surface of human civilization and not draw attention to themselves. "Define 'trouble'?"

Rynn gave me a pointed stare and banged the brass ring a second time. "Last time I had to drag him out of a Bangkok whorehouse."

I frowned. "Isn't that kind of par for the course with you guys though?"

He shook his head. "Trust me, he figured out a way to make it a problem. We didn't part on good terms, and I didn't bother telling him we were coming either, so we're going to make this quick—"

"Whoa, wait a minute—we're crashing his party?"

"Artemis is more amenable when he's off his game."

The massive doors swung open. I stumbled back a step, not because of the massive bald bodyguard who stepped outside but because of the sheer volume of noise— music and otherwise—that crashed over me, along with a cloud of incense reminiscent of amber and burnt sandalwood. The massive doors and walls had to have been reinforced, because standing outside, I hadn't heard a damned thing. I caught a glimpse of people piled into the main hall just past the entrance—flashes of bright colors and metallics that all seemed to meld into one giant kaleidoscope.

I shook my head. Too much sensory overload. I had the urge to get the hell away. I would have tripped back down the front steps if Rynn hadn't caught me. He swore, but it was barely audible over the noise. Whereas before he'd looked apprehensive, now he just looked pissed. "I don't believe it—I don't know how many times I've told him—stay still, Alix, it will pass."

Yeah, right, sure it would. "Forgive me if I'm not fucking convinced."

The man at the front door was watching us, his face impassive at the attempts to collect myself. He was a little over six feet tall and dressed in a dark suit that contrasted with his dark olive skin color, which hinted at Middle Eastern descent. Even under the suit I could tell he was large enough to moonlight as a boxer. He gave each of us a once-over, his eyes dismissing me immediately but lingering on Rynn.

Without a word he opened the door and stepped aside. Rynn nodded and stepped in. I followed—or tried to.

The bodyguard gently, but in a way that made no mistake about his intention, blocked my way.

"Hey, come on—look at me! Would I be dressed like this if I wasn't with him?"

The bodyguard ignored me and turned to Rynn. "*Seereet?*" There was that goddamn word again . . .

Rynn didn't look particularly happy about being asked. He glanced from me to the guard and nodded, repeating the only snippet of supernatural dialect I could actually replicate with any chance of accuracy ... What am I talking about? I barely reproduce any language with any form of accuracy.

I didn't have time to ponder it though. The guard stepped out of the way and let me through.

Inside the entrance, the smell and noise were even more overpowering. I shook my head, trying to clear my thoughts. I'd never experienced anything quite like it. I checked to see if the guard had followed us in, but he'd taken his post back by the door, reminding me of a statue. He didn't even look like he was breathing.

I pulled Rynn closer so I could whisper ... well, loudly whisper. "I'm guessing he's not human."

Rynn snorted. "If you think for a second he's human, I've got a bridge for sale."

"Stealing my lines now, Rynn—you've got to be nervous," but I said it with a confidence I didn't feel.

He didn't answer that one, and I didn't expect him to. We stepped out of the entrance and into the main hall. I froze in my tracks.

Opulence. I don't know 'bout you, but to me the word conjures up images of Louis XIV palaces and ballrooms filled with antiques covered in more gold leaf than sense dictates. Hell, the word itself means "excess" ...

But this ballroom crammed full with people? Well, let's say it had the Louis XIV thing going on ... and Roman statues, and a staircase that looked like it belonged in *Gone with the Wind,* and 1960s glam decor—hell, there was even some Goth rock art thrown in.

The only right way to describe it was an explosion of eclecticism ... with a paintball gun ... and paint balloons, lots and lots of paint balloons.

The scent of amber and burnt sandalwood intensified. I realized the sandalwood reminded me of Rynn's cologne, though the burnt tone was a distinct departure.

"Opulence took one hell of an acid trip," I said.

Rynn was as immobilized as I was, but whereas I was shocked by the sheer . . . well . . . this made Cirque de Soleil look tame . . . Rynn just looked more pissed.

"Son of a bitch—is that guy wearing anything but body paint?"

Rynn swore. Loud. "I don't believe it—"

"No, seriously, I can't tell, I mean if it is, they've done one hell of a—"

"I didn't believe Artemis would pull this off in public." I noticed Rynn's hand had moved from the small of my back to my arm, and his grip had tightened.

"Alix, I'm serious this time, don't leave my side and don't take any food or drink," Rynn said and began scanning the room. "Come on, I want to get this over with as soon as possible."

And with that, we entered the den of Artemis Bast, rock star extraordinaire.

The place was packed to the brim with young, beautiful people— men and women—dancing, drinking, laughing. There was a surrealism to it; even though I was standing there, it was as if I was caught up in a whirlwind of noise and color. And there was something disturbing as hell . . . I just couldn't put my finger on what it was—or why my head was getting light.

Had to be the nerves . . . or the noise . . . or lights . . .

Wait a minute—was that Corona on a platter? My eyes followed a plate filled with bottles, each and every single one stuffed with a bright green lime.

The waiter caught me looking and brought over the plate. He was another man with a shaved head and beautiful dark skin, the color of coffee. He reminded me of the guard at the door but so much more beautiful . . . and that smile. He offered me the tray . . . who the hell was I to refuse? This was a party after all . . . the lights danced across the tray . . . purples and neon pink . . . I reached out.

Someone stopped me before my hand brushed the glass bottle. They grabbed my shoulders and began to shake me.

"Alix?" Rynn said.

I blinked. His eyes were bright blue . . . There was something important about that . . . Why though?

His eyes brightened, and my eyes focused. A warm wave washed over me, pushing back the psychedelic fog.

Shit. I snapped out of it and shook my head.

He was still staring at me, his eyes still a bright blue. "Rynn, what the hell is going on in here?" Something wasn't right, and not just the party aspect; it was wrong on so many other levels. "And what's wrong with these people? Are they even human?"

Rynn's mouth curled up in a snarl. "Oh most of them are human. My cousin likes to make a spectacle of himself—and surround himself in one. I didn't think he'd go this far—"

OK, yeah, not at all cryptic, I thought as another person wearing paint in lieu of clothes walked by, taking one of the drinks from a platter . . . which weren't Coronas at all but champagne flutes filled with an amber liquid. "Well, what the hell is it? Is it an incubus thing?" That thought didn't sit well with me; incubi and succubi were supposed to be benign on the supernatural sliding scale of dangerous. This sure as hell didn't qualify as benign in my books.

More people filled in around us, all human if Rynn was to be believed. I wasn't seeing it. Don't get me wrong, I'm no stranger to a good party, but this . . .

Rynn swore as another person just about slammed into him and brushed up against me. Another wave of euphoria hit me in a manic rush . . .

Shit.

"It's passed along by contact?"

Rynn pulled me out of the way into a corner. Now he was looking worried. "It's an incense of sorts," he said. "Incubi and succubi are fond of it, though it only has this euphoric effect on humans. It permeates food and water. My idiot cousin saw fit to douse an entire room with it. That's what you see in the glasses and smell in the air . . ." He swore and tried to block someone from crashing into me, but the dress made it a losing battle.

"And you brought me here dressed like this? And you think I'm reckless!?" Another rush hit me, and I balanced on Rynn.

"I swear, if I had known Artemis had gone this far—"

A pair of girls riveted their eyes towards Rynn as the name Artemis left his lips. They giggled . . . and began to whisper . . . creepy, like epic creepy . . . *except it might be kind of cool to meet Artemis . . . wasn't that Rynn's cousin?*

I pressed my hand against my forehead. *OK, Owl, get control over it, anything stupid you start to think is probably that drug . . .*

Two servers walked by holding a plate of the long-stemmed glasses. They exchanged a glance as they passed by Rynn and me, setting off towards a side hallway I hadn't noticed before. They didn't seem to be affected by the incense. Had to be supernaturals . . . not nymphs or incubi . . . something worse? I shivered—I'd have to describe them to Nadya later and see what she thought.

"Here there be monsters," I whispered.

Rynn glanced down at me—he actually looked worried now. "Alix—I'm sorry, this was a bad call. I didn't think Artemis would be this idiotic—" He touched the side of my face and made me look at him again. My head started to clear . . .

A woman, maybe a year or two younger than me, with cascading, brown highlighted hair and even worse balance in stilettos, fell towards me.

Rynn caught her instead, though he didn't look happy about it. He searched around the room again, more intensely scanning the upper floor as he tried to stand the woman up.

The woman smiled at Rynn. "You kind of look like him," the woman said in a breathy bedroom voice that even through my haze sounded overboard.

For his part, Rynn tried to push the girl back up, but with a laugh she leaned in. "I'm Violet," she said, and ran her finger along Rynn's arm, shifting her expression from intoxicated to alert and coy. "Have you seen him yet? I've been trying to find him all night," she said, her fingernails, fake and painted a shade of purple that had to be after her namesake, dug into Rynn's sleeve.

There was something wrong with this picture . . . I just couldn't remember what . . .

The girl glanced over and reached for me.

Shit—

I tried jumping back out of range, but all my motor skills weren't at my disposal . . . well, that, and let's face it, heels are death for running.

Her fingers brushed the skin on my arm before she leaned herself back into Rynn, where she focused her attention. Well, as focused as she could be through half-lidded eyes.

The euphoria pushed its way through my defenses, flooding all my senses.

Come on, Owl, get a grip . . .

I closed my eyes and tried to force out the noise, but there was no escape. When I opened my eyes, the deluge sent a rush of pleasure down my spine.

I looked back to where Rynn should be. He was gone. "Rynn?" I yelled, and had to grab the wall to steady myself as another rush hit me.

OK, this train was derailing fast . . .

"Alix!" I heard him scream. I found him a few feet away, trying to peel off Violet. He screamed for me again . . . there were too many people to reach him in time . . . I thought I saw his eyes turn blue, but that had to be a mistake. Rynn's eyes were gray—

I shook my head as my brain fought for control. Rynn, I had to get back to Rynn . . . I took a step towards him but stumbled. It was as if the floor reached out and pulled me down. I fell on my knees—hard. I knew it, my brain knew it—I just didn't feel it.

More people moved around me. I stared at my hands . . . were they . . . gold? No, it was something reflecting off the ceiling. I glanced up at the gold bowl hanging above me, a sacrificial bowl, circa Alexander the Great.

Son of a bitch . . . one just went up for auction a few months ago, was that it? I tried to focus in on it better, but it kept rippling in and out of detail. Had to be the lights . . . it couldn't hurt to check out the place though. Rynn's cousin might even have a decent art collection; he was an incubus, after all. Must have collected something good over the past couple hundred years—or however long incubi lived . . .

"Alix!"

Rynn's voice cut through the fog and euphoria this time. I blinked, trying to clear my eyes, and looked up. There was no ancient gold dish, only a beat-up chandelier. Jesus Christ, I needed to get the hell out of here before I did something stupid.

"Don't move. Stay there," Rynn yelled, but he was no longer trying to just untangle himself from Violet. More people had closed in around him. He wouldn't make it through in time.

Every ounce of my brain not high on the damn incense was desperate to escape while it still could.

"Sorry, but I need to get the hell out of here," I said, though I wasn't sure if I said it loud enough for Rynn to hear me.

I pushed myself back up to standing. Now where the hell was that exit?

My eyes landed on a hallway not too far away from me. Had it been there before? I steadied myself against the wall, the textured wallpaper prickling against my hand like pins, repulsing me back towards the room.

I frowned. To hell with that. Ignoring the sensation, I made my way towards the empty hall.

"Alix!" Rynn yelled. I didn't even look over my shoulder. I'd worry about Rynn once I was out of this room—once my head was clear . . .

I made it to the hallway and reached my hand out towards the arch. Something like a pool rippled underneath my fingers—not entirely real. I faltered, and the last bit of my thoughts not wrapped up in the incense reared its head. *You need out.*

I took a deep breath and stepped through.

Silence flooded over me.

Oh my God . . . I could breathe again. I closed my eyes and leaned against the wall as the sensation left me. I'd just catch my breath, then find Rynn . . .

"I'm surprised you made it past the wallpaper. Most people can't stand the texture. Feels sharp against the fingers, or so I've been told," a man said beside me, his voice carrying an accent I recognized—like Rynn's, though this voice was deeper and rougher. I opened my eyes and spun around as fast as my body was willing.

Artemis Bast leaned against the wall beside me. The resemblance to Rynn was uncanny, as far as facial features went—even the same cropped blond hair, but the comparison ended there. The leather pants, tattoos, gold-paint-splattered burnout T-shirt, a single gold stud earring, not to mention his expression and the way he stood—everything would have been foreign on Rynn. And green eyes. Artemis had green eyes instead of Rynn's gray/blue.

He didn't smile or come any closer, just watched me as he took a swig from a bottle of Jack Daniel's. The way he watched me—it was almost cruel. Attractive—I'd be an idiot and a liar if I said he wasn't something to look at—but make no mistake about it, underneath the surface was thinly masked cruelty.

I had to admit though, if someone asked me what an incubus looked like, I'd point out this guy over Rynn any day of the week.

Here there be monsters.

I stepped out of Artemis's range, but, not altogether having my senses back, I tripped on my heel. The wall caught me, which was a damn good thing, because Artemis sure as hell didn't make any move to help.

I nodded at the ballroom. "So, is that what has-been rock stars do for kicks out here? No offense, but it seems kind of easy." Yup. That's me. When faced with unknown supernaturals, my go-to is to start throwing insults. Good to see I hadn't lost my form or touch, by the way Artemis glared.

Nothing like getting insulted by someone who shouldn't have had the mental capacity to string them together, and trust me, with the left-over head rush, I shouldn't have had the capacity . . .

He tilted his head to the side, giving me a critical once-over. "Interesting," he said, glancing back towards the party. "They usually don't make it this far—and the ones that do are . . ." He paused, as if searching for the phrase he wanted to use.

I swallowed and, using the wall for balance, edged back another few steps. I did not like how Artemis was watching me. "Let me guess. Interesting?"

Artemis arched an eyebrow, again reminding me of Rynn. "More interesting than my cousin's tastes usually run, and let's leave it at that, shall we?" Artemis took a step towards me, the hint of a frown touching his face.

What I wouldn't give for an exit. I could run, but where? Back into kaleidoscope fun land? No thanks. I settled for backing up another few steps, still using the wall as my prop. I used the opportunity to check out the ballroom. It looked like I was staring through a pool of water, where everything was unnaturally warped on the other side.

Great, more supernatural bullshit magic.

Clear the hell up, brain, so we can get us out of this mess.

Artemis followed me, like a cat or snake moving in on prey. "Now, who might you be, and what on earth are you doing with my cousin? Better yet, you can start with what the hell he's after."

"Why don't you ask him yourself?" I said.

I'd almost have called Artemis's expression a smile if not for the fact that the sentiment didn't come close to reaching his eyes. "Because I'm asking you. And you can damn well do better than that."

Artemis was regarding me now with more interest than I was comfortable with.

"You know, I'm pretty sure I can make you tell me," he said. "In fact, I'm pretty sure you'll be more than happy to tell me every secret you've ever had. What do you think about that?"

I swore as he closed in and his eyes flashed green.

I shut mine tight before he could pull off the incubus bullshit.

There's nothing I hate more then being backed into a corner by supernaturals. You could say it's a sore spot with me . . .

What was it Rynn had said? Artemis was easier to handle when he was off his game? *Well, let's throw him off his game then, shall we?*

I stopped backing up, crossed my arms, and picked a classic Pink Floyd poster on the wall behind him to stare at. "How bout this, Artemis? You lay off the incubus bullshit, and I won't kick you in the sweet spot? Then maybe we can talk." I kept my eyes fixated on the rainbow triangle—and no, the irony didn't escape me.

Out of the corner of my eye I saw Artemis arch an eyebrow, but no flashes of green. "Sweet spot—now where would that be exactly?" he said.

I smiled. I love it when the bad guys ask that.

A hand clamped down on my shoulder. "Artemis, you really don't want to know the answer to that one, and if you don't believe me, there's a number of vampires who can vouch for it," Rynn said.

I let out the breath I'd been holding. I wasn't sure I'd have been able to do any damage in this state.

Artemis looked from me to Rynn and smiled. "I'll take your word for it then," he said, then added, "what, cousin, no phone call?"

Rynn smiled back. "You know me. I prefer to drop in. More entertaining that way."

Artemis laughed, as if amused, and glanced down the hallway. "Come on, then—you can chastise me in my office, since that's what you like to do. If you haven't noticed, I have a party to get back to." He turned his back on us and headed down the hallway.

I caught Rynn's arm as he started to follow. "You couldn't have warned me about him?" I said under my breath.

"I heard that," Artemis sang out from up ahead.

Rynn frowned but didn't look at me—his eyes were focused on Artemis's back. "I told you we didn't part on good terms," he whispered.

"Yeah, bad terms I got—not the blood feud part."

Rynn's jaw tightened. "We don't have a blood feud—"

I still wasn't budging. "Not from where I was standing two minutes ago."

"I heard that too," Artemis yelled from up ahead. "You might want to stop whispering, since it's serving you no fucking purpose."

This time Rynn did look at me. "Alix, trust me. I know what I'm doing."

"No offense, but all evidence tonight would point to the exact opposite—"

"Oh come on, you two," Artemis yelled from somewhere down the hall. "It can wait till later. I'm getting bored holding the door open."

Rynn looked at me, pleading . . . Damn it. I swore and reminded myself that according to Rynn, Artemis held the keys to getting me into Daphne's mansion and halfway to clearing my name. Asshole incubus, or IAA and homicidal Naga . . .

You know, it hasn't escaped my attention that the choices I've been forced to make lately really suck.

"I so need a new job—and next time, I arrange my own outfit," I said. "Something with actual pockets."

We followed Artemis into his office.

It was less opulent than the rest of the mansion—more business, less rocker—with a dozen or so platinum and gold records and a few concert posters decorating the walls. At the back was a large oak desk on which Artemis placed two tumblers. He slid the glasses across the desk towards me and Rynn, then sat in the leather chair.

He held up his bottle of Jack Daniel's. I stole a quick glance at Rynn, but he didn't give me a hint either way. I nodded; not that whiskey was my drink of choice, but I would take what I could get at this point.

Artemis poured and slid the glasses towards us. He gave me a slow once-over before turning his full attention on Rynn. "Rynn," he said, "what have I done to deserve your illustrious company this time?"

"I'm calling in one of the many favors you owe me."

Artemis's smile still didn't drop, but instead of acknowledging Rynn, he turned his attention on me. "Sorry, dear, but typical Rynn here never bothered introducing us."

I shook my head to clear the shock. "Charity," I said, using one of my more benign aliases.

The corner of Artemis's mouth quirked up. "Charity," he said, rolling the word over, as if testing it for validity. "Interesting . . . choice."

Rynn's arm went around my shoulder again, something I wasn't used to from him—not in public, anyways. I don't think he'd ever shown anything close to territorial male behavior. I didn't count his gripe with Carpe, because Rynn didn't like elves period.

Artemis continued sizing me up, then held up the bottle. "Bottoms up," he said, and took a swig. I noted Rynn picked up his glass, so I followed suit.

"Now what the hell do you want? And please explain, dear cousin, why you get to parade your human conquests around while I have mine—"

Rynn snapped at Artemis in supernatural—a warning, from the tone, but Artemis interrupted Rynn before he could finish, rolling his eyes. "Oh for God's sake, will you please speak English? If not for my ears, then at least for the girl's. Oh come on—don't look at me like that, the rules hardly apply to her anymore. She's had enough bloody vampire pheromones to drown a cow in. Though you don't look like a cow, dear," he said, holding up the bottle towards me. "You're quite fetching, it's really just a figure of speech."

"You know the rules, Artemis, which is why I can't fathom what the hell you're doing—"

"Oh come off it—I'm not breaking any rules. Every last one of them is here of their own free will, and they come and go as they please. I'm not keeping them here." The corner of Artemis's mouth twitched up. "And you're one to talk," he said, pointing at me with the bottle again. "The only ones who work their way past my party veils are the vampire junkies, and I never let them through the front door, which, let's not mince words here—she's had her fair share of vampires—"

"Whoa, wait a minute—*so* not a vampire pheromone junkie here," I said.

Artemis faced me. "Yet you know what I'm talking about—interesting." His eyes widened in mock surprise as he turned back to Rynn. "By the way, what you're doing dragging her around with you is what the rest of us call slumming it. You're welcome for the life lesson—"

"Hey, asshole, right here," I said, waving my hand.

"Never mind, dear. I withdraw the remark. Now what is this favor you so desperately need, cousin?" He took another swig from the bottle. "And if you're here, it's desperate, so don't bother denying it."

"I need to get into Daphne Sylph's mansion," I said.

Artemis snorted. "You don't exactly come across as the Hollywood fan type, and you do realize you're in the wrong house—"

"Yeah, no shit. But Rynn here seems to think you can get me in, and apparently you owe him a favor, so . . . ?" I held up my hands. "Deal or no, incubus?"

He laughed. "Oh now you're fun. What did you say your name was again? Charity?"

The cousins stared each other down, but whereas Rynn looked like he wanted to punch Artemis, Artemis was examining the situation, his green eyes dancing between me and Rynn.

Artemis leaned back in his chair and crossed his arms. "What the hell has Daphne done to piss you off this time?"

Rynn shrugged. "Nothing of consequence—more importantly, none of your business." I didn't miss the warning, so there was no way Artemis could have.

"You know what Daphne will do if you get within a mile of her place?"

"Which is why I'm asking for your help."

Artemis took another swig of the Jack Daniel's while he considered Rynn's proposal. "So I take the girl into Daphne's and that's it? We're square?"

"Clean slate," Rynn said through clenched teeth.

"Well, then how can I possibly refuse?" Artemis's green eyes turned back on me. "But just her, not you."

"The deal is for both of us."

Artemis snorted. "Both of you would be suspicious, and knowing you, Daphne will not take kindly to whatever it is you have in store."

"Artemis—"

"Oh stop worrying. I'll get her in and bring her back in one piece as well—though I'm still curious as to why the hell for."

Rynn didn't answer. Artemis just shrugged and nodded at me. "Bring her back tomorrow night around nine p.m. She cleans up, I imagine?"

I snorted. "Do I clean up? What the hell is that supposed to—" But Rynn covered my mouth before I could say anything really offensive.

Artemis glanced up, apparently fascinated with a spot on the ceiling. "My God, Rynn, I wouldn't believe it if I hadn't seen it for myself, but you actually seem to be getting more interesting with age."

"Fuck off," Rynn said, grabbing my hand before helping me out of the office. "And clean up your fucking mansion."

Artemis just laughed and gave me a measured look. "Charity," he said, and lifted the Jack Daniel's. "Until tomorrow, and whatever nefarious deeds my illustrious cousin has you doing on his behalf."

I was about to correct Artemis's assumption that I worked for Rynn, but I stopped when Rynn gave a slight shake of his head. Maybe there was an advantage to keeping Artemis in the dark.

Old wise thieves proverb: Quit while the going is still good.

"Not even a thank-you?" Artemis yelled, leaning out his office door.

"You owe me. I'm doing you a favor."

"This makes us square," Artemis yelled behind us.

"Just be sober!"

"Don't count on it!"

The incense hit me again. Oh shit . . . the party. I'd almost forgotten. I stopped in my tracks. "Whoa, hold up—"

"Just keep walking," he said, stepping up our pace.

Yeah, this I was putting my foot down on. I dug both heels into the carpet. "No way. I'm not going back out there into kaleidoscope happy land."

That earned me another laugh from Artemis, who'd come to watch us leave. "Kaleidoscope happy land—oh that's good. I might have to use that for my next album title. Are you sure you plan on keeping her, Rynn? You can always leave her here. I'll give you another one—Violet was quite taken with the family resemblance."

Rynn shot Artemis a look of death and steered me out.

"Nice meeting you, *Charity*. Make sure you're not late, I hate to be kept waiting."

Rynn's eyes briefly flashed.

Oh no, I'd had enough of the flashy eyes for one night. "Hey—yeah—just wait a minute."

"I'm just making it so the incense won't affect you as much—provided we move quickly."

Yeah, not that I didn't appreciate the sentiment . . . Using supernaturals to get me out of supernatural problems had indirectly led to my current predicament. Human Owl didn't approve of the solution, thank you very much. There had to be an easier way than letting Rynn mess with my mind—however noninvasive and well-intentioned he was—or getting high as a kite and stumbling my way out. "The ballroom is the worst of it, right?"

Rynn nodded. Artemis was still watching us, amusement replacing the cruelty.

Great, just fantastic. Now I amused him. Well, let's see if I could use that to my advantage.

"Hey, asshole incubus?"

Artemis arched an eyebrow.

"Got a back door? Preferably the opposite direction from the happy kaleidoscope crazy hour?"

Rynn swore, but Artemis laughed outright, pointing down the hall. "Through the kitchen, there's a back door that opens onto the porch."

OK, now we were getting somewhere. Fast, now that was the second thing. I pulled off my shoes and handed them to Rynn.

"Out the back door it is," I said.

Artemis laughed behind us. "It's been a slice, *Charity*. See you tomorrow."

We exited back into the hall, and almost immediately the euphoria hit—though, as suspected, not nearly as powerfully outside the epicenter. At least I knew it was coming this time, so it didn't have a chance to creep up through my thoughts.

"And Artemis thinks vampire pheromones are bad?"

Rynn frowned. "Similar effect—except this wears off almost immediately, and it's not exactly addictive."

"What do you mean 'not exactly'?"

"You saw those people. They come back for more because they think it's a good party." I didn't miss the vehemence in his voice.

"What does he do to them?" I asked.

Rynn didn't say anything at first.

"Oh come on. He wouldn't go to all that trouble if he didn't get something out of it—"

"He feeds off of them, all right? That's all." He shook his head. "I'm not in the mood to talk about it right now. Ask me later." Yeah . . . no one's that angry about nothing at all.

We reached the kitchen—almost home free. I spun at the sound of humming and the smell of a heavy floral perfume.

A woman helping herself to a bottle of champagne emerged from behind the fridge. Her eyes widened with frantic need as she saw us.

It was the same girl who'd thrown herself at Rynn and practically confided her life goal of sleeping with as many rock stars as she could. Violet.

"I heard you met him?" she said, the fanatic euphoria lighting up her face. She reached out her hand and tried to brush my arm, but this time I managed to put Rynn between us. On the one hand, I felt bad for him, but on the other, I didn't need another psychedelic trip.

Violet either didn't care or notice.

"Violet? Violet dear, where did you get off to?" Artemis called out from down the hall.

She tilted her head towards the sound of his voice. With something besides Rynn catching her attention, she flitted back into the hallway like a vapid, drunk butterfly.

Not that I make a habit of being a good Samaritan, but Violet was in no condition to be doing anything. "Violet—hey Violet." I tried going after her, but Rynn stopped me.

"You can't. She's here of her own free will."

"This," I said, indicating the house, "is not free will, and I think you know that as well as I do."

His face darkened. "I don't like it either, believe me, but there's nothing we can do about it. Artemis is unfortunately not breaking a single rule." He sighed. "I should have known better."

I glanced back to where Violet had gone, but there wasn't much I could do at this point—the only thing I was likely to do was crawl through the mansion looking for treasure . . .

Rynn made me look at him. No flash of blue, but still, it helped me focus.

"We need to *leave*," he said.

I nodded. Whoever Violet was—to Artemis, to the people here, to people outside this warped playland—there was nothing I could do for her . . . not right now anyways.

We reached our jeep. I don't think I've ever been as happy about being in the open air as I was when we pulled away from the Hollywood Hills and Artemis Bast's mansion. It might have been the tail end of incense euphoria, but I had a lot of questions about the incubi I was going to need answered once I got my thoughts back together. I had a sinking suspicion Rynn had glossed over just how dangerous they could be. I know better than to start an argument half cut. Off-again lesson number two . . .

"How come the more I try to do the right thing, the more monsters I run into?"

"Because the monsters were always there." He shook his head. "You just have a way of poking them where they least expect it."

Somehow I don't think he was talking about just Artemis Bast, and I remembered Nadya's theory, born of her uncanny nose for trouble, that there was more going on than anyone was letting on.

"You know those things you keep asking me about the supernatural, and I keep saying you really don't want to know?" he continued.

I ran over the biggest offenders in my head: goblin culinary habits in the modern world, vampire blood banks, ghoul feeding stations—I mean, they had to exist, how else would an entire corpse-eating species go unnoticed? With YouTube the way it was, all it'd take would be one ghoul dragging a body out of a morgue or graveyard, and all hell would break loose. Even the IAA couldn't keep a handle on YouTube.

"This is definitely one of those things," Rynn said.

I sat back in my seat and let Rynn drive, hoping what was left of the euphoria cleared the hell out. "Some party," I said.

This time Rynn didn't say anything back.

What the hell had I gotten myself into this time?

8

World Quest and Other Distractions

Noon, hiding out in the hotel lobby

I curled up on the chair and pulled my laptop closer to make sure the couple behind me couldn't see what I was doing. Call me self-conscious, but I draw the line at letting people watch me play World Quest over my shoulder. I'm not that much of a social lost cause. Besides, there's something to be said for a luxury hotel lobby; the Wi-Fi works, and the work areas feel like a higher-end version of IKEA.

The biggest reason for hiding out down here, though, was the fact that I was still fighting with Rynn. World Quest helps me think . . . and work through my thoughts. Like Nadya, Rynn didn't maybe appreciate that as much as he should.

And for the record, I do not use World Quest to avoid adult conversations about my relationships with actual people—incubi included.

At least I felt better this morning in my black snakeskin leather jacket and matching leather boots. I still looked like I belonged here, just on my terms, not L.A.'s. I cringed thinking about last night's outfit. "Never again, Captain," I said, and he mewed from the carrier—the designer one Nadya had wrangled in Egypt.

Another perk about staying in high-end hotels—they were used to putting up with crazy people and their pets.

Oh God, I'm doomed to a life of playing video games by myself, except for my cat.

Captain looked around the lobby again and then at me—and mewed. His food dish was still upstairs . . . so was the litter box. He had a point.

"Look, we'll go back up in another half hour. Just let's give Rynn a while longer to cool off."

FYI—that incubus incense shit Artemis laced his entire mansion with? Coming down's a real bitch, and it leaves one hell of a hangover. I'd been in a bad mood and probably said a few things I shouldn't have. You'd think someone like Artemis, who'd probably been alive for a couple hundred years, would have found something that didn't mess humans up quite that much.

The worst part about the latest fight with Rynn was that I'd started it for no reason. I'd accused him of not telling me about the Artemis kaleidoscope crazy hour on purpose . . . and lying to me about incubi not being dangerous. After seeing Artemis, I'd called Rynn on that being a load of shit. It had been a low blow. Rynn hadn't let me out of his sight while the damn incense worked its way out of my system, and he'd felt guilty enough about exposing me to it.

Goddamn it, why the hell couldn't I pull my punches? At least the verbal ones? Rynn did.

It hadn't been like this when he'd been in Japan . . .

And I'd only seen him every few months . . .

And I'd thought he was human . . .

And Artemis's spectacle hadn't demonstrated how *harmless* was open to interpretation . . . I was still seriously trying to process everything I'd seen last night, with mixed results.

I was starting to remember why I used to have that damn rule about no goddamned supernaturals. Because humans end up maimed and dead, that's why!

I shrunk further into the chair. I'd tried to apologize after I'd yelled, but Rynn hadn't wanted my apology. Empty promises don't mean a hell of a lot to someone who can tell exactly what you really feel.

Artemis's words to Rynn kept repeating in my head: *"Slumming it even for you."*

Rynn had said something to me once about being attracted to things that were broken.

Normally I don't care that I'm broken . . . I know it, I admit it, I embrace it. Let's face it: I'm not normal. I don't know how a normal relationship is supposed to work—hell, facing Alexander and his cronies would actually be easier than facing Rynn right now.

The thing that bothered me the most about our fight was that for once Rynn hadn't called me a train wreck.

I hadn't called him a whore either.

I held up my coffee mug for the waitress. More caffeine and World Quest, that's what my god-awful hangover needed.

When I glanced back down, a message from Carpe was scrolling across my screen. The lobby wasn't private enough that I could talk, so I'd limited our conversation to chat—I was starting to think it wasn't that bad an idea in general. Carpe tended to keep his mouth shut about the damn spell book when he actually had to put in the effort to type it out.

OK, what the hell is up? Carpe wrote.

Nothing's up. I just had a rough day at work. Except that we were trolling a goblin cave for loot. A nice, generic goblin cave, with no archaeological significance whatsoever . . .

This blew.

Captain picked up his head from his carrier, mewed louder this time, and began sniffing the air.

I hazarded what I hoped was a subtle glance around the hotel lobby, every nerve on edge.

All I saw were tourists and people on business, no sign of vampire junkies or the telltale scent of rotting lily of the valley. Not wanting to risk a scene, I grasped Captain's red leash until he settled back down. Rynn had told me Maus were bred by the Egyptians to hunt vampires in packs. Captain disagreed and felt it should be a solo operation. It was still a point of contention and training between the two of us.

False alarm. Still . . . I fired off a text message to Nadya. *Any pings on Alexander and the Paris boys lately?* Better safe than sorry.

Technically Mr. Kurosawa had a truce with Alexander and the vampire powers that said they couldn't kill me. In practice, that just meant Alexander couldn't get caught. If Alexander got wind I was in L.A., he might risk it.

I was starting to wonder whether protection from the vampires was worth it. *Three years, Owl—three years and then you're free* . . . provided I managed to clear my name and convince both Mr. Kurosawa and the IAA I wasn't the thief breaking into the City of the Dead.

I put my forehead against my keyboard. This is exactly what I got for facing my problems and trying to come up with adult solutions. And Rynn wondered why the hell I avoided adult conversations . . .

My World Quest screen pinged again.

Hey? You playing or not?

I snorted at Carpe's message and took one last look around the lobby. Considering Captain wasn't growling and trying to chew his way out of the carrier, it was probably residual vampire he was picking up.

I went back to the game screen. *Of course I'm still playing. Why wouldn't I want to play? I mean, it's generic goblins? What's not to like?*

Seriously, Byzantine, get your ass back in the game or fuck the hell off— this crappy quest is in fact entirely your fault and you don't hear me bitching and whining.

Not what I need to hear right now, Carpe . . . yet another problem blamed on me. I counted ten goblins left.

I took a sip of my coffee and faded Byzantine into the shadows in preparation for a backstab. Then I came out with one of my most powerful attacks—a swipe of a magic staff I'd picked up on a much better and more lucrative dungeon crawl. One of those one-a-day deals that wipes out an entire playing field of enemies in a digital haze of lightning and fire.

Yes, it was overkill.

The screen lit up, and in a moment all that was left of the goblin cave was a few scorched skeletons and what treasure they'd been carrying.

Happy? I wrote back.

Stop being such a fucking princess.

I ignored Carpe and started to search the cave for loot. Maybe I'd get lucky and the goblins had killed a new player who'd gone out and supped themselves up with armor, weapons, and magic gear from the real-money in-game store.

My phone pinged before I could open the first bag. Carpe was pissed enough as it was, so I planned on ignoring the call—until I saw it was Hermes.

Keeping one eye on the screen, I checked the message.

Dear Owl—I can fit you into my schedule now. Hermes

Yeah, not likely. I wouldn't hear the end of it if I ditched the game now, especially after that stunt I just pulled . . .

Bad timing, Hermes—Now's no good. How bout 30? Better yet, pick a spot, I'll come meet you. Giving my location out to relative strangers fuels my paranoia. Now . . . let's see if there isn't a secret stash in here somewhere . . . newbie players need loot drop too, right?

My phone pinged again with Hermes's response.

Dear Owl, I think I'll meet you. No offense, but you drag trouble behind you like a gator tows seaweed through a swamp.

Yeah, still not happening. *You think I'm giving you the hotel I'm staying at you might as well pony up some cash for magic beans.*

Dear Owl, Doing my best to stay polite here. Not asking again. Give me your hotel, I'll swing by, we'll talk.

Yeah. No. I started to type my response and noted Captain chirped. Probably a game light flashing . . . or he had to go to the litter box. "Dude, just give me a sec—"

"Will you just look the fuck up already?" said a male voice, medium tenor, with a mild American accent.

Son of a bitch. I looked up and swore at the guy standing in front of me: late twenties/early thirties, light red hair that came down just past his ears, dressed like a bike messenger, complete with bag, and perpetual smile filled with very good white teeth. Cute in an outdoorsy, nondescript kind of way, except for the bright red hair. That would have stood out anywhere.

He smiled and stuck out his hand. "Hi there. Hermes," he said, then took the seat across from me.

"Umm, yeah, OK. Please, just take a seat."

Captain chirped again, louder this time, so I glanced down. He was alert and curious but not a frantic, hissing mess. OK, Hermes wasn't a vampire. I counted that as a positive.

"You realize finding this hotel wasn't easy?" he said.

I frowned. "That's the point. And how the hell do I know you're even Hermes?"

Nonplussed at my question, Hermes waved a waitress down as she walked by. "Two Coronas—that's what you drink, right?"

I nodded. Slowly. I still hadn't decided if I should run. I figured I could at least wait until the Corona arrived. Between me and my double on the cruise ship, I was having surprising luck in the weaponizing bottles department.

"In fact, couldn't track you," Hermes said. "Had to track your boyfriend. Nice-looking guy, by the way, even for an incubus. He could do a lot better. You can't."

"Ummm, fuck off?"

He didn't leave though, just leaned back in the leather chair. "So here's my question: at what point did you wake up and say, *Hey, I want to be a complete and utter fuckup*?" he said, open, friendly smile still on his face.

"All right, where do you get off calling me the fuckup?"

Hermes ignored me and kept going. "Like seriously, out of all my clients—and trust me, there are some seriously messed-up cats on my list right now—you're the one who decided to fuck the IAA. I mean, how does someone do that? Do you just wake up and say, *Hey, I know, let's fuck everyone's business*?"

Oh for Christ's sake . . . I was officially sick and tired of everyone—including the IAA—blaming me for a bunch of thefts that some asshole was pinning on me. "First off, whatever the IAA is saying, it's not me—"

Hermes snorted. "I know that. You wouldn't have been asking about the pieces if you'd taken them. You'd be running—knowing you, really far, really fast."

"OK—wait a minute. Back up here. If you know it's not me, why do you even care?"

"Because you're the one in the eye of the storm, so you're the one they're looking for, and not just the IAA. The supernaturals are getting pissed about it too, which, by the way, makes up a hell of a lot of my business. It's not just you thieves."

Captain meowed from his carrier, probably wanting to know why no one was paying attention to him. Hermes reached in and gave Captain a pat. More surprisingly, Captain let him. "Like the cat, by the way. You realize if the IAA decides to crack down, I could be out of business?"

I think I preferred Hermes as a digital entity. "Like I give a flying fuck. As you pointed out, I've got enough problems. Worry about your own skin."

"Seriously? We're going there? Already? And where's your sense of community?" That perpetual smile was starting to unnerve me. Botched Botox?

"Hey, I'm all for honor amongst thieves, but the golden rule is watch thine own goddamn back."

A corner of Hermes's mouth twitched up in sarcasm. "OK, that is so not the first rule of thieves—"

"Prove it, Hermes—oh that's right. You can't."

For the first time since he sat down, his smile fell. "Goddamn it, the worst part about you thieves is you warp and twist the rules any which way that suits you. Jesus, I mean, who does that?" He paused while the waitress delivered our drinks. "No offense, kid, but you seriously need to start taking some advice."

I took a swing of my Corona. I needed it—though I briefly wondered how the alcohol, caffeine, and incense comedown would mix. "Really? Let me guess, yours is the advice I should take?"

He shrugged. "Honestly? At this point, I think you could take anyone's advice and it'd be better than your own."

I got up to leave.

"Just relax," Hermes said, pulling a small laptop out of his messenger bag, one that looked as if a grab bag of tech parts had been thrown together at a late-night engineering party—one with lots of beer. "I found something. I won't even charge you for it as a sign of goodwill." He shook his head while he typed, then passed the screen to me.

On the screen was a job list I knew of but had never used—it was hosted on Black Pit Freelance, a website on the dark net, where people went to post illegal jobs and heists—either to recruit or off-load. It was a bad scene, and not because of the thieves. It was full of FBI and IAA agents setting up fake accounts and combing the posts. Only rookies and the desperate trawled for work there.

Highlighted on Hermes's screen was a post from about two months back, looking for someone willing to do a retrieval in Syria. The coordinates and photos in the bottom left no doubt about it—it was for a job at the Syrian City of the Dead.

"Son of a bitch, you found the original job posting—"

"Ah! Don't get excited. It's all bogus accounts. To be honest, I thought it was another idiot IAA or FBI agent trying to draw a few rookies out. Too high-stakes for the pros. The poster and the guy who responded— Red Shirt one—closed their accounts after a couple hours."

Set up a new bogus account for each job and delete it as soon as terms are agreed upon—preferably from a location the IAA had a hard time getting agents into.

I had no way to trace the original poster, but at least I knew where the job had originated.

"What about Daphne Sylph?" I asked.

Hermes shook his head. "If she was involved, it was through an intermediary—and I doubt it, because I hacked her email. Just curious," he added. "If she was behind it, she kept it quiet, and between you and me, I don't think she's that smart. In my humble opinion, she's holding it for someone or bought it after the fact."

Which meant someone had not only targeted the City of the Dead but they also hadn't wanted to end up on anyone's radar. I swore. This was not the scenario I'd been hoping for. It neither cleared my name nor got me closer to the real thief. Guilty by default.

Hermes put the laptop away. "Like I said, not much. Piqued my interest though. Especially with you involved. Seriously, Owl, people are pissed. There's a reason I don't deal in cursed items."

I glared. "Neither do I."

"Hey, not me you have to convince. It's the supernaturals and the IAA."

Hermes shrugged, fumbled something out of his front pocket—an off-white business card with embossed gold lettering on both sides—and extended it to me, balanced between two fingers. "I wasn't going to give you this, buuuttt I figure you deserve some kind of frequent flyer bonus." He stood and added, "You're turning into one hell of a long shot. Smarter people than me bet you'd be dead long before now."

Oh God, there was a betting pool on me now? "Let me guess, how soon until Owl ends up in jail?"

"Dead, actually." Hermes's expression turned serious. "Just be glad you're proving entertaining enough to attract some attention. If you're going to be a colossal fuckup, might as well be an interesting one. Seriously, though—I've got big money on you coming through this game, and I'm going to be pissed if I lose." He nodded at the card. "Just remember that, kid."

I took the card, and a static shock coursed through me. I suck at spotting the supernatural, but even I know magic when I touch it.

Shit . . .

On the card was Hermes's name and number followed by the statement *Good for one get out of jail free. All attempts to forge more uses will null and void this card. Yes, it's been a problem, you fucking thieves.*

I turned the card over. On the back, in blue pen, was written, *Stop fucking around, kid.*

Oh shit . . . Yeah, no, this wasn't a dangerous situation at all . . .

I looked up at Hermes. "What are you?"

He grinned. It wasn't unfriendly or friendly. "A bit like clothes with no price tags; if you have to ask, you probably can't afford it." He bent down to give Captain a scratch. "Just do me a favor and don't waste the card, OK? It'll piss me off. You get, like, one from me—and let's face it, chances are good you'll be dead before you rate a second."

The perpetual smile didn't falter as he polished off the beer and headed out of the lobby.

Fuuuccckkkk. Oh I was so not telling Rynn and Nadya about this . . . no way, I'd never live it down.

"BTW?" Hermes said.

I glanced up. He'd stopped a few feet away and turned back around to face me.

"I'll be really disappointed if you ditch the boyfriend. He's one of the few things keeping you alive. Like I said, I've got money on this." And with one last wave, Hermes left.

Oh I was so screwed . . . I finished off my beer as I watched Hermes go. I hate it when people have a point. "What do you think, Captain?"

In response, he gave me a forlorn mew from inside his carrier. If he'd wanted his litter box and food dish before, he really wanted them now. I took it as a sign to go back upstairs and try to act like an adult. Before any more supernaturals who found my current predicament mildly amusing walked through the door . . .

I hate supernaturals.

I'm out, Carpe, I typed into the game window. *I've got things to do, and let's face it, this quest blows.* I closed the game screen before Carpe could respond.

While packing up my laptop, I noticed a news alert tag on my phone. I monitor a handful of sites and accounts that report actual news, not the latest *Voice* results. "Unknown flu strikes two undocumented workers from overseas. Pathogen remains unidentified though authorities suggest it is not contagious. Any suspected flu cases should be reported to doctors immediately—"

I opened the link, but the report was little more than a Reuters footnote. I shoved my phone in my pocket and headed for the elevator. There was no reason to think it had anything to do with the curse . . . still, I'd keep my eye on the news and tell Nadya to do the same.

Time to be a grown-up and face Rynn.

I didn't even lose my nerve on the way to the room. Rynn was sitting at the desk, working on his own laptop.

"Hey?" I said.

He didn't look up at first, just kept staring at the screen. "If you've come back to yell some more, please save it until I'm finished."

I drew in a deep breath. *Come on, Alix—make the effort, open up . . .* Who was I kidding? Rynn and I spent most of our time dancing around issues, and most of the time that was my fault.

Why did adult relationships have to be . . . well, work?

I pulled a chair up beside him. "On a scale from one to ten, how badly did I mess up this morning?"

Rynn glanced back up from the screen and lifted both eyebrows.

"All right. A scale from one to twenty, then?"

He swore under his breath and went back to checking his email—a lot of names I didn't recognize, and most of them from the last couple of days. Odd. Rynn wasn't much for email . . .

"I'm not playing this game with you, Alix. Not right now. I'll probably say something I'll regret, and I'm still set on only having one of us in the relationship who does that."

Straight, simple gray eyes.

OK, first relationship, then everything else. "It's not your fault," I said.

Rynn glanced back up at me, not quite able to hide his surprise.

I shook my head. "What happened with Artemis? There's no way you could have known exactly what was behind the door."

He shook his head and went back to an email. "I could have warned you he'd done something like that before. Should have," he started.

I shook my head. "No. You can't."

Again, he couldn't quite mask the surprise.

"I don't like it, and I doubt I'm going to stop asking questions, but I do grasp that most of whatever goes on in supernatural society isn't anything I'm supposed to know about. I'm not an idiot." Just dense, argumentative, and carrying a beacon over my head that broadcasts, *Please, supernaturals, come fuck up my life.*

Rynn watched me, a frown touching his face. "Who are you, and what have you done with Alix?"

Ha. Very funny. "It's called making an attempt."

He held up his hands. "I'm not complaining—just surprised."

I sat back in the chair. "At what point did I completely fuck this up?"

"The IAA or—"

"I don't mean Egypt. You were right, that was all me. If I had been honest, we might have avoided that fiasco. I was mad at you and Nadya for vetoing my jobs and wanted to lash out, so instead of talking I figured I'd get the message across by raiding a temple. Good idea on paper, bad idea in practice, I take responsibility for that one. I meant this—us?"

He looked back at the screen before saying, "Caring about people and relationships comes with strings, ones you aren't used to. And you still have issues with me not being human," he added.

True . . .

"And more than half the time when I say something I'm right, and your ego doesn't like being wrong."

"Yeah, OK, I get the point." Why does the universe force me into situations I don't want to be in—like the whole supernatural thing? It's as if there was a goddamn new monster at every turn. "And it's not half—maybe forty, and I'm being generous."

Rynn touched my mouth. "I've been keeping score. Closer to sixty."

. . . *Because you like lying to yourself, Owl, and the universe probably thinks you should stop. It might have a point.*

"Only you would keep score," I said.

A silence fell between us as he went back to checking his email. Finally he broke the quiet by saying, "It's not that I don't trust your judgment . . ."

It was my turn to look skeptical.

"All right, I have issues with some of your tactical judgments, but it's not just the IAA anymore. There are things going on behind the scenes in my world that you're not aware of." The computer chimed with another email, stealing back Rynn's attention. He swore as he read it and shook his head.

"Let's just say Oricho's stunt did more damage than any of us realized, and I fear there's a chain reaction." There was a defiance on his face I hadn't seen before. "The thefts are related, though I don't know how yet. You're caught in the middle, but I'm finding more and more there's very little I can do about it."

We were back to dancing around facts again, but maybe there was a way to help without breaking any of the supernatural rules. Isn't that what Hermes had hinted at? Actually getting into the game instead of screaming foul at it and Rynn? "Does it have anything to do with Artemis?" I asked.

Rynn snorted. "No, Artemis is the least of my worries . . ." Uncharacteristically Rynn trailed off. Again, we were delving into things I wasn't supposed to know about.

There were two possible reactions for me here. One was to get indignant and point out that the rules sucked and weren't fair, but I was starting to think Rynn maybe felt worse about leaving me in the dark about his problems than I'd considered.

"Alix? Whatever Artemis said, you're not broken. Don't ever forget that."

I felt the knot from earlier dispel in my stomach. Maybe there was something I could do . . . provided I kept to things I was already aware about instead of getting pissed about the things that I was in the dark about.

"All right, let's approach this differently than we have been." I nodded at Rynn's laptop. "Why don't you tell me what you can?"

He was silent while he considered it. "What have you gleaned about our politics from the elf?" he said finally.

"You'd be surprised what I get out of the elf. He loses his temper every time I call the head elf a Grand Poobah."

Rynn frowned but nodded. "I think I can work with that."

9

Rock Stars and Other Assorted Denizens of L.A.

9:00 p.m., stealing artifacts; finally, my goddamned job

Rynn stopped the car just outside Artemis's mansion.

"Are you certain you want to do this?" he asked me, mouth drawn in a tight line.

If I thought this whole plan over any more, chances were good I'd back out. I shook my head. "It's settled. This might be the only chance to get inside without orchestrating an out-and-out B&E. And I'd rather get the artifacts now, while I still know where they are—provided I can trust Artemis not to kill me or throw the crazy drug at me."

"You . . . can," Rynn said, taking his time with each word. "Artemis is the black sheep of the family, but he's never really hurt anyone. He's not exactly what I'd call responsible, which is why you need to keep an eye on him. More likely he'll get distracted and chase after some actress."

Somehow that didn't have the desired effect of calming my nerves . . .

We walked in silence across the front lawn, which was illuminated by motion-sensor floodlights. Somehow that just seemed . . . mundane for a supernatural. I mean, you pick those up at Home Depot.

"You scare me when you stop talking," Rynn said. "It usually means you're about to do something stupid."

I didn't have an answer to that one. Even Captain raised his head from my purse and meowed.

I glared at him. "You're supposed to keep quiet."

Rynn shook his head. "What happens if there's a vampire at the party? You think you'll be able to control him?"

Control Captain at a cocktail party with vampires? Hmmm, let's think about that one. "He's not there as a party favor, he's there so I get a head start." I'd noticed that while Captain only had the urge to search and destroy vampires, he showed some interest in most supernaturals we crossed paths with. I was hoping we could use it to our advantage.

Rynn shook his head. "This is going to be an unmitigated disaster, isn't it?"

"Between you and me, the question in jobs like this isn't if, it's when. And hopefully not until I'm already running away with the artifacts." And without a ballroom full of supernaturals on my tail . . .

From what Rynn had told me of the two supernatural factions—well, to be perfectly honest, there were really three, two minor and one major—it was kind of terrifying just how supernatural politics worked.

The two political sides consisted of two minorities with a few major backers—like, say, dragons. One side was dead set on keeping supernaturals away from mainstream human eyes; that was the faction Rynn, Lady Siyu, and Mr. Kurosawa belonged to. The other faction, again a minor but very vocal group, thought things were great back in the good old days, when supernaturals played warlord and kept humans at their feet . . . in some cases *on* their feet, as slippers. Political disputes were handled between the two minority sides. The side in charge was the one who could kick the shit out of the other side.

Everyone else? The vast majority of supernaturals, like Artemis and Daphne, didn't like the idea of getting the shit kicked out of them by a bigger monster. They could care less who was in charge, so long as it didn't affect their day-to-day activities and no one asked them to show up for a fight.

Putting aside the fact that minorities with big mouths ran the show, the other problem with this political system was obvious. As soon as one side weakened, the other made a play for power. Four heavy hitters for the "keep humans out of the loop" faction had been hit by Oricho's scroll debacle a few months back, including Rynn, Mr. Kurosawa, Lady Siyu, and Oricho himself. Everyone else in North America got hit too, but according to Rynn, he and the other three took the brunt of it.

Rynn figured most supernaturals were watching to see where the tide ebbed and would flip their loyalties accordingly. Politics through apathy. Great.

"Just don't do anything stupid," Rynn said.

"Any other words of advice?"

"Yes. Watch out for Daphne. She's dangerous. The less she notices you, the better. And whatever you do, don't touch the items. That's what Artemis is for."

Well, there we were in agreement. Damn straight I wasn't going to be touching any cursed items.

I'd have had a rebuttal to that effect, but we were at the door.

Before Rynn could knock, the door swung open. Much to my relief, no trace of incense. Artemis leaned out, dressed much as he had been the night before: leather pants paired with a black and gold torn T-shirt, and of course the prerequisite jewelry. I couldn't be sure in the light, but it looked like the tips of his hair had been painted gold to match the shirt. He also wore a deep frown.

"Can we please get a fucking move on? As much as Daphne likes to show everyone a good time, I'd rather not have to spend all night there," Artemis said, to Rynn more than me.

Rynn replied in supernatural, using what sounded to me like a harsh, chastising tone.

Artemis only rolled his eyes. "Yes, yes—I know. I have to bring her back, otherwise you'll kick the shit out of me. Save the speech, I've heard it before," Artemis said as he stepped past both of us and headed towards the garage, where a red convertible was waiting. "I'll make sure I give your regards to Daphne—my guess is her response will be 'fuck off.'"

Red Corvette? No, that wasn't predictable at all . . .

I glanced up at Rynn and nodded at his retreating cousin. "How much can I really trust him?"

"It depends—"

"On?"

"How convinced he is I can still kill him."

Great, just fucking fantastic.

Rynn kissed me quickly and whispered one last thing. "If you don't get the artifacts by midnight, run. I'll be outside, near the road."

"Why midnight?"

He glanced back at Artemis. "Because that's when the masks come off."

"Please. People. I'm fucking bored over here!" Artemis yelled at us, gunning the engine for effect.

"Oh knock it off, I'm coming already," I yelled back.

Artemis swore but shut up, which was the desired effect.

"Stay past midnight, I get turned into a pulverized pumpkin—got it." I waved at Rynn and headed over to the car as Artemis gunned the engine again.

Captain mewed, and I gave the bag a pat. "You heard Rynn, Captain. Get ready for a disaster."

I made a point of not talking to Artemis on the way over. I was watching for landmarks, in case I needed to get out fast. As we rounded onto a palm-tree-lined road that led up into the Hollywood Hills, Artemis broke our comfortably uncomfortable silence.

"I believe we may have gotten off on the wrong foot," he said.

I made a somewhat agreeable sound but kept staring at the passing houses.

"You know, this would go a hell of a lot smoother if we spoke to each other," he said.

"Un hunh? Is that so ..." I wasn't having much luck with landmarks. The houses and trees were all starting to blend together in the darkness.

"Sorry?" I said, realizing Artemis had asked me a question that required more than a one-word answer.

"I asked what my illustrious cousin had to say about me. Some of it had to be interesting."

I shrugged. "Nothing that wasn't in the tabloids already."

Artemis laughed. "Well, at least they're accurate."

I snorted. "I highly doubt that."

"I disagree. Best news reporting in the world. They're not afraid to get their hands dirty hacking into email accounts, phone records, cameras in hotels. Brilliant reporting," he said. "And you must have other, more interesting questions?"

The houses started looking increasingly expensive, with more distance between the driveways and less visibility from the street. Almost there, I figured, meaning I'd only have to put up with Artemis a few more minutes.

"How is my cousin doing, by the way? Familial curiosity. He's not one to pick up the phone."

Oh for Christ's— "All right, fine. You want to talk? You can start by telling me what Daphne is," I said. That ought to shut him up. Supernaturals couldn't talk about other supernaturals.

"I thought it'd be obvious—she's a siren. Most of the stories are true, except for the singing, which her recording attempts debunked spectacularly. But her voice will ensnare human men and even some supernaturals. Doesn't work on females though, or incubi, or succubi."

I looked away from the window to stare at Artemis, who was splitting his attention between the road and me, a relatively innocent expression on his face. I say relatively, because I'm not sure Artemis did innocent.

"Seriously? Aren't you not supposed to answer?" I said.

He shrugged. "It's the only thing you're really interested in. Besides, Daphne will be royally pissed if she figures out you're one of Rynn's."

"One of Rynn's?"

Artemis's lip twitched. "Figure of speech—most incubi don't tend to practice monogamy. No fucking point, since the more energy the better, but some integrate more with humans than others.

"The warning is relevant though. Most of them will smell incubus on you. Not exactly a problem, since most don't know Rynn, and that's about as good an explanation as you could have for being here. They'll just figure you're one of mine, but Daphne?" Artemis whistled for effect. "Well, Daphne and Rynn go back a long way, and the memories aren't pleasant. Needless to say, a siren won't be able to resist taking a bit of vengeance out of you."

Artemis pulled into a driveway behind a series of other cars, all on the flashy, versus luxury, end. From what little Rynn had explained of Artemis, he had a habit of lending everything an opulent air, something that clashed with Rynn's understated nature.

My God, I was referring to Rynn as understated . . .

Artemis smiled at the valet who rushed up to take the car.

We both got out, me feeling less confident than I had a few minutes back now that I was actually standing in supernatural central.

"You've got nothing to worry about from me," Artemis said, flashing me half a smile, uncannily like Rynn, as he tossed the keys over his shoulder. "Unless you want to, that is. You know, worried about what I might do to you." He held out his arm.

I shook my head and walked past him to where the guests were entering the mansion, which was even larger than his. "You realize that's not doing anything for me? I'm not interested."

"That's not entirely true. And you'd be the first."

"Bullshit."

He raised his hands. "True story."

I ignored him. Telling him I really wasn't interested again would only egg him on. I'd known guys like Artemis at my grad school dorm—where replying itself was considered a form of flirting.

"Oh come on, is that it?"

I shook my head. I wanted to get this over with, not serve as his entertainment for the night. "I'm just disappointed. I knew grad students who had better game than you. You're what? Two, three hundred years old at least? I just figured you'd have your routine a little more polished by now."

Artemis dodged in front of me, blocking my way—which wasn't hard, considering the crowd. "But that's the point, isn't it, Charity? Part of the game, appeal to the target's comfort zone, just challenging you enough to get your blood going? Coming in with all guns blazing doesn't always get the job done. Sometimes it's the tools you leave in the box, not the ones you take out."

I rolled my eyes. OK, this was starting to bother me now. "Just keep up your end of the bargain and get me in."

Artemis smiled. "More than happy to. With a name like Charity, they'll just figure you're the call girl of the week."

"Fuck off."

Artemis, enjoying this way more than I was comfortable with, put his arm around my shoulder and pulled me in close as we reached the hostess checking guests off the list.

"Don't shoot the messenger," Artemis said. "You and Rynn asked me for help." He winked at the hostess, who was in her early twenties, with a dark bob and flapper dress. She initially seemed indifferent, but that changed as soon as Artemis leaned in to help her find his name.

Dear sweet Jesus, I think I might hate rock stars.

I shouldn't.

Seriously, we have a surprising number of things in common: they drink, I drink; I prefer to shop out of a catalogue, and they're happy to wear whatever's left on the floor in the wake of last night's party. Definitely more parallels than tangents.

By the time the girl had checked us in, she was giving Artemis more than a friendly smile.

"Yeah, that's not at all creepy," I said when we were out of her earshot.

He shrugged. "Just trying to give you a bit of an education into the incubus mind, Charity."

"And by creepy I'm including the sexual innuendo," I whispered as we entered the ballroom. The sheer volume around us would hide our conversation in a normal crowd, but I didn't want to be picking up the attention of stray supernaturals. "And Rynn doesn't pull any of the garbage you just did."

Apparently that was what Artemis had been waiting for, because he gave me a slow smile.

"*That* just proves Rynn's even better at it than I am," he said, and continued ahead of me into the expansive ballroom full of booze, dancing, art, and a mixed crowd of masked supernaturals and humans. Damn, there couldn't be this many supernaturals in Hollywood, could there? I decided not to ask Artemis. I wasn't sure whether I'd like the answer, and I already wasn't happy with the direction our conversation was steering.

As much as I pestered Rynn and Carpe about supernaturals, for some reason I didn't think I wanted to learn anything else about incubi from Artemis.

"Let's just get this job over with, Captain," I said to my bag. Now that we were inside, I had more important things to concentrate on. There was a hell of a lot of decent artwork in here. Say what you would about Daphne Sylph's movie career, but the siren had taste.

My eyes fell on a tapestry hanging from the high ceiling. It depicted Viking seafarers marooned on an island with a beautiful woman who had a head full of thick red dreadlocks . . . and bore a striking resemblance to Daphne. Twelfth century, restored, if the colors and patterns used were any indication . . . if the restoration was any good, it was worth a few hundred thousand dollars . . .

I swore as someone grabbed my elbow.

To my dismay, it was Artemis. I'd figured he'd ditch me as soon as we passed through the doors. No such luck.

"Where the hell is your mask?" he said. His wasn't one of the Venetian numbers with frills and giant noses but a flatter, simpler one in black with gold detail.

"I hate masks," I whispered. "They cut my visibility." I'd tried explaining that to Rynn too. "Besides, what's the big deal? How many people are actually going to be wearing masks? Don't they prefer having their faces photographed?"

Artemis frowned. "Not at this party. Here," he said, and towed me to a corner. "Put it on now before anyone else notices."

I fished the one Rynn had given me out of my purse. It was more ornate than Artemis's, with a beaklike nose, but the real kick was the white and spotted feathers arranged around the eyes—just like an owl. I'd thought it was bad taste, but Rynn had gotten a kick out of it.

Artemis waited until I strapped it on.

"Happy?"

Artemis arched an eyebrow. "*Thrilled.*"

I ignored him and went back to searching the ballroom. There were two obvious exits leading outside: the hallway we came in through and a pair of glass doors that led out to the gardens, maybe a pool.

I didn't want to get too ahead of myself planning alternative escape routes. I needed to steal the damn item first. *One thing at a time, Owl.*

"So tell me, what else did my illustrious cousin tell you about me?" Artemis asked.

I forced a smile. Three hallways leading out of the ballroom. Two on the opposite side of the room, which led further back into the mansion, and one that ran parallel to the gardens. Considering that one had a constant stream of waiters entering and exiting, I put my money on the other two. "Something about dragging you out of a Bangkok whorehouse," I told Artemis.

He laughed and snatched two flutes of champagne from a passing server, handing one to me. "Did he now? I suppose that was one of my more spectacular low points, but a low point nonetheless." He smiled, eerily reminiscent of Rynn. "I promise I'm on my best behavior."

I downed the champagne. "Weren't you supposed to stay sober?" I asked as Artemis grabbed another flute.

He shrugged and waved the glass at me. "I took it as a suggestion, and calling the kettle black, isn't it? Speaking of which, you seem an adventurous, devil-may-care sort of girl. What the hell are you doing with my cousin?"

I glared. I so didn't have time for this. "He makes a really good martini, all right."

Artemis shrugged. "I make a great martini."

"Dude, I saw the vodka in your fridge. Not even midshelf." I started pushing my way into the crowd, hoping to get a better look at the halls. I tried not to think of the supernaturals I might be jostling. I also hoped Artemis would take a hint and go chase an actress.

Apparently I was way too entertaining, and he followed. "All right then, Charity—if that is indeed your name—what has my cousin told you about incubi?"

"Who says he's told me anything? I hear that's against the rules."

"Hardly seems fair now, does it? Get involved with someone, to be left in the dark, rather like . . ." Artemis watched me. ". . . a possession—no, wait, I have it. *Pet.*" He inclined his head and watched me, a more malicious smile dancing across his features. "Yes, that's how it is, isn't it?"

"Not even close," I said through clenched teeth.

Now, if I was an ancient artifact being held in a siren's mansion, down which hall would I be? Over the left hall entrance was a fresco I recognized from the haphazard entertainment TV tour of Daphne's private exhibit. Of course it was the only hallway being guarded.

Well, if I was a priceless artifact, that's definitely where I would be.

Come to think of it, now that I had my bearings, the fresco wasn't half bad either. Definitely older than I'd thought—medieval, Levant features from the Middle Ages . . .

Come on, Alix, focus, just the artifacts.

"You do know how incubi and succubi reproduce, don't you? I'd at least expect him to tell you that much."

"OK, not discussing my sex life with you. Besides, incubi and succubi are essentially the same species, right? You do the math."

Artemis pressed another champagne flute into my hand. "If you're not going to drink, at least pretend you are. And you'd think that, wouldn't you? Genetically we're similar enough. Succubi are the female of our species, if you care to call it that, but we're parasitic off humans in more ways than one. Probably to make sure . . ." He trailed off, and I wasn't sure whether it was the topic or the crowd breaking out in laughter near the glass doors.

He recovered, though. "Regardless, we use a go-between, and hence why incubi and succubi tend to integrate with humans better than everyone else." He looked at me but waved the champagne flute around the crowd. "Except the dragon. But he likes humans for the treasure, and they're so accommodating to just drop it off at his doorstep. In fact, I've rather got the same game going here. Women and men just more or less flock to my doorstep. Daphne has the same racket going on here, for that matter.

"You aren't supposed to know any of that, by the way," Artemis added as he reached for another glass of champagne off a passing silver tray. "Probably be in quite a bit of trouble if the dragon and Naga ever find out."

Oh for— I spun on Artemis. "Then why the hell are you telling me?"

He shrugged and swirled the second flute; he had one in each hand now. "Easy. You don't think very well of me, and unless I start dressing and behaving like my cousin—which isn't going to happen—that is unlikely to change. I do, however, have information, and that is something you like very much."

The way he watched me and swirled the two drinks sent a chill down my spine. "Besides, Charity, it's more interesting this way. Especially when I hand you back off to my cousin. I'm sure he'll be in for an earful after this. I can feel the curiosity pouring off you—oh don't give me that look. Your poker face needs a shocking amount of work." After a pause, he added, "I'm also curious just how far I can push the rules right now. Consider it a thought experiment, so to speak."

"Stop the incubus bullshit," I said.

"Now why on earth would I do that when it's so much fun?"

"Look, don't you have anything better to do than heckle me? Don't you have pretty young starlets and groupies to go chase?"

"So cynical for one so young. And as a matter of fact, I need a stronger drink. Wait here," he said before disappearing into the crowd.

Finally. As soon as I was certain Artemis was out of sight, I beelined for the hall beneath the tapestry.

Shit. I stopped short of stumbling into a group of admirers surrounding none other than Daphne Sylph. Tonight her hair was a mix of bright red and blond dreadlocks that hung down to the middle of her back. A little alternative, but she managed to make it look high fashion. She was also dressed in a floor-length white silk dress—not that I'm a fan of white, but with that hair?

She stopped laughing and scanned the crowd, as if looking for someone. I ducked behind a taller couple before she saw me, but not before I got a good look at her face. Not a day over twenty.

"Do you want me to introduce you?" Artemis whispered in my ear.

I swore and jumped back out of reflex. "Could you not sneak up on me like that? And no, I don't want to meet her. I like my body parts attached, thank you very much."

Some thieves like to toss in a personal touch, like introducing themselves to their victims beforehand or leaving a note—something like that. Just to let people know they really cared who they were robbing. Not me. All the personal touch does is make it that much more personal for them to hunt you down.

I nodded towards Daphne. "In her case, the camera really doesn't lie."

Artemis shrugged. "I suppose, though it depends what you're looking for. Trust me, she had her heyday a long time ago. Try Rome. I think Caligula's court was her last big coup—"

"You just said you weren't supposed to be telling me this!"

Artemis had replaced his champagne flutes with a tumbler of clear liquor, which he sipped. "No, but I'm bored. And that's where her feud with Rynn came in, in case you were wondering. Something about Daphne changing the course of civilization, being found out—"

Caligula? That was two thousand years ago. I'd figured Rynn had been around for a couple hundred years on account of the incubus thing, but two thousand years?

Artemis swished his glass so the ice clinked the sides. "Think it was a colossal waste of his effort, to be honest."

I pushed thoughts of Rynn's age aside. Even if Artemis was telling the truth I could worry about how old Rynn was later. "Why? Because we're too stupid to figure out a bunch of supernaturals are rounding us up like cattle?"

"Nice analogy, but for your information, no. Because you all would have been dead from lead poisoning long before we ever got around to altering history."

I looked away. Artemis was an unsettling mix. Unlike most supernaturals I run into, he wasn't trying to kill me, but that was more a circumstance of boredom and his deal with Rynn. Out of those two, I put boredom higher up on the list. Artemis was more likely to grab a good seat while Rome burned than he was to try and stop it. Come to think of it, if he was telling the truth about Caligula, he might have done exactly that.

Oh you got to be kidding me . . . The crowd had migrated away from us, removing my cover. Daphne was looking straight at me. I swore and as discreetly as possible turned my face away and ducked behind Artemis. "Not that it hasn't been a slice, but I need an opening out of this ballroom now," I whispered to him.

He was fixated on the other side of the room. "I figured Rynn didn't send you to celebrity watch," he whispered back. "Don't worry, I've handled it about . . ." He trailed off as he glanced down at his phone.

A commotion spilled through the glass doors that led to the garden.

". . . now. Wonderful, they're on time," he said, nodding at the commotion.

Three guards, two of which had been manning the hallway, raced past us as flashes of light hit the crowd and guests yelled. Daphne strode behind them.

Paparazzi.

Bingo . . . got to love it when opportunity screams rather than knocks. Might even make it easier to sneak out of here if they lasted that long.

I spotted a pile of tablecloths by the ice sculptures—call it a thief's instinct.

I couldn't touch the cursed artifacts, but those should do the trick.

Oh screw it, this was my heist. If—scratch that, *when*—this went sideways, the less Artemis knew about the pieces, the better.

I glanced over at my drunken incubus escort. "You ready for me to reveal the great task we need you for tonight?" I said.

Artemis leaned in. "*Dying* to know."

"Great." I grabbed myself a glass of champagne and downed it in one gulp—the first had been weak, and I needed steady hands. "Now see Daphne over there?" The siren had entered into the paparazzi fray and had the photographers eating out of her hands. No one protested as she and her guards led them out back—probably to drown them in the pool.

"Hard to miss with that hair, isn't she?"

"Fantastic." I slapped Artemis on the shoulder. "Go keep her distracted."

Artemis narrowed his eyes at me. "Knowing my cousin, that's not what I picture he had in mind."

"Well, frankly, I feel better without you breathing over my shoulder," I said, and headed towards the now unguarded hall.

Artemis grabbed my shoulder, stopping me in my tracks.

"Look, Artemis—" I started as he spun me around. His expression threw me off. There was a frown etched on his face . . . and sincerity.

"Just remember, I told Rynn I won't save you. You'd do well to remember that, and it goes without saying whatever he has you doing here isn't worth it."

OK, Rynn's evil—well, more like debauched—cousin warning me away from Rynn was one hell of a tangent.

"You know," he said, "there's one thing that hasn't changed about Rynn over the years, and I have to admit I admire this about him."

I frowned. "And what would that be?"

"He always did prefer the broken ones."

With that, Artemis tipped his head back as he finished his drink and headed off for Daphne.

As strange as his warning was, Daphne would have the paparazzi cleared shortly. No time for pondering things I really didn't care about right now.

I grabbed the tablecloths and slipped through the hallway where treasure awaited.

I balanced my cell phone under my ear as I stood in front of the plexiglass case that held the three artifacts. "So seriously, which vial do you want me to use here? Green one, right?" I wracked my memory, trying to remember if that one held the concentrated hydrochloric acid.

"No, that's for fiberglass," Nadya answered. "This is bulletproof plexi, so you'll need something stronger. Just go with the red one—and be careful. The weight sensors are still there."

Captain was sitting on the sleeve of vials Nadya had made me take. I swore and pulled them out from under him—with minimal complaining. "Finesse is your department, not mine. Speaking of which, so is dressing up in heels and schmoozing with people. Care to explain why the hell you aren't standing here instead of me?"

"Because I have a deep-rooted instinct to run away from trouble, not into it. Now move before the paparazzi are dealt with." And with that she hung up the phone.

Retinal scanners, lasers, acid-proof plastics . . . In my mind, if it takes two separate PhDs to break into a box, go with the simplest method— just break the damn box and run.

Searching through the sleeve I found not one but two red vials: one with a red label on a white tube, the other with a white label on a red tube.

Oh you've got to be fucking kidding me . . .

Use the red vial, Owl. For all I knew, one of the red tubes held nitro-glycerine, and I'd just blow myself up.

Nuts to this . . . Nadya could keep her chemistry kit.

"Stay there," I whispered to Captain as I fished out a plug-in–like adaptor and headed for the nearest three-pronged socket.

The room wasn't filled with lasers, or weight plates, or any of the stuff you hear about in the movies, but the box was sealed shut electronically to create a vacuum for the artifacts. Inside was a weight sensor.

There were two ways to handle this particular situation; the elegant way, which was dissolving part of the box with Nadya's chemicals and taking the items, or my way. My way involved brute force and blowing the fuse box behind the vacuum. Elegance is for show-offs and thieves with way too much time on their hands—well, and Nadya, but she doesn't count; she's in a class all her own.

The prong in my bag would be certain to short out the fuse to the entire room—maybe even the entire building if the place was wired badly.

I plugged the adaptor into a socket near the door and turned the in-nocuous green light on. The entire room went dark. Including the green light in the artifact display case.

Flashlight in hand, I headed back to the case, where Captain was waiting on the pile of tablecloths.

Now all I needed to do was get the physical backup lock open. I put my flashlight between my teeth and started fitting my picks—flat, screwdriver-like tools I kept for wedging things open—into the lock.

Without any effort on my part, it opened.

Son of a bitch, it was already open—but the pieces were still in the case. Could Daphne have forgotten to lock it?

"I'm really starting to wonder what the hell my cousin is up to these days," Artemis said.

I swore and fumbled my pick. Artemis was leaning against the doorway, holding his drink.

"I thought I told you to keep Daphne busy," I said.

He shrugged. "It was a boring party." He indicated the case with his drink. "And Rynn's not one for petty thefts."

I snorted and retrieved my pick. "Well, at least we're agreed on one thing. This isn't a petty theft—shit," I said as the case hood slid back down. I didn't want to wedge my fingers underneath with the artifacts so close.

"Are you all right?" Artemis asked.

"Yeah, everything is fine, no thanks to you sneaking up on me." This time the glass case gave and I popped it open, being careful not to touch any of the items inside, not even the material they were laid out on. Now all I needed to do was wrap the three pieces up. What was the best angle to get them from?

"If I'd known you were here to steal something . . ." Artemis said, his brow furrowing. OK, that looked a bit like Rynn.

"You said it yourself—you're just here to get me in. My neck is my own responsibility."

"Again, let me point out you left out the *thieving* part. I just thought you were here as a spy or some other such of Rynn's nonsense."

I didn't have time or inclination to justify my actions to the debauched wonder. Someone might have noticed the fuse. "Look—just stand over there and keep quiet for a second, will you?"

All right, here we go . . . I grabbed the tablecloth and doubled it around my hand. Wrap up the artifacts, nice and easy, then into my bag . . . I felt a bead of sweat form on my forehead as I layered the tablecloth over my hand one more time—I didn't want my skin coming into contact with the pieces through some kind of supernatural technicality . . . I thought about asking Artemis to do it, but that struck me as a worse-than-usual idea.

I took a quick breath and readied my hands, hidden well underneath the tablecloth.

"You know, you and I aren't that unalike."

I stopped before I could grab the flint. So much for shutting up. "How do you figure that?" I said, my eyes on the pieces, ready to grab again, even though I could feel Artemis staring at me.

"Neither of us likes to play by the rules. They aren't particularly fun."

There was something about the way he said it. "Somehow I don't think our versions of fun are on the same page," I said.

Artemis laughed.

I held my breath as I leveled the piece of flint off the pedestal, then exhaled only after the flint was wrapped in the tablecloth and lightning didn't strike me down. I deposited it into an airtight bag and dropped that in the pocket of Captain's carrier only after I'd made him crawl out. No sense risking my cat getting cursed.

OK, two more and I was home free . . . now for the stone bowl . . .

I frowned. The bowl was larger and would be trickier not to touch with my bare hands. "Look, Artemis, can't you watch the hallway or something?" *Or do something otherwise useful so I don't accidently curse myself?*

"I'll whistle if someone is on their way," he said.

"No! No whistling. If someone comes by, just try to buy me time." *All right, big breath, Owl . . .* Gripping the edge, I tilted the bowl in beside the flint piece. Captain was eyeing his now half-filled carrier. He looked up and gave me a perturbed mew.

"You're walking out of here," I told him. He mewed again.

Now for the grand finale. I scooped the knife up with the tablecloth. For an early Bronze Age sword, the weight was well . . . off. Very carefully I undid the tablecloth.

"Oh you've got to be kidding me . . ." Don't get me wrong, it was a good replica, about as close to the one in photos as you could get, but checking the weight and getting a good look at it?

Close up, the etched symbols were too clean and the weight and sheen of the metal was off for the crude smelting characteristic of Copper Age transitions. If a real pro had been hired to make an authentic replica, I might not have known. Whoever had made this was almost good enough, but perhaps they hadn't had enough time.

Well, now I knew why the case had been unlocked. Someone had beat me to the sword and, for some reason, had left the other artifacts.

No sense worrying about what I couldn't do now. Not with a ball-room full of supernaturals. I'd take what I could get while the going was still good.

A long, drawn-out, shrill whistle echoed from the doorway.

"I thought I told you no—" I cut myself short.

It was Daphne standing in the doorway, in all her red-and-gold dreadlocked glory. She pursed her bright red lips and whistled again as she took in the surroundings—namely me, Captain, and the now empty case.

Artemis hadn't even been able to watch the hall properly . . . and now he was nowhere to be seen.

"Wow, now look at you. I haven't had a thief drop in on me in ages. Who sent you?" she said, her voice neither sweet nor beautiful, but carrying a deep, throaty texture you couldn't help but pay attention to.

I swallowed. "Would you believe this is my off weekend and I just happened to crash?"

Daphne let out another sharp whistle as she considered what I'd said. "The dragon? No matter, you'll tell me. Too bad they sent a girl though. Means I have to think out of the box, and that gets painful," she said, and took a step forward. Behind her followed two dark-skinned supernaturals, the same kind I'd seen at Artemis's. Together, the three of them fanned out around the room, closing me in. "Painful for you, that is. Not me."

I had two choices: try to reason with her, or run like hell and hope the door on the other side of the room wasn't a closet. I went with the latter. I grabbed my bag full of artifacts and bolted past the other display cases, Captain close on my heels.

Daphne let out a piercing shriek behind me, and I heard the body-guards' boots hitting the ground. I shunted my bag onto my shoulder and covered my ears as I ran. I thought sirens were supposed to lure you in with songs, not boil your eardrums.

I slammed into the door at a dead run, knocking it open and stumbling into another hallway. There was a staircase leading up on my right, and more hallway to my left. I went for the staircase. Most of the guards and supernaturals would be on the lower floors for the party, and I was more likely to slip out a window than bolt past a full ballroom.

That and no one ever expects thieves to go up . . . except in this case. I came to a halt on the third step as the sound of heavy footsteps hit the floor above. Big, bulky, armed footsteps. Captain hissed.

"Supernatural horde it is," I told him.

We ran back down and turned left as the door to the exhibit room crashed open. The footsteps upstairs got louder and closer.

Captain and I both skidded to a halt.

The corner had looped us back around to the ballroom, and an entire room turned towards me.

Something told me we were past midnight. I got a good, long look in those few seconds of inaction. Goblins, trolls—recognized that one . . . I was pretty sure I saw a Naga in back. Teeth. There were a lot of serrated teeth. Black, green, white even. Not something I would have thought.

I noticed one nearby—he/she/it had reflective white skin and was tall, with black eyes and a tuft of white and green leaflets shooting out at odd angles from the top of their head.

Hunh, so that's what a daikon demon looks like.

It's amazing the things that pop into your head when you think you might be about to die.

Daphne screeched behind me, breaking our impasse.

The entire horde moved towards me as one as Daphne closed in behind me, her dreadlocks streaming around her head with a life of their own.

If Rynn asked me to pinpoint when everything became a disaster, this was definitely it.

"You've got a great art collection," I tried.

Daphne smiled, but it looked more like she was baring her teeth—serrated teeth. Son of a bitch, what the hell was it with supernaturals and the sharp teeth? Rynn better not be hiding serrated teeth somewhere—and speaking of incubi, where the hell was Artemis?

"You know, it's funny you stealing those artifacts from me. Considering you stole them for me in the first place," Daphne said.

"Whoa? I'm sorry? I did not steal *anything* for you—especially not these," I said, shaking the bag holding the artifacts.

Daphne only smiled. "That's not what my paper trail says." Louder, for the crowd, she added, "Not only does Mr. Kurosawa's Owl steal dangerous artifacts, she sneaks back in to try and cover her mistakes."

The way she was smiling . . . she knew I wasn't the thief; what's more, she knew I was being set up . . .

"Funny, considering you're the one holding the cursed artifacts." I knew as soon as I said it that it'd been the wrong thing to say. Daphne was way too happy about it.

"No dear, that would be you. And I was only doing the dragon's job retrieving them from reckless and incompetent human hands."

Screw reasoning, it was a losing battle. Whatever Daphne was angling for with the rest of the supernaturals here, she had the upper hand. Time to get the hell out.

For once, Captain was two big steps ahead of me. He bolted through what I'd assumed was a broom closet. It wasn't—it was some sort of servants' wing.

At this point I was game for anything. I raced after my cat.

Daphne screeched, and it sounded like the entire ballroom picked up after me. That worked in my favor—a few hundred monsters all trying to squeeze through a narrow doorway at the same time would slow the mob down.

Captain skidded to a stop along the hardwood floor halfway down the hallway and lifted his nose up to sniff the air.

"I thought you knew where you were going!" I said.

He mewed and bolted down a left arm of the smaller passage.

I swore. Not the direction I would have picked, but here's hoping Captain could smell freedom better than me. Not that I had many options left . . . no windows or vents, and I could hear that damn horde right behind me.

At the end of the passage, Captain stopped again and started sniffing and scratching madly at the bottom of a door.

I shook my head. "Dude, I'm trusting you," I said, and opened it. Captain shot through, and I followed after. No more than three steps in, rotting lily of the valley hit me, right before Captain howled.

Shit. Using the door handle as an anchor, I stopped. "Bad cat! Get back here!"

It was too late though. Captain launched himself at the vampire standing at the other end—dressed in a server's outfit, of all things.

Well, local vampires wouldn't know about the wonder of a Mau's poisonous bite. This vampire did though. He waited until the last minute of Captain's leap, then, faster than a human would have been able to, caught him in a canvas bag.

Damn it. Had to be one of Alexander's. I scanned the room for something to attack the vampire with—a chair, painting, baseball-sized stone sculpture . . . The poker at the fireplace caught my eye. That'd do.

Captain shrieked, and the vampire swore in French as my cat did his best to tear his way out of the bag.

Before I could launch myself at the fireplace poker though, a bag found its way over my head—the same kind they'd caught Captain with.

I yelled and tried to push it off, but a cord pulled it tight around my neck. The lily of the valley scent got stronger as someone, not much taller than me, leaned in to whisper, "Miss me much, little birdie?" Female. Valley girl accent.

Bindi. Psychotic surfer vampire chick from hell. Before I could throw an insult at her, a baseball bat collided with my stomach, knocking the wind out of me and doubling me over.

I held my breath against the vampire pheromones. *OK, Alix, think.* Three vampires: Bindi holding me, the one with the baseball bat, and the one trying to contain Captain. Captain and I could manage three vampires; all I had to do was get out of the bag.

I threw my head back where I thought Bindi's face might be and was rewarded with a crunch of cartilage and Bindi's resulting growl. She let go of my arms, and I started to untie the burlap hood.

A sickly sweet smell hit me that wasn't vampire pheromone. More like sweetened acetone. Ether. They'd doused the bags with ether. Shit.

I raced to get the bag off, but it was no use—the ether and pheromones permeated my lungs and nose. With the two of them mixed, I'd pass out any moment. "Captain?" I tried.

I got a mew, but it was faint; they'd doused him too.

The last thought that hit me was I hoped they didn't hand us over to Daphne's horde. Then again, considering my last conversation with Alexander, the horde might be the gentler way to go.

10

Vampires of the Sunset Strip

Time: No fucking clue
Place: Urine, beer, and gross negligence of eardrums say nightclub

Or the basement of a dive bar, take your pick. It was the mix of beer and urine that gave it away. Funny how alcohol dulls the smell of urine . . . I've never wondered about that relationship before, but there you go.

I leaned my head back against the concrete wall as Captain let out another forlorn mew.

Only his head poked out the top of a burlap bag. He wasn't impressed. So unimpressed that a few minutes earlier, he'd decided to pee all over the bag. And himself. I added ammonia to the regular dive bar smells that permeated the closet-sized room. Way to get the message across to our vampire captors, Captain. Why hadn't I thought of that?

"You realize this is all your fault? You were supposed to find us an exit, not vampires."

He meowed again and looked at me expectantly.

I held up my hands, both tied with a zip cord. "I get it, you want out, but I can't exactly help you here." I'd already tried slipping out of them, but the vampires had gotten smart since last time. They'd switched from plastic to metal.

Assholes.

At least I couldn't smell any rotting lily of the valley, though that could just mean they had something worse in store.

Try to think about the positives, Alix . . .

Well, Captain was in here with me, but my bag, along with the two cursed items and one very authentic-looking fake, was gone.

That was positive, right? I couldn't accidently curse myself anymore.

Oh hell, I give up.

The door opened and Bindi stepped through. I held my breath against the pheromones that assaulted my nose.

Vampires . . . how do I say this accurately? They're like the cockroaches of the supernatural world. Vampires hold the exalted position of being one of the only supernaturals that starts off human. Most of what you've heard in the movies or read in stories is exaggerated and overblown. First off, vampires don't have superstrength. They excrete a narcotic-like pheromone that delivers their victims into a euphoric high where they'd be hard-pressed to throw a punch, let alone run. It's also more addictive than heroin. Vampire junkies, as I like to call them, are those who follow their vampire sugar daddies around waiting for the next hit.

As for the rest of the legends? Holy water is a complete bust, so are crosses, though sunlight has its uses. It depends how old the vampire is—the really old ones go up in seconds, but the young ones still sustain nasty burns from a good dose of UV light. Same thing goes for the allergic reactions to garlic.

Like cockroaches though, you might kill a few, but most just crawl off into a dark hole to lick their wounds, breed, and return another day.

Oh yeah, and they hate Captain. Maus were bred by the ancient Egyptians to attack vampires on sight. Their bites are poisonous to vampires and elicit one hell of an allergic reaction. As evidenced by the scar left on Alexander's face, the poison nullifies some of the healing—and Alexander was a few hundred years old.

They like to play dress-up too; designer suits, expensive shoes—you know, Eurotrash. Though apparently Bindi was in a class of her own. She was still dressed like a university surfer chick in a pair of dock shorts, tank top, and flip-flops, with her shoulder-length blond hair in tangled waves.

"Wow, they let you walk around dressed like that? What, did Alexander add a surfing department to his cronies? You look ridiculous, by the way."

As I expected, Bindi didn't take the jab well. Her mouth twisted into a snarl—not a subtle one but a full-on, fang-baring snarl.

Bindi was what I like to call batshit crazy. She'd been a few baskets shy of a picnic when human, and vampirism hadn't helped. An archaeologist PhD student by trade, she'd been roped into a plot to steal artifacts for a powerful vampire in exchange for being turned. Already well on her way to full-blown sociopath, Bindi had killed a bunch of her innocent dig mates to prove just how dedicated she was.

She balled up her fists and stepped inside the closet, but she was very careful to stay out of range of Captain, who, for his part, had doubled his efforts to tear his way out of the bag. He'd escalated from hissing to spitting.

"I was sent to tell you the master is on his way," Bindi said.

I made a derisive noise. "The only people in the world who call Alexander 'master' are you and him, and that includes vampires. Now, go woman up and start calling him 'dipshit' and 'asshole' like the rest of us—"

She snarled and took a step closer towards me. "Stop screwing your face up and show some respect."

I snorted. "Or what?"

"Or I'll eat your cat and make . . ." Bindi suddenly looked disgusted and glanced around the room. "What is that *smell*?" she said, and covered up her nose.

"What—the cat pee? Your fault for not including a litter box."

"Oh my God, that is the foulest—" I didn't hear the rest as Bindi succumbed to a coughing fit.

Hunh. Note to self: Captain's pee was bad for vampires too.

Being a young vampire, Bindi's pheromones hadn't hit me full force yet. With her doubled over, maybe I could crawl out of here—at least until I could find some wire cutters.

Captain wiggled in his bag and bunny-hopped towards a still-doubled-over Bindi. I held my breath, hoping she didn't notice as he made two more hops, each time wiggling furiously, then launching the sack towards his target. He latched on to her bare leg.

Bindi straightened, the anger and viciousness replaced by panic and excruciating pain. She shrieked and dropped to her knees . . . which was a stupid idea on her part, since it allowed Captain to sink his teeth in deeper—which he did.

Her leg began to turn an unhealthy shade of purple. "Get it off me, get it off me!" she yelled, batting at Captain's head.

"You know that only pisses him off," I offered. "If you stay still, he might let go." He wouldn't, but hopefully the level of pain was high enough that Bindi would believe anything.

She continued to shriek, but her struggling lightened a notch and she stopped smacking him. "It's not working!"

Let's hope the pain was real bad. I held up my hands. "Untie the zip cord and I can get him off." I'd actually untie Captain so he could get his claws in. I'd seen vampire's pass out from Captain bites before.

"Do you think I'm stupid?" she said.

Considering you let the vampire-hunting cat bite you? "It's that, or let him keep going," I said. The entire calf and knee were purple now. "You know his bites leave scars—look at Alexander's face."

That did it. Red tears streaming down her face, she leaned towards me. Nothing like pain to cloud judgment.

"Enough!"

I turned my attention to the doorway, where Alexander stood in all his Eurotrash glory. Bindi looked too, but she was still whimpering and grasping her leg, trying to block the purple color now creeping up her thigh.

I gave Alexander my best nonchalant look, but the sickly sweet lily of the valley ebbing off him hit me. So much so that Alexander, with chestnut hair that fell a little past his shoulders, struck me as moderately attractive, even with the pink scar marring the right side of his face. His expensive suit and leather shoes were worth more than my Winnebago.

Like Bindi, Alexander noticed the smell, barely hiding his disgust as he pulled out a handkerchief and held it to his nose.

I nodded at Bindi, still whimpering with Captain attached to her leg. "You're really letting the dress code slide, Alexander."

He frowned and tsked as he took in the room before turning to Bindi. "I thought I told you to stay away from the Mau," he said, his thick French accent on full display. As far as I could tell, Alexander had been made roughly three hundred years ago in Paris. He'd picked up English but had never lost the accent.

Bindi stopped whimpering long enough to snarl at me. "She tricked me."

"I tricked you? Oh come on, Bindi." I held up my wrists. "I'm a prisoner—of *vampires*. Of course I tried to trick you." I turned my attention to Alexander. "Come on, you must be desperate if you let her in—"

He strode over to where Bindi—weeping now—was cradling her leg, then he picked up Captain by the scruff of his neck. "Get the cat off, or I will do it for you."

I swore under my breath and hoped Captain listened this time. I whistled twice. Captain turned his bright yellow eyes on me. "Captain, heel—let go of the vampire," I said.

He growled, deep and throaty.

"Let go now, otherwise the other vampire is going to eat you."

That did the trick, but not the way I'd hoped. Captain had been so wrapped up in trying to devour Bindi's leg that he hadn't noticed Alexander. Now he did. Captain released Bindi, let out a howl and, contorting his body, made a grab for Alexander.

Alexander shook Captain and held both my cat and the cat pee-drenched bag away from his suit, thereby avoiding Captain's teeth.

I breathed a sigh of relief. As much as I would have enjoyed seeing Alexander's hand ravaged by Captain's teeth, there were now two vampires, and I was still tied up and starting to feel the effects of pheromones. I didn't like Captain's odds right now if he pissed off Alexander—as it was, I already didn't like our odds.

Alexander deposited Captain's bag beside me and turned to deal with Bindi, who was still weeping. I couldn't see or hear what was said, but she immediately got up and fled the broom closet.

Alexander closed the door behind her, drowning out the music as Captain continued to growl. He removed something from his pocket . . . it looked like something to fit over my mouth.

In spite of my haze, my panic nerves still lit up. I twisted away as Alexander fit the contraption over my head, but that's the bitch about vampire pheromones—they zap your strength.

I held my breath until my lungs were burning and I couldn't hold out anymore . . . there was no more trace of rotting lily of the valley. A gas mask? I tested the air, taking in a deeper breath. Sure enough, it was clean.

What the hell was Alexander giving me a gas mask for?

It must have registered in my eyes, because Alexander said, "See? I am not unreasonable. Now we may have a civilized conversation on . . . how would you say? Fair ground?"

I glared. Alexander planned on having a civilized conversation with me about as much as Captain planned on curling up on his lap. "What the hell are you up to?" I said.

Alexander tsked as he pulled up a footstool and sat on the far side of the room— about as far as he could get from a screeching Captain. "So skeptical and angry for one so young."

Alexander and I have a history. Before I'd known Alexander was a vampire, he'd been a client of mine. A good client; he'd never asked questions, paid me on time, and had been gifted with more money than sense. Or at least that's what I'd assumed when he'd asked me to retrieve a sarcophagus from underneath Ephesus, telling me under no circumstances to open it because of a vampire. This part I'm not proud of: assuming he was short a few baskets of a picnic, hiding treasure, or both, I'd opened the sarcophagus. In broad daylight. The ancient vampire had dissolved into ash, putting me on Alexander's shit list for vaporizing his Grand Poobah.

Resealing the sarcophagus and collecting payment before they could get the lid off probably hadn't helped matters.

Regardless, I knew from experience that the best way to get information out of Alexander was to piss him the hell off. Vampire Psychology with Owl 101.

"Go to hell," I told him.

Alexander didn't get mad. He smiled, just enough to expose the tips of his fangs, and held up my purse-turned-cat-carrier. "I wish to know why were you stealing these particular artifacts from the siren this evening."

Now, that was unexpected . . . and, to be honest, threw me for a loop. What did Alexander care about Daphne's artifacts?

He jiggled the bag, waiting.

Alexander and his vampires hadn't been at the party for me, they'd been after the artifacts as well. Now I knew why the case had been open and who was likely responsible for the fake. "What the hell do you want with the artifacts?" I said.

The smile on Alexander's face fell, but only for a moment. "Never mind my concern," he said, albeit more strained than before. "I am asking you."

This nice version of Alexander was unnerving me. "You don't do questions; you do threats and intimidation. So I'll ask you again, what the hell do you know about the pieces?"

Alexander's mood was falling. "Would you prefer it if I started straight off with the torture and threats?"

I gambled. "You guys beat me to the exhibit. You put the fake knife in there, didn't you? What, did I stumble in before you could get the rest of them?"

Alexander frowned. "Never mind my interest, the topic at hand is yours."

"No. You want to have a civilized conversation with me? Fine, you go first."

He swore in French. "This is getting us nowhere—tell me what you were doing."

"Or else what?" I snorted. "Come on, you gave me a gas mask, for Christ's sake—what kind of vampire does that?"

"I'm trying to be reasonable so we can come to a mutually beneficial exchange of information."

"How stupid do I look? You don't do reasonable."

Captain bleated, as if in agreement.

Alexander sighed, closed his eyes, and counted to ten. I think he added something derogatory in there, but my French is bad on a good day.

After he finished counting, Alexander opened the bag. "Since you wish me to start and I have no wish of remaining here all evening in you and your horrendous cat's company—" He pulled the bowl out first, holding it too close to my face for comfort. I drew in a sharp breath and leaned back.

Alexander smiled. "Ahh. We both see you are not so ignorant," he said, and placed the bowl near my feet. Alexander and his cronies had removed my shoes when they'd placed me in here. Restrained bare feet on wet floor that near a cursed item—you do the math. I felt a bead of sweat form on my neck.

From what Lady Siyu had suggested, only the higher-up supernaturals should be able to handle the cursed items. Alexander as a vampire had started off as human—that type of supernatural tended to have a harder time with magic. Hell, magic curse was how they ended up not human in the first place. "How come you can handle those?"

Alexander's smile widened. "Because, *ma chérie,* as a vampire I am already cursed. Only one curse at a time, you could say—rather like one of your 'coupons.'"

I would have rolled my eyes at his attempt at colloquial phrases—a bad habit of his—but I was too busy watching the bag and the remaining items.

Vampires feed off fear. They live for it, they can smell it. Alexander was practically salivating. "However, you do not have the same . . . immunity." He withdrew the flint next and arranged it on the other side of my feet, corralling them between the cursed items. He leaned as close as he dared without coming in range of Captain. "Now, unless you wish to test the truth behind the curses, you will tell me where you found them and why you deigned to remove them from their resting place." He extended his foot so it was almost touching the bowl.

Oh for God's sake, not Alexander too . . .

"If by 'resting place' you mean Daphne Sylph's display room, I found out about it like everyone else in this century. Google."

A sharp breath escaped between his pursed lips. "I think you take me for a fool, *ma chérie*." And with that, he pushed the bowl forward with the tip of his expensive Italian leather shoes. "Now, their proper resting place?"

Shit. I curled my toes back out of reflex. I was watching his feet, not his face . . . "Look, I know you're probably going to find this hard to believe, but I didn't actually break into the City of the Dead. It was someone else—pretending to be me."

"You who takes me for the idiot again." This time he pushed the flint closer, and once again I shifted my feet. I'd run out of space soon.

"Look—I realize everyone is having a hard time believing it wasn't me, especially since apparently some asshole is selling artifacts under my name, but this is some other asshole . . . impersonating me . . ."

"Then why are they now again in your possession? I find that a rather unlikely coincidence."

"Because I had nothing better to do on a Friday night—hey!" I yelled as he pushed the bowl closer.

"Whereas others may find you funny, I do not."

Asshole. "If I was the thief who stole them in the first place, would

I bother breaking into Daphne's—a siren, I might add—to steal them back?"

Alexander regarded me, a frown touching his face. "If the dragon was angry enough? Perhaps, especially if you did the theft behind his back, which I well know you are wont to do."

Open one sarcophagus . . . I shook my head. "OK, despite the fact that was the most intelligent thing I've ever heard you say—the answer is no, for one very good, logical reason."

"And what would that be, *chérie*?"

This time I leaned in, just so Alexander could see I meant it. "Simple—if the dragon thought for one second I actually stole those items and sold them behind his back, I'd be dead already—or halfway across some deserted wasteland."

Alexander sat back, considering what I'd said. "Agreed. The dragon would not suffer you to live for taking these items without his approval."

If it hadn't been for those last few words . . . "Oh come on—you seriously think the dragon would want those things unearthed?"

"If he thought they posed a greater threat running wild and free? Certainly."

I rolled my eyes. "OK, yeah—" Especially since Mr. Kurosawa had done almost that exact same thing before making me fetch the scroll. "But that's not the case here. And you still haven't told me what the hell you want with them."

Alexander still looked skeptical. He reached out and pushed the bowl closer again.

I swore. The worst part was Alexander wouldn't be breaking rules if I ended up cursed. He wasn't allowed to kill me, specifically—where supernatural deals were concerned, "made me touch an ancient cursed artifact" was gray area.

He edged his foot towards the flint piece.

OK, now time to panic . . . "Look, Alexander, my phone is in the front pocket. Call Mr. Kurosawa, he'll back up my story."

Instead of pushing the piece of flint towards me though, he pulled it back and placed it back in the bag. I didn't like the smile that spread across his face or the blackening of his eyes.

"From what I understand, Owl, I believe your agreement with Mr. Kurosawa means that you need to retrieve the three items? Yes? Then find the thief?"

I hadn't told Alexander about the thief. A cold chill ran up my spine.

Alexander continued. "I wonder what will happen if I call Mr. Kurosawa and mention I saw you take the pieces and disappear. I am certain Daphne will back up the story. Why have suspicion fall on me and my vampires, when you were so conveniently in my way? And as for what I want with the pieces, it is, as you say, none of your goddamn business." The evil look I expected from Alexander filled his eyes.

Great, one thief uses me as a scapegoat, and everyone else figures it's a free-for-all. "You goddamn low-life son of a bitch—let me out and give me those pieces back."

Alexander held both hands out to the side. "Or what? What do you suggest you can do from there?" He crouched down inches away from me. "Absolutely nothing," he said, and tapped the top of the gas mask. "I believe I shall leave this on. I wonder whether letting my children bite first will be more painful that way."

"You son of a bitch—I *helped* you in Bali—"

His polite demeanor fell as he snarled, "You locked us in a pit for days while you paraded the fact outside. We vampires have some pride."

"Oh *get over* yourself. You'd have backed yourself into a corner with the Contingency if it hadn't been for me." The Contingency being the group in charge of vampires.

"Consider this my retribution for the embarrassment. Let us see how you like being locked up and useless in a hole for *three* days."

Evil, fucking, no-good vampires. Not that I'd really expected anything else, but still . . . "Retribution? You assholes were trying to kill me. Hell, I handed over Bindi and Red. I ought to get some credit for that—"

Alexander spread out his hands. "What is the expression? Ah, I know, 'Like I give a flying fuck.'" He made sure to flash his teeth, just to remind me what he could really do if he wanted. "And perhaps after a little misuse at the hands of my fledglings, I shall let you and your wretched cat roam free." He shrugged. "Or perhaps you will be a vampire by then, who can say?" And with that, Alexander got up to leave, bag in hand.

"Hey! Come back and say that when I'm holding a UV light and my cat isn't tied up, asshole!"

But having made his point, Alexander left.

I leaned my head against the wall and started to work on my restraints. I wouldn't break them, but maybe with enough sweat I could pull my wrist through—minus some skin. Or, if I was really lucky, Rynn had been able to GPS my phone, unless Alexander had buried me and it under floors of concrete with no reception.

Damn it, when did Alexander get smart?

Captain mewed.

"Yeah, I know. Not exactly how I'd hoped to see the Sunset Strip, either," I said. At least the gas mask meant I couldn't smell Captain's retaliation urine anymore.

Small comforts.

By my guess, roughly an hour had passed. The music was still going up top, so not closing time yet—*if* the Sunset Strip ever closed. . . . That was a sobering and unsettling thought.

Oh yeah, and my hands were bleeding. Did that count for progress? Probably not, since my hands were still bound by the metal twist ties.

Captain, however, was sitting on my restrained legs, wondering why the hell I wasn't up yet. Apparently no carrier or burlap sack could withstand the determined wrath of Captain. Now, if he could only pick locks . . .

Hermes's comment about me being a fuckup came to mind.

However long I'd been here, my ears were on edge, and I heard the scrape against the door before the handle began to turn.

Feeding time, and me with my wrists all nicely bloodied up as an appetizer. Captain, also hearing the noise, wriggled his hind end.

Maybe there'd only be one or two. I nodded to the spot behind the door, and Captain obliged. The one bonus to being in a vampire den for the past hour was that Captain had acclimatized to the pheromones and had stopped growling at everything.

The door creaked open an inch, and Captain readied himself.

"*Wait,*" I mouthed. Another few inches open . . .

The door opened and Captain pounced, claws first, as Artemis stuck his head through.

Captain, realizing midair he wasn't attacking a vampire, sheathed his claws and more or less bounced off Artemis's stomach. I say more or less because Captain packs a punch.

Artemis and Captain watched each other, Artemis wary and Captain . . . well, Captain just waiting. "Did the cat . . . ?" he said, pointing.

"Long story. Short version: he thought you were a vampire." My relief at seeing him and not a vampire was warp-speed short-lived. "Artemis, you had one lousy job to do! Warn me if anyone was coming!"

Artemis raised a finger. "I said I'd keep watch—which I did. It just so happens I also said I wasn't going to risk my neck saving you, which, by the way, confronting Daphne would have been."

"Then why the hell did you offer?"

"Because I didn't actually think she'd come herself! Besides, I came to get you out, didn't I?"

I shook my head and held out my wrists. Worst incubus escort ever. Well . . . no, not in that way—forget it. "Just please say you have a knife."

Artemis pulled out a box cutter and slit the metal binds. "Come on, we need to leave now," he said, pulling me up and out the door.

"One second. I need my bag."

"Seriously? Get my cousin to buy you a new one. We're not rifling around a vampire den."

"Yes seriously." I pulled away, towards a side door. Artemis tried to grab my arm again, but I danced out of the way.

"Shit," he said. "Look, the only reason I'm here is so my dear cousin doesn't kill me for letting you out of my sight. Now come on. I have no intention of tangling with a pack of vampires. In case you haven't noticed, I'm not exactly my cousin." He snarled the last few words.

I didn't budge. "Well, I'm as good as dead without the items, so consider it saving your own skin."

Artemis swore, but instead of trying to grab me, he checked the hallway. "All right, this way. I think I saw an office when I came in."

"How did you make it past the vampires anyways?"

"Hmmm—oh I got one of the girls to bring me down. They've got human employees—for the daytime shifts they have to. The young vampires get cranky during the day, and it's bad for business when beer delivery men keep disappearing. Vampire pheromones coursing through their blood does make them easy targets though. Doesn't quite seem fair."

"Wait—you got downstairs seducing some poor bar staff?"

Artemis glanced over his shoulder. "I wouldn't be so quick to the pity party. She did say she was a big fan."

Even if Artemis saw me roll my eyes, somehow I doubted he cared.

He shoved me into a side storage room full of beer kegs as a pair of girls came down the stairs. The growl I had to muffle from Captain told me these were vampires—or at least full-blown junkies.

As soon as they turned the corner, Artemis led me a little ways up the hall to a door marked OFFICE. Through the window I could see my bag sitting on the desk. I tried the door. Locked. "Shit—got a lock pick handy?"

"I've got a better idea," Artemis said, and forced the door open. He shrugged when I stared at him. "Being stronger than humans occasionally has its uses."

I ducked into the room and grabbed my bag first. Now for the artifacts . . . I started searching the drawers.

"Hurry it up, more people are coming."

"Vampires, not people."

"In this instance, the difference is a moot point. I told Rynn I'd get you out, not save you from a horde of vampires."

"Great, go on. I'm out, so not your problem."

Artemis snorted. "If only. Unfortunately my cousin will beg to differ."

I ignored him. *Come on, brain, if I were a bag of loot, where would I be?* My World Quest reflexes kicked in and I started opening the closets and throwing books off shelves . . . I spotted a white satchel behind a row of books on the third shelf.

Artemis was still keeping watch and swore. "There's two coming down the stairs," he whispered. "I can hear the panic and adrenaline— and what the hell are you doing?"

"Making sure everything is still here." Inside the bag were the bowl, flint, and fake sword. I shoved them inside my bag and thought about giving the room a cursory look for the real sword, but Artemis motioned for me to squat on the other side of the door while team number two walked by at a crawl. They began sticking their heads in each room. Shit . . . The woman looked through the office window but didn't spot us. I tightened my hold on Captain's scruff, doing my best to muffle his growl until they moved down to the storage room.

Artemis grabbed me and shoved me out of the room. "Up the stairs, before they get thorough."

Vampires shouted behind us, but we had the head start. Captain squirmed under my arm as I pushed the door to the upstairs club open. The place was packed—mostly a punk crowd here to see the punk band on stage. I could barely hear the lead singer screaming over the drum and guitars—though this was a bar band, and that might have been the point.

Well, best way to lose the vampires was to blend in with the flock of sheep.

It was standing room only, so I pushed my way in. Artemis, figuring I wasn't moving fast enough, darted around me. Why the hell hadn't I thought to grab my damn shoes?

I did my best to make sure no one jostled the artifacts or Captain too badly. If I was smart, I'd have given the bag to Artemis to carry, but visions of the pieces rolling across the floor coming into contact with multiple people stopped me.

Even in the dim lighting, Artemis still managed to garner looks from the crowd. "You stick out like a sore thumb," I said.

"That's because when I'm in a dive bar, I'm usually drinking," he yelled over his shoulder, and reached back to grab me. "Hurry it up—I'm not about to end up on the vampires' shit list."

We were getting close to the front of the club and hadn't been spotted by the vampires yet. We probably would have made it to the door in a few more steps if I hadn't caught sight of a familiar face; a petite brunette in a lawyer-black suit, the same one who'd been standing outside the catacomb dig in Egypt.

Our eyes met, and she lifted her hand, signaling to other agents.

Shit. And me with the bag of goods slung over my shoulder . . . I grabbed Artemis by the collar of his jacket and ground to a halt, almost slipping on spilled beer in the process.

Off balance, Artemis glared at me over his shoulder.

"IAA," I shouted, and pointed at the entrance, where more suits had appeared.

Artemis swore. "Is there anyone you don't manage to piss off?" He altered our course towards the signs that indicated washrooms.

Fantastic; more urine and stale beer.

I did my best to keep up. Artemis wasn't exactly in "let's keep the band together" mode; more like "save my own goddamned skin." Considering how often his band Kaliope split up, that didn't surprise me.

I slid across spilled beer to a precarious stop behind Artemis before ducking after him into a washroom.

He raced to the cracked porcelain sink. It groaned under his weight as he used it to get a look outside the small bathroom window—the kind you find lining the top of a basement wall.

"It's only a small drop to the fire escape," he said, and held out his hand for me.

There was a loud bang on the washroom door. IAA or vampires—

either one was a problem at this point. Didn't need to warn me twice. I was a little more cautious in my bare feet, but I managed to scramble up. The pipes groaned again under the added weight. Somehow I didn't think the sink would work quite the same after this.

"You've got a lot of experience sneaking out of bars," I said.

"Necessity breeds expertise," he said, and braced both hands to push me up. "Come on, that lock won't hold long."

Like Artemis said, the fire stairs were only a three-foot drop. You'd think that'd be a concern for a bar, but this place was cash and carry. I dropped down on bare feet and held up my hands for Captain, then the artifacts. I was already racing down the stairs when I heard Artemis drop down behind me.

"Run before the vampires wise up and run out the back," he yelled down the stairs after me. Ignoring the protest the soles of my feet were making, I concentrated on taking the steps faster until I reached the pavement. Artemis had almost caught up, but I heard a door break up above. Shit. I hoped it was the vampires—the IAA was worse; they had guns.

"Which way?"

Across the road, a car lit up and gunned its engine. I shielded my eyes against the floodlights—UV floodlights . . . a jeep, military grade, with an open hood easy to jump into, and able to go off-road if needed.

Rynn.

I bolted for the car, not bothering to wait for Artemis. I needn't have worried; Artemis outpaced me and hopped into the front seat. He wasn't kidding when he said he had no intention of being caught by vampires.

I tossed the bag of artifacts and Captain in before diving into the backseat. I saw a group of people braced at the front of the bar, staying out of the range of the UV headlights. As soon as I was in, Rynn hit the gas, and the jeep careened through the crowd of vampires, who scattered. Like I said, not supernatural juggernauts. Cockroaches. I didn't bother looking to see if the IAA made it out the bathroom window.

Only once we were woven into traffic did Rynn glance over his shoulder at me.

"Are you all right?" he said, his face knit with worry.

"She's fine. I told you I'd get her out," Artemis said.

Rynn glared at him, not bothering to hide his anger and something else—disgust, contempt. I wasn't certain, because those weren't things Rynn usually expressed. "I'm fine," I said, and held up the bag. "Guess who else was after these?"

By the time I finished catching Rynn up, we were well on the highway, heading towards an airfield, and no one was following us.

We still had a ways to go before we reached the plane, where we'd ditch the jeep—and Artemis—and be on our way back to Las Vegas, the first half of my problem solved. . . . Well, partially solved, since I only had a fake sword . . .

I opened the bag—carefully—and removed the sword, now wrapped in an archaeology-grade muslin. Credit where credit was due; at least Alexander knew how to take care of the shit I used to steal for him.

I started to unwrap it, thinking I'd get the flashlight out and examine it once it was sitting in my lap. Might give me an idea who Alexander had on his payroll as a forger. The muslin came loose, and I reached to turn the bronze sword over. If the artist left a mark, it'd be on the handle . . .

It tingled as I touched it, and a shot of static electricity traveled up my arm and didn't stop until it transversed my entire body.

Captain's head perked up and he chirped, ears tipped forward. Both Rynn and Artemis turned in their seats, nostrils flaring and eyes glowing blue and green, respectively, at the scent of magic.

Unbelieving, I took another look at the sword in my lap. "No, No, No . . ." It wasn't possible—I'd been sure . . . I rifled through the side pocket of my purse until the flashlight was in my hand.

"Alix, what the hell did you just do?" Rynn said.

I would have said something, but panic set in first. "No, this isn't possible, this is a nightmare." I turned the flashlight on, still shaking my head. "I don't understand, I checked the sword," I added, still trying to convince myself that what just happened hadn't.

Sitting unwrapped in my lap was not the fake I'd taken from Daphne's collection but the real, cursed bronze sword. I spotted a note written in tight script.

In case you do manage to escape my den, my dear Owl—which, knowing you and your infernal cat, is a distinct possibility—I took the liberty to reunite the true sword with its friends in hopes your reckless nature will prevail. If I cannot have my revenge, I can take comfort knowing you'll die a painful death. Beneath Alexander's scrawled and overly fancy signature was a ten-digit L.A. number and *P.S: Give me a call. No hard feelings. It's never personal.*

"Not personal?" I crumpled up the note and shoved it back in my pocket. "Goddamned vampires. Psychos, every one of them. The son of a bitch cursed me."

11

Cursed

Time: Who cares? I'm cursed.
Las Vegas

I don't know what pissed me off more; the fact that I'd been stupid enough to pick up a cursed artifact, or the fact that Alexander outsmarted me. I think the latter.

We hadn't said much on the flight back after "How could you be so stupid?" and "Do you have any idea what you've done?" I might even have been angry at Rynn except that (A) Rynn had a point, and (B) he only went really silent when he was worried.

I'd been so certain the sword in my bag was a fake . . .

My phone chimed a drawn-out, metallic hiss, followed by a roar. It was something I'd picked up off a '90s video game—the battle roar of their version of snake people. Rynn shook his head at me, but I just shrugged. If I can't derive some humor from working for a Naga and a dragon, I might as well be dead . . . no wait. That was already happening.

I stopped to read Lady Siyu's message twice and just about threw my phone at the wall. I would have if I didn't need Carpe to get the fuck back to me on what his elf brain knew about ancient curses—like three hours ago.

In answer to Rynn's unspoken question, I said, "They're never happy with what they get."

I shoved my phone in my pocket to get rid of the throwing temptation and headed for the elevator. Rynn followed close on my heels. Unlike last time, he'd be able to run some interference with Mr. Kurosawa and Lady Siyu. I almost wished he wasn't coming with me. At the end of the day, I'm not sure how much interference he'd be able to run.

"Whatever you do, do not piss off Mr. Kurosawa—and let me do the talking," he said.

"Trust me, I've got bigger things to worry about than mouthing off to the dragon this time."

"*Or* Lady Siyu."

"That I can't promise—"

"Alix!" Nadya raced out of the Garden Café bar, laptop in hand. With her formfitting "casual" black jeans and usual red wig absent in favor of her natural brown hair, she turned more than a few heads. If Nadya had pulled anything resembling an all-nighter, I sure as hell couldn't tell.

The elevator door opened, and Rynn held it until Nadya could duck inside, laptop under her arm.

"Bartender not biting yet?" I asked.

Nadya glared.

So did Rynn. "Don't you have better things to do than seduce my staff?"

She gave him a noncommittal shrug before turning back to me.

"Two of my contacts came through when I told them about the City of the Dead. Don't worry, I didn't mention you, just hinted the site might have been opened and sent them some of the new photos. That was enough; the Russian branch of the IAA takes their curses and supernatural plagues seriously. They're trying to get the site shut down, but your old supervisor, Dr. Sanders, who signed off on the dig?" She shook her head. "He has vanished. Both my guys have been unable to get in contact with him. They think the signatures may be falsified."

Yeah, Dr. Sanders was a patronizing, self-important fool, but he wasn't separated from his phone or email—not for long anyways. If the Russian IAA couldn't get in touch with him, then chances were good something bad had happened.

"Do we have any idea which of his fleet of postdocs is in charge of the dig yet?"

Nadya shook her head. "No, and they find that peculiar as well—and before you even ask, no, I haven't found anything useful about lifting the curse."

I swore. God, I hoped Carpe or Mr. Kurosawa pulled through.

"How long?" I asked, my throat dry, even though I was pretty damn sure we knew the answer already from the old dig notes.

"Maybe a few days until you begin to show symptoms. Then," she shrugged, "a week at most."

Again, the way you know the good friends from the bad ones? The good ones tell you the truth you need to hear, no matter how much it sucks.

Rynn was having a hard time reining in his temper now. "Alix, so help me God, why on earth did you risk—"

But he didn't get the chance to finish the sentence, because Nadya whirled on him in all her high-end-hostess glory. "That's enough. It's not her fault."

OK . . . that wasn't what I expected . . . "Nadya, I knew better—"

This time she whirled on me. "You were certain the knife was a fake?"

"I—yeah, it was a fake."

"How do you know?" she asked, her accent coming through thicker with her anger, reminding me of an old Russian professor who used to enjoy putting us on the spot.

Uh . . . where did I start? "First off, the weight wasn't anywhere near right—the copper content should have been higher, since they hadn't figured out the tin yet, which you damn well know. Second, there was the sheen. It didn't match a five-thousand-year-old artifact, even one with magic. There should have been way more pitting. On top of that, the carvings—"

She didn't wait for me to finish before she whirled back on Rynn. "Alix knew exactly what she was doing—the knife she took was fake. Alexander made the switch. It's Alexander's fault."

He wasn't focused on Nadya though; he was watching me. "She shouldn't have tried opening it in the backseat—"

She made a clicking noise. "Why? Because she should suspect Alexander's smart enough to replace the fake one she already identified? No one in their right mind could predict something like that. Alexander isn't that smart." She shook her head. "I'm half of a mind he had help. He shouldn't have known Alix would do that—it's something you or I expect, but Alexander?"

Rynn wasn't happy, but Nadya wasn't stepping down.

I thought about what she'd said. After my disaster in Egypt, I'd been real fast to blame my own reckless streak, but this time . . . You know what, this fuckup wasn't on me. "How the hell could I have known? I'm an antiquities thief, not a spy. The only reason I pulled the knife out was so I could get some clues as to who'd forged it."

Nadya nodded, as if I was confirming her own suspicions.

"You're blaming Alix for doing the right thing under the circumstances," she said. "I would have done exactly the same thing."

Rynn looked for a moment like he might argue, but with Nadya and me . . . he backed down. "You're right, you couldn't have predicted the switch. I shouldn't be this upset with you," he conceded.

Nadya settled against the elevator wall, satisfied.

Still, he didn't sound or look convinced enough—not to me.

That . . . bothered me, more than I cared to admit. I knew what I was doing when it came to antiquities. I'm brilliant at spotting fakes—one of the reasons I make sure I document my stuff as well as I do.

My phone chimed again, but this time it rang with the first few notes of the Lord of the Rings theme.

"Please don't say that's the elf," Rynn said.

I shrugged. "Fine, I won't tell you it's Carpe," I said, and fished my phone out of my pocket. Hopefully the damned elf had something.

Nothing useful yet—give me another couple days . . . still have a few rocks to overturn.

Shit. *Fat good that does me*—I wrote back. I didn't really blame Carpe—solutions to ancient curses were a needle in a haystack. Even supernaturals had thought it best to leave curses buried over the past couple centuries. For good reason. Like genie wishes, magic tends to backfire spectacularly.

Not the answer I wanted to hear, but still better than "you've got seven days, good luck with that."

The elevator doors opened to the twenty-third floor—Mr. Kurosawa's casino.

I stopped Nadya from following us out. "Trust me. You want to sit this one out. They're pissed."

She looked like she was about to protest, so I handed her Captain's carrier. "Don't do it for me, do it for Captain. He wasn't the idiot who decided to go to Algiers and Egypt."

She took the carrier tentatively, then nodded. "I'll follow up with a couple academic leads. They'd never talk to you, but they might still speak with me."

The elevator doors slid shut, leaving me and Rynn outside the black and gold casino doors. Rynn took my arm and gently steered me towards them. "Stop panicking, Alix. You're making me nervous."

"Make you a deal. Get rid of the dragon and the Naga, and I'll stop panicking."

That at least got a smile out of him—a strained smile, but the first I'd seen since I'd managed to curse myself.

"Mr. Kurosawa says Lady Siyu is proficient with curse lore, so she may know how to counteract it."

"Great, the supernatural who openly wants me dead is the expert on curses. I'm *fucked*."

"You're not fucked, not yet. We haven't exhausted all our options. On the bright side, you returned all the pieces, so they can't be upset about that."

Small comfort. "Somehow I don't think that buys me much leeway with these two. Not after Daphne's."

—w—

Lady Siyu was waiting for us on the other side of the doors, and she looked pissed. That I'd expected, not the complete lack of composure. I couldn't look away from her collar . . . my God . . . was it crooked? Come to think of it, Lady Siyu looked downright disheveled . . . for her, that is.

"Explain yoursssself," she said.

"Lady Siyu, I thought you'd be jumping for joy. Not only did I manage to retrieve all three artifacts, I cursed myself in the process. I ought to be dead in seven—no, wait, make that six more days. Oh yeah, and Daphne told a room full of supernaturals I was the thief—"

"*Enough!*" Her hands clenched at her sides, the red fingernails digging into her pale skin. "Why did you touch the pieces yourself when you were specifically told not to?"

OK, asking the obvious now . . . in spite of myself and being very familiar with her temper and disdain for, well, me, I frowned. "Wow, let me see. Minor act of rebellion against my Snake God overlord?" Lady Siyu's snarl didn't dissipate, so I added, "Trust me, I'm a hell of a lot more pissed off about it than you."

Lady Siyu snarled something in supernatural to Rynn.

That was . . . unusual. I'd never seen her actually show anything but polite coldness to him before—not to his face, anyways.

Apparently, Rynn knew something I didn't. He stepped past a still fuming Lady Siyu into the slot machine maze without a word.

OK, I wasn't even pretending to understand what supernatural bullshit had just transpired. Left with a choice between Rynn and Lady Siyu?

I gave Lady Siyu a wide berth and caught up to Rynn. "Since when can you find your way through this?" I asked him.

"Since I never told you because you're a *thief*."

I heard Lady Siyu's heels click behind us a heartbeat later, but she kept her distance.

We took a right turn that hadn't been there last time. I swear the place reorganized every time I walked through. Another right turn later and we arrived at Mr. Kurosawa's private lounge.

The first thing I noticed was that the décor had changed since the last time. The off-white and gold light fixtures were now deep red with a smattering of gold, casting the space in gold-flecked red light. Instead of the white leather couch, Mr. Kurosawa was sitting on a bloodred version, and the modern mirrored coffee table had been replaced by a wooden base topped with a slick black surface. It still reflected the room, but more akin to through a looking glass darkly. The white marble bar had also been replaced with a darker red—almost black—shade, run through with gold flecks. Mr. Kurosawa himself was dressed in a designer black suit, but his skin was tinged a deep maroon and his eyes were pools of black. Smoke rose off his skin in waves.

God, I hoped to hell that wasn't directed at me.

As my eyes adapted to the low light, my stomach churned. The three artifacts were laid out on the bar. Reflexively I took a step back, hitting Rynn, who deftly placed himself between me and the maze.

"Never run from predators," he whispered in my ear. "They'll always give chase." For a moment I wondered if he was only talking about my present company. Mostly though I was glad he'd had the foresight to warn me. I don't think I'd last very long in that maze.

The hairs on the back of my arms rose as Lady Siyu took her place beside me.

"Did she retrieve the right artifacts?" Rynn said, speaking to Lady Siyu but keeping his eyes on Mr. Kurosawa.

She glanced over at the bar as she continued past us to join Mr. Kurosawa, and I noted she'd recovered her usual cold composure. "Yes, Owl obtained the correct artifacts," she said. Her lip curled at the corner, exposing a fang. "The wonders never cease," she added.

"My dear God, Lady Siyu learned sarcasm." I'd have added something else, but she silenced me with a hiss.

"That was *not* an invitation to speak, thief."

Sensing my frustration building, Rynn nudged me from behind.

You know what? Screw best behavior. If Lady Siyu was my great hope for lifting the curse, I might as well drop dead now. Contrary to popular belief, I don't have a death wish. I like living—it means I still have something left to lose. And snark was the only defense I had holding back the tears right now.

Rynn tensed as I faced Mr. Kurosawa. "Are all snakes this unpersonable, or is it just her?" I asked.

Rynn swore under his breath. Two thick plumes of smoke rose from each of Mr. Kurosawa's nostrils. "Please, explain what occurred," he said to me.

—⁂—

Lady Siyu was not impressed with the logic of my explanation, and she launched in as soon as I'd finished. "I specifically told you the items were not to be handled by humans. What part of those instructions did you fail to wrap your brain around—"

"Enough," Mr. Kurosawa said. A look passed between him and her, and with a last snarl at me, she retreated back into the maze. Only once the click of her heels faded did Mr. Kurosawa turn his still black eyes back on me and Rynn.

"Lady Siyu is . . . concerned," he finally decided on, "that the information passed on by her informant was false and therefore her conclusions concerning your guilt in the thefts is incorrect. We have determined in your absence that you must not be the thief who broke into the city. As you have otherwise fulfilled your side of our most recent bargain, Lady Siyu will attempt to lift the curse—"

I snorted. I know, it was stupid, but come on. Lady Siyu, help me stay alive? Not if someone threatened to rip out her bleak, black heart...

Rynn shoved me between the shoulder blades a little less gently.

"*In* compensation for her errors in judgment," Mr. Kurosawa continued, then waited for me to say something.

There were a number of things I thought about saying. *I won't hold my breath* topped the list, but I realized I hadn't actually fulfilled my side of the bargain, only half. I still had no idea who the thief was.

Mr. Kurosawa concluding our agreement before I delivered? Not a chance.

"There's been another theft, hasn't there? While I was in L.A.," I said.

He inclined his head and smiled. I noted his usual white, human-looking teeth were two rows of black, razor-sharp serrated points. "While both the IAA and vampires were tracking you, the thief returned to the city."

Of course they had, why not? Drop the artifacts off in L.A. and back to Syria. I couldn't have pulled off two continents like that ... Son of a bitch—I *hate* not being the best antiquities thief on the job.

Wait a minute ... "Do you have a copy of all the thefts? The ones that the IAA attributed to me?" I asked. Mr. Kurosawa nodded and handed me the tablet.

I checked the dates, adding in the delivery to L.A. "There's more than one thief," I said.

Mr. Kurosawa nodded.

"What went missing this time?" I noted a dry feeling at the back of my throat and hoped it was just my nerves acting up and not the curse taking hold.

"That is something I do not know. Whatever was removed, this time it was neither excavated nor documented yet."

I pushed back the emotional part of my brain that wanted to pulverize this thieving collective; they were careful, specific, targeting items with precision. All under the noses of a number of supernaturals: Hermes, Mr. Kurosawa, Lady Siyu, Daphne, hell, even the vampires.

I know I attract trouble, but there was more going on here than just theft.

I glanced up at Rynn, who mouthed, "*Be careful.*" More plumes of smoke rose off Mr. Kurosawa, and I wondered if the décor change might have been because the darker colors showed fewer scorch marks. Dragons struggle to control their human forms at the best of times.

I'd done a few rounds with Mr. Kurosawa before. It wasn't pretty. Short version, I'd get my ass handed to me. On the other hand, chances were good I'd be dead by the end of the week anyways . . . What was the worst that could happen at this point?

"What is the real chance Lady Siyu will be able to remove the curse?"

"It is difficult to determine at this time," he said. "Lady Siyu is an expert, but these curses are ancient."

"Correct me if I'm wrong, but there's a group of thieves running around stealing dangerous artifacts under my name, and an entire contingent of supernaturals who think this is a great argument to start wielding their powers over hapless humans everywhere since we can't be trusted." And I was starting to think the two things were not so coincidental as they appeared.

Rynn swore loudly behind me. Mr. Kurosawa growled but didn't eat me.

"Just listen to my proposition." I held up both hands and hoped I'd guessed correctly how desperate the situation had become.

"Let me go to Syria," I started, and before either could argue, I steamrolled on. "If there is a set of instructions saying how to lift the curse, I'll find it in the city." Ancient curses had a nasty habit of backfiring spectacularly. As a result, most curses kept the instructions to undo them nearby.

"Something is going on in the IAA, and I think it's linked with the thieves and whatever the hell is going on between you and the rest of the supernaturals. I'm dead in a week anyways. What's the worst that could happen?"

Rynn didn't bother hiding the fact that he wasn't happy about my proposal.

"Indeed, what do you have to lose?" Mr. Kurosawa said. He stood up and nodded to Rynn, and the next thing I knew Rynn was leading me back towards the maze, moving a little too fast for my liking.

"Owl?"

I glanced back over my shoulder. Mr. Kurosawa was regarding me with an unreadable expression. "Do humans always see treasure around every corner?"

I thought about how best to answer that. "If you ever played a video game, you'd know it's a pretty common theme. The bigger the monster, the better the lock, the trickier the trap." I shrugged. "Most people assume the treasure inside is pretty damn good."

Mr. Kurosawa nodded. "Then if I wanted to devise a trap for humans, the same principle would apply?"

I nodded, not certain where Mr. Kurosawa was going with this.

"Do you know why it's called the City of the Dead?" he asked.

"I'm guessing because the city was built as a burial site. It was never meant for the living."

"In part. It was also built for the deity the early Qaraoun worshiped."

I wouldn't go so far as to say deity—more like whichever supernatural happened to be masquerading as a god at the time.

"And you are only partially right. Our legends say burial in the city was a form of human sacrifice, a fate worse than death, to spend an eternity in servitude to their god."

Unpleasant, but still not an uncommon practice, especially in ancient times, even up to the medieval periods. There are enough supernaturals that feed off human corpses that setting up shop as a minor god wasn't a bad business model . . . except for the way he said it and his measured look. "Have you never wondered why their neighbors, the Natufians, slept on top of their dead?"

The Natufians had been interesting that way. They were one of the early groups who, instead of using burial cites, literally buried their dead under their beds. Cemented in, but the visual is still a bit creepy. "I was told it was so the ghosts of the Natufian ancestors would protect their living descendents from monsters while they slept," I said.

He smiled. "You are mistaken. It was to protect their dead ancestors from the Qaraoun. Think on that, Owl, before you decide to deliver yourself to the temple, curse or no curse."

And with that, Mr. Kurosawa disappeared into the shadows.

Supernaturals, curses, ancient gods, and thieves pretending to be me. This just kept getting better and better.

12

Drinking

11:00 p.m., the poolside bar at the Japanese Circus.
If you have a better idea, go right ahead.

I did my best to tune out Rynn and Nadya. Considering the tequila and Corona buzz I had going on, it was proving more difficult than it should have been. Hell, maybe that was the first symptom. Lack of concentration . . .

It'd hit me in the last hour.

I was going to die.

And not a drop-dead-unexpectedly kind of death. The nasty, painful, oozing kind.

"Syria is too dangerous at the moment," Rynn said.

"She's got less than a week. We don't have time to go the long way," Nadya said. I took another sip of my Mexican happy hour—tequila-spiked Corona; swig the beer, add lime, then the tequila. Saves time. I was wallowing over my computer screen, a jumble of archaeology notes, aerial maps, and incomplete temple maps . . . which were worse than useless . . .

"You're more likely to get killed the first step you take inside the borders—"

After that the conversation divulged into Russian cursing. Or maybe I was completely fucked and this was just the second symptom . . . everyone around me started speaking in Russian.

Oh God, I hoped that wasn't the second symptom.

I took solace in the fact that for once they were yelling at each other, not me.

Nadya and Rynn were arguing over the best way to storm the City of the Dead so we could find instructions to help us undo the curse. Forgive me if I wasn't fucking into it. What the hell had I been thinking telling Mr. Kurosawa I'd go to Syria?

Even if we got into Syria without getting shot at, which frankly was pretty unlikely at this point, I still didn't have a map of the city itself, and with my current World Quest ban, I wasn't getting one anytime soon.

"What if we use a low-flying cargo plane?" Nadya said, my buzzed brain picking back up on the conversation.

"You do realize every tribe, militia, and army behind those borders shoots small aircraft down for target practice?" Rynn said, lowering his voice as a couple walked up to the bar to order.

"At least getting shot down is a faster alternative than choking on my own blood," I added under my breath.

I went to take another sip of my Corona. It was empty. On a positive note, no one was attempting to regulate just how much alcohol I shoved into my five-foot-four, cursed circulatory system. I looked for Nadya's current favorite bartender but didn't spot him. Had to be waiting on someone else but me . . .

Never one to have my drinking streak broken, I leaned over the bar and helped myself to the tequila bottle . . . and another Corona.

Now, where were the damn limes?

"Alix, are you even listening to us?" Nadya said.

English, definitely English. Hallucinating Russian was not the second symptom of the curse. Oh joy of joys.

Now, if I were a lime, where would I be? "No, Nadya, I'm not. I'm drinking because I'm going to die." Who the hell was going to look after

Captain? Nadya would just overfeed him, and then there was the whole vampire thing . . .

Nadya yelled at me in Russian fast enough I wouldn't have caught it even if I'd been sober. I shrugged, lifted the Corona, and was rewarded with more angry Russian.

"She says drunken participation is still better than none," Rynn said. "And I agree." He retrieved the tequila bottle before I could take advantage of it and hopped behind the empty bar before I could take advantage of that too.

He found the limes though—win some, lose some.

"How many Mexican happy hours does that make now?" he asked, before letting go of a tequila shot he poured for me.

I shrugged. "Three. I think."

"Last one."

"Seriously? Why exactly are we choosing now to care about the state of my liver? Dead in . . ." I used my fingers to count. "Six days, remember?"

"First, you aren't dying. Between Lady Siyu and the temple in Syria, we'll figure out a way to reverse the curse."

"Do you have any idea what the chances are of either of those things actually happening?" And people call me the optimistic nut job . . .

"*Secondly,* we're getting on a plane before the IAA figures out where we're heading. I have no intention of spending the little amount of sleep I have left holding your head while you pray to the porcelain gods."

Rynn leaned in, took a swig of my beer himself, then added the tequila shot for me. "Alix, you're not going to die."

"Unless you're hungover for the next five days, in which case yes, you will die, either your liver or the curse, whichever gets you first," Nadya added.

I'm sure there was a point made in there . . .

"Look, even if we get to the temple, I have no idea where the artifacts were taken from. There isn't a proper map—anywhere." I flicked the open files on my laptop, just to get my point across.

"We stand even less chance if you can't stop wallowing in self-pity and help us come up with a plan," she said.

When I didn't have a snarky comment, Rynn added, "Let's worry about one thing at a time. Ignore the map for now and help us figure out how we're going to get into the temple."

I took another sip of beer and thought about it. If I were a thief, how would I get my ass into the temple? "First, we need to get into Syria without raising any alarms; that's what the thieves have to be doing. Livestock and cargo planes are too predictable. Even sneaking in with livestock would have raised an alarm somewhere by now. The IAA isn't completely incompetent—they'll be watching the borders."

So how were the thieves getting in and out? Greece? No, too many thieves. Same thing went for Croatia and the Barbary Coast. They'd be combing those already . . . Hell, if the entire Mediterranean coast wasn't crawling with IAA agents, I'd be shocked. Same thing went for flights anywhere across the Mediterranean, Middle East, and Europe.

I took another sip and stared at the map on my screen as if that might illuminate the answer . . .

I don't know if it was the alcohol or the fact that I was toeing the blurry line between sober and drunk, but it struck me how the thieves had been avoiding the IAA where I'd just about been snagged.

"What if they aren't using any of the routes we've come up with?" I said.

Both Rynn and Nadya stared at me as if I sounded as drunk as I probably was.

I grabbed Nadya's notebook, tore a clean sheet out, and started to draw a haphazard map of the Mediterranean, Syria, and Turkey.

"We've been assuming all along they're using the Mediterranean or the Black Sea to get in and out."

"It's the only logical way. The IAA would be watching the land borders and airports too closely, you said so yourself."

"But that's just it. The IAA is so thick along those coasts that I don't think we can get back in that way again. We keep figuring these guys are geniuses—what if they're not? I mean, the fact that they even risked the city tells me they're idiots—idiots with a golden goose shoved up their asses, but still."

Nadya tsked. "Golden egg, the goose does not fit," she corrected me.

"Assuming they're not using those two ports of entry then," Rynn said.

I pointed to the East African coast that bordered the Red Sea and traced my finger down to the sharp point where it drained into the Indian Ocean. "I think they're dumber than we thought. I think they're using the one place the IAA won't dare go."

"The Somali coast," Rynn said.

I nodded.

Nadya weighed the pros and cons over in her head. "But that would be . . ."

"Suicide?" I filled in. Maybe it was a good thing I was halfway drunk—I don't think the third idiotic way in and out would have crossed my mind otherwise. "Eventually, sure, but these guys have already managed to sneak into the city twice without getting themselves cursed or otherwise killed. Maybe their luck just hasn't caught up with them yet," I said. Nadya looked like she was working on an argument, so I added, "It is the only place the IAA won't go."

Fun fact about the largest antiquities society in the known world: they might not be scared of curses, supernaturals, and thieves, but throw pirates in the mix? Historically they haven't fared well, not since Roman times.

"All right," Nadya said. "That still doesn't help us get into the dig and find the tomb."

"I thought that was your specialty," Rynn said.

Nadya and I exchanged a look. Where to start? "All right, working backwards—and this is all assuming we can even find the tomb where these things were originally hidden—there are a whole wonder of things we have to worry about."

"Such as?"

I started the count off. "Ancient booby traps, for one. Without a reliable map, we'll have to find all of them manually."

Nadya jumped in. "And those are just the physical ones—trapdoors, weapons, pits. Who knows about the supernatural versions? Magic, more curses—"

"Not to mention the inadvertent traps. You know how much goblins and trolls like these kinds of mountains."

Nadya nodded. "But before we're even inside, we need to get past the IAA."

"Usually that'd be the easier part. Nadya and I would just sneak in."

Nadya snorted. "I do not play games with the IAA; you would sneak in, I would stay as far away as possible."

I rolled my eyes. "Regardless, hiding in plain sight is out."

"How many people guard the dig site at night?" Rynn asked.

"Depends. I can't see them using more than a skeleton crew in the middle of the mountains, even for a site that dangerous."

Nadya nodded. "In this terrain, a large team of guards would attract more unwanted attention than it would turn away." She gave me a pointed look. "They might be keeping the archaeologists working through the night however."

I'd been worried about that. Because of the time frame . . . and well, now that Nadya's Russian contacts were well and thoroughly breathing down their necks, they'd want to finish as soon as possible.

"OK, so, let's say a handful of guards and a night crew of archaeologists—probably half with a shift change."

Rynn nodded. "Let me worry about getting them out of the way; you two worry about getting in and out again."

"That still leaves of course the small matter of getting into the mountains without people shooting at us." It was Murphy's Law that most of the places in the world with the really cool dig sites were in the middle of civil wars. In that case, both sides figured they had something to gain by shooting the foreigners—either because they didn't like you, or because they could pin it on the other side . . .

"What about entering as medical? Doctors Without Borders or Red Cross?"

Both Nadya and I shook our heads.

"We've tried that—better on paper than in practice. For some reason, everyone still shoots the doctors. Nadya was right on that point—livestock is way better."

"No one ever shoots livestock—too valuable. Stomachs over curing bacterial infections any day," Nadya concurred.

Rynn closed his eyes. "I'm going to ignore how much sense that just made. Well, I've still got a few favors owed and a contact on that side of the continent who will be interested in what's occurring in the city. I'll come up with something that hopefully doesn't involve being shot at or hiding under the feet of ruminants." He shook his head.

"There's one more thing that none of us has touched on," I said. "Any resident or interfering supernaturals." I looked hopefully at Rynn.

He shook his head. "My contact can help us get in, but I'm afraid his knowledge of the city is as limited as mine. And there is no guarantee Daphne and Alexander won't make a claim."

I also wasn't comfortable with how little I knew about Alexander and Daphne's interest in the pieces. "I have an idea how to keep those two occupied for the next few days and out of my hair," I said, and fished the note Alexander had left me, cringing as I touched it. Before Rynn could stop me, I dialed.

A tentative female voice answered the phone. "Hello?"

Bindi. "Does Alexander still have you answering the phones?"

"You? How dare you disturb—"

"Oh knock it off, princess. Look, I don't want to talk to your boss, I just want you to give him a message for me."

She swore, but I was pretty sure I heard the crinkling of paper. "What?"

"Tell your asshole boss Daphne Sylph is buying more pieces. They should be arriving any day." Before Bindi could slide in any questions, I hung up.

"Call up Artemis for me," I said.

When Rynn opened his mouth to argue, I added, "Trust me."

He pulled out his own phone and dialed. I put it on speakerphone.

"Hello?" came a woman's light voice on the third ring. There was a slight laugh to her voice. I thought I recognized it. "Violet?" I asked.

"Speaking," she said, laughing again.

"Violet, put Artemis on—tell him it's Charity." While I waited a few moments, I heard muffled voices in the background.

"It isn't enough to ruin my weekend—what the hell do you want now?" came Artemis's voice.

"Wow, what is this? Violet's second, third night in a row? Not your style, Artemis."

"Styles change," he said, not even slightly perturbed.

"Is she drunk?"

"Secret to tolerating anyone past a few days is to get them good and drunk—besides, she's not nearly as interesting as you. And you still haven't told me what the hell you're bothering me for."

"Real simple. Deliver a message to Daphne for me. You two are still on speaking terms, right?"

"Marginally. What is it?"

"Tell her the vampire Alexander, den on the Sunset Strip, has the City of the Dead artifacts and is planning on intercepting more coming into the city," I said.

There was a pause on the other end. "I thought I made it perfectly clear to my cousin we were all squared up."

Rynn opened his mouth, but I held my finger to my lips. "Yup, you are, Artemis—but this is a message you want to deliver."

"And why, pray tell, would that be?"

"Well, for one, it'll put you back in her good books. But two, and this is the real kicker, so you can see the look on her face when you tell her the real Owl sent it."

With that, I hung up the phone. Rynn glared at me and shook his head. "It'll never work. They'll figure it out."

"You'd be surprised. Neither of them will be able to resist checking it out, and as soon as one of them throws the first punch?" I shrugged. "They'll figure it out eventually, but hopefully not until the curse is lifted and the other thieves are shut down."

And the dig site closed ... there was that small matter ... I still wasn't sure whether the IAA could be trusted to do it themselves anymore.

Now here came the fun part. I drained my beer-and-tequila numbing goodness number four. "While we're still on the topic of stupid plans, how do you two propose we sneak past the pirates and into Syria?"

—✺—

Do you ever feel like you're having the same conversation over and over again without getting anywhere new?

Smart person would say it was time to change the conversation. Or that was my plan when I closed my hotel room door.

Nadya was smart. She'd stayed downstairs ... OK, well, not smart, since this was her Hail Mary to get Rynn's bartender ...

God, I hope she and Rynn hadn't bet money on it.

I frowned when I saw Captain sitting on the kitchen table. *Not* howling for food ... I picked out the green plastic shrapnel scattered across the carpet. It was his toy—something the vet had convinced me to buy, a ball that doled out treats in reward for exercise.

"You destroyed the toy and ate all the treats?" I said.

He mewed.

Figured. "I can't leave you anywhere."

I dumped my laptop on the kitchen table, ignoring Captain's run for the kitchen. Yeah, not going to happen.

"What's up with him?" Rynn asked when Captain darted around his feet as he entered. He glanced between the toy and Captain. "It is impressive the cat was able to get it in that many pieces."

"Yeah, don't give him ideas."

All right—important conversations ...

"It's not so much the important aspect, Alix, it's altering the conversation we've been having," Rynn said, kneeling in the kitchen, where he was now petting the damn cat.

Damn it. Sometimes, especially when I'm nervous, Rynn picks up on my emotions and figures out what I'm going to say before I do. I hate it when he does that.

"You don't hate it. You figure I won't give you credit for it," he added.

I leaned against the kitchen table and forced my brain to reorganize. Think Zen thoughts—alcohol-fueled Zen thoughts . . .

"You know I pick up even more when you've been drinking?"

One bonus to dating an incubus was that I never lied about what I was feeling.

That streak didn't go both ways though.

"You know, it wasn't until this afternoon I figured out what was really bothering you about Los Angeles," I said.

Rynn came over until he was close—touching distance but not quite touching. Again, he knew my personal quirks; I don't like having important conversations when I'm touching him. Obvious reasons, the whole incubi thing puts me at a hell of a disadvantage. I took a deep breath and focused on his face. Still the same as when I'd met him at Gaijin Cloud in Japan almost two years ago, except wearing a less amicable expression than he used to . . . then again, maybe not. I'm pretty sure I had heavy champagne glasses on a few times . . .

I don't know why it occurred to me now, not before, but I wondered if Rynn even did age. Mortality and imminent death do crazy things.

"Alix, you can't break up with me when you're drunk and upset. It doesn't go well."

"OK, I did that—once—and I said I wouldn't do it again, so I'm not."

Rynn watched me, still wary. "You were thinking about it."

"OK, I do not act on every impulse that filters through my brain—and that was before I realized that you weren't mad about the curse, you were upset about something else," I said.

I watched his face as he went on the defensive. Me talking about his emotions was, well . . . let's face it, I don't read anyone's emotions well.

"Alix—" he started, but I kept going. It was my turn to show some semblance of maturity in this relationship.

"It took me a while to figure out—till this evening actually—that you weren't angry at me. You were pissed off at yourself." My God, for someone as halfway to stumbling drunk as I was, my brain was fantastically lucid—a side benefit of tequila? One can hope.

OK, here goes. Honest conversation . . . "Why didn't you tell me how many supernaturals were involved in this? From the start?" I asked, careful to keep my voice neutral.

"Alix—"

And there was the wariness I'd picked up in his voice before and mistaken for anger. Funny how sometimes perception is everything.

"Don't tell me you didn't know, it's why you've been touchy since Mr. Kurosawa and Lady Siyu accused me of stealing the artifacts."

"My hands were tied. If it got back to anyone that you knew and I'd told you—"

I'd heard this part before, so I didn't wait for him to finish. The one thing I'd learned about supernaturals in the last few months was that you sure as hell had to read between the lines.

"There is no actual rule about telling humans about the supernatural, is there? Not in any official capacity, anyway."

Sometimes silence is a more powerful affirmation than words.

When I'd finally figured it out—through Artemis, no less—I'd felt betrayed, hurt, just sick to my stomach more than anything. I don't like being lied to. It's kind of a sore point with me.

But then I'd realized I'd created part of the problem—not on purpose, but inadvertently. I breathed and forced my temper to step back from the precarious ledge it was threatening to leap off of.

"You still think I hate supernaturals?" I said.

Rynn gave me a measured stare.

"All right, most supernaturals. I'll give you that. Though I'd argue it's a little more case specific than across the board."

Rynn shook his head. "The more you know about our world, the more you'll be held responsible by others who are less than kind." He reached out to touch my face. "You chose not to participate. Vehemently, as I recall."

I closed my eyes. "Which means anything to do with the supernatural becomes your responsibility."

Like I said, it'd taken me a while to read between those lines. Rynn had taken it upon himself to act as filter between me and all the supernatural . . . well . . . bullshit. The problem was we both still had to deal with it. I'd been doing so since the day I'd pissed off a pack of vampires. Pretending none of it existed just turned me into a pawn. Just like I'd been in archaeology. I'm starting to see the wisdom of the statement "History repeats itself."

Sticking my head in the sand doesn't make the monsters go away. It just means I get blindsided and Rynn has to run interference. *All right, Alix, let's see if we can curb that trend, shall we?*

"I'm not saying I want, need, or am ready to know everything, but the way we're going now is making both you and me miserable." Different reasons, mind you—me because it had likely gotten me killed, and Rynn because he was getting sick of holding all the responsibility for the entire supernatural world's response every time I gave it a good kick in the balls—which I had a habit of doing.

"What sucks the most about this is it's taken me three months to wrap my head around it. Why the hell didn't you say something?"

"I told you I was selfish," he said. "I thought if you knew how entrenched in this world you'd become—"

"I'd leave." If Rynn had a relationship fear, that was it.

"Well, actually, you've left on a number of occasions—"

"OK, enough about the on-off thing—" I took another breath though and changed the subject back to the issue at hand. "The less I knew, the less I could be held accountable for."

He nodded again and watched me, his eyes a solid gray.

I knew I'd been spending too much time with supernaturals; the logic made sense.

"I knew you'd figure it out eventually, I just never thought—"

"Never thought I'd end up cursed?" Yeah, neither had I. "Hindsight really is twenty-twenty," I said. My emotions were already coming up to the forefront, a place I was not comfortable having them. I tried to break away. Rynn wouldn't let me.

"You avoid these conversations like the plague—no, I'm not criticizing you, that's the way you are." Rynn stepped in close enough so I could feel his breath on my face. I wondered sometimes if I could feel the whole energy thing, but my imagination plays tricks on me at the best of times. Rynn touched his forehead to mine. "Why are you bringing this up tonight?"

I cared about him. I didn't want him to leave. I wasn't ready for that yet, for all my complaining and arguing. I've had enough people try and succeed at using me, so I could make a few accommodations to one of two people who were on my side. The supernatural thing? Well, that had fallen to the wayside three months ago.

Come to think of it, I'm amazed how much I've grown over the past few months. I'm becoming an interesting person. Not well adjusted, but someone who occasionally sees through the messes they create.

Be damned if I was smart enough to say any of that. My decision-making skills rival that of a sea slug . . . the sea slug might win, since it usually runs from danger, or at least has the whole poisoning capability . . .

I managed to look Rynn in the eyes. "Because it's important. For all I know, the first symptoms of the curse could start tomorrow, and trying to have any serious conversation then? Well, it'd fall into my bad idea category."

"What's the first sign?" he asked. When I didn't say anything, he kissed me—the kind that's designed to show the other person that the giver doesn't care what's actually at stake.

I bit my lip and pushed him away. "Fever and hallucinations, Rynn." If you were looking for the match that lit my tequila/Corona streak, that was it.

I sat down at the computer so I had an excuse not to look at Rynn.

"Alix?" he tried.

I frowned at the reflection in the computer screen. Captain had elevated his mooching to the next level and was standing on the counter, dragging the cat food bag out of the cupboard.

Not important, don't turn around, let him do it. The next owner—Rynn or Nadya—would probably do a better job regulating his food. Let's face it, I'm a pushover.

"Alix?" Rynn said again.

"What?" *Please don't make me turn around, not right now . . .* I figured if I thought it loud enough in my head, Rynn was bound to pick something up. See? Not only have I accepted the whole supernatural boyfriend thing, I've found a use for it.

He didn't turn me around, but he did come up behind me and lean his chin on my shoulder. "You aren't going to die. Nadya isn't going to let you die. She'll have no one to drink with except older Japanese men and attractive young hosts. Besides, I think you owe her money."

That I snorted at.

"I'm not going to let you die either," he added. That was all he said, and I had to admit I was thankful. Some things I was ready for—other things, well, not so much. It's still me, after all.

"Are you coming to bed?" he asked.

I shook my head, still not willing to look at him. "I just have a couple things I need to do on my end."

Rynn retreated into the bedroom, closing the door behind him. I still didn't look away from the screen. If I didn't turn around, I could still treat this like a game. And right now that was exactly what I had to do.

The World Quest login screen flickered into existence. I logged the Byzantine Thief in and pinged Carpe—in rapid succession, to get my point across.

While I waited, I pulled Hermes's card out of my pocket. The message on the back had changed. *Better, but still the long shot.* I shoved the card back in my pocket. Either the hallucinations were kicking in, or I was on the right track.

My computer chimed. *OK, Owl, nut up, and get your damned map to the City of the Dead.* Like hell I was dragging Nadya and Rynn into this blind—not if I could help it.

I still don't have anything new. As soon as I do— Carpe wrote.

Besides, I had something to barter.

Carpe, you still want me to get you that spell book? I wrote.

A few moments later, my headset chimed as Carpe turned on sound. "Is that a trick question?" he asked, his voice loaded with suspicion.

"No trick. But you're going to have to do something for me—and it's big, so listen real damn close."

"Name it," he said.

"Make World Quest your bitch."

13

I Hate This Arcade Shit

Time: Ahh, 2:00, 3:00 a.m.? Where did I put that spare Corona?

"Byzantine?" Carpe said over my headset as I rifled through my fridge. In lieu of beer, I went with soda, though all things considering, I needed a beer.

"What?" My God, if that turret re-spawned one more time ... There were no gun turrets in ancient Byzantine. First moving architecture, now historically inaccurate spontaneous additions. The game designers had hit a new low.

"I've got the turret figured out I think," Carpe said. "They looped the program in, assholes."

I sighed and rolled the can of soda over my forehead. Yeah, well the programmers were pretty pissed at us right now.

If I have a religion, it's World Quest, a perfectly accurate depiction of archaeological sites around the world, flying in the face of every last tenet of the IAA.

Real shame we had to break it.

But, like I kept telling myself, this was an emergency, and not just mine. If artifacts were left to flow unchecked out of the city, it was only a matter of time before the body count started.

Meaning I needed that fucking map yesterday.

Cold soda still pressed against my forehead, I sat back down and did my best not to think about the fever burning inside me. It wasn't a malfunctioning air conditioner; I'd checked that when I'd first noticed the heat. It was the start of the curse. *Manage it, Owl, pretend it isn't there. That's the best way to deal.* "Well, you know, Carpe, we did hack their system." Three hours ago. Initially Carpe figured it'd be a quick run in the park—he got rid of the bad guys, opened up the level, and locked the developers out. We should have hit the temple, retrieved the map, and escaped in half an hour.

The developers were better programmers than Carpe had assumed. It had cost us. Three hours, to be exact. Hence, me sitting in front of my laptop holding a can of cold soda against my forehead.

"No more bad guys?" The turrets had been a stroke of brilliance on the developers' part in response to Carpe's bunnies. From what I understood, Carpe had introduced a viral piece of code—my definition, not his—that turned all bad guys into bunnies. The game designers still hadn't figured out how to remove it; the worst we'd faced had been a storm of bunnies—more annoying than anything else.

With the turret gone, I made Byzantine crawl up the escarpment. Another surprise—the developers had figured out how to collapse the tunnel after we'd dispatched the goblin horde . . . by turning them into bunnies.

"Oh shit—" I dodged Byzantine out of the way as another carpet buzzed me. The developers hadn't figured out how to re-spawn monsters, but, between the turrets and the damn flying carpets, they had figured out how to make the game architecture lethal. I held the cold soda up to my forehead again. At least the carpets were marginally in keeping with the time period.

The designers were being unreasonable. Dying of magic curse or pissing them off. Hard choice, but I'd rather not be dead.

Besides, World Quest was about the only entity in the archaeology periphery I hadn't pissed off yet. They'd been due.

"Byzantine, I think they might be through your computer's firewall," Carpe said.

"I thought they were after you. You know, after you dropped that worm in their server and took World Quest offline?" We actually hadn't had a choice on that one. The developers had put a bounty on our heads after the first twenty minutes. It was the only way to lock out other players. Well, that or just kill everyone's characters, but that'd take too long and probably ruin a lot of people's nights, so, server it was.

"Weakest link. No offense, but your firewalls aren't . . . well . . . mine."

I focused back on the wall Byzantine was scaling. "I don't care how, just fix it—I'm almost in the city." That map was mere minutes away.

The World Quest version of the city predated the Christian Church and was all ancient stone walls and ominous caves and towers. Heavily guarded by the Byzantine army until Carpe turned them into—you guessed it—bunnies.

I swore again as the carpet wound back around. I rolled the Byzantine Thief over the ledge and onto the first of seven stone pillars, old and crumbling during the Byzantine Empire.

Byzantine dove and rolled as the carpet dive-bombed in, raining large, cannonball-shaped stones over the temple ruins. All this trouble just because the developers had been monitoring the entire Lebanon mountain range. I mean seriously, Carpe and I were two players . . .

"Lousy damn luck," I said as another bead of sweat rolled down my lip and I chased it away with the back of my hand. When I got a couple free seconds, I'd crank the air conditioner again. In the meantime, I took another swig of cold soda. Should have gotten ice . . .

Hello, there, now what might you be? I peered at the game screen, where Byzantine had landed at the base of a ruined pillar. One of the tiles was cracked, and I could just make out a pixelated black patch underneath instead of the uniform gray of the rocks. Like there was a hollow space beneath.

"Carpe, get up here. I think I found us an entrance, but I'll need you to lift this tile magically."

"All right, wait five. Stand lookout for carpets while I get these guys off your laptop's tail."

I started to comb the area for sticks and anything else I might use to get the tile opened—or break it. My eyes blurred over, just for a second—goddamn it.

Figuring I had a breather while the developers fought a losing battle with Carpe in hacking lore, I got up and went over to the control panel, where I cranked the air conditioner from medium to high.

"Byzantine! Check your character!"

I raced back to my screen. The nearest pillar teetered precariously from side to side.

I danced Byzantine out of the way before it toppled over, but not fast enough. A piece of rubble smacked into my back, downing my hit points to less than half. Before I could reclaim my footing and down a healing potion, the next nearest pillar started to tilt. "Goddamn it—" I dodged out of its way and looked for a spot where I could safely down the second-to-last potion in my inventory. "Carpe, hurry up and get up here. I'm down to one potion."

"You have like what? Two resurrection scrolls?"

"That's not the point." Though out of reflex I opened up my current inventory to see if I had both of them with me; I had a habit of leaving one hidden so gamers couldn't loot one off my corpse while I was using the first. The things you have to worry about in PVP areas.

"No. That's not possible," I said as I searched my inventory. The scrolls weren't there, either of them. Oh that was dirty.

"What?"

"My scrolls are gone. Those bastards got into my inventory—"

"What? Shit—mine are gone too."

I frowned. "I thought you used your last one three months ago." Carpe had gotten himself killed during a really stupid engagement with an ancient Aztec god.

"Surprise?" he tried. "Now neither of us has a way to regenerate if they manage to kill us."

"Well, can we hack their character sheets and kill them off?"

"OK, that's overreacting. Oh damn. You're not going to like this."

"Out with it."

"They figured a way around my 'Bunnies of Evil' worm."

"Carpe, we really have to work on your names—shit."

Where before there'd been a pair of white bunnies, now stood two black knights, breathing smoke and holding giant axes. The kind I've avoided entire games series to never meet.

"Whoa, what are those?" Carpe asked.

"Don't know and not about to get the monster sheets to find out," I said as Byzantine rolled between twin blades as they crashed into the stones tiles in tandem, clipping my back and dropping my health bar back down to next to nothing.

"Byzantine, you still alive?" Carpe said.

"Depends on your definition," I said, eyeing my health bar.

The two knights recovered their swords faster than game physics should have allowed and came at me again. All I could do was bolt out of the way before the swords swung back down in their deadly arcs.

"Do not come up here—I repeat, whatever you do, do not come up here." Hell, I didn't want to be up here anymore. Oh no—wait.

The knights might be defying game physics, but the stone tiles in the ancient temple weren't. Where the knights' swords had swung, nearly dealing a lethal blow to me, the stone tiles had crumbled under impact.

That's what you get hacking a game on the fly.

"Carpe—hang tight, I've got an idea."

I wiped another bead of sweat off my face.

Using Hide in Plain Sight, I maneuvered Byzantine to the edge of the temple. Now, time to test the NPC intelligence level on these suckers. Two was one too many swinging swords for what I needed, so . . .

I slid my avatar out of plain sight and, hovering the cursor over the Gesture button, hit Enter in rapid succession.

Byzantine began waving and jumping at the giant knights.

Both raised their swords and started towards me. I danced to the side and checked their foot movements. There was no deviation from their slow walk towards me. I smiled. Generic AI. I waited until the last minute, when the lead knight raised the sword over my head.

I vaulted over the ledge and caught a hook partway down.

The knight did exactly what I expected a generic game AI to do: it stepped over the edge after me.

One knight down, one left to use. I edged away from the second sword as it crashed against the cliff edge. I then vaulted my avatar up a few feet away. "Get ready, Carpe, I'm going to need a portal to nowhere real soon."

I dodged Byzantine around the knight's feet, over to the pillar and the cracked stone tile.

The knight, like a good AI, wandered over. There was a burst of white beside my character, and Carpe solidified beside me.

"All right, when do you want this portal?" he asked.

"See the giant knight?"

"Hard to miss, since he doesn't belong in the damn game."

"All right, as soon as he drops the sword. Don't worry, I'm pretty sure there's a passage underneath." The game designers might be able to hide architecture, but they couldn't redesign it on the fly while Carpe had their server tied up.

"Do you have any idea how stupid a plan that is?"

"They want us dead. At this point, poor tactical choices are a moot point."

The sword rose over the knight's head, and he bellowed out smoke.

"You're too far to the right," Carpe yelled into my headset.

"No I'm not—"

"Yes you are—"

"No I'm—damn it." I slid to the right, but not soon enough. The knight's sword sliced my avatar's arm on the way down.

"Told you so."

And to boot, the knight had missed the tile.

"Carpe, portal now!" I said as the knight bolted after me.

"I can't, not with you two moving. I've got another idea. Stand back."

I knew that tone of voice. I tossed on my dragon eye goggles and checked Carpe's casting effect range. I was well within it. Normally not a problem, but I wasn't willing to bet the party immunity factor would be on—especially if the designers knew how we played. We're more of a drop-a-few-fireballs-and-see-what-hasn't-melted kind of team. Gold and gemstones are good for that.

"What are you casting?"

"Fireball. Figure it'll trash the knight and the stone."

Shit. I sat up. "Yeah—hold off, I'm in range."

"Ahh—kind of a no on that one. Spell's halfway cast. I'd have to scratch a fifth level off my list."

"Dude, saving a fucking spell slot is not going to help you if you kill me!"

"A fifth-level Fireball spell isn't going to kill you. Drain by half maybe—oh."

"No shit. Check your fucking teammate's health bar first next time."

"Look, maybe I can re-spawn you, or you could try to down a potion fast," Carpe offered.

"Never mind, I'll save myself."

Come on, Byzantine, don't fail me now . . . I stumbled out of the spell's effect range just ahead of the blast, but my health bar flashed red anyways. "No—that's not good, get out of the red." I madly equipped my last health potion and waited for the smoke on the screen to clear.

There was a crater-sized hole in the middle of the temple ruins. The knight was nowhere to be seen.

I breathed a sigh of relief and leaned back in my chair. Man oh man that was close. I took the pause in action to grab soda number two and filled a large glass with ice.

"Well, it worked," Carpe said.

Yeah, well . . . less fireball would have been nice. No point telling Carpe that though. Past "you're not dead" and "it worked," I didn't think it'd get me anywhere. "Bottoms up," I said, and hopped into the now exposed tunnel before Carpe could argue.

The tunnel beneath us had been lined with carved brick to keep the earth at bay. There were two ends; one that led further into the mountain, and one that led back in the direction we'd come from.

Right, into the mountain we go. I pulled out a torch and lit it. At least the game designers hadn't completely raided our equipment.

We maybe had five minutes of solitude before Carpe's voice chimed up.

"Ummm, were those there before?"

I heard the gleeful squeal right before the first scrape. I turned towards Carpe and caught the first glimpse of rusted metal in the shadows. It was covered in a half-assed poison charm. Great, goblins.

"Just what we needed right now. Goblin horde at three o'clock." Raided you for gold after they killed you and used your entrails as finger paint. There was an entire out-of-game wall dedicated to goblin art. If you had a good eye, you could tell which styles came from which tribe.

"I think we should turn back," Carpe said.

I glanced back down at the map in the right-hand corner of my screen, which revealed more of itself as we progressed through the temple. A quarter of the map left, all forward. Just a few minutes more.

"Any chance you've got another portal on you?" I said.

"What? No. Fuck off."

"I need to know what's in the center of this ruin so I can figure out where the artifacts are coming from."

"The deal was map for book, not kill my character off—hey!"

The tunnel shook.

"I do not like that. They're up to something," Carpe said.

I brushed away more sweat. "We're almost inside; what's the worst that can happen? They've already banned us."

The screen shook again, this time loosening a few rocks. A crack formed in the sealed stone door blocking the way. For a second my hopes rose—until I realized the giant stone door was poised not to crack or open but fall forward—on us.

"Carpe! Door—"

"All right, you two." The voice over my headset was medium-tone male, soft American accent, Midwest—Michigan, maybe. "We've just about had it."

One of the game designers.

"Hey asshole, you had your chance—this is a private chat line," I said.

"You hacked our server," a second, deeper male voice said, with a thicker accent. Texas maybe.

"It's an emergency—" I started.

"Bullshit," said Texas.

"We mean business. Get the hell out of our game," chimed the more-educated-sounding Michigan.

"Like I said last time, I can't do that." Not only was I hot but now my head was pounding too.

"I don't fucking believe this," Texan said.

"Look, if you don't believe me, ask Carpe Diem. It's a matter of life and death that I get into that tomb, so will you two whiny programmers get the fuck out of my way?" I thought about adding that I meant that in the most respectable way possible—they had built World Quest after all—but figured I missed the boat to ingratiate myself already.

"Stealing stuff from the Syrian City of the Dead isn't a matter of life and death," said Michigan.

Goddamn it. "Look, I got cursed accidently—as in not my fault. And it's another thief breaking into the temple, not me."

"She's lying through her teeth," said Texas. "Smoke her."

"Now see, that's the kind of response that gets your game hacked!"

Carpe groaned.

"Last chance, Byzantine Thief. Get the fuck off our server," said Michigan.

I don't do well with ultimatums. "No, this is *your* last chance. Give me the fucking map of the city so I can get this fucking curse lifted, you miserly assho—"

There was an electric hiss as the programmers' com spike went dead.

"Shit, Byzantine, something is up," Carpe said. Sure enough, the screen shook and flickered with gray lines.

So close, just beyond that door—maybe another fireball blast would do the trick . . .

The screen flickered again.

"Byzantine, if we both die, I don't know how long it's going to take me to resurrect our characters . . . as it stands, I can still hack our way back in."

So close . . . "I thought you were the best hacker in the world."

"One of the best! I'm not lord of the internet!"

That decided it for me. "All right, teleport us out of here," I said.

Light flickered around our characters as Carpe casted his spell. Then everything went dead.

And I mean everything; my laptop, the lights, the fridge, the air conditioner—

"Carpe?"

No answer. I took off my headset. Captain, figuring something was up, came out of the bedroom, followed closely by Rynn.

The bastards had figured out a way to cut the power to the casino. There was something wrong about the darkness though—it was too dark.

Horns and sirens drifted up from the strip below.

They wouldn't have . . . I swore and checked outside the window. The buildings, streetlights—except for headlights, all of Vegas was dark.

"Oh that's overkill—"

"Alix, why do I get the funny feeling you have something to do with the power?" Rynn said, coming up beside me.

I turned away from the window and stumbled into him as my headache flared; he'd been standing closer than I'd realized.

"Ah, yeah—long story about that. It was the World Quest developers—"

Rynn peered down at me, his brow furrowed.

"OK, it was my fault, but it was an emergency."

Rynn touched my forehead with the back of his hand. "You need to get in the shower now."

"No, I need to get back up on World Quest," I told him. Maybe Carpe could hack us back in . . . I ducked out of the way but tripped over my own feet. Rynn caught me, his expression of worry deepening.

"Stop it, you're burning up."

I stopped. In fact, I got a good look at myself in the mirror, all sweat-soaked, five feet four inches of me. Who was I kidding? I wasn't going to be any more use tonight in World Quest.

I let Rynn lead me to the shower. Alix Hiboux, welcome to your curse.

14

To Catch a Thief. No, Not Me. The Real Thief.

Noon, somewhere over the Eastern Sahara

Ever flown over a desert?

I figure the closest comparison is flying over the Arctic on a cloudless day. Except for the color, snow dunes look an awful lot like sand dunes.

I turned away from the port window and tried to get comfortable in the ... well ... not seat. Let's go with pile of bags and blankets and leave it on a positive note. This was a significant change from the modes of transportation I'd gotten used to as of late—luxury cruises, private jets ...

Cargo plane.

The cargo plane itself didn't bug me. It was a relief to be somewhere I felt safe.

It was the damn chickens. The rooster especially kept crowing and pulling me out of my hard-won sleep, which I was trying to catch up on. After the power on the Vegas Strip was leveled, we bumped up our departure time. No one blamed me outright. They were just happy to have me gone.

Oh yeah, and there was the small issue of my curse. After Rynn had corralled me into taking a long, cold shower to lower my body temperature, he'd gotten out the heavy-duty Tylenol. The fever had gotten under control—mostly—as had the headaches. I hadn't had any hallucinations. Maybe I'd get lucky and it'd stay that way.

Yeah, I don't think I'm that lucky either.

No sooner did I start to doze off than the right engine coughed and the rooster voiced his displeasure.

Captain's claws dug into my shoulder as he growled. I'd newly discovered Captain's tolerance for livestock. The hens he was fine with—it was the damn rooster. "Why does it have to be chickens?" I said.

"You said livestock," Rynn said, not bothering to open his eyes to look up. After the flight from Las Vegas to South Africa, we all needed to catch up on sleep.

I needed to be more specific next time . . .

I settled back in and did my best to ignore the yellow dinghy hanging from the inside of the cargo deck. Yellow rafts and cargo planes . . . well, you've seen the movie. That whole ride-the-dinghy-out-of-a-crashing-plane? Doesn't work, though that never stops people from trying . . .

Captain started to creep down my shoulder, towards the crates. Again.

I grabbed his tail and towed him back across Rynn's assortment of canvas bags. As I turned, my elbow bit into a gun. Oh yeah. I'd forgotten about that.

"When I said we needed to go in as someone the locals wouldn't shoot at . . ." I held up the rifle fitted with a scope; God, I hoped it wasn't real—or loaded. ". . . I'm pretty sure 'mercenary' wasn't what I meant."

Rynn glanced up. Unlike me, dressed in cargo pants and a Kevlar jacket, Nadya and Rynn actually looked like mercenaries. I'd forgotten just how easily Rynn slid in and out of his mercenary persona—and how different he looked. Until he'd gotten tired of shooting at people, he'd been an enforcer of sorts for supernaturals. He was always careful to keep his host image at the forefront, and most days you'd never suspect his secret history. Maybe that was what made him good at it. Hide in "plane" sight, as I always say . . .

However, seeing mercenary Rynn wasn't nearly as frightening as seeing how well Nadya fit the part. Hell, not only did she look like a mercenary but she also managed to make the whole thing look fashionable.

Me, on the other hand . . .

"Just pretend it is costume night at the Space Station Deluxe," Nadya said, referring to the upscale hostess bar she ran in Tokyo. "And try to look like you know what you're doing."

Easier said than done. Not exactly a five-foot-nine glamazon who looked just as good in Kevlar as she did in a miniskirt.

"Just relax and please, for the love of God, let me do the talking," Rynn said before settling back into the seat and pulling his hood down.

I tried to settle back in, but my paranoia about curse symptoms resurfaced. If all the notes on the previous victims were right, the hallucinations were next. Maybe paranoia was a hallucination . . . hell, the first symptoms were poorly documented, since the dig members hadn't known they'd been cursed to begin with.

"I think you've orchestrated a disaster," I said to Rynn.

"Right back at you."

"Whore."

"Train wreck."

Not being able to sleep, I glanced out at the Sahara below, Captain's leash wrapped tight around my hand. Still a few hours left. I grabbed a thermos of coffee then pulled out my laptop; if I couldn't sleep, at least I could get my bearings on where we were. Maybe Carpe had gotten back into World Quest and found me the damn map. Provided our characters weren't toast.

I hooked up my satellite phone and opened our private chat line. *Hey—any news on World Quest?* I typed.

For once, Carpe's response wasn't instantaneous. *Can you give me, like, half an hour? I'm kind of busy.*

Ah, no? *Asshole, me dying is more important than whatever the hell you're doing.* Mostly he'd never find another player willing to let him skim off the top of our loot. *Have you patched back into the World Quest server yet?*

Not yet. Like I said, something else came up. Look—gimme a sec, I'm seriously in the middle of something.

Before I could argue back, Carpe logged out.

I snorted, took another sip of coffee, and glanced out the window at the sand dunes passing below. For fun I pulled up the map on my screen. We'd reached southern Egypt. Something about that bugged me, even though we were still headed in the right direction. I saw the green light flash in the bottom-left corner of my screen, telling me Carpe was back. I switched to audio.

"Hey, do I need to remind you we have a deal—no map, no book?" I said. Not least of which was because there was no chance I'd be alive at the end of the week if I didn't make it into the city . . . and let's face it, even with the map I could still end up dead. Lesser things had killed better archaeologists, not to mention there might not be a way to reverse the curse.

"Yeah, yeah—look, can we please have this conversation . . . shit." Then I heard the electric snap telling me he'd signed off.

Get back online, you slimy elf—Oh shit. The right engine coughed, and the plane bucked to the right. I swore again as my laptop and satellite phone slid to the floor.

Both Rynn and Nadya sat up.

"What the hell was that?" Rynn said.

"I don't know, but the engine doesn't sound happy," I said.

The plane banked again, and I heard the pilot swear loudly in the cockpit.

Wait a minute. I recognized that voice . . . Oh no. Please be a hallucination. "Rynn, who's flying the plane?"

Rynn glanced up at me, then at the door.

"We don't know who's flying the plane, do we?" I said.

Rynn shook his head as the engine—the left this time—coughed and sputtered smoke.

Shit.

I scrambled up, dumping Captain, who'd firmly dug his claws into my thigh. "Get the door open."

I reached it first and wrenched it open as the plane banked forward, spilling me into the cockpit.

Sitting in the pilot's seat, wearing an old cargo jacket, a baseball cap to cover his ears, and an oversized pair of aviators, was none other than Carpe. In the pilot's seat. Without a copilot.

"Carpe," I said, untangling myself from him and grabbing the collar of his jacket, "I really, *really* hope you're a hallucination—"

"Will you let go of me? I'm a very experienced pilot, thank you very much. I've clocked more hours in simulation than most pilots." He grabbed at my wrists and tried to dislodge them.

"A video game does *not* mean you can fly a plane," I said.

"I beg to differ," he said, insulted. "I got us this far, didn't I?"

"Fine, you can tell us why the left engine is smoking then," Rynn said, coming up behind me.

Carpe swallowed and glanced sideways at the instruments as they began to blink red and beep loudly. He glanced at the controls again and his laptop. "There are mitigating circumstances, namely I didn't account for all the sand," he started.

"What does that mean exactly?" I yelled as the engine sputtered again.

Carpe swallowed and lifted his dark brown eyebrows. "It means buckle up." I really would have liked to hit him. Fear of dying by ejection through the cockpit window won out though.

Apparently Rynn had the same thought process, because after exchanging a look, we both dove for the hatch back into the cargo section.

Nadya was standing in the cargo bay, dealing with an irate and bellowing Captain. "Why is my nose itching?" she yelled so as to be heard over the sputtering engines—both now streaming black smoke that registered as burned rubber in my nose.

"Because we're about to crash," I said.

"Because the damned elf is flying the plane," Rynn yelled, shoving me towards my seat.

Nadya swore, tossed an indignant Captain at me, and dove for our bags of computer equipment.

The plane banked again, and I had to jump to save my laptop from crashing into the hold wall.

"Rynn? Parachutes?" I said as he dove for the pile of canvas bags. "Shouldn't we be jumping out?"

"Not enough altitude—strap in." He grabbed two of the larger canvas bags and held them up, before deciding the heavier one on the left would be better served tied down. He checked the window and swore before grabbing the next piece of essential equipment.

Nadya went for the yellow rubber inflatable hanging from the wall. I grabbed her before she could pull it down, shaking my head. "Trust me, bad idea."

She abandoned the dinghy and tied more of our equipment to the steel rings in the floor before strapping herself in.

I grabbed Captain's leash. He took one look at the developing chaos and sought shelter in the carrier. Smart cat. I tied it to the empty seat beside me and buckled in for dear life.

Rynn strapped one last bag in before following suit. I hoped the most dangerous of the bags was bolted down.

The plane sputtered twice more before the nose dipped and my stomach leapt, the way it does on a roller coaster. I think I counted three, maybe four, seconds until we clipped the first sand dune.

Planes clipping sand dunes? Let me cross that off your bucket list for you; doesn't matter if you're strapped in, it still hurts like a son of a bitch.

My teeth and jaw were still hurting when another giant mountain of sand flickered by the window and the entire plane jolted and veered to the right. The plane came to a wrenching halt—the rending of metal assaulting our ears—as it collided into the next sand dune.

I figure I sat there for a couple of minutes. I wasn't dead, and from the groans nearby, neither were Nadya and Rynn. That struck me as dumb luck more than anything else.

The plane had lodged into a sand dune. Nadya and Rynn were both looking up at me, suspended above them. The window behind them only showed sand.

All my limbs were still working, so I first let Captain out of his carrier—he leapt down about as gracefully as you'd expect from a cat carrying an extra few pounds. I struggled to get the belt undone, then I dropped down.

"Oomph." I landed on my knees nowhere near as gracefully as Captain, but in one piece and with no broken bones. This was a plane crash, not ballet; I couldn't be bothered with making it look pretty.

Rynn and Nadya climbed out of their seats next. It took all three of us to pry the cargo door open.

Our plane was sticking out of the top of a dune. Only the left wing was still attached, more or less. The other wing was sticking out of the neighboring dune.

"Where are we?" Nadya said.

Good question. "Last thing my GPS told me, we were in southern Egypt, near the Sudanese border."

Nadya swore in Russian.

Rynn added, "Well, we're ready to deal with insurgents and freedom fighters—just not the ones we'd been planning on." He frowned and looked at me. "Are you sure about the location?"

I nodded and tossed him my satellite phone with the GPS. "See for yourself."

He studied it. "How the hell did we end up that far off course? The flight plan was supposed to skirt Egypt along the coast, not travel inland."

Carpe . . .

Now where the hell was he . . . shit.

The front section of the plane had not made friends with the sand; it was buried in the dune. Something kicked the pilot's door. Carpe yelled something, but it was muffled by the metal.

"I vote we leave him in there," Rynn said.

"I second," Nadya added.

I was halfway inclined to agree with both of them. As much as I wanted to pummel Carpe myself, leaving him locked up in that tin can for a while might do him some good.

More helpless pounding on the metal.

Damn it. "OK, as great as that sounds right now, none of us actually wants to be responsible for accidently letting Carpe die," I said.

Rynn glanced up at me. "Speak for yourself. I think it's a fantastic idea."

"Me too," added Nadya.

I sighed. All right, neither of them actually meant that . . . "OK, no. Not leaving the elf to die. Come on," I added, and started to climb up what was left of the cargo plane's door to get to the damn elf. It had to be the fever. I was not used to being the voice of reason. Rynn followed me up and grabbed hold of the other side of the door.

I banged it. "Hey, asshole who crashed the plane . . . get back."

"On three," Rynn said. "One, two—three." Both of us pulled, and the door gave way. Carpe pushed his head out.

I'd never met Carpe in person before. I'd only ever seen him once over the computer camera when I'd been pissed enough to drop his firewall, and I'd had no chance or intention of attempting that again.

Carpe looked much the same as I remembered: pointed ears, dark brown hair past his shoulders. Whereas Rynn's features were attractive in a youthful but still male way, Carpe struck me as more androgynous—like a grunge kid from the '90s on a nature kick. Kind of a hippy computer hacker . . . Oh forget it, Carpe didn't quite fit well into any box.

I'd be lying if I said he wasn't cute—taller than I'd expected from the photo.

He extended his hand out towards me. "Much appreciat—Damn it!"

Rynn grabbed him by the collar and tossed him out of the plane.

Carpe hit the sand—hard. Rynn hopped down after him.

"Carpe, isn't it?" Rynn said, closing in on him. "What the hell were you doing flying our plane?"

Carpe held up one arm in defense while he tried to scramble back, though since it was sand, he wasn't getting much traction. "Look, I can explain—"

"Fantastic. You've got two minutes to convince me not to shoot you."

Carpe's fear vanished as his face contorted in indignant anger. "Two minutes? You can't be serious—"

Rynn took his gun out and shot at the sand near Carpe's leg. Nadya, me, Carpe—all of us jumped, though Carpe jumped the highest.

"Jesus, you shot me!"

"I shot *at* you; in the same vicinity. If I have to do it again, chances are my aim will get worse." He then shrugged, reconsidering. "Or better."

Carpe glared at me, still indignant. "Seriously, Owl, do you see the violence here?" He turned his attention back to Rynn. "All you incubi do is hit things."

Rynn smiled. "If I thought for a second you actually knew what you just said, I might laugh," he said as he glanced down at his watch. "One minute thirty seconds left."

Carpe stared at me, pleading. "Owl, please."

I held up my hands. "Hey, I'm just the archaeologist. You want to steal our cargo plane, you get to talk to the mercenary incubus."

"OK, OK. Just point the gun somewhere else."

Rynn obliged, and Carpe pleaded to me once more. "All right, when I figured out you were going to the City of the Dead to try and get out of the curse you got yourself into—"

"You mean Alexander tricked me into."

Carpe waved his hand as if the details weren't particularly relevant. Not exactly ingratiating me to his cause . . .

"I got to thinking that it was going to be a long shot, even if we got the map from World Quest. No offense, but there's a very good chance you're going to die anyways—hey, it's the truth!" Carpe yelled as Rynn kicked sand at him. "On a side note, I was wondering how you'd get there. I ruled out North Africa and Europe—too much IAA, then it occurred to me you might be coming from the south. When I checked which flight you were on—"

"Whoa, wait, you cyber-stalked me to find out what flight I was taking?"

He shrugged. "Not really cyber-stalking. More like I walked by a house and the lights were on with the drapes—"

"You idiot, that's called peeping. It's just as bad—no, worse than cyber-stalking."

He seemed to consider that. "Well maybe people shouldn't leave their data that accessible—"

"Thirty seconds," Rynn said. "Now what the hell were you doing flying our plane?"

"Fine—Jesus, you have serious anger issues, you know that?" he said, but I noted he sped up. "When I realized which way you were going, I figured the tomb and my book were right along the way—"

I closed my eyes. My God, could Carpe be that much of a selfish asshole?

"Granted, we didn't land as close as I wanted, but a bit of a walk and we should be able to retrieve my book before nightfall." He glanced back at the plane. "I also didn't figure on crashing. It'll take some work to get you to the city—I feel bad about that. Oh, almost forgot." He rifled around in his jacket until he produced a folded sheet of paper and offered it to me. "See, I even have a map. I know how much you prefer raiding tombs with a map."

I stared at the piece of paper.

Rynn leaned in close enough to whisper, "Now, I'm not one who told you so—"

"Yes you are," I whispered back.

"But if you'd have listened to me about trusting elves in the first place, we wouldn't have ended up with this little demonstration."

I shook my head and held out my hand to Rynn. "Give me your gun," I said.

"Why?"

"So I can shoot the elf."

Carpe must have picked up on some of our exchange, because he frowned and decided it'd be a good idea to keep talking. "We'll have plenty of time to get to the city. I brought my laptop so we can deal with World Quest. As soon as you have my book."

"Have you ever been in a tomb?" I said to him, my jaw clenched.

"We're counting World Quest, right?"

"World Quest is about as close to a real tomb as the flight simulator is to a cargo plane," I said, waving my hand at the spectacular wreck behind us.

"In all fairness—"

"So let me get this straight, just so we're all on the same page and we remove all minutiae of misunderstanding. You figured since the agreement was the City of the Dead map for the Egyptian spell book, it'd be a better idea to derail any chance I have of lifting my curse to get your damn book first because in your estimation I'm going to die anyways? That's the reasoning we're using?"

Carpe frowned. "OK, in my defense the spell book is a life-and-death situation—and for more people than just you. Who cursed yourself. And I'm not that callous. I plan on staying to help with the city."

Rynn snorted.

That was it. I launched myself at Carpe, landing on his chest. "Why, you lousy, no-good excuse for a teammate—"

The Kevlar worked to my advantage; I was heavier than expected. Carpe gasped as I knocked the wind right out of him.

I didn't waste time. My fingers closed around Carpe's neck. "I am going to *die* because of your obsession with a book—a stupid *book,* you evil excuse for pixie—"

"It's just a detour! We're practically there already—we do them all the time in game. What am I supposed to do if you die?" he said, trying to dislodge my hands and roll out of my grasp.

"I don't care! I'll be dead, that's the point!"

Carpe managed to break my grip, so I punched him in the face. "You were supposed to be working on getting me that map. Not hijacking our plane!"

I wound up to punch Carpe again, but Rynn and Nadya pulled me off. Carpe scrambled up.

"You stay there," Rynn said to Carpe while he held me with both hands. Maybe I could get Captain to attack the damn elf. All of a sudden, my vision clouded like television static. I sunk to my knees.

"Alix?" Rynn said, concern edging his voice.

The static cleared somewhat, and I looked up.

Rynn was frowning at me, the concern I'd heard in his voice gone. "You know the elf is right?" he said.

"W-what?"

"Let's face it, you're not exactly competent when it comes to the whole theft game. Otherwise we wouldn't be here in the first place."

I shook my head. Yeah, I mean, I believed that, but Rynn didn't. Did he?

Sharp pain streaked through my head again, and I grabbed both sides. Rynn didn't seem to notice or care; he kept going.

"And while we're at it, you do know I'm only tagging along out of pity?"

That got my attention, even though my head was killing me.

"Why are you telling me this?" I said.

Rynn shrugged, his face devoid of any warmth. "Because no one lies to themselves quite like you do, Alix. It's the only reason you haven't figured out yet why I'm really here—"

My head flooded with another round of painful static, so I closed my eyes, trying to pinch it away.

"Alix?" Rynn said, again and again. Someone was shaking my shoulders.

"You know where you can go, Rynn—" I opened up my eyes and stopped.

I was on my back in the sand, Nadya, Rynn, and—to my dismay—Carpe looking down at me.

I sat up, the noise in my head downgraded to a dull thrum. "What the hell just happened?"

"You tell us," Nadya said. "One minute we were pulling you off Carpe, the next you were on your back, talking to no one." She frowned as she said it and put a hand to my forehead. "You are burning up again."

Shit. "The hallucinations started."

Nadya nodded and helped me up. "We need to get moving. They'll only get worse."

Carpe stepped in front of me. "Agree to get my book, and I'll start on the World Quest server right now. I can get the map and anything they have on it—I promise. Your chances aren't great with it, but they're nonexistent without it."

Rynn said something to Carpe in supernatural and stepped towards him.

Unfortunately Carpe was right about the map. "Fine," I said.

Both Carpe and Rynn looked at me, shocked. "We'll get your damn book, but on two conditions," I added.

Carpe's guard went up. "What are they?"

"One, we give it until nightfall. No book, we head to Syria, and not one more peep out of you and no more attempts to derail us."

He nodded, still wary.

"Two, you better be damn sure you can get me that map, because if I get your book and lose half a day and there's no map, you'll have me to deal with."

"Oh if he doesn't get you the map, Alix, don't worry—I'll shoot him for you. With the poisoned crossbow bolts," Rynn said.

Carpe flinched at that but nodded. "I can get you the map—I swear."

He climbed back into the cockpit to retrieve his things. A chicken hopped out, and I swore. I'd forgotten about the chickens—I'd feel bad about leaving them here. "Guys, what do we do about the chickens?"

"We have protocols for that," Carpe answered from inside the cockpit. "They've got food and water in the plane. It might get cold, but someone should be able to attend them in a day or so."

"He's serious," Rynn piped up as he pulled two more canvas bags out of the cargo hold. "The elves have strange priorities."

"Innocent living creatures that fall in harm's way are always a priority," Carpe said, sticking his head back out. "They are our sacred responsibility," he added as he emerged again, giving Rynn and Nadya a wide berth.

I frowned. "Yet you hijacked our plane to fetch a book while I'm *dying*?"

Carpe hopped down and retrieved his bag from Rynn. "Yes, but none of you are innocent—except maybe the cat, and even he's borderline."

I glanced down at Captain, whose hackles were raised in Carpe's direction. Well, he had that part marginally right . . . I exchanged a quick glance with Rynn.

"*Told you so,*" he mouthed before handing me a single bag, leaving him and Nadya to each take two. Normally I'd argue, but under the circumstances . . .

"It should be this way," Carpe said, and set off ahead of us.

It wouldn't have bothered me so much if he hadn't sounded so cheerful. I set off after him, ignoring Rynn's smirk. "Fifty bucks says you try to kill him again before we reach the temple," he said.

"You're on."

"Awful confident."

I shook my head. "Only because I figure you'll beat me to it."

"Train wreck."

"Whore," I said under my breath. "Hey, Carpe?" I waited until he looked over his shoulder. "Just remember, if I end up dead after all this, you can be damn sure I'll be coming back to haunt you."

Carpe swallowed, and the cheeriness dropped a peg as we set off over the sand dunes.

Nadya caught up to me as Rynn kept a close eye on Carpe. "Alix, I'm not one for violence, but my nose says we should have done what Rynn said and shot the elf. Nothing good can come from a creature who values chickens over humans and cats."

She had a point. Half of me was disappointed in Carpe, but on the other hand, we were ruthless with each other in game. I guess I always figured he'd be different in person. "Nadya, to be honest, I'll be amazed if we even make it to Carpe's temple. I'm just waiting to see what'll go wrong next."

I didn't even bother checking Hermes's card. I didn't want to know what it said.

15

Pyramids

7:00 p.m., OK, so not really pyramids, but close

When people think ancient Egypt, the Nile by the border of Sudan isn't the first thing that comes to mind. More like Cairo; maybe the Valley of the Kings if they watch TV specials.

They'd be making a big omission. The Nile was the backbone and lifeblood of ancient Egypt and didn't recognize the arbitrary borders we use today.

We were just north of the Sudanese-Egyptian border in a deserted section of the Nile. We were about twenty kilometers or so south of the Abu Simbel river temples, a pair of temples carved into the Nile cliffs during the reigns of Ramses II and Nefertari in the twelfth century BC. And no, I don't mean Nefertiti. Different queen. Interesting story about Nefertiti though; she and her husband tried to put a supernatural masquerading as a god into power. The other Egyptians didn't like that very much . . .

Off topic . . . The point was, the river temples are glorious—designed as monuments to stand the test of time, attracting hordes of tourists even today.

This temple, the one I was about to break into, had been built by Ramses II's court sorcerer and vizier, Passer. Whereas the river temples had been designed as monuments, Passer, the High Priest of Magic, had designed this one with the idea of never being found—he'd gone to extreme lengths, even having a fake body buried in his name elsewhere.

You know, it's the ones who get lost to history you need to worry about . . . Like deadly poisonous snakes camouflaged in tall grass, the last thing you want to do is stumble into one. The fact that the IAA had set a two-kilometer perimeter around this place should be warning enough to stay away.

"Move, Captain," I said as I scooted up closer to the edge of the sandstone out-crop twenty feet up from the river and lifted my binoculars to scan the cliff face on the opposite side of the Nile. There were four inconsequential sandstone pillars carved into the rock face flanking a rectangular entrance camouflaged by a recessed piece of sandstone. If you didn't know exactly where and what to look for, the entrance of Passer's tomb appeared like just another solid piece of the cliff, the door and pillars bleeding seamlessly into the rest of the sandstone.

Oh this was a bad idea . . .

I shielded my eyes against the light reflecting off the water's surface. The sun was almost below the horizon now—just a little bit longer. Nice part about this section of the Nile, the water didn't smell . . . and there were no crocodiles. Considering what we were planning, that was probably a good thing. I pulled my cargo jacket closed. I was into the chills part of my fever now.

"Well, Carpe, you were right about reaching the temple by nightfall," I said. Sitting a little ways away from the edge of the embankment, he glanced up from his laptop and frowned at me. Apparently elves weren't used to the kind of treatment we were in the habit of showing people who crashed our plane.

"Now all you need to be is right about how to handle the sorcerer's mummy and we might actually get out alive." Personally, I was hoping not to run into the mummy at all. From the map Carpe had given me, there were an awful lot of side tunnels and passageways to hide in.

With my luck, the mummy would walk in right while I was lifting the damn book.

"What do you think?" Nadya said, sliding in beside me and nodding at the hidden temple entrance. Both she and Rynn had taken to ignoring Carpe. It seemed about the only way to prevent us from dissolving into threats of physical violence.

"Considering there's a skeleton crew of IAA guards who are patrolling from further back than we are, I say the going is about as good as we're going to get."

I noted Nadya had my infrared binoculars out already, anticipating the need for them shortly—in the next hour or so, give or take the sunset. "You ever been here before?" I asked.

She shook her head. "You?"

I shook my head. Contrary to popular belief, I wasn't that stupid. The more inconsequential the temples looked, the bigger the monsters . . .

Rynn came up on my other side, also shooting a glare at Carpe before crouching down next to me. "There's next to no one here," he said. "There's the watchtower a kilometer downriver, but that's all I could find. Not even the IAA wants to piss off the sorcerer's mummy."

Fantastic . . .

Rynn frowned and nodded towards the temple. "Why do you think he designed it this way?"

The last of the sun set behind the sand. Time to get going before the chills got much worse. "Same reason this place looks like it's in the middle of nowhere," I said, squeezing his shoulder as I stood up. "To keep the thieves out."

I slid my backpack on and helped Nadya roll out the yellow dinghy we'd salvaged from the plane. I whistled for Captain. He popped out from under a rock, already wearing his harness. I wouldn't worry about the leash until we were ready to cross. I doubted there were vampires hanging out by the bank, not with Passer. It was the water I was worried about; Captain wasn't a huge fan of water.

Carpe glanced up from his laptop, perturbed. "I still think I should come with you—"

"No!" Nadya and I both answered as we unrolled the dinghy.

He looked awful dejected for someone who'd just downed our airplane.

"Look, Carpe—it will be much better for us if you stay out here and work on World Quest. Worst-case scenario, if we get into trouble, you'll be more help out here anyways." And that had some truth to it. Considering Nadya and I had only been studying the tomb map for a couple hours—and I wasn't at my performance best—it was a distinct possibility we'd need Carpe to do some online tomb reconnaissance on the fly.

I was also less tempted to punch him over a headset.

"Just stay online," I said, tapping my earpiece. "And do whatever the hell Rynn says."

Nadya lowered herself over the ledge to the riverbed, while Rynn held me back.

"Keep your line open to channel one—I've got the elf on channel two." There was a reluctance and warning on the end of that statement.

I snorted. "Don't worry, the elf is on a need-to-use basis. What about our ride into Syria?" We'd missed whatever checkpoint Rynn had set up with his contact.

"They're aware of the situation. Not happy about the elf, but they'll come to us."

"What are these guys exactly?"

Rynn had been sparse on the details except that they could handle themselves.

"About the only people coming out on top of the Syrian civil war. The Jinn."

"At this rate I'll be amazed if we make it to the City of the Dead before I dissolve into a hallucinating pile of human wreck."

"We can leave the elf here and go now, Alix, just say the word."

I glanced to where Carpe was sitting. I wondered how good elf hearing was.

I shook my head. "I need the World Quest map too much—and Nadya and I should be able to handle this." Initially I'd considered taking

Rynn, but as useful as he'd be dealing with the mummy, the traps and inscriptions were another matter. Just because Rynn was supernatural didn't mean he knew everything, and Egypt wasn't his forte. "Just make sure the elf is working on my map. He seriously got elves to rescue the chickens?"

"Oh yes. Nothing about picking us up, mind you—"

Like some warped, twisted version of Buddhism . . . "Just try not to shoot him before he finishes the job."

"What if he double-crosses us?" Rynn said that a little too fast for it to be spontaneous.

"How could he possibly screw us over even more?"

Deadpanning, Rynn said, "But just think. What if his elven friends need help rescuing all those chickens?"

I shook my head and glanced over at Carpe, still typing away on his damn computer. "The worst part is I don't think you're joking."

Out of all the moments in the last couple hours, Rynn picked that one to snake his arm around my waist and kiss me. Not our usual "there were people around" version but the kind he usually saved for behind closed doors . . . or if there isn't anyone around we particularly care about seeing us. That's happened a couple times . . . and no, I'm not the instigator, Rynn is . . . not that I'm complaining.

This was definitely one of those. In fact, it caught me so off guard I opened my eyes partway through.

Rynn's arms might have been wrapped around me and his face might have been pressed against mine, but he sure as hell wasn't watching me. He was looking at the damn elf, and not nicely. I caught Carpe glance away as soon as he saw me look.

Oh for Christ's sake . . . I pushed Rynn away, breaking off our kiss. "Seriously?" I said, nodding towards Carpe.

Rynn shrugged but didn't offer up any defense.

Yeah, not getting off that easy. "Out of all the nymphs and attractive bartenders hanging around the Japanese Circus, you're jealous over the damn elf? Seriously, are you sure I'm the only one hallucinating?"

He shrugged, but there was a ghost of a smile on his face. "The bartenders work for me and you don't like the nymphs. You talk to the elf on a daily basis."

"No, I talk to you and Nadya on a daily basis. I play World Quest with Carpe, and it's a couple times a week, not every day. And he crashed our plane and is holding my map hostage!"

Rynn wasn't fazed one damn bit. His smile widened as he waved at Carpe, who glanced back down at his screen, though I could have sworn his face was red. "Besides," Rynn added, "I really hate elves."

I shook my head and grabbed Captain, encouraging him into the backpack. "I'm not even going to dignify that one." I grabbed the rope and followed Nadya down to the bank.

Rynn jealous over the backstabbing elf—who I was tempted to punch. Again. I mean, Carpe wasn't horrible to look at—in a kind of yoga-retreat way. He was slighter than Rynn, which made sense, with the perma-computer chair and vegetarianism—not that Rynn was a super athlete or anything . . .

Jesus, what was I doing, comparing Rynn and Carpe?

"What was that about?" Nadya asked once I touched down on the bank.

"Nothing, except I think the curse is rubbing off on Rynn. He's jealous—of *Carpe*."

Nadya didn't say anything, instead becoming engrossed in the inflation of the yellow raft.

"Seriously? Not you too."

Nadya shrugged. "Well, you do spend a lot of time on World Quest."

"And in the bar, and on dig sites."

"Not the same thing, and you know it."

I snorted. Rynn worried about Carpe. If it wasn't for the fact that I didn't have a headache, I'd be willing to bet I'd hallucinated it. I hunkered down with Nadya and Captain to wait for nightfall and our signal to cross.

Well, considering the IAA in the tower hadn't spotted us yet, maybe our luck was on the up. On a lark, I checked Hermes's card to see if the message had changed.

Don't hold your breath.

I shoved it back in my pocket. Great, just fucking fantastic . . .

———ɯ———

The nice thing about the desert is it gets dark fast. With only the artificial light from the IAA tower, the stars were out and bright. I like looking at stars. I don't get the chance in Las Vegas and Seattle with the city lights.

On a positive note, the night had cooled down, but my fever was running hot again.

"It is dark enough to go now, no?" Nadya whispered beside me.

"Have to wait for Rynn's signal. Does us no good to get across and have the IAA waiting for us with guns when we stroll out," I said, and added, "though it'd sure be nice if he'd hurry up on that."

"I heard that," Rynn said into my headset. "Take a look over at the tower, *carefully*. They watch that river for boats."

"Don't get spotted, we got it the first time." I rolled onto my back and edged out from underneath our hiding spot—a river-worn stone ledge. I focused my goggles until I could see the tower and its front door. "All right, I see the tower."

"Now watch the door. There will be guards entering the lighthouse any minute."

Like clockwork, I watched as the two guards did indeed round the tower and enter through the front entrance.

"They're in," I said.

"That's the guard change—there should be two coming out any minute. Once that happens, go. I can drop the infrared camera and give you about twenty minutes without raising any major alarms."

"How the hell do you plan on doing that?" The IAA was notorious about sounding alarms for next to nothing.

"Easy, the generator is outside. I'll run a power surge through it—out here, with the temperature fluctuation, a blown fuse isn't far-fetched."

"Rynn, I hate being the voice of reason here, but depending on the IAA not to act—"

"Will work because I'm watching the tower and the elf is tracking their communications."

"I thought Carpe was breaking into World Quest."

"With proper motivation, the elf can do two things at once," he said.

I decided not to ask what motivation Rynn used. Still pissed about Carpe hijacking and crashing our cargo plane . . .

The door to the tower opened and two guards walked out.

"Rynn, they're out."

"Go."

Nadya and I shoved the dinghy into the river and leapt on board. I winced as the boat splashed into the water—more noise than I would have liked. The boat started floating downstream, and I kept my eyes on the tower to see if we'd been seen . . . nothing except the flicker of flashlights and the tower disappearing from my immediate sight . . . come to think of it, we were leaving the tower behind awful fast.

Shit, we were being dragged downstream.

Nadya swore and tossed me a paddle. "Go, before they get back online."

We'd figured that between the two of us, it'd take ten minutes to get across, leaving five to ten to stow the bright yellow boat and make it inside. We hadn't taken into account battling the current.

I started paddling. Captain, figuring there was now water involved, bellowed from inside my bag to be let out. "No, your claws will puncture the boat—then you'll really be wet . . . ow!" I tried to dislodge Captain as his claws sunk through the canvas into my back.

"Keep paddling," Nadya said. "We're veering to the left, and the current is dragging us off target."

I swore and got my paddle back in the water, fighting the current as Captain the wonder cat found new ways to torture my back.

The sound of sand scraping against the rubber raft told us we'd made it. We both leapt out of the boat and dragged it onshore. I got my backpack off.

"How much time?" I said, out of breath . . . we had to have four or five minutes left, right?

"You've got three," Rynn replied.

"Shit—" Not only did we have to run back to the entrance, which we hadn't planned on, but we also had to hide the damn boat and paddles first. Tying it up wasn't an option. They'd see it once they got the cameras back on. Letting it float upstream was tempting, but I wasn't willing to test that current or swim across with Captain puncturing my head. I pulled the air tube and started compressing like mad.

"Up there," Nadya hissed, pointing to another sandstone ledge. I tossed her the paddles while I pushed the rest of the air out.

"You've got two minutes left, move."

Damn it, why won't air pockets leave? Oh hell, it was good enough. I rolled the dinghy up as best I could.

"Alix, the boat!"

I tossed the deflated raft to Nadya, who shoved it deep into a ledge.

"Time?" I said to Rynn.

"A minute. And you need to run."

Damn it . . . "Come on," I said to Nadya, and scrambled up the ledge. A head rush hit me as I pulled myself up—but if it was the curse or the exertion I didn't have time to sit back and contemplate.

Nadya scrambled up ahead of me and broke into a dead run for the entrance.

I swore and took off after her, forcing my legs to keep up with Nadya's longer stride.

"Run faster, Alix."

"I hate running," I said.

"Don't care, and it's thirty seconds now," came Rynn's voice.

I let Captain out of my backpack. "Work off those cat treats," I told him, and kept running.

Nadya reached the entrance first and slid behind the recessed rock wall ahead of me. With my goggles I could just make out the entrance/ optical illusion.

I grabbed Captain by the harness before he could overshoot and pulled him in after me.

I collapsed against the wall beside Nadya. "Let's not do that again," I managed to squeeze out between breaths.

"Do not say that, you will jinx it," she said.

While the two of us recouped, I flipped on my flashlight and started to look around.

What had been absent in decoration outside Passer's temple was made up twofold inside. Like the river temple entrances, this one was lined with statues of the Egyptian pantheon, but it distinguished itself with a more cavernous room. If this hall was any indication, the entire complex had been built as if someone really did intend to spend a few thousand years living here. I couldn't tell for sure with my flashlight, but if I had to guess, I'd say the hieroglyph reliefs beat the river temples in number and intricacy as well. "You seeing what I'm seeing, Nadya?"

She nodded, taking in the expansiveness the same way I was. "The outside might not be much, but this puts the Ramses and Nefertari river temples to shame."

Carefully, using the map as a guide, we headed into the next chamber. My flashlight showed this one had the same high ceilings as the first, but it stretched out into the cliff side farther than my flashlight beam reached. Statues of the Egyptian pantheon had been used to shore up the ceiling, in lieu of more traditional pillars with hieroglyphs.

I wondered how much of Ramses and Nefertari's budget had been diverted Passer's way.

"Main chamber," Nadya said, glancing down at my map.

The map showed four exits from this room. The one at the back led to the burial room—where all the treasure was—and the left and right ones led to the living quarters and workroom, respectively. All the traps listed on the map were on the way to the burial chamber—no big surprise there. We'd try the workroom first, then treasure and burial rooms, then the living quarters. "Hopefully Passer follows the designed living layout and we find the book in the workroom minus him," I said.

Nadya snorted but didn't argue the search plan. Captain stayed close. When there aren't any vampires, he's a surprisingly attentive cat.

Flashlights out, we wound our way through the pillars. I counted the gods I recognized off the top of my head: Horus, Anubis, Aken, Ammit, Osiris, Nebthet... "Every Egyptian god of the underworld is on display," I said to Nadya.

My earpiece clicked as someone switched the line on. "Passer was known for his obsession with the underworld—particularly the goddess Ammit," came Carpe, of all people.

Ammit was the crocodile-headed god of the underworld. No hell for those judged unworthy, just the eating and vanquishing of the soul. I did not need to know about Passer's obsession with the soul-eating crocodile goddess right now, thank you very much. "Not helping," I said, wondering how he'd gotten online. Must have switched to line two by accident. I went to switch back to line one, only to find it was already on line one.

"I thought you two were discussing Egyptian gods," he replied.

"Carpe, what the hell are you doing on Rynn's line?"

"It's quiet out here and I wanted to see what was going on. I thought I could help."

Oh for Christ's...

"This is not one of Alix's video games," Nadya said.

"Yet I'm the one who knew about the crocodile goddess. And I call bullshit about relevancy, Alix. The obsession is totally relevant and hints at the types of traps you're likely to encounter—"

OK, point made, but I wasn't about to acknowledge it. "Put Rynn back on and go back to getting the map of Syria—need I remind you, the *only* reason we are here."

Carpe and I were going to have a little talk when we got out of here about the difference between video games and real life—

I swore as pain spiked through my head...

Nadya was staring at me, an intense look in her eyes.

"If Rynn and Carpe are going to fight over you, you could have the decency to tell them to do so in private."

Wait . . . what? "I think you are grossly misunderstanding the dynamics here—" Besides, the bickering had more to do with Rynn hating the elf, and Carpe being . . . well . . . Carpe, the backstabbing elf.

Nadya snorted, and her lip curled up in a sneer. "I suppose you could just keep leading them on. That does fit with your cruel streak. Rynn will win, by the way—he's more devious than the elf, and when push comes to shove isn't afraid to get his hands dirty."

"OK, pretty sure that's not a compliment—"

Nadya didn't let me finish. "I still haven't forgotten what happens to your friends. I'll run before I'll let you lock me in a tomb," she said as she quirked her head to the side. "Maybe I should lock you in here instead."

A chill ran down the back of my neck, and in spite of my fever I clenched my fists. That was way the hell out of bounds. "Not OK bringing up Marie, not now—"

The pain flared again, forcing me to shut my eyes and clasp both sides of my head until it dissipated. Nadya was watching me with concern. Captain sniffed my shoes and mewed.

"Why would I bring up Marie?" Nadya said.

Nausea hit me as a metallic taste filled my mouth. I covered my mouth to stop myself from puking. Hallucination number two—and I was starting to see a pattern. "Nothing, just the curse rearing its ugly head."

She frowned but nodded. "We should keep moving and find this stupid book before it happens again."

I couldn't have agreed more.

We reached the entrance passageway to Passer's workroom. The ceiling was lower, only six feet compared to the ten of the main chamber. Nadya and I both checked for traps—twice—before stepping inside.

If you were an ancient Egyptian wielding a substantial amount of power, one of the benefits of a temple like this over a pyramid was the fact that it was harder to find—and had more ways for potential thieves to get lost. Contrary to popular belief, there was not a lot of room inside pyramids. Lots of crawl spaces though, but you were more likely to find a dead end you couldn't turn yourself around in than treasure.

Temples offered more variety—and booby traps.

Nadya swore as she tripped over a raised tile. I stopped her before she could take another step forward and shone my flashlight down. It was a four-by-four plate depicting a particularly gruesome funeral ceremony, where a man was having his soul devoured by none other than Ammit. I scanned ahead. The floor up until the next room was covered in the larger plate tiles—three per row. Out of the first six, four depicted scenes of the underworld; a deceased's soul being weighed against the feather of Maat followed by said deceased's lackluster soul being eaten by Ammit, the jackal-headed Anubis fighting with a god I didn't recognize, and finally one of Osiris rising from his bier. Two of the tiles—on opposite ends, a row apart—did not fit with the narrative. A picture of the cat goddess Bast, a sun god and protector of the pharaoh, at the far right of the first row, and the scarab beetle Khepry, bringer of the dawn, on the far left of the second row.

I crouched to check the edges. Sure enough, they were mobile. "How much do you want to bet you step on the wrong tile a trap goes off?"

Nadya swore. "I thought the elf said there were no traps this way."

"I think it was an educated guess more than anything else." I switched to line two. "Hey Carpe, plate trap, aisle one on the way to the storeroom. I need to know what it does."

"Oh now you want my help—"

"I can still turn around," I interrupted.

"Just a sec," he said, followed by manic typing on the other end. "Ahh, either the floor collapses, plummeting you to your death, or the roof collapses from above."

"Well, which is it?"

"I don't know. I'm translating from old architect notes."

"So go into World Quest and find out," I said.

"I can't do that. It isn't ethical—"

"Ethical? You already broke World Quest. Teleport your avatar over to Egypt and find out what the trap does."

"The Syrian City of the Dead is an exception. I bartered that for the book, which I already told you is a matter of utmost importance—life and death. It was an ethical exception I was willing to make."

"So is this, you good-for-nothing elf! And might I point out if we die, you also don't get your book?"

"So not the same. Besides, you already know it's a trap—block crushes you from above or the floor drops. Don't step on the wrong tile—I have complete faith in you. Now get back to finding my book, and I'll get back to getting your map," he said, and the line snapped dead.

"Goddamn son of an elven bitch—" I didn't have nearly enough insults for elves. I switched back to line one.

"What are you doing?" Nadya asked.

"Getting Rynn to 'persuade' it out of him," I said. The line snapped open. "Hey Rynn, feel like beating up Carpe?"

But Rynn wasn't on the other line. It was Carpe. Again.

"Yeah, hacking Rynn's comm system is nothing compared to World Quest. Suck it up, princess."

"Put Rynn on right now or I'm—goddamn it!" The comm line snapped dead.

No concept of the real world . . . "I swear, if we get out of here, I'm going to give Carpe a black eye to go with his nose."

"Not if I get to him first," Nadya said.

No point in dreaming about ways to do bodily harm to Carpe now. I looked at the pictures again. Either the two sun gods were safe, or it was the other way around and the underworld gods were safe . . . time to test my theory.

I pulled my pick out of my bag and carefully pressed the wooden handle down on the tile showing Bast.

Nothing happened.

So far so good. I pressed harder, with more confidence. Still nothing happened.

I said a fast prayer to no one in particular and stepped on the tile. Safe.

The next one was a little harder, since it required me to jump to the other side of the hall. I leapt and landed on the scarab beetle—wavering, but otherwise safe.

Now for the next row. This time the lineup was the four sons of Horus—depictions of the sacred organ jars, underworld if I've ever seen it. Sekhmet, another cat god, was next—definitely sun. My flashlight beam danced over the third one. A gazelle.

"Nadya, what the hell does the gazelle represent?" I whispered.

"The goddess of the Nile, Satet."

"Satet? That doesn't make any sense. Satet's another sun god."

"Sekhmet is also a god of war, maybe that's the distinction."

Maybe . . . Still, I'd rather know for sure. I reached for my comm to contact Carpe. Instead, my head reeled as another surge of pain struck—a bad one, like right before I started hallucinating. I did not want to be standing on the death plates. "Think fast, Nadya, which one?"

"Ah, Satet, the Nile. It's safest—"

All right, Nile it was. The Nile tile was diagonal to the scarab beetle I was standing on, so the jump was easy.

I landed on the tile and breathed a sigh of relief when nothing happened. I turned my flashlight on the next row. Horus this time, Kuk the frog and serpent god of darkness, and Isis—

The ceiling started to shake.

How the hell had the Nile been wrong? It occurred to me as the first bit of ceiling crumbled that the order had been switched—two sun, one underworld. "Shit, it was the four sons of Horus." More ceiling crumbled, and I heard the first bang above. Something was coming down a chute, and I had no plans on being here when it landed.

"Nadya, fast—Horus, Kuk, and Isis—"

Another bang against granite sounded above, shaking the temple hall. Well, that was that answered. Ceiling it was . . . Oh hell, screw picking the right tile.

I bolted across Isis, running straight for the end. The ceiling behind me collapsed, and the floor shook as something heavy struck it.

I hit the fifth row of tiles, but instead of something crashing from above, the tile cracked under my feet, spilling me onto my knees as it buckled inwards. Passer hadn't used one or the other trap, he'd used both.

I did the only thing I could—roll over the cracking tiles and dive for it. The wind was knocked out of me as I collided with solid wall.

"Alix!" Nadya yelled across the pile of stone and pit between us. Considering I'd just collapsed a major artery of the temple, there was no point staying quiet now.

"Yeah—alive," I said, wincing as I pulled myself up, my head protesting the movement. I aimed my flashlight down the hall. No mummy. "And I can see the workroom from here." All I had to do was check for the book, then figure a way back across. "We brought rope, right?" I asked.

"If you didn't, I'm sure I have some lying around. Never want to be caught without rope. All sorts of lovely uses," came a familiar voice with a dry texture and faint British accent.

Caracalla, the Roman mummy I'd dealt with back in the Alexandria catacombs, stepped out of the shadows. I aimed the flashlight at his face, but unlike in the catacombs, Caracalla didn't jump back. The bone I'd rammed through his head was gone, replaced by a pair of dark sunglasses. I wrinkled my nose at the smell of sewer. I'd forgotten just how much he smelled . . .

He made a clicking noise, almost like a laugh. "Now what a pleasant surprise, you turning up here. I was promised that might be the case, but I never dreamed so soon." His mouth widened into a grin. "Seems I made quite a lucrative deal."

This had to be a hallucination. There was no way Caracalla was here. This was Passer's tomb, the court sorcerer of Ramses II, for Christ's sake. Caracalla was a minor mummy from the Ptolemaic age of Egypt—he barely counted as a real mummy.

I swallowed hard and backed towards the workroom as Caracalla took another step towards me. "Where's Passer? This is his temple."

Caracalla torqued his head to the side, but the sinew was so dry it was an unnatural movement.

"Him? Ahh, I suppose you would expect him to be here. I'm afraid you are a few days too late. Funny story, after you destroyed my tomb, the IAA swarmed in. I decided it was getting much too crowded and was time to move house, so to speak. As luck would have it, I stumbled across a rather curious benefactor, one who offered me—well, you, to be perfectly honest. Skeptical though I was they'd be able to deliver you, he did throw in this lovely new tomb—much more spacious, no flooding, none of the noise." Caracalla took another step forward. "As for Passer, when I arrived I found him sleeping in his crypt. I believe he gave up the will to exist many years ago. I'm proud to admit I helped him along." His eyes glowed red and he took another step closer, blocking off the pit—not that I planned to try and jump it.

"How's that for a half-rate mummy?"

Of course an insult thrown out in the heat of the moment came back to bite me . . .

"Now now dear, what's wrong? 'Cat have your tongue' is the saying I think they use?"

The headache was back full swing . . . what was the chance I was actually dealing with Caracalla? "You're a figment of my imagination," I tried.

"Doubt that, but let's test the theory." Caracalla might have grinned—it was hard to tell with part of his skull torn up. Regardless, he swiped at me with his hand. Exposed finger bones sharpened into daggerlike points grazed my jacket.

He was real. "Nadya, we have a problem," I said as I ducked a second swipe.

Running out of dodging space, I did the only thing I could—flashlight in hand, I ran for the workroom.

Unlike the reliefs carved elsewhere in the temple, the workroom was decorated in painted hieroglyphs uncannily preserved by lack of light and exposure. There was a slab of rectangular black granite in the center large enough to fit a human. I darted around the other side, putting it between me and Caracalla. I got a look at a few of the painted scenes—jars, organs; like an instructional on mummification.

"I see you found the preparation chamber," Caracalla said. He darted to the left, then right, trying to make me run within range. Nope, not working—I was happy to wait him out behind the slab of granite.

"I never saw the point of waiting until people were dead to start the process. So much more personal and intimate when the subject is still alive."

With the lull in Caracalla's feinting around the table, I had a breath's worth of break to change my comm channel. "Rynn, need help—"

It wasn't Rynn who answered though. "Let me guess, you want him to force me to break into World Quest?"

I swore as Caracalla darted around the side after me. "Carpe, put Rynn on now!"

"Not until you promise—"

"Now! Or as soon as this mummy kills me, I swear to God I'm coming back for you."

There was a soft click, not the electric snap that signified Carpe hanging up. "Alix?" came Rynn's voice about the same time I found an unused urn under the table and launched it at Caracalla's head.

"Mummy." It was all I managed to get out before Caracalla resumed his chase.

"Tell me what's happening."

I ducked as Caracalla threw a discarded piece of tablet. "Fewer questions, more help—" I said.

"DMSO cocktail tranquilizer, left pocket of Nadya's backpack—it will work on Passer."

"Nadya?" I yelled as I dodged a piece of broken tablet thrown at my shoulder.

"I've got it—I can't see enough to shoot though. You'll need to come my way."

Time to figure out who was smarter: me or a two-thousand-year-old mummy.

I darted left, then right—further into Caracalla's reach than was safe. He took the bait and chased around my end. I dropped to all fours and slid under the table . . . My fingers brushed parchment—a leather-bound book.

Maybe this wasn't a complete waste after all. Hoping it was Carpe's spell book, I grabbed it before bolting back into the hall as Caracalla growled behind me.

"Get ready," I said to Nadya as I bolted for the hall.

Caracalla was still growling, but I didn't bother checking over my shoulder. I didn't want to see how close he was.

"Alix, I need you closer—and use your flashlight, I can't see a damn thing."

Use your flashlight on the mummy chasing you while running . . . Yeah, that was going to go well . . .

I skidded to a stop a foot away from the pit and aimed the flashlight at Caracalla.

"Duck," Nadya yelled.

I dropped to the floor and heard the pop of the tranquilizer gun. Three yellow-tailed darts lodged into Caracalla's face and chest.

He plucked out a dart from his forehead and examined it. "Hmmm, interesting weapon," he said, sniffing the concoction pooling at the tip with what was left of his nose.

"Rynn, it isn't working."

"Did you miss?"

"No, there are two darts sticking out of his chest. Caracalla isn't even fazed. He's just more curious than anything else."

"Wait—Caracalla? Are you hallucinating again? This is Passer's temple."

"Apparently Caracalla took out Passer and moved in after I trashed his tomb, because apparently someone suggested I might be stopping in. Know anything about that, Carpe?"

"Hey! I don't sell people to mummies!" Carpe said.

"You hijacked our plane, not a giant leap," I said.

"You think I enjoy stealing airplanes and getting punched by friends who now hate me?"

"We are so not friends anymore," I said, keeping my eyes on Cara-calla.

"*Enough,*" Rynn said. "As much as I hate to say it, the elf wouldn't have sold you out to the mummy."

"Who did?"

"Someone else who wants the book. I wasn't screwing around when I said this was life and death. And you seriously think I enjoy coercing my friends into doing things they don't want to do, Alix?" Carpe added.

"Yes!"

"Knock it off, both of you. I didn't pack anything for Caracalla," Rynn said.

He added something else after that, which I'm sure would have been useful, but my attention was on the mummy, who tossed the dart to the side and started towards me again.

"I'm curious, now that you've given it your all, I wonder what will you try next?"

"Alix!" I turned in time to catch the rope Nadya threw. I wound it around my arm, testing the anchor to a statue. It held.

Now or never. I shoved the book in my jacket and leapt off the edge of the pit. I grunted as I hit the wall on the opposite side. Nadya started pulling the rope up while I climbed.

"Clever," Caracalla said. "But you forget one important detail."

"What? That you're a half-rate mummy?"

"I can jump." He took three strides back before leaping over the pit, landing a few feet away from us.

I really need to learn to keep my mouth shut. . . . I backed up in one direction while Nadya backed up in the other. Catching the movement, Caracalla turned his attention on her.

Yeah, not happening. I picked up a piece of granite and chucked it at his head. "Hey, half-rate mummy, over here!"

If there's one thing I've learned over the years, it's that monsters are predictable. They don't like being insulted. Caracalla turned back towards me and closed in. Not that I had a plan or anything.

I tapped my comm. "Rynn, any ideas you have about defeating this guy would be awesome about now."

But before Rynn had a chance to answer, Captain barreled out in front of me, hackles up and hissing a storm at Caracalla. Yeah, monsters are predictable. Cats not so much.

"Captain, not a vampire!" I started.

Captain, in the throes of attack cat, wasn't having any of it.

I searched for a rock, anything to throw at Caracalla before Captain reached him.

But as Captain hissed and spit, Caracalla backed up . . .

Now, Maus have no effect on mummies whatsoever. Mummies being scared of cats was a myth, based on some nonsense of cats being guardians of the underworld. Scourge of vampires everywhere, yes, but guardian of the underworld Captain was not.

Through a combination of whatever was firing through Captain's walnut-sized brain and whatever the hell Caracalla believed Captain could do to him, the effect was the same. Caracalla was backing up towards the pit's edge.

Well, when opportunity presents itself . . . I kicked Caracalla in the sweet spot, grabbed my cat by his harness, and pushed Caracalla over the edge.

Nadya stared at me, jaw open.

"Start running. I have a sinking suspicion he might crawl out."

We tore back towards the entrance and I pressed the communicator. "Rynn?"

I thought I heard his voice, but there was static. Shit, must be the part of the temple we were in. I pressed line two and tried Carpe—no answer either. Figures, he waits until I need to talk to him not to answer.

A small, cautious part of my brain thought we should make sure the coast was clear of IAA before bolting out in the open. Most of my brain agreed full heartedly we did not want to be in this temple when Caracalla crawled out of the pit . . .

I crossed the entrance a few paces ahead of Nadya and Captain.

Meaning I hit the trip wire first.

I landed flat on my face. I was aware of Nadya pulling up short behind me, cursing in Russian, and heard the click of safeties that told me multiple guns were pointed in our direction.

Damn, I hate the IAA . . .

I ignored the ringing in my head and pushed myself onto my forearms, hoping to get a good look at how many agents were pointing guns at us.

It wasn't the IAA, or local Egyptians—not even Sudanese. Too tall and not the right ethnic background. If it wasn't for where we were, I would have sworn we were surrounded by a group of Somalians.

What the hell would the Somali be doing staking out a tomb?

I pushed myself up to kneeling and looked to see who was in charge. Captain was nowhere to be seen. Here's hoping he stayed hidden until Rynn and Carpe showed up.

One of the men, the shortest of the lot and the only one not pointing a gun at me, stepped forward, a fixed smile never leaving his face.

"You have something of mine. How fortuitous. And here we thought we would have to retrieve it ourselves." His English was good and the accent suggested he'd been educated in London. He crouched down to pick up the spell book that had spilled out from my jacket.

"Who the hell are you?" I asked.

His smile widened. "Why, the Owl, of course. Antiquities thief extraordinaire."

You know I often find myself saying things couldn't possibly get worse.

I need to stop that. I also need to come up with a filter. "Oh you got to be fucking kidding me. You're the assholes pretending to be the Owl?"

I didn't get much more past that. A gun butt to the head will do that to you.

Well . . . at least for once it wasn't the supernaturals taking potshots at me.

This time it was Somali pirates.

16

Pirates

Oh sweet Jesus, why does everything hurt?

Fun observation: coming to with a killer headache and my hands tied behind my back isn't as much a shock as it used to be ... though as I tried pulling my cramped legs in, I realized they were tied together as well.

Hunh. That was new. Come to think of it, so was the cage.

Why is it I always get knocked out anyways? Gun butt to the head this time, too, if I remembered correctly ...

I tried to shift my legs into a more comfortable position and found two things; first, my ribs hurt like a son of a bitch. On the bright side, the foggy memory of someone landing a kick to my stomach hadn't been a figment of my imagination.

The second thing I noted though was less expected; my legs were tied real tight, pins-and-needles-inducing tight. And I wasn't all by my lonesome. I was tied back to back with someone else stuck in the cage, and in my opinion done with an excess amount of rope.

"Pssst, Nadya?" I whispered, hazarding a guess.

"Good, you are awake finally," she said, and turned her head so she could see me out of the corner of her eye.

"I think someone went to a hell of a lot of trouble to make sure we didn't up and try to walk out of here," I said.

This time she replied in a string of Russian insults I don't feel like translating or repeating right now. I don't shy away from cursing, but even I have my limits.

The fact that Nadya hadn't made any progress on her own told me someone really had gone to a lot of trouble. I filed that away in the "interesting" category.

"I don't know about you, Alix, but I'm about ready to go above and beyond their expectations."

"Oh I've well and already reached that point," I said, and started scanning my immediate surroundings.

We were in a tent, the green khaki, military-grade kind, built to house a lot of equipment for short periods of time then get packed right back up. As far as its contents went, if it wasn't for the small issue of being tied up in a cage, I'd be singing happy birthday to me. To quote World Quest, the place was a treasure whore's dream. These guys had enough antiquities loot to rival the Smithsonian.

Captain, Rynn, and Carpe, however, were nowhere to be seen—at least not in my periphery.

"What happened to everyone else?" I asked.

"They found Rynn ahead of us, but I haven't seen him since the truck. I don't know what happened to Captain; he ran back into the temple after you tripped."

I nodded, more for myself than Nadya. I was happy they hadn't grabbed Captain. Him I could go back for later . . .

"The elf got away," Nadya added derisively.

So much for sticking around to help. "Somehow Carpe saving his own skin doesn't surprise me," I said, though at least I had the satisfaction of knowing he didn't have his book—the pirates did.

Speaking of which . . . I was about to ask Nadya if she'd had a chance to talk to Rynn and come up with a tentative game plan, but I didn't get the chance, courtesy of muffled voices and footsteps outside the tent.

"Someone's coming," Nadya said.

"Look, just follow my lead," I said.

Nadya snorted. "You are feverish and delusional. We follow my lead."

"Yeah, but for better or worse, I have more experience dealing with people who tie me up and threaten to kill me. We're using my methods."

She struggled in order to see me. "Your methods involve pissing people off more than they already are."

"It works, doesn't it? And keeping them happy is a moot point. They already know who we are—or did you forget the ropes and cage?"

I'm sure she would have kept the argument going, but the voices outside the tent became voices inside it.

Showtime.

I let out a loud whistle. "Hey, Nadya, there's more loot in here than the British Museum—how many trucks do you figure we need?"

She swore and did her best to elbow me. It might have packed a punch considering the condition of my rib, but she couldn't get much of a windup.

Louder this time I added, "I mean, look at all this stuff. I think those might actually be terra-cotta warriors over there. Think we could get a few out without them knowing?" I wasn't lying about that one either. There was one standing in front of half-unpacked cargo crates. Curse aside, I could spend a week cataloguing this stuff . . .

The footsteps picked up the pace.

"They are going to shoot you," Nadya whispered.

"No, they're not," I whispered back. "If they were, they'd have done it already." Yet another sentence I should not be that comfortable saying. For the benefit of whoever was making their way over, I added, "And aren't you just a little bit curious why they have us so trussed up?"

"Quiet in there," said one of the new players to the party. I couldn't see him, but his voice alone told me plenty. An unfamiliar, soft-accented English, mixed with a quick pronunciation and the ease with which the phrase rolled out, told me he was no stranger to the language. That was good. The more everyone understands each other, the less trigger-happy they are. The high pitch hinted at something else as well.

"Hey, great, you speak English. Would you believe we were on a hike and got lost in that cave? I know, crazy American tourists—"

"I said be quiet," the male voice said, with more emphasis this time. He rounded the cage, and I got my first look at one of our captors.

If I hadn't been tied up in a cage, I'd have felt bad for the kid—and he was a kid. Even if the voice hadn't given it away, his face did. He was tall for his age, but if he was a day over twelve, I was a dancing bear.

I made a point of looking him in the eye—something I'd learned when bartering with vampires. Funny thing about a kid pirate, they don't have the eyes of a kid anymore.

Or maybe that was the fever and hallucinations hitting me again.

Regardless, the rifle slung over his shoulder didn't escape my notice; neither did the way he played with the strap and butt.

Despite the English, I added trigger-happy back into the equation and decided to forgo the dumb tourist routine. "Why are we here?" I asked.

The kid frowned at me. "I told you. No speaking."

I made a point of not breaking eye contact even though the kid was glaring at me. Harder to shoot someone while you're looking them in the eye—mechanically, not ethically. Like I said, jaded . . . "Look, all I'm asking, kid, is why we're here. I'm not asking you to let me out—" His frown deepened, so I added, "Ransoming tourists? Figure we have money on us? Just curious."

"You are to stop speaking now, or I will make you."

"Oh come on, you've already got us tied up in a cage. A little overkill, isn't it? What's the harm in telling us—"

The kid swung the gun off his shoulder and rammed the tip into my side right about where my sore rib was. "OK, kid—you made your point, I'll shut up."

"Do not call me a child. I am the one with the gun, and I am the one in charge. You will do what *I* say," he said, and pointed a finger at his chest. It was the kind of aggression you get from a kitten or puppy when it's done playing—a kitten with a loaded rifle and not afraid to use it, but still the uncomfortable analogy stands . . .

If I'd had my hands free, I would have lifted them in surrender. No sense risking another prod with a loaded gun from a twelve-year-old unhappy pirate. Instead, I said absolutely nothing, showing the kid that yes, he was in charge.

He waited, watching me before standing up and slowly walking around the cage, checking the lock and rope knots.

Oh very interesting.

I waited until the footsteps faded and the canvas of the tent once again muffled the retreating voices.

"How frequently does he come in?" I said to Nadya.

"Every thirty minutes or so. I've been counting—four times since we got here."

So I'd been passed out for two hours or so.

Yeah, they definitely knew who we were—or who I was, at least. No way Somali pirates would go to all this trouble for two foreign girls. Which begged the question: who was pulling the strings?

"You're lucky he didn't shoot you," she said.

"They wouldn't bother tying us up if they were planning on killing us." I probably should have added *yet* to that statement . . . if I was being completely honest.

"Note, I said shoot, not kill. The two can be mutually exclusive."

"If he was going to hurt me, he'd have hit me with the butt of his gun. Someone told him not to." I craned my neck around to see if I could get a better look at what was on Nadya's side. I caught a glimpse of yet more crates and boxes piled high. They really had a hodgepodge of goods from just about every corner of the world. I was impressed in spite of my predicament. It takes a lot of effort to amass this many antiquities in one spot. "What else do we know besides they have no problem giving children guns?"

I felt Nadya shake her head. "Surprisingly little. I got the distinct impression on the way over here they were told to knock you out."

"How'd they get Rynn?"

"We didn't have a chance to speak. But I think it was deliberate. He only had two guns on him."

Yeah, well Rynn had better know what he was doing with the pirates. Carpe's whereabouts just worried me in general. I think the only place I trusted the elf was a few thousand miles away in front of a computer screen.

More muffled voices traveled from outside.

"How much do you want to bet the guy in charge is about to walk in now that I'm awake?"

I felt Nadya shrug. "Fifty-fifty they send someone lower down the ladder. Just in case we managed to get out."

"You're on."

Sure enough, the voices cleared as the tent flap opened.

"Two?" I asked, guessing from the number of distinct voices I thought I'd heard.

"No, three—"

"Why, hello, my guests. My little brother tells me you are both awake now," one of the men said, followed by an enthusiastic clap.

Definitely an adult, but not the deep, menacing, testosterone-fueled voice of the kind of tyrant I'd associate with running a band of pirates. It was more what I'd expect in a courtroom—or a business merger—or maybe even politics. If I had to guess, I'd bet on it being the same man who'd greeted us outside the temple, the same one claiming to be me.

When something surprises you, sometimes the best course of action is to hold your tongue until you have a better grip on your surroundings. I decided to wait until I got a better look at him.

Yes, I'm capable of rational thought.

The three men stepped around to my side of the cage. The first two looked like pirates—tall, muscular, large men decorated with guns and knives and a worn mismatch of fatigues. It was the third man who drew my attention. A foot or so shorter than his companions and less muscular, he was in fact the same one who had greeted us, except now he was dressed in a crisp, short-sleeved khaki shirt with matching shorts— expensive, if my tutelage with Nadya was any help. Whereas the other two pirates wore stoic expressions, on this man's face was what could best be described as a politician's smile. In fact, if it weren't for my current predicament, I'd guess businessman on safari over pirate any day.

"My name is Odawaa Siad Barre, and I am the one in charge." He raised his hand to point behind him. "These behind me are my men and will shoot you if you do something I do not like." The smile didn't falter as he added, "Do we understand each other?"

The tingling down the back of my neck rose four notches on the Spidey scale. Someone like this didn't become king of the pirates because they threatened and intimidated people. That was the job of the two in back. Someone like Odawaa rose to power through his wits.

"Crystal," I said.

Apparently Odawaa liked that answer. He crouched down to the dirt floor, arranging himself carefully and deliberately into a cross-legged position. It was a message; he didn't need to sit above me to know he had the upper hand.

It's the really dangerous ones who know posturing is for those who need to overcompensate.

"That is very good. Misunderstandings are unpleasant and unfortunately lead to people losing their fingers."

Odawaa's muscle stood a few paces behind, scowling. I didn't miss their hands on the guns. Or the assortment of knives.

"Imagine my surprise earlier this evening when I and my men came across two American women rummaging around old unmarked ruins," he said, and tsked. "Very dangerous for tourists this far south."

Now who was wasting time pretending . . . "Yeah, that's us. Just a couple of tourists running around unmarked dig sites in the middle of the night. What do you want?"

Odawaa smiled, but this time it wasn't friendly. "At first I thought

I would ransom you back to your government. Two lone women who travel with an armed guard must be worth something." He rubbed his fingertips together, the universal sign for money.

He thought Rynn was a bodyguard and didn't seem to know about Carpe—or my cat. That was good.

"But then, I thought to myself, What are two young women doing out here in the middle of nowhere?" He feigned surprise. "I thought, Perhaps they are archaeologists with the IAA. I had better check, I know how particular they can be. I thought, I will ask my good friend." He pulled out a cell phone and turned the screen around so I could see the picture. It was me—unconscious, with my mouth open and drooling.

"Imagine how much more surprised I was after sending this picture to find I was playing host to the famed thief Owl."

Yeah, I couldn't quite hide my own expression at that statement. I lifted my bound wrists as far as I could. "I think our cultures have very differing definitions of 'host.'"

Odawaa's smile widened. "I was told to expect a strange sense of humor. Though I believe it is me who does the laughing. We are—how would you say?—great admirers of your work. Imitation is the best form of flattery, no?"

Strange didn't begin to cover this. I nodded at the crates and boxes surrounding us. "A bit upscale for Somali pirates, isn't this?"

Odawaa's smile and businesslike swagger didn't drop, not for a second, as he shrugged. "Governments get very upset when we steal ships, and it's no secret that the good ships carry more guns now as well. I find that they are much less concerned about vanishing antiquities, and there are no guns. It is a very lucrative business, as I believe you are already aware."

Great—not only were pirates getting involved in the antiquities trade but they were also impersonating me to do it. Fantastic.

"Look, Odawaa, neither of us are idiots." I hoped, though according to Rynn and Nadya, my omission from that club was tentative at best. "My head is killing me and I'm kind of on a time line here. What do you want?"

He gestured towards me. "Perhaps I simply wanted to see the legend—and my competition."

I shook my head. "No. You'd just shoot me. It'd be easier and less messy. What do you want?" I said, and gave the question more emphasis.

He turned to his men and tsked. One of them handed him a tablet and a large-grid notebook, the kind archaeologists use to map locations and track dig items.

"Two of my men are dead and three more are dying," Odawaa said. "All the same symptoms, all the same time, but do you want to know what the truly interesting thing is? They were on different continents. Two in Syria, one in my beloved home of Somalia, and two in Los Angeles, California. Strange coincidence, no?"

A familiar chill ran up my spine. When I didn't say anything, he continued, "I asked myself, Odawaa, what did these men have in common? Health? No. Women? More possible but also no. Something they ate? But how could they have shared food on different sides of the world?"

He lowered his head like one of the large predators the African continent is famous for. "The only thing these men had in common was that all handled the artifacts from the IAA's city in Syria. I want to know why." He turned the tablet around. I recognized an article I'd seen in L.A. only a few days before, though it seemed much longer. It was an update on the two foreign undocumented workers who had fallen ill and been quarantined. Both were now dead, and the health authorities were still investigating and warning people to report in to a hospital if experiencing flulike symptoms.

Yeah, that chilled feeling only got worse. I swallowed my nerves. "So? Ask your friend at the IAA. You know damn well I haven't set foot in the city."

Odawaa grinned and laughed, making a show of slapping his legs and gesturing to his men as if we were sharing in a great joke. "You know, I did just that. They say it is merely coincidence. Many viruses float around in Africa, which is true." He dropped all pretence of friendliness. "But they kill more than five men. I want to know what you know of this disease that kills like a poison and the IAA need to lie about."

So many ways to answer that question . . . "Do you believe in curses, Mr. Barre?" I asked.

He smiled. " 'Mr. Barre'—I think I like that—Owl. Do I believe in curses?" He nodded at the men standing behind him, still holding their guns. "You see my men? They only speak a few words of English and believe in all manner of things, from curses to demons." To prove his point, he asked them a question in what I guessed was Somali. Both men's hands left the hilts of their guns, and they made the sign of the cross.

Odawaa turned back to me. "You see? Very superstitious. Me? Before my country imploded and this line of work found me, I studied tropical diseases in London, of all places. They may not know better, but you and I? We do."

"No offense, but how the hell does a doctor end up king of the pirates?" I said.

He smiled. "At the risk of quoting old children's tales, I decided I'd rather be the thing that goes bump in the night than the one waiting to be eaten, and the only things that go bump in the night in Somalia are the pirates, so here I am. Who knew I would have such a talent for this line of work?"

The universe in its unholy wrath rains down all sorts of surprises on the unsuspecting . . . as much as I was pissed Odawaa and his crew were using me as their business model, I'm not the one who could judge him for joining the side with all the guns after the government collapsed.

I also didn't want to spend an extended period of time with an ex-MD who'd crawled the ranks to Head Somali Pirate . . .

"Now, I tell you all this because my contact believes I am just another superstitious thug of a pirate. I ask you again, what do you know of this hemorrhagic fever that lives in the old caverns and acts like a poison? What disease is this that hides on old stone and drowns its victims in their own blood?"

Hemorrhagic fever. That was bad, and also not what the previous teams/victims had called it in their dig notes . . . then again, they hadn't had a doctor on team.

Bigger problem; how the hell did I explain to someone who knew better than to believe in supernatural monsters and curses that what his men were experiencing was a supernatural curse?

"I am not accustomed to waiting for answers, Owl," Odawaa said, and I saw the men behind him shift.

Failing to tell him anything would be a bad idea—he knew his diseases, and he knew damn well the curse was linked to the dig site—and no amount of lying would get me around that. So I'd just have to lie around the truth . . .

Besides, telling the pirate his contact had screwed him over was just another way to screw them over—and maybe find out who the hell was in charge. Win-win.

"OK, you're right. There is a disease in the Syrian temple," I said, choosing my words with care as I licked the sweat off my lips. "It's why the dig site is supposed to be closed. The artifacts they had you remove were probably contaminated—which I'm guessing is why they hired a bunch of uneducated pirates to handle it for them." That would also have given whoever in the IAA orchestrated this fiasco the time and window to get themselves an airtight alibi. If I were an evil archaeologist trying to release dangerous artifacts into the world at large, that's what I'd do . . .

"Am I right?" I asked. "They made your men go inside and get the artifacts for them, while they stayed safe outside?"

Odawaa leaned towards the cage. He spat out the words, "What kind of disease?"

The first rule of lying convincingly is to never divulge details you don't understand—especially to someone who knows a hell of a lot more than you do. "Ah, yeah, not so big on the details—"

"It's a bacterium," Nadya said, interrupting what I'm sure would have been a plane crash of a lie. "Long living, not sure what species, forms cysts around itself, able to survive years like that—apparently hundreds of years. Like Owl says, the dig was supposed to be closed off. We don't know who authorized opening it up."

Thank God one of us showed up to pathology class.

Odawaa considered what Nadya said, then nodded. "That would make the most sense . . ." He then looked back at me. "They knew about this, you say?"

"Oh yeah, they've got dig notes from as recently as thirty years back." Though they sure as hell hadn't used the words *hemorrhagic fever* . . . "Think of it this way, Mr. Barre: they wanted whatever was in that temple, and you and your pirates are a hell of a lot more expendable than their archaeologists."

Odawaa said something to his companions in Somali and without another word to us stood up.

"Hey! We told you what you want to know." Sort of—or the most believable version. "Your turn. What the hell do you plan on doing with us?"

He ignored us and headed for the tent exit. The stale smell of uncirculated air hit me, along with a shot of adrenaline. Not the kind of place I wanted to die a slow death in.

"Hey—if getting back at the IAA is what you want, let me out. They'll really hate that."

I heard his footsteps stop. "Oh I thought about handing you over to the IAA. That is certainly what my contact requested, though you've been useful to me, and I hate to waste a useful resource."

He stepped back into view and motioned at the crates and already unpacked items stacked upon them. "All of these artifacts, much smaller and easier to negotiate than ships. More profit, less risk to me and my men. The problem was I never understood much about old relics. I was always better with diseases, broken bones." He shrugged. "Cirro was our archaeologist who was in charge of making sure all these items were real enough. He spent three years studying in the United States and brought back many curious stories about the infamous Owl. A promising student who threw away her potential by falsifying research, then had no choice but to become a thief."

Oh buddy, if you knew the half of it. As I suspected, an undergraduate had been behind the cursed items getting out. I'm sure someone owed me a beer for that. If and when we got out of here . . .

Odawaa frowned. "There was a medical student I knew, my classmate, 'Johnny Boy' we used to call him—fun fellow, well liked. He used to cheat on exams. At first it was every now and then, but he found he got ahead, and then it was a given he would cheat. Graduated too, became a well-known and respectable doctor. Do you know what you and Johnny Boy have in common?"

I felt Nadya tense behind me . . . "No," I said, "and you talk too much."

Odawaa's smile was back. "Eventually the lies caught up with him. They always do."

I snorted. "If bad things have a habit of catching up, I'd hate to see what the universe has in store for you."

He shook his head and held open the tent flaps. "The world does not always catch up with bad people, that is its way. Only the ones who are so caught up in their own lies and half-truths they no longer know the difference. My archaeologist, Cirro, very sad. He died five days ago. I have no idea where any of these items go or what they are." He whistled to the two guards, and they both hung back by our cage.

"If you think for one second I'm helping the guys who've been masquerading as me for the past month—"

"Not all people really believe we are the Owl," Odawaa said. "Partly because the messenger, Hermes, would not be bribed, but mostly due to a strange practice you have of authenticating all of your merchandise. Very hard to replicate, Cirro told me, the mark of a very good archaeologist. But now with you here, we can have our items delivered by this Hermes and offer the authentic Owl experience."

"You can keep on being my second-rate, cheap impression for all I care—hey!" I yelled as one of the guards kicked the cage near my face.

Odawaa laughed. "You know, I was very gifted in surgery. It has been a few years, but I believe my methods will convince you to cooperate. Chloroform only goes so far to dull the pain—hard to determine the doses with my current equipment. Of course, we need you in one piece. Not so with your friend and companion."

"And I'll bet you'll let them walk free if I help?"

"Please, let us be honest with our barter. We both know none of you will be walking free. A quick death is better than torture, however."

I swallowed. "First off, you don't have a fraction of the equipment we'd need."

He arched an eyebrow, driving a sick feeling into my stomach. "You misunderstand me. I do not need you to authenticate these, I need you to make it look like you have authenticated them." His smile widened. "We are pirates, after all." He whistled to his men, who approached the cage. "My men, Bhotaan and Odiye, will let you out and make sure you get to work. They speak no English, so they will not be able to answer any questions, and they have a tendency to shoot first and ask questions later. If you do not cooperate, they will shoot. Stray bullets get lodged in the strangest places. You will not want to watch me try to remove them from you or your friend."

"You seriously expect—shit." As if to prove the point, the second guard this time delivered a kick to the cage.

Odawaa turned his back on us. "You two can start with the items out on the crates," he said, and then he was gone.

"Finally. I could not wait for him to shut up," Nadya said.

"Well, there are two things we know now that we didn't before," I said as the first guard opened our cage.

"What's that?"

"These pirates don't have any idea what they're involved in." Furthermore, someone inside the IAA did.

A bunch of pirates selling off highly dangerous supernatural artifacts. Under less dire circumstances, I might think it comical. "I don't know about you, Nadya, but I have no intention of being here when the supernaturals start showing up looking for their shit." I also had a sinking suspicion Rynn's imprisonment by the pirates was a temporary predicament.

"Ditto," Nadya said.

The guards cut the rope, and I rubbed circulation back into my wrists and ankles. "In the meantime though, I'm game to rummage around the pirate treasure. Do some souvenir shopping?"

"Let me know where to sign up."

And with that we started our survey of the epic loot.

If it wasn't for the fact that these were pirates who were seriously screwing me over, I might feel sorry for them.

I picked up the Tibetan scroll—it was nicely preserved. Until these assholes had gotten hold of it, I'm sure someone had kept it locked up in an airtight room ... probably in a Tibetan temple ...

I held it up to the light sifting through a corner of the tent. Yup, definitely a spell scroll. "That makes four on my side," I said to Nadya.

"And that's only what's out of the boxes," she replied from inside the wooden crate she was crouched in.

I picked up a gold Buddha statue that was roughly the size of Captain. Again supposedly from Tibet—nice piece, hard to find; the Chinese made a point of destroying a lot of the Buddhist artifacts during the Cultural Revolution.

Nadya looked up from the crate. "Don't tell me they got a hold of a real prayer statue?"

"Supposed to be." I flipped it over and checked the bottom with a flashlight I'd found on the desk. There was a small divot in the gold—showing gray metal underneath. Gold leaf. "Would be a hell of a lot more impressed if it was real."

"Another fake? How many does that make now?"

"Sixty-forty split in favor of the fakes. This one's good though. They've got the tarnish and wear right on it. Might even be an old forgery from a hundred years or so ago." And I was somehow supposed to create the paperwork saying it was real, when it took me less than a minute to figure out it was a fake?

"Make it look authentic ... What do they think I am, magic?" I placed the statue into the largest and first of the three piles. The harmless fakes.

Initially we hadn't planned on organizing the pirates' treasure room. We'd planned on royally screwing things up and maybe pocketing a few things while we figured out a way out or Rynn caused a commotion—whichever came first. It was a decent—if random—amassment of antiquities.

But Odawaa hadn't been kidding. His two men were definitely trigger-happy. They'd already put a bullet in one of the crates when we'd gotten too close to the tent flap. We'd been planning on bolting, but that was beside the point.

It was when we'd stumbled across the supernatural artifacts that we'd rethought our approach.

I picked up another item—a goblet with gold details and a handful of sapphires. I hit it with the infrared light; most supernaturals could see infrared. Lines of painted magic lit up. "Hey, Nadya—got another one. Ever heard of a magic Persian goblet?"

She stood up so she could see me. I held up the goblet for her inspection, and she frowned. "Is it covered with sapphires? And pass me the infrared laser."

"Yes, around the rim," I said, and tossed the penlight overhand.

She caught the laser and disappeared back inside the crate. "Twelfth century, Goblet of the Peri. There's an incantation that makes the goblet cure all poison."

Be more impressed if it turned liquid into wine ... better yet, beer ... I could use one about now. "And if you fuck it up?"

"If you fuck it up, the goblet poisons you. The Peri toed the line between angels and demons. They weren't giving anything away for free."

Right. Dangerous stuff pile it was. "That's what, ten total?"

Nadya crawled back out of the crate. "Eleven. This one has a golem, pre-Christian, Jerusalem."

Jesus Christ, where the hell were they finding all this stuff? "It's a wonder they all aren't dead yet," I said.

Supernatural magic is designed for use by supernaturals only. Usually it's written in blood or some other fluid of dubious origin spiked with magic. It's also written in their languages—either the common tongue that just about everyone except the vampires spoke, or something species-specific.

Humans trying to speak supernatural and invoke their magic almost always backfired in spectacular explosions and magic gone wild, though every few decades some IAA idiot in the supernatural department decided it was a good idea to have a go invoking a charm, something as harmless-looking as the Goblet of Peri. Of course, this time was going to be different. They knew where the last guy went wrong . . .

If they were lucky, they turned a half dozen people into rabbits or goats. If they were unlucky, a few buildings exploded . . . proving spectacularly why no one should ever try it again . . . which translated into roughly thirty years.

Nadya frowned at me. "Alix, you are not looking well."

I wasn't feeling well either. The chills and sweats had gotten more manageable, but I wasn't convinced that was a good sign. My skin had grown clammy, and though I'd been doing my best to hide it, I was now soaked in sweat.

Worrying about Rynn wasn't helping. Supernaturals are hard to kill, not invincible. It was a distinct possibility the pirates had incapacitated him and we'd have to save him.

I heard footsteps outside, and a moment later Odawaa stepped through the tent flap, carrying something under his arm.

Carpe's book—I'd wondered what had happened to that.

"What is this?" he asked, handing it to me.

I made a big show of examining it, then shrugged. "It's an old Egyptian book, well preserved, authentic."

"I'll tell you what I think," Odawaa continued. "I think you know something I do not about its value."

"Where's my bodyguard?" I countered.

Odawaa smiled. "Maybe I shot him."

I could feel the sweat pilling on my forehead now . . . I hoped he didn't notice or chalked it up to working in the heat. "Then I guess I don't know anything."

Odawaa pulled out a handgun. Not the flashier, more intimidating rifles his men carried but a gun you pull out when you're faced with the very real inconvenience of having to shoot someone. He pointed it at Nadya's head. "I do not believe you."

"I can translate it for you," Nadya piped up. "In fact, I'm better with languages than she is."

The way Nadya said *languages* . . .

Odawaa narrowed his eyes. "Why would you help us?"

She jerked her head in my direction. "Because she has a bad habit of getting people killed and I'm more interested in my own neck."

He seemed to consider that, then offered her the book before turning to his men.

I shook my head at Nadya, indicating I thought it was a bad idea. Blown up by misfiring magic was worse than pirates.

But she either didn't see me—doubtful—or was ignoring me.

I watched as she opened the book and flipped through the pages, settling on one I didn't like the look of. A curse . . . a sleep spell, by the looks of it.

"Nadya, bad—ow!" I turned to the guard, who'd rammed me again with the gun.

"No speaking to your friend," Odawaa called.

While the guards were concentrating on me, I caught Nadya mouth the words, "*Let me try to invoke it, all right?*"

Not that I had a choice. Oh this was going to be an unmitigated disaster.

Nadya started to read out loud from the page, under her breath, pronouncing the ancient Egyptian deity supernatural words until she'd spoken the last one.

I waited, all my muscles tensed. Nothing happened. We were still in one piece, which was a bonus, but Odawaa and his men were still awake.

And then the wind picked up.

"Is that supposed to happen?" I whispered to Nadya.

"I don't know, you tell me—you're the one with experience in curses—"

"Well, I don't see any of them sleeping yet."

"Here, let me try another one."

"Try another one?" I grabbed for the book, and yelling from Odawaa's right- and left-hand men ensued. "Are you out of your mind?"

"If you had read it, there would be shrapnel already. Alix, let go of the book before they shoot us."

"No, you let go!"

I'm sure either Odawaa or one of his men would have shot at us eventually, except that the crate Nadya had been in minutes before—the one holding the golem—shifted.

Everyone in the room froze, including Nadya and I, with both our hands on Carpe's spell book.

"I thought you said that was a sleeping spell you read."

"It was."

"Then why is the golem moving?"

Nadya inclined her head and let out a breath. "Unforeseen magical misfire?"

The crate shifted again—this time with more force rocking the crate from side to side.

The two men holding the rifles both crossed their chests, said fast prayers, and backed up towards the exit—pointing the guns at the crate instead of us.

Odawaa turned to face us. "What manner of trick is this?"

"Yeah—I'd follow what your men are doing and back up," I said as Nadya and I made for the stack of unopened crates behind us.

Odawaa barked a command at his men. They stopped short of running out of the tent, but this was the first time I saw any inkling of dissension, with both of them barking right back. Superstition one, modern science, zero.

Odawaa aimed his gun at me, not even a trace of the friendly façade left. "I do not know what trick this is, but you will bring it to an end now, or I will shoot you both."

To give you an idea how badly the thing in the box scared us, neither of us stopped backing up. "Odawaa, trust me, if we could stop it, we would," I said. We were almost at the crates.

Odawaa's gun fired in the sand near my feet. Still I didn't stop.

"You can either stand here and shoot us, or run," I said. "I *strongly* suggest you run."

The gun fired again, this time grazing my shoe. Well, it's not like I hadn't tried to warn him . . .

The crate cracked along its front as the first stone foot hit the ground.

That was it for Odawaa's two men. They bolted for the entrance, ignoring Odawaa as he screamed after them.

I shared the sentiment. Gun or not, negotiations were over. "You know all that stuff you don't believe in?" I said to him, nodding at the crate. "That's it." And despite the gun still aimed at us, Nadya and I dove behind the nearest intact crate.

Golems are . . . well . . . not a good idea is what it boils down to. Supernaturals used to make them to act as guards—ancient vampires were quite fond of them, as were genies and anything else that might have reason to hide from humans while they were sleeping. The problem is golems work on a primitive binary code, and you don't always get what you pay for.

This one was big and made of rock. It stood about seven feet tall and had been sculpted without many features. Its torso consisted of a large, pendulous midsection, attached to a featureless head and rounded limbs. The whole thing reminded me of the Mesopotamian fertility gods. Golems weren't built to look pretty, they were built to pound threats into roadkill.

Peering from behind the crate, Nadya and I stayed as still as possible. Golems responded to movement. Hopefully it would go for Odawaa, who was yelling for reinforcements steps away from the tent exit.

No such luck. It took two more steps out of the crate, but instead of running after Odawaa, it swiveled its stone head. Three unnaturally black pits chiseled into the front of its head focused in on us.

"If we split up and run, we might short-circuit it," Nadya said.

"Or it could squish us."

Turns out we didn't have to test that theory. Odawaa's reinforcements arrived and opened fire.

Like I said, golems work on binary logic. The guns going off overrode whatever proximity programming we'd triggered. Stone grating against stone, the golem swiveled and charged towards Odawaa and his men.

We took the opportunity to duck behind another crate while the bullets slapped against the oncoming golem, not that they were doing much good. Think rock-paper-scissors, except with bullets instead of scissors. Rock still wins.

Like idiots, they kept firing. I swore. You don't try to defeat a golem, you run— fast—preferably into tight spots it can't fit its limbs through. There's a reason golems are found in tombs with a doorway smaller than they are.

As much as I'd have liked to get even with Odawaa and his band of merry pirates for pretending to be me . . .

"Odawaa, you idiot, you don't shoot golems, you run!" I yelled.

Odawaa turned his gun in my direction. "There is no such thing as golems," he snarled, a maniacal look on his face.

It's the smart, sane ones who go ballistic when faced with their first supernatural.

"Don't you think that's a pretty fucking moot point—oh shit." I ducked back down as Odawaa opened fire, bullets peppering the crates.

A high-pitched shriek echoed around the room, and I hazarded a peek back over the box in time to see the golem toss one of the pirates. I winced as bone met tent pole with a crunch. The man didn't get back up—or move.

Odawaa's sanity might've been getting a hell of a challenge today, but he wasn't stupid. He and the remaining pirate abandoned their shooting and went for the tent flap.

Only problem was the tent wouldn't halt a golem.

Come to think of it, the best bet was to follow their lead while the golem was busy. The crates were in the center of the room. We might be able to make a run for it and slide under the canvas.

I peeked over the edge to see where the golem was in time to see it bat Odawaa's remaining man in our direction. I swore and ducked back down as the body collided with our crate. Bone cracking against plywood.

Yeah, not running. I heard Odawaa scream, I think, but I didn't dare look—not with the golem lobbing human projectiles in our direction.

"That thing moves a hell of a lot faster than I thought it would," I said to Nadya.

"Yes, its speed and agility are an unforeseen complication."

"Unforeseen complication? Nadya, the *golem* is an unforeseen complication."

She shrugged. "Like I said. Now stop worrying about how the golem got activated and start worrying about a way out—one that does not involve running by the golem."

I frowned. "Me find a way? I was the one who told you not to read from Carpe's goddamned magic book. *You* find a way out . . ."

The yelling and screaming had stopped.

Nadya frowned. "Go see what it is doing," she said.

"No, *you* go see what it's doing, it's already thrown someone at me—oomph!" Without ceremony, Nadya shoved me so that I had no choice but to peek over the edge. Damn it, I needed to remember to push first next time . . .

No sign of Odawaa—or his body—and the tent flap had been torn off. Whether he'd gotten out or been thrown was up for debate. The golem was standing there, perfectly still. For whatever reason, programming or misfire, it had decided for the moment that this was the area it was supposed to protect. "I think it's deactivated," I said.

At the sound of my voice, its head swiveled around, the three black pits fixating on our crate.

I swore and ducked back down. What I needed was something that would trigger the attack response, get it going in one direction while we went the other . . . I scanned the things in reach. Vase? No, too expensive—I wasn't that desperate yet. Buddha? The gold plate probably wouldn't register as an attack—wait a minute . . .

I slid my hand between the crates as silently as I could and reached for the rifle strapped across the collapsed man's chest. Eww, there was blood. Oh man, I signed up to be an antiquities thief specifically to avoid blood and shooting.

My fingers closed around the back of the gun strap, and I untangled it from the body.

Only problem was I didn't know a goddamn thing about rifles. "Do you know how to use this?" I asked, handing it to Nadya.

She checked the gun. "It's a Kalashnikov—that's a yes," she added when I gave her an exasperated look.

"Is it ready to fire?" I'm not one for guns—in my experience, unless you really know what you're doing, the bad guys end up with the weapons—pointed at me.

She nodded, but a frown touched her face.

"Fantastic. I know exactly the distraction. Shoot the metal crates on the golem's left," I said.

"That's a terrible idea—"

"Fine, I'll do it." I took back the gun and leveled the bullet end over the crate. "No!" Nadya yelled.

It was too late. I'd already pulled the trigger.

My plan had been to aim at the metal storage boxes piled on the far side of the tent and draw the golem's attention away from us, leaving a short but clear pathway to freedom . . .

Fun fact: bullets ricochet when you shoot them at some types of metal. And the Kalashnikov is an automatic.

I swore and ducked back behind the crate with Nadya as the bullets rained back down on the artifacts and fakes, including the false Buddha statue. The pieces—brittle metal under the gold leaf—clattered to the ground all around us.

I knew I should have thrown the statue . . . maybe the golem hadn't noticed?

I heard the granite on granite swivel as it charged.

Nadya shoved me to the left while she took off to the right. With two of us to chase, it might just short-circuit long enough to give us time to make it out under the tent flap.

The golem's head swiveled towards me.

If the golem thought this was its new lair, then as soon as we slid under the tent flap, the off switch should be triggered. Or it might start rampaging through the pirates' camp, but at this point I was desperate.

"Hurry up!" Nadya yelled. I checked over my shoulder and saw she was halfway under the tent. The golem had caught up.

The end of the tent was only a few feet away. Oh hell, I hoped I didn't mess this up, otherwise I was going to be a sand popsicle . . .

The golem raised its arm to swing, and I dove. Maybe it was the fever, maybe it was just my personal brand of bad luck, but instead of sliding under the canvas, I slipped in the sand, the golem's arms braced overhead.

There was no way I'd crawl out in time. I closed my eyes and winced. So that was how it ended; the great Owl smashed by an accidently triggered golem . . .

Before the golem could swing its rock hand down on me, a strong hand snatched my wrist and pulled me under the tent and out to safety. I felt the ground shake as the golem's fist struck the sand. I looked up into Rynn's face.

"Hi Alix, found a golem, I see?" he said, smiling.

Relief washed over me. "Let it never be said you don't have good timing."

But before I could do anything too embarrassing, Rynn turned to the man standing behind him. Not one of the pirates, but familiar-looking . . . dark skin with a blue tinge to it, no hair, tall.

"I told you they'd be where the pirates were screaming 'Monster,'" Rynn said.

The man frowned at me, and I realized why he looked familiar. He was a ringer for the guards who'd been stationed at both Artemis's and Daphne's homes. A genie.

Rynn's genie friend frowned at me and used the one word of supernatural I recognized. *Seereet.* Rynn shrugged at him in response, and the genie turned back to me. "She is very small for someone to cause that much trouble. I would caution you to find another human."

"Hey!" I said.

Rynn patted the genie on the back. "Don't mind Nomun, Alix, he means no harm. He's an air genie. Not much of a filter either. Owes me a gambling debt, so he'll be getting us into Syria."

The genie shook his head at me, still not looking convinced. "I must say, incubus, as a point of honor I should offer to extinguish this one for you. So much trouble—"

"Yeah, I can really see the 'no harm' part, Rynn," I said, backing up as the genie peered down at me.

The genie threw back his head and laughed. "You were right, incubus, she is very gullible."

Oh you've got to be fucking kidding me. I glared at Rynn, who couldn't quite cover a laugh. "You thought that was funny?"

Nomun leaned down and patted my shoulder. "Please take no offense. I offered to get you out of harm's way, but he claimed you would be just as likely to throw something at me as the golem." He added to Rynn, "The pirates are dismantled for now, though no sign of their leader. If we leave now and the wind is good, we will get there before nightfall."

"We need to grab the elf first—and the Mau," Rynn said. "I left them back at Passer's temple. They should be fine provided the elf didn't do anything stupid."

Shit . . . "No, wait—I need back in there," I said. "We can't leave without Carpe's stupid book, and I'm not leaving the pirates with the dig notes." Thief or not, an archaeologist would have kept a map and inventory. We'd also know if more cursed artifacts had been sold.

Nomun nodded. "I'll deal with the golem," he said. He frowned and shook his head as he headed into the tent ahead of me. "So much trouble for one so small."

"Yeah, yeah," I called after him.

As soon as Nomun disappeared into the tent, I shook my head at Rynn. "I got to admit, I'm a little disappointed. An incubus held in captivity by a pack of pirates."

"Who said anything about captivity?" Rynn said, arching a blond eyebrow.

I frowned. "What the hell else could you have been doing for the past couple hours?"

Rynn's smile widened. "How bout you come meet my entourage."

"*What* entourage?"

17

The Syrian City of the Dead

7:00 p.m., at the feet of Moses the Abyssinian

I had to hand it to Nomun, he got us into Syria and to the mountain undetected, though I don't think I'll ever step foot on a cargo plane again. Nomun could make very old planes do things they shouldn't—like fly.

A fat lot of good getting here had done us, what with all the IAA crawling around . . . I was still trying to figure out how the hell they'd gotten all the vehicles in there, on account of there being no roads.

"I cannot believe we left the terra-cotta warriors behind," I said to Nadya, who was sitting beside me. At the moment she had the binoculars. "A pair, Nadya."

She jabbed me in the arm. "You do not need a terra-cotta warrior."

I wiped sweat off my forehead and did my best to cover the wet cough I'd developed. It had started in the last couple hours, along with a killer sore throat—no pun intended. I was having a hard time keeping the hemorrhagic fever part out of my mind. "I beg to differ, especially if I get out alive."

Nadya skewered me with one look.

"Do you have any idea how long I've had my eye out for one of those? A pair!"

The skewering didn't stop. "We'll be in China again."

"You know, that's what people used to say about Nirvana concerts. No terra-cotta warriors—happy?" I said, and stifled another cough.

She shook her head and got up, heading over to where Carpe and Captain were hiding.

We were encamped on mountain steps dug out on the opposite side of the ravine that housed the Deir Mar Musa Monastery, maybe a thousand or so meters away, give or take. Both sides of the ravine were covered in paths that wound their way to nowhere, making that distance not mean a hell of a lot. In fact, the entire mountain range surrounding the Monastery of Saint Moses was filled with similar footpaths, which is what you get when you let the sheep and goats do the urban planning.

My head hurt. And despite the fact that I was running a permanent fever now, I was freezing from the altitude. We'd been on lookout for over an hour now—Rynn and his genie friend were not willing to do anything until nightfall. We had no idea what Odawaa might or might not have told the IAA—or if he was still alive.

By my guess, I was also about due for another hallucination. That was going to be a joy . . .

I checked my watch. 7:00 p.m. Time to see what the IAA had planned for dinner. "Gimme those," I said, and grabbed the binoculars hanging from Rynn's neck as he slid into Nadya's place. After my hallucination with Caracalla, no one was willing to leave me on my own for any stretch of time . . .

"Damn it, will you ask before taking things?" Rynn said.

"Thief, remember?"

Using the binoculars, I focused in on the collection of tents and off-road jeeps surrounding the monastery and the footbridge spanning the ravine.

IAA agents and a handful of archaeologists milled around the jeeps and tarps before heading into the stone monastery buildings, light escaping from the stone windows.

Now, if I could just figure out who the hell was in charge. One of Sanders's postdocs had to be milling around . . . even if I spotted a grad student I recognized, it'd be better than nothing.

"Oh man, this just keeps getting better and better," I said as I picked out a man wearing an old, secondhand military cargo jacket—it was supposed to be ironic, whatever the hell that meant—and shoulder-length light brown hair. I was half convinced he highlighted it.

Out of all the postdocs, of course it had to be him.

Nadya crouched down on my other side. "Far left, entrance to the monastery," I told her. A moment later she swore.

"If we're looking for the link of who's in charge, that's him," I said.

"Who is it?" Rynn asked, taking his binoculars back.

"He's Dr. Cooper Hill," Nadya said. "One of Dr. Sanders's most celebrated researchers, also used to be Alix's and my acting supervisor."

Rynn smirked. I ignored it. "Also happens to be the most cutthroat postdoc on his payroll." I should have known he was involved. "I ruled him out initially because of the curse involved. Cooper isn't stupid, but more than that, he doesn't usually get his hands dirty."

"No, he'd prefer to throw hapless grad students under the bus," Nadya said. Yeah, then hijack the paperwork, falsify a few signatures and dig reports—hell, I'm amazed he hadn't tried to pin drugs on me as well.

"What about the professor in charge?" Rynn asked.

I shook my head. "Past making sure they're turning in publishable research papers, Dr. Sanders can't be bothered checking what the hell his postdocs are doing. Besides, the IAA treats Hill like some sort of archaeology god." With Dr. Sanders's signature on the paperwork and Cooper's clean record and talent for finding hapless and willing scapegoats, no wonder the IAA hadn't bothered looking too closely into the reopening of the dig . . .

When I caught Rynn frowning at me, I added, "He's good," lest he read any meaning into it. "We'll have to be careful—he's got a talent for keeping track of what goes on at his dig sites. If something's out of place, he'll know."

"Hill was responsible for getting Alix thrown out of grad school," Nadya offered. "He was the one who convinced her to retract her research after it uncovered the Aztec mummy."

"Gee thanks, Nadya." Not exactly something I'd wanted Rynn to know about. Mostly because it was embarrassing. "*Retract your thesis, Alix, there'll be a nice compensation pack in Ephesus for you . . .*" Needless to say there had been no travel plans to Turkey, only a one-way ticket to Siberia.

I've got one hell of a talent for trusting the wrong people.

"Alix was particularly stupid, she was practically in love with Hill, followed him around like a lost puppy."

Goddamn it—"Enough, Nadya!" I felt my face turning red as Rynn narrowed in on me. I did my best to put the conversation away from my idiocy and back on track. "Regardless of his dubious ethics, I'm still surprised Cooper's involved. He usually keeps a degree's worth of separation from anything remotely dangerous."

"Cooper? You're on a first-name basis?" Rynn asked, phrasing it innocently, though I knew damn well it was anything but.

I frowned right back. "If *Dr. Hill* is down there, it means he's in charge of whatever the hell they've got going on. No way the thieves could have gotten in and out without him knowing and sounding the alarm." As a point of reference, I purposely stayed away from his digs.

Rynn was finding my discomfort way too entertaining. I switched my attention back to Nadya. "See if you can find where Carpe is. We need that map. *Now.*" Carpe was off with our friendly neighborhood genie, Nomun. Apparently the agreement to get us into the city meant through the front gate. Not that I was complaining; I think Carpe was more afraid of the genie than Rynn . . .

As soon as Nadya was out of earshot, Rynn set in on me. "So Dr. Hill is the postdoc who ruined your life?"

I nodded and did my best to stifle another coughing fit. "Yup, that's about it."

Rynn seemed to consider that. "No offense, but present company excluded, you have horrible taste in men."

"Right back at you," I said.

"What is that supposed to mean?"

I nodded in the direction Nadya had headed, where Nomun was also overseeing Rynn's collection of pirates. "Funny, when you said you'd been working on the pirates, I didn't think you meant it quite so literally."

He frowned. "I was pressed for time. Besides, they're enthralled, not mind controlled. I'm not doing any permanent damage, and it's not like I had a lot of options. Deal with it."

"So the best solution you could come up with was to make the five of them fall madly in love with you?" Turns out Rynn hadn't had to fight any of the pirates. Once he'd had enough of them enthralled, they'd just let him out. "You realize it's not helping the case that you aren't a whore," I said.

"Will you please, for the love of God, stop with the whore jokes? At least until we get out of this mess? And only one of them thinks he's in love with me. The other four don't play for that particular team, and to be honest, I don't think number five thought he did either. They're more like extreme super fans. And who are you to complain? I put up with the stealing."

"The point is you enthralled a pack of pirates." When I said it like that, it sounded like collecting baseball cards. "It's creepy, all right."

"For the love of— Trust me, this isn't a walk in the park. It's disturbing being inside their heads, even on an emotional level. Granted, you'd be worse—"

"Wait a minute, how the hell am I worse than pirates?"

I watched as Rynn weighed his answer. "They're mean and enjoy violence—it's uncomfortable, but I can manage. You're a roller coaster of conflicting emotions on a good day. It'd take more effort than I'm willing to expend to manage what goes on inside your head."

Not sure how I felt about that assessment . . . "Just so we're all clear on this though, you *could* do that to me, the whole enthralling thing?"

"I already promised I wouldn't. Can we please drop the pirates?" he said, then gave me a critical look. "To be honest, I'm amazed you're taking it this well."

"Blame it on the fever. I'll freak out once I've got the curse lifted." Not to mention the over-a-few-thousand-years-old detail Artemis had hinted at back at Daphne's. That is, if I got the curse lifted . . . which reminded me, I might never have the chance to ask Rynn again . . .

"What the hell does *seereet* mean?" I said.

"I prefer the game where you try to guess where I'm from."

I shook my head. "Odds are not in my favor. I have it on questionable authority you were around for Caligula. Borders change too much over a couple thousand years—"

Rynn swore.

"You can thank your cousin for that tidbit. Come on. *Seereet* means 'thrall' or 'incubus dinner,' doesn't it?"

"Alix—not now."

"You might as well tell me. Come on—'nonsupernatural'?"

"My God, if I didn't—" Rynn made an exasperated noise and drew in a breath. "There is no direct translation for *seereet*. It's an old word, and it's a description used for someone's energy—aura, you might call it, but that's a human word as well and not completely accurate."

I knew it. They'd been calling me some derogatory word for humans to my face . . . "Spit it out. What have all the supernaturals been calling me?"

He swayed his head from side to side, weighing his answer. "The closest translation would be—"

"Thief, it's thief, isn't it?"

"Train wreck," he said.

Oh . . . Somehow I hadn't seen that one coming. "I have the aura of a train wreck?" Somehow that was a bit of a letdown.

"Not exactly, but close enough."

Hunh. I picked up the binoculars and started surveying the monastery again. The supernaturals had been calling me "train wreck" to my face . . .

Rynn gave me a wary look. "I didn't tell people to call you that, I swear—"

It was my turn to shake my head. "No. I heard you the first time. It's an aura thing." Though I decided it was time to switch subjects. I jerked my head in the thralls' direction. "Are you sure we can trust them?"

Rynn shrugged. "As far as you can trust anyone enthralled against their will—"

Someone cleared their throat.

I put down the binoculars. Carpe stood behind us with Nadya . . . and Nadya looked pissed.

"Carpe, where's my World Quest map of the Syrian temple?" I said, letting the threat come through in my voice.

He cleared his throat again and glanced warily at Rynn. "There's been a complication—" he started.

I'd had it with his bullshit. First the detour to Egypt, now this. I didn't let him finish. Instead, I jumped up and pinned him to the cliff wall behind us. The nice thing about elves is they're light. "Let's just be real clear on something before another word leaves your mouth—if you even come *close* to insinuating I just wasted two days and my life chasing after *your* book and you can't get my map—"

"No. I can get the map! Just stop strangling me and I'll explain."

Against my better judgment, I let Carpe go.

He rubbed his neck for a moment and glared at me. "The programmers have agreed to give us the map. It's just that they want to have a meeting with us on World Quest—to negotiate . . ."

"I told you to make World Quest your bitch. Where the hell do you figure negotiate fits into that?"

He straightened up. "It means we won't be stealing, and they promise they'll give us the map. They just want to talk."

I closed my eyes. *Deep breath, Owl* . . . "Fine, get them online now so I can tell them to give me my fucking map."

"It's not technically your map, and it's not that simple—"

I opened my eyes and narrowed them at him. He fidgeted but tread onwards. "Look, they want to meet with us in an hour and a half. As a piece of goodwill, they won't remove our characters or ban us . . ."

"So let me get this straight. You have your spell book and I'll *maybe* have a map in an hour and a half if the game designers decide to give it to us in a place of their choosing?"

"They'll give us the map, but all bets are off if we no show. Sorry, but that's the best I could do in line with my own ethics."

The best he could do? I held out my hand. "Rynn, give me your gun," I said.

"Why?"

"So I can shoot the elf and take my goddamn spell book back."

Rynn and Nadya tried to grab me, but on account of my extreme sweatiness I slipped through their grasp, knocked Carpe to the ground, and straddled him. Considering Carpe was taller and heavier than me, I was surprised I'd knocked him over. "Give me my book back!"

"I'll get you your map, I give you my word!"

"In an hour and a half I could be dead!" I wound up to hit him.

The fever had slowed me down, and he was able to hook my leg and flip me over. He pinned me down. Not hard, just enough to keep me from hitting him. "Will you please listen—What are you doing?"

I didn't have enough strength to throw Carpe, so I was doing the next best thing—reaching around and grabbing his backpack zipper. "Getting my spell book back until you give me the fucking map." I reached inside and felt around . . . found it. I started to pull it out, when Carpe grabbed my arm.

I used the fact that Carpe wasn't trying to hurt me to my advantage. I grabbed both sides of his collar and crossed my arms, hoping chokes worked as well on elves as they did on humans.

"Will you stop that? It's a matter of life and death that I deliver the spell book into the right hands—" Carpe forced his hand between my fist and his neck, buying his carotid artery a little more time.

"So is my map."

It was at that point Rynn and Nadya hauled us apart.

I noted the genie, Nomun, had made an appearance as well and was watching from a little ways away.

"You'll get your damn map soon enough," Carpe said to me, sitting up and rubbing his throat.

"It'll be too late," I said. I was doing a passable job pretending I was OK, but it was a show. I was weak, and my vision was acting up.

Carpe's face softened. "Look, I want you to get the curse lifted as well—as much as those two do—"

I snorted.

"But I'm not stealing it from the developers when they've offered me an alternative." He stood up. He actually looked mad; he was even clenching his fists by his side.

Granted, so was I.

"Enough, both of you," Rynn said, stepping between us. He pointed at Carpe first. "Give the book to Nomun. If you deliver the map, you can have the book. If not—" He shrugged.

Carpe glared at Rynn. "You know perfectly well I need that—"

"I *know* you traded Alix for a very specific map, which you have yet to produce. No map, no book. Only fair."

Carpe swore but pulled the book the rest of the way out of his backpack and handed it to Nomun.

Rynn turned to me next. "Alix—"

"It doesn't matter if he gets the map in an hour and a half, if I wait any longer I might start bleeding out of my nose. I need to be in there now, map or not."

"There are two of you, no?" Nomun said, frowning.

Nadya shook her head. "Alix is the trap and tomb expert—I'm translation."

"Nadya can pick up some of the slack, but not if I'm a drooling mess." This was what I got for going on Carpe's damn goose chase. I should have ditched him in Egypt . . .

"What if we went in now and you logged in once you were inside? We have a general idea where to go, no?" Nadya said.

I weighed that idea. The pirates' notes on the dig had been surprisingly sparse, as if someone had given them most of the directions. Still, I had a general idea where under the monastery I was headed. It was the details about the catacombs underneath, the city itself, I needed.

"If we go now, we can use the thralls as a distraction," Rynn added. "It'll buy you time to get in. Nomun, can you get us in closer undetected?"

The genie looked over the encampment and nodded. "Close, yes, but not to the gates, not if you wish to remain secret."

Rynn turned to me. "Alix, it's your call."

Risk getting caught in an IAA camp or put my trust in Lady Siyu being sufficiently motivated and capable of finding her own cure . . .

I grabbed my pack and shoved my laptop inside, since I'd be needing it.

Most of the lights in the monastery were on now that dusk had rolled into the mountains. I nodded at Nadya and Rynn. "Well, it certainly is prettier with the lights on. What do you say we wander over and take a look?"

Nadya grabbed her bag. "I thought you'd never ask."

There certainly were a lot of IAA agents milling around. Funny how it looked like a lot less from a half mile away . . .

"I think I preferred the IAA when you could just stroll right in," I whispered to Nadya.

We crouched behind an old stone wall that kept us hidden in the dark but wouldn't provide an iota of cover if they started shooting. On top of that, my stomach was still churning after Nomun had dropped us off by way of air genie travel, which, by the way, is unnerving as hell . . .

I tapped my earpiece. Miraculously I hadn't broken it yet. "Any bright ideas how to get inside?" I asked Rynn. Nomun had dropped him and his pirates off on the other side of the monastery, where the mountain offered more cover.

"At this point? Not without alerting every agent in the area," Rynn said.

Nadya jabbed me in the side and pointed towards the main entrance as Cooper walked in accompanied by two other people, one of which was Odawaa, much to my dismay.

"Damn it, I'd really hoped the golem had gotten him," I said.

On the bright side, Odawaa looked pissed and was having heated words with Cooper—probably about the disposable pirates.

I focused in on the third person following a few feet behind, who didn't follow Odawaa and Cooper in but instead hung back by the entrance. Wait a minute . . . the gait, hunched shoulders, general meek stance. "Nadya, guy by the door," I said, just to make sure I wasn't hallucinating.

She peeked over the crumbling wall. "What is Benji doing here?" she said after a moment. "I thought he was in Egypt."

"That's exactly why he's here. You said yourself your Russian contacts were putting pressure on them to close this dig down, right? Where better to fly more manpower in from but Egypt? Benji knows his tombs, and it's faster than flying someone in from overseas. Probably grabbed a few extra hands from Turkey and Israel too."

In fact, the archaeologists were running around like worker ants. Burning the candle at both ends—dangerous and stupid. Dig sites—especially cursed ones—induced sleep deprivation in the best of grad students all on their own; working them like this was a recipe for disaster. On top of that, how the hell could the IAA expect to keep track of them all?

That and the addition of Benji to the equation gave me an idea . . .

"Change of plan," I whispered. "I think I found us a better way in."

She gave me a wary look. "How come I get the distinct impression I'm not going to like this?"

I smiled and pulled my hood up. "Because it's a little out of the box." I tapped my comm again. "Rynn, I think I know how to get inside. How about a distraction your way?" If they were focused on the mountainside, they wouldn't be looking in our direction.

"The deal was to go in together."

"Trust me, will you? Besides, you'll be next to useless in the tomb, and we need someone out here to tell us what the hell Odawaa and Cooper are up to."

"You don't want to risk being spotted."

"I'll be fine. I'm not going on a vengeance streak against my former boss," . . . who ruined my life, completely annihilated any trust I had for authority figures . . . stole my goddamned thesis project I'd worked on for three years straight. . . .

"You forget I know you, Alix."

I opened my mouth to say something snarky back, but there was no accusation or judgment in Rynn's voice.

I let out my breath and calmed my nerves as I watched Cooper step outside to talk to Benji. I couldn't bring myself to lie—not even a white one. "I'll try to avoid him . . . no promises though if the opportunity presents itself." There was a pause on Rynn's end, so I added, "I've managed to stay alive for the past twenty-seven years all on my own—I can handle a few more hours. Just trust me, will you?"

"All right, one distraction coming up. Odawaa being there gives me an idea."

I waited for what seemed like an awfully long five minutes.

I saw the flash before something exploded in the hills, and the next thing I knew there was screaming and gunfire. All the nearby IAA rushed towards the other side of the monastery. Odawaa and Cooper came out and jogged towards the commotion.

Now or never.

I threw my backpack over my shoulders. Captain mewed inside. "This time no vampires. I mean it. I don't care what the hell you catch smell of."

Captain mewed in acknowledgment, but I'm not sure it was in agreement.

We waited for two nearby guards to rush by before jumping the fence and entering the throng of panicked archaeology grads—unfamiliar to both the IAA and each other—every last one looking as worn out as we did.

Heads down, we hightailed it to the main entrance. Benji was hugging the nice, sturdy stone wall, where he had easy access to rooms that had stood thousands of years through earthquakes, wars, and other disasters. Good for Benji; he was learning to find good hiding spots from monsters and shrapnel.

My hand fell on Benji's shoulder, and I squeezed. "Hey, fancy meeting you here."

He spun around, his face drained white as if he'd seen a ghost. There were heavy bags under his eyes, a few days' worth of stubble, and his normally neat hair was greasy.

"You look awful," I said, and it was true; he looked worse than when I'd seen him a few days ago in Egypt.

He opened his mouth to say something, but before he could, Nadya clamped her hand over his mouth and together we pulled him into a darkened, unguarded side alcove just inside the monastery proper. I made the universal symbol for *Shhh* and, slowly, Nadya removed her hand from his mouth.

"Alix—what the hell?" Benji started.

"Knock off the high horse. I'm not the one opening up a cursed dig site."

He glared as he pushed greasy bangs out of his face. "I'm not here by choice. They moved me and ten other archaeologists in two days ago, and we've been working nonstop. Now get the hell out of here before I get in trouble. I almost got sent to Siberia for Alexandria."

"I'm sorry, you must not have heard the cursed part."

"You think I don't know? Everyone knows the site's cursed, and they have us excavating anyways. It's not my call—"

"They're selling cursed artifacts, Benji," Nadya said.

Just when I thought his face couldn't get whiter . . . "Bullshit." Funny thing, he said the words but didn't sound so convinced.

I pulled out my laptop and showed him the pieces sold to Daphne, then I filled him in on Odawaa.

His face got whiter. "There's no way the IAA knows this is going on," he started.

"It's Cooper and his pirates."

"Cooper said he was a local consultant, to avoid skirmishes."

"Funny, he told me he was Owl, international antiquities thief for hire. Funny story, the IAA has spent the past week hunting me down for selling cursed items from this dig site."

"We don't even know all the artifacts he smuggled out yet," Nadya said.

Benji searched through the pictures, then looked up at me as if I were to blame. I sympathized with him—really, I did. If it hadn't been for the curse and my fever, I'd have left him the hell alone.

No, that's a lie. I might sympathize with Benji, but I couldn't let Cooper and Odawaa take more artifacts out of the city. I've got a lot of personality faults, but letting them inadvertently kill people with something they couldn't possibly protect themselves from? I'm not that far gone yet.

"What do you want?" he said.

"We need to get me into the lower catacombs—where they're finding the Neolithic stuff," I said.

"What! No—" He tried to run, but Nadya stopped him.

"Benji, if we don't get into the catacombs and cut off the supply, more people are going to die. What if we've only seen the tip of the iceberg?"

"You want to end up in an IAA holding cell? Fine, go ahead and save the world, I'm getting the hell out of—"

All three of us shut up and flattened up against the wall as three guards shone their flashlights into the main monastery room. More yelling in both English and Somali reached us.

I would have loved to know what the hell Rynn had orchestrated out there . . . And in spite of myself, I hoped the enthralled pirates hadn't gotten maimed or killed in the process. Pirates getting hurt by a golem while keeping us locked in a cage was one thing, enthralled pirates getting used as cannon fodder was another.

I waited until the flashlights retreated before I uncovered Benji's mouth again. "Look, if this was just a hate on for me, that'd be fine, but five people are already dead from the curse." Granted, most of them were pirates impersonating me, but I saw no need to put that small detail forward. "Sorry, Benji, you can be a good guy or bad guy, not both."

He swore. "Fine, but only because I didn't sign up for people to end up dead." He checked that the coast was clear in the main hall and nodded for us to follow him. "The entrance is down this way," he said.

We froze as footsteps sounded behind us, followed by Cooper's Midwest accent and Odawaa's raised voice. Nadya and I pulled our hoods further down. "Quick, give us something to do—now," I added, pushing Benji in the back of his shoulder to break the panic setting in. After a moment of hesitation, he grabbed two notebooks off the table and shoved them at us.

"Benji, go secure the catacombs, will you? We're shutting down for the night," Cooper said without giving me or Nadya a second look.

What did I say about shipping in archaeologists? Gets hard to tell us apart.

Benji nodded and started towards the back. When I'd been in grad school, Cooper had had one really bad habit; he'd always had his face buried in his phone. Still did . . . I exchanged a quick look with Nadya. Not an opportunity I could resist . . .

It wasn't much of an effort to knock the chair over in front of Cooper. Nadya did the honors on that one. The real trick was nudging the dig kit in front of his feet as he stumbled, still looking at his phone.

Out of reflex, Cooper dropped his phone to catch himself. It skidded across the room and under a table.

Benji and I ran over to get it, both of us edging under the table while Nadya apologized in a heavily altered voice.

"Did you just steal Cooper's phone?" Benji asked.

"It's where he still keeps everything, isn't it? Here, gimme yours—"

"No!"

"Now, or I'll hand your number and address over to Bindi."

"You wouldn't dare."

I pulled my own phone out. "Vampire on speed dial. Try me."

He forked over his phone. Same IAA-issue make and model as Cooper's. I turned his over, opened up the back, and cracked the battery before handing it back. "Here, give this back to him." With the battery trashed, it'd take him a while to figure out it wasn't his phone. I pocketed Cooper's.

Benji handed the phone over to Cooper. I wonder if he would have thought better of it if he hadn't still been in shock from, well, everything.

We continued on down a set of stairs that led into what looked and smelled like a cellar. It wasn't until the fourth or fifth step down that Nadya stopped. "Alix, are you picking up a signal anymore?"

I checked my earpiece. "Carpe? Rynn? Can you hear me?"

"Just barely," came Carpe's voice.

I swore. Not having the ability to contact Carpe completely screwed my ability to log onto World Quest in twenty minutes and get my damn map. I kicked the wall. So close . . .

"Wait, I have an idea—Nadya is with you, right? Can she find a spot closer to the surface? I might be able to bounce the signal—use one of you as a receiver for the other."

I looked at Benji. He nodded. "There's a storage room off to the side. No one will check," he said.

Benji headed back upstairs with Nadya, returning a moment later.

"Can you hear me now, Carpe?"

"Loud and clear."

"All right, Nadya, if things get hectic up there—"

"I'll be the first one to leave. Likewise, Alix."

"All I need is five minutes with these guys. I'll let you know as soon as I've got the map. Then go find Rynn and get out of here."

I helped Benji pull a stone plate off the floor, revealing another drop down into a shorter and narrower stone passage. Not ominous by design, just that a few thousand years ago people were much shorter. "It's down there," he said.

I let Benji go first and still made damn sure I checked for traps; I only trusted Benji so far.

As soon as the coast was clear, I let Captain out of the backpack. One thing Captain was great at finding—besides vampires—was traps. Plus, he was too light to set any off. Ancients were pretty good about making sure small mammals wouldn't set off their traps, otherwise some lazy thief would figure out all he had to do was release a bag of rats down the tunnel and follow after the trap-triggering bonanza . . . provided one of the traps wasn't a giant block that blocked the entire tunnel. Then you were screwed.

"Why the hell did you drag me down here with you? I'm not a thief, and contrary to what you seem to think, I don't want to end up in Siberia," Benji said when we'd gone a few feet down the circular winding tunnel.

Maybe it was the fever talking, but it struck me I could have ended up like Benji—friendless, scared, running. Or worse, I could have ended up like Cooper.

The difference was I had friends who cared about me . . . and had crazy access to military satellites.

I flipped off my comm. "Relax, there's a very good reason I brought you down here with me," I said. The fact that Nadya had to stay up top ended up being serendipitous good luck. That I was stuck with Benji was less good luck, but you can't win them all.

Benji warily watched me; this was the part I knew Rynn and Nadya— my friends—wouldn't go for. Benji would. Benji hated my guts.

"I plan on sealing these tunnels off for good so more cursed artifacts don't find their way out."

Benji, in spite of his hate for me, managed to look mollified. "How do you plan on doing that?"

"Easy," I said, and patted my bag. "Because in about fifteen minutes, I'm going to know where all the big traps are."

"And?"

"And I'm going to set them off."

Yeah . . . Nadya and Rynn wouldn't have gone for that one.

For a second I thought Benji was going to say no, but then he nodded. "What do you need from me?"

"Get us into the first section of the catacombs and find us a spot to hide while I get the map."

"And you promise the dig site will get shut down?"

"Think of it this way. If for some reason I can't get the traps to shut the place down, I'll make damn sure everyone in the IAA and the news outlets knows exactly who's responsible," I said, and held up Cooper's phone. If I had to go out, I was going to go out with one hell of a bang— one that would screw the IAA and Cooper.

Benji nodded and turned down the left wing. "Follow me. I know a shortcut."

18

Dead Gods

9:00 p.m. Where the hell was Carpe?

I swore as I stumbled over another uneven section of floor. The one bitch about old ruins is they never planned or accommodated for ground settling. My head was killing me, and on top of that my vision was now coming in and out of focus—hence the more frequent tripping.

Lucky for me Benji hadn't caught on just how bad off I was. No need to give him anything to tip his flight-or-fight response. As it was, he was jumpy under the best of circumstances.

A wave of light-headedness hit me, and I steadied myself against the wall—yet another part of the curse I was becoming more familiar with. I felt Captain wind around my feet.

"You really need to revisit your priorities."

I frowned. The voice wasn't Benji's—not whiny enough; it reminded me of an old Egyptologist professor back in my undergrad years.

"Seriously, you need a life overhaul."

There it was again. I looked to find Benji—he was farther along, examining a section of floor.

Captain was sitting behind me—watching me, patiently. I frowned. My cat didn't do patient. There was no way, but still . . . "Did you . . . *say* something?"

Captain shook his ruff out and looked straight back at me. "Slow on the uptake, aren't you?" he said, his lips molding around his teeth to form the words. "But seriously, you should really revisit your life goals. I think at some point you really derailed things."

I closed my eyes. Great, now my *cat* was giving me life advice . . .

"And maybe spend some time reflecting. I try to be positive, but I think we both know the chances of survival are not in your favor right now. I mean, my kind are the guardians of the underworld; I think I know a couple things about death."

I frowned. "OK, you're a cat. You chase vampires and apparently the odd mummy—not exactly a tactical genius that should be doling out life advice."

"Hey, you said it; I have a brain the size of a walnut. All things considering, I'm doing fucking spectacularly."

I don't know what was worse: Captain giving me relatively coherent life advice, or me arguing with him.

This wasn't happening, just another hallucination. *Wait it out, Alix, it'll go away . . .*

"Oh and you should give me more treats. Like now. On account of you dying."

"You're a figment of my imagination." I said it more for myself than my cat.

"And tell Nadya to take me off the diet. It's cruel and unusual punishment, and completely unnecessary."

Captain blurred out of focus. Either that meant the hallucination was almost over, or I was about to start bleeding out of my ears . . . I squeezed my eyes shut and hoped for the former.

"Alix? Hey, Alix?"

Someone was shaking my shoulders. Hard.

I opened my eyes. Benji stood in front of me, searching my face, and

OWL and the City of Angels   331

not with concern. "You were just standing there mumbling to yourself," he said. It was phrased as a statement, but I didn't miss the open-ended question.

Note to self, when hallucinating don't talk to the imaginary people. Or cats.

Captain, still sitting behind me, let out a baleful meow. "Just light-headed with the air down here—needed a breather is all."

Benji let me go, but I don't know how convinced he was on the fine part . . . then again, maybe he was just worried a monster was about to jump out at us. Considering the location and company, I could forgive him on that one.

And that was another hallucination down. I was starting to see a pattern; the people I cared about pointing out the things I was most afraid they thought about me. Well, that and the idea of my cat speaking in general scared the shit out of me.

Manifestations of my own paranoia. Fantastic.

"Let's keep going," I said, nodding at the three-way junction up ahead. "You said there was a hall coming up?"

Benji took the left fork. "It's a cistern with some inscriptions left on the pillars and walls, but that's as far as I've gone. Past that?" He shrugged.

I checked my phone clock. Two minutes to go until my meeting. The cistern would do. I followed Benji, placing my feet where he did. After finding a spot to sit, I pulled my laptop out. Time to see if our signal hop worked . . .

"Carpe, I hope to hell you can still hear me," I said.

"Loud and clear. Log in and head to the Dead Orc. I need to teleport our characters to the meeting location."

"Provided the game designers don't delete them as soon as we log in. You think a phone call or email would have been a hell of a lot easier," I mumbled, but I did as Carpe asked.

"You think I didn't try that already? They said in game was the only way."

In World Quest there are only a handful of places you can re-spawn;

bars are the place of choice. I watched as the Byzantine Thief fazed into existence amongst the other players on-screen. So far so good. Thank God bars weren't PVP zones anymore.

"I'm not dead yet," I said.

"Hold on, teleporting. Special destination spell, so don't mess with your screen."

My screen shifted as the Byzantine Thief materialized alongside Carpe on a small mountain path leading up to what looked like a ski lodge, with a distinct Himalayan feel. The mountain path was narrow enough that I had to roll to save my character from sliding down the steep mountain cliff.

"Damn. I've heard of this place," Carpe said. "Just, I'd never thought to actually end up here in game."

"Where are we? It's not showing up on my world map—at all." My headache flared again, and I winced as I tried to focus on my screen.

Carpe turned his character around, taking in the scenery—and probably a lot of screen shots. Below us was a valley spotted with a lake and other dwellings.

"Owl, you don't understand, we're not only off-map, we're, like, in the mythical realm of off-map. This is the game makers' house."

Wait a minute—that rang a bell. Something I'd heard at an archaeology conference a few years back after a lot of beer. I winced again as the headache struck a second time and my vision blurred.

"Byzantine, welcome to the Himalayas and the gates of Shangri-la."

Now, I might have been having a hell of a time focusing, but that detail blazed a trail through my brain. Shangri-la was a mythical location. Like Valhalla, it wasn't supposed to actually exist.

Except here it was. In World Quest.

If there was one thing I'd learned over my years playing, everything in the game had a basis in reality. Shangri-la was real, and Carpe and Byzantine were standing on the edge of it. All I needed to do was get a dot on my map . . .

"Ow—son of a bitch!" I grasped both ears as the headache reared, ugly. "Owl?" I heard Carpe say, though his voice sounded muffled.

"Yeah, fine—" Just your run-of-the-mill curse . . . The pain abated, and I opened my eyes.

You know, on the one hand I knew perfectly well I was sitting in an ancient cistern built underneath a cursed monastery in Syria . . . but my eyes, nose, and brain were convinced I was standing on a Himalayan mountaintop. I looked down. Instead of a laptop, I was looking at Byzantine's climbing gear. Carpe's elf—an uncanny rendition of the real one—stood beside me.

Of all the times for me to hallucinate . . .

Well, no choice but to roll with it. "Let's just get this over with before I freeze." The Byzantine Thief wasn't exactly dressed for snow-filled mountains. Damn it, I couldn't even screen-shot to try and analyze the topography later on. Shangri-la, right there in front of me . . .

The chalet door opened, and a man wearing Buddhist robes paired with a cowboy hat stuck his head outside. "You're late," the one I'd dubbed Texas said.

I was late? . . . Asshole. "Yeah, just be happy I'm not raiding Shangri-la down there." I started walking for the chalet. Damn, these hallucinations were getting awful real. Couldn't be a good sign . . .

Texas spit on the ground as someone I assumed had to be Michigan stuck his head out. No cowboy hat, but the yellow Buddhist robes were there as well.

"I told you it was a mistake meeting them here," Texas said . . . well, *growled* might be more accurate.

"We're here for negotiations, and the elf is trustwort-oomph!" Michigan was cut short by Texas's elbow to the ribs.

They stood aside, and I entered the chalet in a hallucinated daze. For the next few moments we all stood there, awkwardly looking at each other, Carpe fidgeting his thumbs. "This is the Byzantine Thief, and I'm Carpe Diem. We appreciate you meeting us to negotiate," he said.

Yeah, no time for this right now . . . "Look, let's save the uncomfortable pleasantries. Give me the map to the Syrian City of the Dead, and I'll leave. I won't even raid Shangri-la down there on my way out." Not that I *would* raid Shangri-la on my way out. That was a few too many steps over the ethical gray zone line, even for me.

Not that I wouldn't consider coming back.

Carpe winced. So did Michigan, I noted. "Byzantine—" Carpe started.

"Can you not take no for an answer?" Texas said. "Is that what's going on here?"

I needed to have a long chat with Carpe later about what constituted negotiations and what was a fucking waste of time. "How about you stop trying to fuck me over and give me the goddamn map? That we agreed upon."

"Jesus, no wonder we keep getting censorship notes on you," Michigan said.

"Give me my fucking map."

"You're here to negotiate, not hold us at gunpoint," Texas said.

You know, I wasn't going to say it, but if the shoe fits . . .

I grabbed Carpe—or the Byzantine Thief grabbed Carpe; my brain was having trouble keeping track of what was real and not real right now. "Give me the map or World Quest gets it—"

"Hey—" Carpe started to argue.

"Do you want your spell book or not?"

Carpe gave a disgruntled sigh but settled out of his argument.

Texas looked like he might punch me, and I readied my poisoned daggers. I'd get a good hit on him if he swung first.

Michigan took the opportunity to step between me and Texas. "Enough, both of you—"

"But she—" Texas started.

"She's got a mouth worse than a sailor, and you're offering up a bar fight. What did you expect was going to happen?"

Michigan turned his attention on me next. "All right, Carpe took the liberty of explaining your predicament. We get why you attacked World Quest, and I even get the whole give-the-IAA-the-finger thing you've been doing. We both do, but we also don't want any more attention than we already get. You raiding every site we've mapped out in game is causing us some pretty fucking huge problems."

"To put it in terms and words you might be able to understand, we're real inclusive that way," Texas added.

Michigan glared at Texas before continuing. "Because of the extenuating circumstances—namely, someone letting loose cursed artifacts into the public and you dying—we've agreed to help and not ban your asses. Got it?"

"I'm waiting for the *but*."

I must have picked up some kind of cue from the audio, because Michigan's avatar looked as if he'd aged a few years where he stood. "All right, here's the problem; we don't have the entire map to give you because we never finished the level. We've never been inside."

"On account of us being sane and the whole city being cursed," Texas added.

"Let me get this straight—you two knew you didn't have the map and brought me here anyways? Why didn't you just say that in the first place and save us all the time?"

"Alix—" Carpe started.

I turned on him. "If I'd have known there was no complete map, I'd have never wasted time with your damn book."

Carpe winced.

"Jesus—is she always like this?" Texas asked.

He fidgeted. "Well . . . sort of, but right now we're kind of under extenuating circumstances—"

"*Enough*, Carpe." Oh why, universe, do you derive so much pleasure setting me up for disaster? "All right, what *can* you give us?"

"The only one we figure has been inside the city is whoever is removing the items," Michigan said.

"*If* they aren't dead yet," Texas said.

"We've got a decent layout of the tunnels and rooms, including the cistern you're in right now and most of the big outer traps. Basically anything the IAA had in their archives and a few they didn't."

"Wait a minute—how do you know I'm in a cistern?"

Michigan smiled and pointed at Carpe. "Because he's not the only person here who can hack. Now, I'll send you the file, but we want your word no more breaking World Quest."

"Deal," Carpe said, a little too fast for my liking.

"And no more using our game to steal stuff," Texas added.

"Yeah, I heard you the first twenty times. For the record, I wasn't even trying to steal anything this time—"

He snorted. "Yeah, and the guy in the Mexican whorehouse is just visiting his sister."

Goddamn it . . .

"We're in agreement, then?" Michigan asked.

Carpe and I both nodded, and Michigan extended his hand.

I knew it wasn't really there, but what the hell. It felt so real . . .

And then the Buddhist ski chalet was gone, as was Shangri-la. My character, the Byzantine Thief—or me, if you want to get into validating my hallucinogenic delusions of grandeur—was left standing in the Himalayas.

"Carpe?" But Carpe was nowhere to be seen or heard. Son of a bitch had already left. The temperature dropped, and snow that hadn't been there before started lashing at my face . . .

"Hey, assholes, how do I get out of here?" I yelled.

"Walk down the mountain like everyone else," I heard Texas say.

Walk down the mountain. Damn it, I was not leaving Byzantine here . . .

I turned around to see if there was a portal or launch pad to get the hell out.

I heard a cross between a roar and a growl behind me.

"And watch out for the abominable snowmen," came Texas's voice.

Damn it. I started to run down the mountain path and heard something crash after me.

Come on, brain, positive thoughts, we are not running away from abominable snowmen in the Himalayas . . . I closed my eyes and willed the hallucination to disappear. The cold faded, as did the growling, and my screen came back into focus.

I was back in the catacombs—but the growling had been replaced by yelling . . . Benji's.

"What's wrong with you?" he said, his forehead scrunched.

"What's wrong with me?" What wasn't wrong with me was more like it . . . "I'm fine. Just tired. The last few days of no sleep catching up with me."

Benji stood up and took a step back. He wasn't buying it this time. "Yeah, unh-hunh, and that's why your nose is bleeding."

I held my hand to my face and pulled it back. Sure enough, there was blood. Damn it. I glanced back up at Benji. Oh what the hell . . . "All right. In amongst chasing down cursed artifacts, I may have cursed myself—accidently."

The color drained from his face.

I rolled my eyes. "I'm not contagious—"

His pallor wasn't from fear though, as I soon discovered. It was rage. He threw down his flashlight, cracking the plastic on the stone floor. "I don't—You're not here to save everyone from the artifacts, you're here to save your own neck!"

OK, it was my turn to get angry. "I'm here to do both. Hell, I don't want to see anyone else die—"

"Oh and you'd have come here anyways, I suppose? If you weren't trying to cure yourself?" Benji ran his hands through his hair. "Un-fucking believable."

"I got cursed retrieving the artifacts to get them out of circulation— and you should talk. You're helping them excavate, for Christ's sake!"

He made an exasperated sound. "I don't have a choice."

Funny how five small words I've said myself carried that much weight.

It's when I think I'm at my worst that things click—what Rynn, Nadya . . . hell, even Oricho . . . had said.

"Yeah, you do. You can't stomach the consequences, so you pretend you don't have a choice. It's not the same thing."

The look on his face was still furious, but it wasn't aimed at me anymore—or not entirely.

I took a gamble. "Look, you're more than welcome to try and find your own way out. I won't stop you, but I won't stand half as much of a chance if you don't help me—and I'd really like to make sure nothing else leaves this place."

He swore but grabbed his flashlight and continued back towards the cistern. I checked my phone. The map from the World Quest developers still hadn't downloaded. "Owl?" came Carpe's voice.

"Carpe, Nadya—the World Quest map isn't showing up on my screen."

I heard Carpe typing on the other end. "Sorry, I'm having trouble pushing the file through."

Shit. "All right, I'll need you two to walk me through—meaning traps—sooner rather than later."

"Yeah, yeah," Carpe said.

"With descriptions."

I hoped Carpe got the message, then I set off after Benji. Let's see if we could find out where the hell these artifacts were coming from.

We stepped out of a small rectangular room into another forked section. We'd found inscriptions in the previous rooms, but nothing referring to the sword or the other cursed artifacts.

Looking at the wall, I could have sworn I needed to go left, not right, like Carpe said. "Carpe, are you sure it's a right turn here? It's a dead end—it's the left tunnel that keeps going."

"That's what the map says," he said.

"Hey, Benji. See anything on this right wall, like a lever that might open a door?"

He gave a cursory examination to the wall, cracked floor tiles—even the ceiling. After he checked the seams between the wall and floor, he stood back up, shaking his head. "It's just a wall."

Damn elf . . . "Carpe, it's a dead end—the only way out is to the right."

"Alix, Carpe's right, I can see it on the map—left tunnel," Nadya added.

I sighed. And while I was telling them that wasn't possible, there was a rock wall . . . We'd have to find another way around to the Neolithic chamber.

"Where did you say you found those items again? The ones that went missing from the inventory?" Benji asked.

"Daphne Sylph's private collection in L.A.—two of the pieces, at least. The third one—the bronze sword—reappeared in an L.A. vampire den."

Benji shook his head at the mention of vampires, and I felt no need to elaborate. "Give me Cooper's phone," he said.

"There's no point; I can't download anything."

"No, but you know how he is. He takes more pictures on that thing than is healthy."

"So?"

"So, maybe he took a picture of the place where he took them from? I mean, why not? If he was going to go to all the trouble of having the artifacts stolen—which he must have, because he went to the trouble of filing the reports in the first place. There's no advantage to not keeping a record. Besides, I'm pretty sure he didn't expect you to show up and lift his phone. And besides, the photos would be on his phone's memory—here, give it to me."

I passed Benji Cooper's phone, and he scrolled through the pictures. "Bronze sword—that's the one, isn't it?" he said, holding the phone back out.

I took the phone back and focused in on the image. "That's it exactly." There were five or six more pictures showing the flint and stone bowl, along with some long shots of the room the three had been found in.

"Wait a minute," Benji said, grabbing the phone back and zooming in on the room. "Shit, son of a bitch . . . that's what Cooper wanted with those translations."

I froze. "What translations?"

Benji shook his head and showed me a picture of an old room.

"Cooper asked me to do some translations on some old Aramaic inscriptions he pulled off one of the burial mounds. I didn't think of it at the time because it was way past the Neolithic time point. Figured they were added by the next batch of people who moved in and started building the monastery foundation. There was a lot of term discontinuity though, and parts had been added a hundred years apart—as if someone was making notes."

"And you're just telling me this now?"

"I figured it was a translation mix-up, all right? I didn't think it was related to the cursed items. The items were long gone by the time I got there—and you said yourself they were from the Neolithic sites." He pointed to the image. "*That* room's not Neolithic; it's ancient, but built during Aramaic times."

"All right, what was in them—disjointed shorthand?"

"They were run-of-the-mill burial spells—similar in nature to the Egyptians', but much less refined; not as much detail, and a lot more room for ad-lib."

That made sense—the Egyptians had picked their mummification spells off the supernaturals. From there they'd spread out to other regions, but a lot was lost in ancient games of telephone.

"It was talking about the dead," Benji continued, "but there was some funny stuff that kept slipping in—modifiers and descriptors. It was weird."

Supernatural spells in general were a bad idea. When humans started ad-libbing them, things went worse fast. "What kind of funny stuff?" I asked.

"Ah, images and words I'd associate with recruiting an army. I figured it was just a strange way of referring to a burial site for soldiers—and some stuff on the afterlife I thought might have traveled over from Egypt."

I thought back to what Mr. Kurosawa had said about armies of the dead marching across the plains. There was only one reason ancient humans obsessed about burial rites. The Egyptians, the Norse, Nubians— you name it, all ancients had the same agenda. "Resurrection," I said.

Benji frowned. "Well, yeah, that goes without saying—"

"No, that's the thing I was missing. I figured this place was lived in by some ancient supernatural who used to control humans and terrorize the neighbors. Cooper's forte was never Neolithic cultures in this region. He was always way more interested in the cultures who came after: the Egyptians, the Sumerians, the Aramaics. All the cultures who'd obsessed with the afterlife and obtaining immortality through death."

Oh man, my head hurt considering the implications: it wasn't the supernaturals we needed to worry about, it was what the humans had done with all the cursed and magic garbage the supernaturals had left behind when they'd gotten bored and moved on or died.

I've always said supernatural spells are way more dangerous in the hands of humans, and Cooper had stumbled onto the ancients figuring out a way to get them to work. . . .

Jumping onto that logic, what better way for the supernaturals to get a free pass to come out in the open? If someone like Cooper and who knows who else was running around raising an army of dead, the supernaturals and IAA could kiss the anonymous supernatural underworld good-bye. It'd be well and out in the open.

But how did the three artifacts fit into it?

"Benji, I need to see that room now," I said.

He nodded. "Down the right hall. I think it loops up with one of the other rooms Cooper had me translating—or should."

"Carpe, did you hear that? Change of plans—I need you and Nadya to look for traps on the fly."

"I thought we decided you were going to the Neolithic chamber one level down?" he said.

"Trust me, this is a better idea." That chamber, the original resting place of the knife, would give me a better chance of finding the original curse instructions, but Benji's chamber would tell me what the hell the ancient Aramaeans had been doing and what the hell Cooper was trying to replicate . . .

"Alix?" Benji said.

I ignored him for the moment. "Just make sure we don't stumble into a trap," I said to Carpe.

"Seriously—Alix," Benji said, this time with more trepidation.

I muted my earpiece. "What?"

"What the hell is your cat doing?"

I glanced to where Benji was pointing. Captain was hunched in front of the right-facing tunnel, growling at something past the shadows.

Something growled back and reached out with a corpse's rotting hand.

Dr. Sanders—or what I figured was left of my old supervisor— stepped into the light cast by our flashlights and reached for Captain. He was still wearing the tweed suit and tie I remembered from lectures and team meetings.

He growled and shambled towards us. I scrambled back out of sheer instinct.

Well, now I knew what had happened to him and why he hadn't been more concerned about an ancient cursed dig site being opened up under his name. I doubted he cared much at all what Cooper was doing with this place anymore.

"Is that a-a-" Benji stuttered, stepping back.

"Zombie? Yeah, I was hoping that was obvious." Unfortunately, what I know about the undead can be summed up in World Quest experience.

"What's happening down there?" Nadya said.

"Found Dr. Sanders. He's a zombie." Well, he wasn't rushing us yet. Maybe real zombies didn't rush people like they did in World Quest.

He growled and bared his teeth.

No such luck.

"Do you know anything about them?" I asked Benji, forcing optimism I didn't feel.

He shook his head and opened his mouth, but no words came out. At least he wasn't trying to wedge himself between me and the zombie, like some other archaeology postdoc I know. "Do you think he's contagious, like in the movies?" he asked.

"Those are movies, not real life."

"Then why are you backing up?"

"Because now is not the time to find out."

Captain was still sniffing at Dr. Sanders, curious more than anything why something that was dead was still moving.

The zombie moved faster than should have been possible for something in the throes of rigor mortis and lunged for my cat.

Captain took one look at the zombie's outstretched arms and turned tail. His legs just about skidded out from under him as he propelled himself down the right tunnel.

For once I agreed with my psychotic cat. I grabbed Benji and bolted after Captain. I think the one bonus about fever is you stop noticing mild disturbances, like pain in the legs or shortness of breath. We kept running, Dr. Sanders growling in pursuit.

There was another fork up ahead—this time with three options. "Hey, Nadya, Carpe! Three-way split up ahead—straight, right, and left. Which has a really heavy door? Preferably one that won't kill us?" That last bit wasn't so much for Nadya's benefit as Carpe's.

"Ahhh . . . right tunnel, definitely right," Carpe said.

Right it was. Captain had enough sense to wait for us at the intersection.

Up ahead I could see what looked like the entrance to a chamber.

"Is the genie still there, Carpe?" I said as I slid to a stop across the stone tile floor. Benji careened into me. The chamber held no obvious exit. I hoped that was temporary.

"Yeah, still here," Carpe said.

Nomun and the genies were from this region of the world. "Ask him whether he knows any stories or legends about zombies from the city," I said. Every good archaeologist knows most legends and tales have some basis in reality. Just in this case the dead leaving the city hadn't been the nice, happy version of resurrection people always envision. Still, any stories Nomun had might hold a clue that would tell me how Cooper had raised Dr. Sanders and, more immediately, how to stop him.

"Little thief," came Nomun's voice.

"Stories about dead walking out of the city—any useful details?" I said.

An angled slab of stone sat above the entrance we'd just crossed through. Looked like a door to me. I crouched down and searched the edges for a trigger. Benji caught on and started searching the other side. Dr. Sanders was out of our flashlight range, but we heard him growl.

Eaten by supervisor—not exactly how I wanted to go . . .

"Thief, all I know are old legends. None of the living Jinn have any recollection of those events."

"Legends are all I've got to go on right now anyways. Spit it out." Where the hell was the release for that door? Come on, it had to be in here somewhere . . .

"In the story of the city we tell, the Jinn defeated the king, who held the army of the City of the Dead under his thrall by stealing a magic lamp that allowed him to drive the risen army across the lands. In our stories, the price our betters made us pay for interfering with the humans was banishment to live in the lamp until humans called us. But that does not mean there is a lamp or that it controls the dead. It is a legend to explain away a distasteful aspect of our history."

"Wait a minute," Benji piped up. "There was a lamp in the logs— taken out of this place when it first opened up a couple weeks ago. I should know, I had to handle part of the inscription earlier this week."

A magic lamp. I was starting to think this was less some Neolithic gods' resting place and more a dumping ground for supernaturals to dispose of dangerous magic shit.

"One last word of caution," Nomun added. "In the stories, the risen turned those they touched against their rightful rulers."

Great, these were the biting kind . . .

"What the hell did the inscriptions say?" I asked Benji.

"Partial translation—totally out of context. You think Cooper is a big enough idiot to give a single grad student enough to figure out he was raising an army of the dead? I would have gone to the IAA."

No, of course not. Cooper would have used the army of grad students at his disposal to carry out his plan. Damn it . . . "Carpe, hypothetically, if I had another phone down here, could you get info off it?"

"Whose phone?"

"One I stole. What difference does it make?"

"I might be able to get into the files, but it'll take me awhile. What's the number?"

I read it off as Sanders rounded the bend. The zombie wasn't running, but we were trapped in a dead end.

"Benji, did you find a lever on your side?"

"There isn't any!"

"No one builds a ceiling slab like that unless they intend to drop it." It just meant it was probably on the outside, to lock people in . . .

I grabbed Benji and dragged him back into the hall with me.

"What is wrong with you?" he yelled.

"Lever's outside. You search left, I'll search right—other left!" I said, giving Benji a shove as we collided.

OK, lever, lever . . . I checked every stone slab on my side. Not one gave.

"Nothing here," Benji said.

Maybe it wasn't a lever. "Carpe, any pressure plates down this way?"

Nadya spoke up first. "It looks like there is one back in the tunnel a few feet."

Farther back, in the direction of the zombie . . . I started to crawl out, feeling each stone as I went, to see if it might give. Benji swore but followed suit, covering the ones on the other side.

One of the stones shifted ever so slightly under my hand. That had to be the pressure plate. I pushed with all my weight.

It sunk—slowly at first, and then faster until it sunk a good foot. The ceiling above shook as the wedged, pillarlike slab started to slide down.

I called out to Benji and dove for the entrance, sliding under the lowering slab.

"Shit," Benji yelled. I glanced back. He'd tripped, landing short of the entrance by a foot as Dr. Sanders closed in. If the zombie didn't get him, the pillar would.

I grabbed Benji's hands and hauled him towards me as Dr. Sanders dove on all fours with a burst of speed and wrapped his bony fingers around Benji's sneaker, the joints cracking as they went.

I swore and pulled again. Benji moved but not enough, and Dr. Sanders wasn't letting go.

"Benji, stop screaming and kick him!" I said, and put everything I had left into dragging him under the slab. I got further this time, dragging Dr. Sanders along with him.

I reached under, but Benji wouldn't stop kicking long enough for me to get a hold of Dr. Sanders's hand.

Bone cracked as the slab crushed Dr. Sanders's first vertebra.

I slapped Benji hard in the face. "Sneaker—off!"

That did it. Still yelling at the top of his lungs, he kicked at his sneaker instead of Dr. Sanders's head. His foot slipped free as I pulled, and the two of us fell back.

The rest of the stone slab slid into the groove, squishing what was left of my old supervisor.

We collapsed against the wall—me catching my breath, and Benji reorganizing his sanity.

"The inscriptions," I said after a moment. "You said the room Cooper found that sword in had modifications—what kind?"

"Changing the order of the rituals mostly—adding something in here, taking something away there." He shivered. "I can't believe Cooper turned Dr. Sanders into a zombie."

"What if Cooper isn't looking for one item?" I said. "What if he's trying to re-create whatever this ancient king did with the lamp?" I had Cooper's phone with the images. "The lamp . . . do you know where it is?"

Benji shook his head. "Cooper's been keeping it with him for study."

"The lamp might be enough to make a zombie, but it's not enough for whatever the hell it is Cooper's trying to pull off," I said.

"How the hell do you figure that?"

"Because the dig is still open. Dr. Sanders was left down here, and the rest of you are excavating like mad for one reason and one reason only—he either hasn't figured out how it works, or he's still looking for something."

I grabbed the phone, but there was no picture of the lamp or mention of it in the pictographs that illustrated a ritual for the three items to raise a dead army . . .

Then again, if I were a king who'd figured out how to control an undead army, I probably wouldn't leave all the clues in one place either. As Nomun so well illustrated, the problem with an undead army is its binary loyalty—in this legend's case, whoever had the lamp. Cooper was always a little too fast in his dismissal of data he deemed irrelevant . . .

"I think I know what went wrong and what he's missing," I said.

"You know, I kind of figured that might happen if you made it down here."

A voice I knew—that I'd know anywhere—echoed around the chamber.

Benji and I aimed our flashlights at the ceiling. Above us was a small opening, no more than a vent, carved out of the rock—Cooper's face framed perfectly in it.

"Fuck."

Cooper smiled. "I've been going in circles for a month now on how to get this army of dead to work. I only recently found the lamp. Then I remembered how you figured out where Cleopatra's cuffs were, after everyone else gave up. Those made an awesome paper, by the way—for me, anyways, after your spectacular bail from the academic community.

You know, if you had taken the gig in Siberia, I might have even given you second author."

"You son of a bitch, you set me up in Algeria."

"Didn't let me down either, Alix—knew you wouldn't. Though I would have preferred it if you'd just run straight here after I stuck the IAA on your trail. Two years ago you would have. Didn't think you'd have the wherewithal to go for the artifacts first. Had to do some improvising there with the vampire. He was trying to get the bronze sword anyways, so I told him I'd throw something extra in if he gave you incentive to head this way."

"You got Alexander to curse me?"

His smile widened. "Was surprised how fast he agreed to that one. Barely had to sell him on it."

I know at one point I'd thought Cooper had a really cute all-American surfer sort of look going. Can't imagine why . . .

I shook my head. It hadn't been some nebulous branch of the IAA analyzing my behavior; it had been this backstabber, trying to herd me so I could solve his zombie problem—or lack thereof.

"Here's what I think," Cooper continued. "I think just like finding those cuffs, you've got a damn good idea what I need to get a zombie army up and running."

"Wow, and I'm the one hallucinating . . ." I had to cover my eyes as he shone his flashlight around the room, lingering where Dr. Sanders's hand protruded, still clutching Benji's sneaker.

"I see you found Dr. Sanders. Yeah, he was pretty pissed when he found out I'd opened this place up under his name. Not a risk taker—not like you."

"Fuck off."

"Figured you might say that." He pointed a gun through the vent. "Here's my bet, Hiboux. I think you either know what I'm doing wrong, or you're real close to figuring it out. You tell me—"

I snorted. "And what? You won't shoot me? I'm already dead, moron—or I will be real soon."

"No, I'll shoot Benji. Right now Benji hasn't done anything wrong, and we both know he'll toe whatever line I give him—won't you, Benji?"

Benji swore, but he didn't argue. The problem was, Benji might keep up his end of the bargain, but I knew damn well Cooper would shoot him—or, better yet, get the pirates to make it look like an accident.

Benji glanced at me and gave me a slight shake of his head. He knew. He wasn't nearly as stupid or obedient as Cooper gave him credit for.

Still, maybe I could get Benji a couple minutes of running room. Apparently I sucked at saving people, but I could buy them a head start—how's that for an ego builder?

I feigned scratching my ear so I could tap my earpiece—I couldn't talk to Nadya and Carpe, not directly, but I could maybe route them in to listen . . . all I got though was static. Hopefully that meant Nadya had picked up on Cooper and already bugged out.

Least I could do was stall for time—for Benji and Nadya. "So you think the IAA is going to let you have a zombie army for kicks? As a reward for publishing the most papers last year?"

Cooper's smile didn't drop. "Actually, they'll be enraged after I tell them how the great failure Alix Hiboux snuck in, stole the artifacts, and killed her old supervisor so she could raise her own army."

"Got news for you, I'll be long dead by then—curse, remember?"

"Yeah. That'd be a problem—except I've got an entire team of Owls running around the Mediterranean."

Good luck pulling that one over Lady Siyu and Mr. Kurosawa for any length of time. Army of dead or not, if I was Cooper, I would not want to get in Mr. Kurosawa's bad books . . .

Unless Cooper had no idea who I worked for. That was almost as good as Odawaa throwing Rynn the incubus into a regular run-of-the-mill cell. It'd be funny to imagine what Lady Siyu might do to Cooper if not for the fact that his plans were based on me ending up dead . . .

He also couldn't know I had his phone—and that Carpe was well on his way to hacking it.

Cooper might know the old me real well, but the old me always worked alone. As much as I bitch about Nadya, Rynn, and Carpe—especially Carpe, after that idiotic stunt with the plane—I sure as hell wouldn't want to find myself on the wrong side of any of them.

"Quit stalling," Cooper said.

You know, if it wasn't for the fact that Benji, Captain, and I might get shot, I'd feel sorry for Cooper. He had no idea what he was in for . . .

Cooper shot the ground a few inches from Benji's feet. "I don't know what kind of a distraction you orchestrated out there, but my new, improved pirate Owls are on a schedule. Any more stalling and you'll be dealing with them, not me."

"And they're real safe to have around your students? Hey, how's Odawaa handling his dead pirates?"

Cooper shrugged. "They're pirates; they can be bought. As far as student casualties, I'll just blame everything on you anyways. Tell me what I want to know and I'll even let Benji go. After I make him put you out of your misery."

I licked my lips. There had to be some way to screw Cooper over. "You'll just shoot him after anyways. Let's at least try some honesty here. All I'm doing is buying him running time."

"Now. Or I shoot your cat too," he said, and fired near Captain's feet, forcing him to yelp and dance back.

"Stop with the gun already," I said. When no more loosely aimed bullets fired at Benji or Captain, I took a deep breath and started. "Here's the thing. None of these artifacts were ever meant to raise an army of the dead. It's the result of a couple hundred years' worth of trial and error, courtesy of a brutal kingdom with more ambition than sense."

Cooper frowned, probably trying to figure out whether I was lying or not. "I don't believe you," he said.

I was telling the truth—too risky not to when he had the gun. Besides, if I told the truth and he shot Benji and Captain, there wasn't much incentive left to keep telling the truth.

I shrugged. "Trial and error, a few thousand disposable bodies, you'd be amazed what civilizations come up with. Look at the pyramids. My guess is you got hold of some of the old Jinn tales or found them in the archives—makes no never mind. You figured out there actually was a king who built a zombie army. Courtesy of Dr. Sanders, you now know the lamp will raise dead, but my guess is you had no control over him, am I right?" Now I was speculating—for all I knew, Cooper had let his zombie loose in the tunnels and told it to guard against stray archaeologists.

Cooper waved the gun. "Keep going."

One down, one more hypothesis to clear up. "I only have one question for you. Did you plan to get rid of the knife, bowl, and flint from the beginning, or was that a stroke of creativity to help get me involved?"

Cooper tsked. "You're stalling again," he said, and shot the ground near Captain's tail. Captain jumped and growled at the spot in the sand, not sure where the threat was coming from. I flinched; I have a real problem with anyone threatening my cat . . .

"You need me to string all the pieces together for you, Cooper? The instructions are already in your goddamn notes, which you'd have known already if you'd done a better job going over all the pictograms instead of tossing them off on the grad students in pieces. Do you think the sword, bowl, and flint piece kept appearing in all the references for the dead as suggested party favors?"

"Shit, I need all of them, don't I? Damn it, I wondered if selling them to the vampire and siren was preemptive. Oh well, can't predict everything. Don't suppose you'd like to tell me which order they go in?"

"Go fuck yourself."

"Don't worry about it, Alix. I can take it from here—just like the rest of your projects. It's like you're the golden goose." He aimed the gun at me. "Real sorry about this. You're a hard girl to forget."

"Not you, Cooper. You're easy."

"Like I told Odawaa and the pirates, you've got a hell of a habit of crawling out of tight situations. Not if you're dead though." He paused. "Speaking of hard to forget, Nadya still looks great. Odawaa sent a photo of her too—looked for her but I'm guessing she was smart enough to stay out of your particular brand of shit storm. What's she up to these days?"

"Why not ask me yourself, asshole?"

I saw the shock register on Cooper's face as something heavy connected with his head. Cooper slumped, and then was dragged away. Nadya's head popped through the window in his place.

"You were supposed to run," I said.

"You are not the only one who has difficulty following instructions." She dropped a rope down. "Come on, I've got a way out, but we need to be fast."

I made Benji go first, then tied the end of the rope around my midsection and had them pull me up. I couldn't have made the climb if I'd tried, and as it was, I needed both Nadya and Benji's help crawling out the vent into a more recent wing of the monastery, a cellar of some sort.

"What about Cooper?" Benji asked, nodding at the asshole's prone body.

Nadya shook her head. "No time. Cooper is not stupid. I overheard him tell the pirates to only wait fifteen minutes, and it's been ten already."

I bet the only reason he hadn't brought them along was that he hadn't been sure I'd taken care of Dr. Sanders. After the golem, I didn't think Odawaa would react well to a zombie in a tweed suit.

I started rifling through Cooper's army-issue cargo jacket pockets as voices echoed nearby.

"Alix, we don't have time," Nadya started.

I kept going. Wallet, pocketknife, sunglasses . . . where the hell did Cooper keep it?

Bingo. I found his white plastic access card in his inside pocket. "The gold standard of IAA security clearance everywhere," I said, holding it up. Not useful now, but definitely once we got out of here.

Nadya shook her head and pointed down the monastery hall. "Down this way there are tunnels that should lead into the caves in the cliffs. Rynn and the elf will meet us there."

No sooner had she said it than we heard yelling in Somali and a door banging nearby. Nadya leading the way, we bolted in the opposite direction, Captain close on my heels.

"Did you find the Neolithic inscriptions—the ones mentioning the curse?"

I shook my head. While we now knew who was behind the thefts, as far as saving my own neck, the Syrian City of the Dead had turned out to be nothing more than an epic wild-goose chase. I hadn't even gotten to setting off traps . . . "Someone moved the knife a few thousand years ago. It'd take me months to find it, if it's even here."

Nadya didn't say anything more, but there was a hard set to her mouth as we ran for the exit. We had a short, uneventful run through the basement—the monks who built this place didn't have a need for extensive traps. Go figure. We came out at the caves just outside the camp perimeter, though with the way the IAA was mobilizing, it wouldn't be outside their perimeter for long. . . .

I saw a jeep careen around the side of the mountain towards us, Rynn in the front seat and Carpe hanging on for dear life behind him.

Nadya and I broke into a run as Rynn pulled the jeep up. "You know, for someone who doesn't steal, this is the second time you've hot-wired an IAA jeep," I said.

"Not stealing when they give you the keys."

Damned incubus . . . "What happened to your pirate fan club?"

"Sent them back to Odawaa. Caused quite the internal commotion. They weren't sure who to shoot at for a while there." He glanced back over his shoulder at the mobilizing groups. "However, I think they've figured it out—get in."

"I'm coming with you," Benji said, running up behind us as I tossed Captain in the jeep.

Nadya and I exchanged a glance. The IAA was regrouping around the city. It was not going to take much time at all for them to figure I was involved, and I knew Cooper would be blaming me. There might be a way for Benji to still get out of this with his career intact. Antiquities thief in training Benji was not—lightly corruptible professor with a soft spot for thieves? OK, that I could see. A hell of a lot more useful in the long run.

I gave Nadya the nod, and she retrieved a glass bottle from her coat pocket as I grabbed Benji from behind. He began to struggle, and I cut off his protests with an elbow in the ribs.

Note to self: no grabbing people while cursed... "Relax, Benji, we're doing you a favor," I said. "The IAA won't find you until after Cooper and his pirates are long gone."

Benji could tell his bosses I'd forced him to help me. If I had my way, by the time I was done with Cooper, anything he said would be worthless.

Or he'd have an army of the dead. Either way, Benji's role would be inconsequential.

"Deniable plausibility," Nadya said.

"That's plausible deniability," he said.

Nadya pressed the now damp cloth over his mouth. I shrugged. "Same difference."

Benji passed out and Nadya dropped him to the ground—gently. Though to be honest, roughing him up a little might have helped his case.

Rynn hopped out of the jeep and picked up the bottle Nadya had used. "Where the hell did you two get chloroform?"

"Emergency bottle. I always keep one on me," Nadya said.

"Don't look at me," I said. "I use alcohol with just enough GHB to put them to sleep"... and only when I had absolutely no other choice.

Rynn's frown deepened. "I have an entire arsenal of weaponized pharmaceuticals designed to knock out everything from a human to a vampire, and you two use chloroform and GHB?"

"Move faster next time." I tossed my bag in the jeep and hopped in the backseat alongside Captain. "I know where Cooper's going."

That was one silver lining to this—Cooper needed the rest of the artifacts to get his army to work, but he didn't know we had them in Las Vegas. He'd head to Los Angeles first, where we could cut him off.

Rynn stepped on the gas, and I felt something warm in my front pocket: Hermes's card, which I'd forgotten was still there. I flipped it over.

Doing better, kid, but the odds still aren't great.

19

Best-Laid Plans

Don't ask me the time, I can barely see, let alone think straight . . .
You know, funny difference between humans and supernaturals.

When supernaturals find something magic, they try to take over the world, subjugate humans and/or other supernaturals . . . that sort of thing.

Humans get a hold of magic, and what do they do?

Raise dead things.

Maybe try for world peace? Save the environment? Build an exclusive paradise for you and five friends?

Nope. Dead things.

I mean, *come on*. As a collective species, isn't there something better we could come up with? Nope. Over five thousand years, and all we've managed are mummies, zombies, and a handful of walking skeletons.

I'm starting to understand why some supernaturals can't stand us.

We'd reached L.A., but we still needed to find Cooper—preferably before he tried to raise a zombie army or figure out the pieces were no longer where he thought.

Me? I was trying my damnedest not to hurl in the back of the jeep seat I shared with Nadya and Captain. Amazing how much you notice the gas and motor oil when you're sick, and, considering the world kept spinning, my insides were on fire. Not to mention Captain kept pawing at my face, punctuated with baleful meows. I pushed him away again.

Ever since we'd landed, I'd been trying to keep how bad my symptoms were to myself. I'd found new and entertaining ways to hide my coughs. Half the time I succeeded—though that could just have been me hallucinating.

I could hear Carpe clicking away at his laptop in the front seat. Now that he had his damned spell book, he'd decided to help us. I'm not exactly sure that was lucky on our part, but regardless, he was our best bet of picking up Cooper's digital trail.

From the driver's seat, Rynn was speaking supernatural bullshit over his phone to Nomun. The genie had stayed in Syria. There'd been no time or opportunity to close down the monastery before we fled, but now we knew it was effectively one big, ancient garbage pit, so the Jinn could "intervene" without getting supernatural panties in a bunch. Turns out we'd barely touched the surface of the stuff down there.

Rynn got off his phone and turned to face us at the stoplight. "New IAA showed up at the city. Russian and Turkish."

Nadya sat up. "The Russian and the Turkish departments must have gotten through Cooper's red tape."

"It's next to impossible to revoke permits on a dig without the professor who signed for it," I added for Rynn's benefit. And zombie Dr. Sanders wasn't exactly available for a hearing.

"The IAA have surrounded it," Rynn continued, "but Nomun and the Jinn will make sure they don't get inside."

Granted, the city would be safer in this batch of IAA hands than it had been in the last, but considering what still might be down there, I found my fever-addled brain siding with the genies.

I felt the buzz in my pocket, but it wasn't until I heard the '80s video-game dragon hiss that I realized my phone was ringing.

"Lady Siyu," I said, stifling a cough as I answered. I hoped to hell she'd been able to make use of the pictographs I'd sent before leaving Syria. "Please say you've got a way to lift this curse."

There was a soft, drawn-out hiss on the other end. "In a manner of speaking," she said.

I think I preferred it when she got to the fucking point . . . "That sounds damn close to a 'yes,' but—"

"I believe I have a method to lift it. However, it requires the item that cursed you."

That got me to sit up. We already had the bronze sword; Lady Siyu could cure me. For the first time in days, my hopes rose. "I can't believe you did it," I said with more energy and enthusiasm than my body had to give right now. Considering I was going to be OK, I could care less. "Grab the sword, get on a plane, and come meet us in L.A. so I don't die."

The silence on the other end curbed my elation. Lady Siyu wasn't one for dramatic pauses or minced words. After a moment, she offered, "I am already en route to L.A. and will be landing shortly."

Why the hell was she already on her way to L.A.? "What are you not telling me?" I said.

Another pause. "The siren retrieved the items from me a few days ago."

"You gave them back to her? Are you out of your mind?" I screamed. Everyone in the jeep looked at me. My headache got worse.

"If you would allow me to explain," Lady Siyu said.

"You had me run all the way to L.A., on pain of *death,* to retrieve a bunch of cursed artifacts—stolen under my name, I might add—and you *gave them back*?"

"She had the proper paperwork." Lady Siyu's voice was sharp, with thinly veiled anger.

I leaned back in my seat and ran a hand through my hair. It was greasy from the on-and-off sweating. "I don't fucking believe this."

"I did not have a choice in the matter. The siren admitted to deliberately misleading us, and clarified that you were not the thief she purchased from and are therefore not responsible for removing cursed artifacts from the city. As the major transgression we were accused of was having a human under our employ acquiring dangerous artifacts for public distribution—"

I made a derisive noise.

"She also offered a substantial monetary settlement. My hands were tied," Lady Siyu added. "The siren is one of us. There are no rules against Daphne possessing cursed artifacts."

Only humans acquiring them and selling them . . . a warped version of prohibition. Ever feel like a really expensive doormat? I didn't say anything. What was I supposed to say—*Nice colossal fuckup*?

"If you had completed your task sooner, I would have been able to stall her," she added at my uncharacteristic silence.

"Oh that's just great—blame the human. Real mature." I pinched the bridge of my nose. "Look, if I get the damn knife—*again*—can you get this curse off me? Yes-or-no answer."

"Perhaps, perhaps not. It is too hard to tell until I attempt it, but I believe so." Her voice lowered, lending it a threatening tone. "I have yet to fail in one of Mr. Kurosawa's tasks."

Somehow not comforting . . . "All right, I'll text you when we know where we're headed. You can meet us there," I said, and hung up before she could argue.

I couldn't believe she'd given them back to Daphne . . . proper paperwork my ass. "Lady Siyu's on her way," I said when I realized everyone was still staring at me. "She thinks she can lift the curse." I drew in a big breath to settle my spinning head. "We have a bigger problem though. She gave the items back to Daphne. Cooper still needs to test them out, and he'll want to try it sooner rather than later."

"Where would he take the artifacts then?" Rynn asked.

I shook my head. "Where Cooper can find a ton of zombies in waiting."

"That's all of L.A.," Rynn said.

"That's the point. So we have no idea."

"Hollywood Boulevard," Rynn said after a moment.

"Too predictable. Maybe he's headed to the beach—less obvious."

"Oh come on—the beach? It's an army, not a vacation."

"Hey, we're talking about a zombie army. Raising them from a beach-partying crowd isn't the most far-fetched part of that statement. And how do you know Cooper doesn't want a beach-themed zombie army? Maybe he figures if he's got to look at bodies, they might as well be cute and scantily clad—"

"Stop, both of you," Nadya said, raising her voice over ours.

It did the trick. Only Carpe ignored us, staring at his computer.

As soon as she had our undivided attention, Nadya pushed on. "We are assuming he needs live victims—but the pictures under Deir Mar Musa only show bodies. What if Cooper isn't after living victims? What if he only thinks he needs a repository of dead? Besides, a large living population would cause too much attention."

I pulled out my phone and went over the pictures of the adapted rituals with the three artifacts. Nadya was right. There'd been nothing to indicate living sacrifices. In fact, if the stories Mr. Kurosawa had told me about the ancient Qaraoun stealing the dead of their neighbors had any merit . . .

"What's the biggest graveyard in L.A.?"

"Doesn't need the biggest, just the closest to Daphne and the artifacts," Rynn said. "And that still leaves too many to search."

"I found him," Carpe said. "Hollywood Forever—that's where he's going." He flipped his laptop around so Nadya and I could see the purple dot moving across the digital map.

Somehow, someway, the elf had managed to find Cooper's airport rental car and was tracking it. Carpe tapped another part of the screen. "Hollywood Forever. It's the closest cemetery—a bunch of actors from old 1920s Hollywood are buried there—and it's right on his route."

"How do you know about old cemeteries?" Nadya asked him.

I could have sworn the elf turned his nose up at her. "I like old black-and-white movies," he said. "And I took a tour. Bugsy Siegel and Mel

Blanc are buried there. They have old movie clips and documentaries on kiosks through the park. They even show movies—"

Yeah, and while they discussed Carpe's dubious vacation choices, the purple dot was getting closer. "Look, I don't care if they have rows of dancing bears, he's getting closer. Rynn, step on it."

"We won't beat Cooper," Carpe said.

"Then hope he doesn't have the artifacts from Daphne yet," I said as the car peeled off. I texted Lady Siyu.

On our way to Hollywood Forever Cemetery. We think Cooper's meeting Daphne and maybe Alexander there, since, you know, you gave her the artifacts back.

I pictured her hissing—or maybe even throwing something on the other end . . . No. She'd never lose it enough to throw something. Her response flashed in my screen.

I will arrive shortly. You are ordered not to die before I can attempt to lift the curse—otherwise I will find a way to make your afterlife very unpleasant.

I wondered exactly how Mr. Kurosawa had worded his orders to cure me. If I liked Lady Siyu—or had an iota of professional respect for her—I might have felt sorry.

"There's something I still don't quite get," Carpe said, and turned around in the front seat so he could face me. "Why have the vampire and siren involved themselves?" he said.

I shrugged. "Who can say why the hell Alexander does anything."

Carpe frowned. Or I thought he frowned. Bad light, add curse—you get the picture . . . "Yes, but why would they want an army of dead?"

I shook my head. "I don't think they have any idea what Cooper's actually planning—Daphne and Alexander aren't exactly high up on the supernatural food chain. Alexander knows some antiquities, but the sword and Neolithic objects are beyond him. I should know, I used to work for him. Regardless of what Cooper's told them, my guess is Alexander figures at the very least this is going to cause one hell of a mess."

"But to what purpose?"

Rynn took that one. "To orchestrate the kind of disaster we can't possibly cover—not the IAA, not Mr. Kurosawa, not the Jinn, not me. They don't want to come out in the open, they want license to kill humans at random whenever and however it pleases them."

Nadya snorted. "I wonder what Alexander would think if he understood just what was about to happen to his local food supply."

I laughed and wished I hadn't; I had to cover my mouth to stop from puking. Still, what I'd give to see the look on Alexander's face when he found out he was getting zombies—I was pretty sure vampires need living humans . . .

Come to think of it, why not ask Alexander himself?

I still had his number in my phone, so I pulled it out and dialed. Bindi answered the phone again in classic valley girl. "Hello?"

"Jesus, you've been at this what, three months now? I'd at least expect a *You've reached the phone of dick vampire, who may I ask is calling—*"

"What are you doing?" Rynn yelled from the front.

I covered the mic. "I'm calling Alexander to see if I can't throw a wrench in Cooper's plans."

"Owl—" Alexander purred. "You are still alive. I see your old associate has just as much trouble trying to kill you as I have."

"Hey there, asshole. Just wanted to know how it feels to be next on the vampire Grand Poobah's shit list. Oh yeah—and Captain says hello." I then covered the mic so I could cough.

"I suppose there is a point to this?" Alexander said. The drawn-out French accent told me he wasn't thrilled, but he hadn't hung up yet.

"You're making a big mistake. Cooper is using both you and Daphne. That ritual he's running? All it's going to do is thin your food supply, unless zombies are some weird vampire delicacy now."

Alexander sighed. "And here I thought you might have something useful for me. There is no 'zombie army,' Owl. How do I say this politely? Cease your feverish rambling and find some hole to crawl in and die with a smidgen of grace. I know—it is a stretch, but I have faith you will, how do you say—'Give it your best shot'?" Then he hung up.

"Idiot. Well, don't say I didn't warn you, Alexander," I said to myself.

I dialed Artemis next. On the fourth ring he picked up.

"My God, someone might start to think you were looking to trade up on my cousin. Well, I can't fault your taste," came Artemis's smooth voice.

"Stuff the incubus shit. I need your help."

"This ought to be good. You're starting to bank a lot of favors with me."

I ignored the innuendo . . . how best to convince Artemis to intervene with Daphne? "Hey, soooo—this whole artifact thing kind of stepped up a few notches. Daphne is about to help raise an army of dead."

There was a pause on his end. "All right, a little disaster and mayhem I'll give her, but Daphne is more of the devil-may-care fun sort—she's not stupid enough to get involved in that much of a fuckup. She still remembers the fallout from Caligula."

"Yeah, somehow I don't think Daphne knows the full extent," I said, and gave him the short-short version of what Cooper was trying to pull off. "Think of it this way, if a bunch of old Hollywood zombies start wandering through the Hollywood Hills, it's going to be bad. The supernatural cat will be out of the bag in a bad way, and you'll probably have to curtail your parties." Not that I thought that was necessarily a bad thing, but I was looking for angles here . . . "Cooper is playing both of them, and they're too stupid to realize it."

There was a sigh on Artemis's end. "Christ almighty—all right, no promises, but I'll see what I can do." There was another pause before Artemis added, "Are you certain you want to keep getting involved with this, Charity? It might be wise to save yourself and leave well enough alone," he said before hanging up.

If it hadn't been for the whole unleashing the army of dead on L.A. and needing my damn curse lifted, I might have agreed with him. . . .

What bothered me more and more though was the fact that Cooper was playing the supernaturals. I'd never counted Cooper as stupid enough to play these kinds of games. I don't know what he'd offered them, but it sure as hell wasn't an army of dead. Daphne and Alexander both wanted their leashes loosened when it came to the population at large, but I couldn't see them signing up for something this reckless. Hazard of being on the low end of the supernatural totem pole—if humans thought they were a real threat, they'd take them out first.

There wasn't any more time to ponder what strings Cooper was pulling though as we pulled up to the cemetery gates.

Rynn killed the lights as we parked the jeep. There was no sign of Cooper anywhere—but then, there wasn't any sign of anyone: guards, tourists . . .

"All the lights are off," Carpe said.

I glared at him. "Wow, are all elves as observant as you?"

He frowned back. "I'm sorry, but you have a bad habit of walking into dark places without a torch. I thought it might be a general shortcoming."

"That's World Quest, Carpe."

"Still—"

I rolled my eyes and focused on the area past the gates. I searched for signs of stray flashlight beams in the garden. There was nothing.

"Are we sure he's here?" I asked.

"I've got his rental just past the gates near one of the buildings," Carpe replied.

Great, he was hiding . . .

We piled out of the jeep with me lowering myself carefully over the side and trying to move my legs with something resembling coordination. Instead, I stumbled on my second step and landed on my knees. Concrete, hands, knees—not a good combination . . .

Both Nadya and Rynn watched me. "I'm fine—just slipped," I said. Captain jumped out after me, getting right in my face to sniff me before letting out another meow. I fastened his leash before he could sniff the air—just in case Alexander was lurking somewhere.

I caught Nadya and Rynn exchange a glance, but otherwise they left me alone. All four of us crept towards the gate.

The Hollywood Forever Cemetery was a collection of white mausoleums situated in a sprawling, manicured park. From what Carpe told us, the cemetery had a sordid past, much like the rest of Hollywood. After falling into complete disrepair over an eighty-year period due to a less-than-scrupulous owner, the in-debt cemetery had changed hands, and the new owners were left with the problem of figuring out a way to turn a profit to refill the coffers. Of a *cemetery*. This being L.A., not as hard as you think. They'd managed to fix it up and turn it into a tourist destination of sorts, highlighting some of their more famous residents and using the park itself to show movies.

Well, it'd worked. Even without the lights, the place had the same Hollywood sheen that Artemis's and Daphne's homes had. And somehow made it all the more creepy . . .

"Found him," Rynn said, stopping and motioning for us to crouch down behind the cement pillar that formed the gates. "Past the gates, on the island in the center of the lake." Rynn handed me his night goggles.

Sure enough, in the partial cover of the mausoleum situated on the small man-made island was Cooper—and only Cooper—crouched beside a stone bench. He was trying his best to mask his flashlight. I could see why he'd picked the spot; far enough away from the gates not to draw attention and plenty of things to hide behind.

I scanned the nearby grounds until I spotted the rental SUV a little ways away.

"He's alone. Maybe Odawaa and the pirates found something better to do," I said optimistically. Or Cooper didn't want Odawaa and his crew exposed to more supernatural bullshit than necessary.

"We'll see," was all Rynn said.

The four of us made our way through the gates and across the grounds until we were roughly fifty yards away from the lake—close enough so we could all keep track of Cooper without the night vision and zoom. Bonus—I only stumbled twice. Once we were there though, Rynn had us wait.

"Can we please deal with him before he raises an undead army?" I whispered to Rynn after five minutes had passed of us watching Cooper set up.

"This is too easy," he said. "Alix, stay back here with Captain. It'll be easier without you crashing into things. Nadya, Carpe, you go right, I'll go left. Try to see if there's a route to get closer to him undetected, and keep your eyes open. We'll meet back here," he added.

"Yeah—good idea—crouch in the soft bushes . . ." I lay down near a nice-smelling rosebush as everyone piled off. To be honest, that was about all I could handle. The walk across the cemetery alone had just about done me in. Now if only the world would stop moving . . . No, wait, that was Captain. Pulling at his leash . . .

I sat back up to see where Captain was straining. He grunted, and dug in his hind legs. He wanted to go out in the open. Shit, Alexander . . .

"Captain, no," I said, pulling back the leash. It was no use. Captain turned back and snorted at me before doubling his efforts.

Damn cat. I wrapped the leash around my hand . . .

And heard the gun click right as Captain broke my hold and bolted under the bushes. The weight of a gun barrel pressed against the back of my head, followed by a string of Somali as someone shoved me out from underneath the shrubbery. I looked up at none other than Odawaa.

"Fancy seeing you here, Owl," he said. "I said to Cooper, 'No, she would not be so stupid as to stumble across us again,' but yet here you are." All pretense of camaraderie was gone this time. In fact, there was a fanatic look to his eyes I didn't like.

"You know, for someone who doesn't believe in the supernatural, you sure as hell are up to your neck in a pile of it," I said.

He sneered and gripped my arm much harder than necessary. "I am not some stupid superstitious savage. There is no such thing as magic and monsters," he said, giving me another hard shove.

The funny thing with beliefs is they don't like to be challenged, and I was betting that golem had challenged Odawaa's beliefs big time. Most people have the same reaction when their convictions get confronted; they do their damned best to squash the challenger.

Odawaa herded me out of the bushes towards the mausoleum, where Cooper was standing, waiting.

"Hey there, Alix—or Owl, or whatever the hell you're calling your-self nowadays. Glad you could make it. Why don't you come on up," he said.

"Screw off." I'm sure under other circumstances I'd have come up with something more eloquent, but hey—sometimes simple is the best policy.

Cooper whistled and aimed his flashlight at my face. "Still holding a grudge, eh? Let's try this again. Get up here now, otherwise I'll do to your friends what I did to Dr. Sanders."

Carpe and Nadya stumbled out from behind the mausoleum at the prompting of two pirates. I don't know who looked more miffed at hav-ing a gun in their back. I think Carpe won; he looked more incredulous than pissed. But no sign of Rynn.

"Hey there, Nadya, you look great," Cooper said. "Looking for dig work? I've got a few spaces to fill."

Nadya spat back a stream of Russian insults.

Cooper shrugged before turning his attention back on me. "Never said I was in your league, but can't fault a guy for trying."

Odawaa herded me across the narrow bridge, staying close enough on my heels that I felt his breath on the back of my neck.

He shoved me when we reached the edge, causing me to stumble. Cooper caught me by the shoulders. "You know, I have a lot to thank you for," he said.

I snorted. "For what? My dig notes?"

He smiled and squeezed my shoulder. If I wasn't already shaking from the effort of standing, I would have cringed. "I was thinking more along the lines of how you showed me just how much power I had over all you grad students."

I must have heard that wrong . . . "I'm sorry—what did you just say?"

"Oh I figured I'd get away with it. I mean, grad student, you? Me?" He shrugged. "Not much of a competition there, but I figured I'd pick up some slack for that dig fiasco a few years back, end up on the IAA's radar." He leaned in so his face was almost touching mine. "You didn't even file a complaint. Hell, you just went on the fucking warpath." He gave me back to Odawaa, who bound my arms behind me as Cooper headed over to his makeshift shrine set up across a white stone bench in front of the mausoleum. Odawaa gave me the requisite shove to follow.

"You showed me I can do anything I want provided there's someone to take the fall. No one will do a damn thing, because at the end of the day it's too inconvenient. All thanks to you, Alix." He smiled again and gave me a conspiratorial pat on the shoulder.

"You seriously plan on raising an army of dead in the middle of Hollywood?"

"Everyone needs a hobby." Cooper grabbed my collar and hauled me up onto the bench. I caught a streak of white fur and followed it to where Captain crouched behind a tombstone, switching his tail. I gave him the barest shake of my head and hoped our training wasn't a complete waste of time . . .

"It wouldn't have mattered who I told. The IAA never would have looked into you," I said.

He shrugged as he pulled on a pair of heavy gloves, then carefully removed the lamp from a bag and set it out before me. "Maybe, maybe not. The thing you've got to realize is you're the perfect scapegoat. The IAA hates you. They were more than happy to figure you were in on all those thefts, didn't even stop to think for a second you don't touch the dangerous stuff. I'll turn in your dead body—claim you set off the curse. Hell, I'll come out of this looking like a hero. What was it you used to say about her, Nadya? She attracts trouble?"

Nadya spit in his face.

Cooper wiped it off, unperturbed. "Yeah, that was it. She was right, you know," he said, directing that last bit at me.

I might be dying, but I know my rotting lily of the valley any day of the week. It was faint but there, coming across the cemetery on the breeze. Captain would smell it too. I shook my head at him again. He crouched low behind the tombstone and bared his teeth.

Alexander stepped out of the shadows onto the bridge. A few steps behind him followed Daphne, her red dreadlocks tied into twin elaborate braids that fell down her back over a gold-and-green dress. Over her shoulder she carried a canvas bag.

The artifacts. We were out of stalling time.

I searched the darkened cemetery. Now would be a real good time to start shooting, Rynn . . .

Alexander took the bag from Daphne when he was halfway across the bridge and held it out in front of him like a peace offering. Tonight he was wearing an expensive suit jacket paired with expensive ripped jeans. He fit right in with the rest of the L.A. sleazebags . . . "We've upheld our end of the bargain, Cooper Hill; we assume you are ready to uphold yours?"

Son of a bitch, how could Alexander be that stupid . . . "You *idiots*. What'd he promise you? Cause I'll tell you right now he's lying."

"I see you have the Owl," Alexander said, ignoring me. "The real one, not the pathetic pirate you tried pawning off before. Where is the cat?"

"In the bushes somewhere," Cooper said. "Here, I'll show you." With that, he aimed his gun close to where Captain was hiding and fired.

"You son of a bitch!" I lunged at Cooper, but Odawaa hit the back of my knees with the butt of his gun.

"Don't worry, Alix," Cooper said as Odawaa shoved me towards him. "The vampire wants him alive. And like I said, Alexander and Daphne, as soon as I perform the ritual, you'll be the proud owners of a trio of cursed artifacts that work on other supernaturals."

That was what all this was about. I remembered what Lady Siyu had told me about cursed artifacts not working on supernaturals . . . Since Oricho had read that damn scroll, everyone knew that wasn't entirely true anymore, though I highly doubted Cooper was peddling anything other than snake oil.

And stupid of him to piss off a siren and a vampire . . . though once zombies started walking around, I don't know that they'd care—they'd have bigger problems.

The rotting lily of the valley was stronger now, permeating the air around me. I wondered why Cooper wasn't wearing a mask. Maybe he didn't have as much experience with vampires as I did. I caught one of the pirates trying to shake the pheromones off. I tried to catch Nadya's eyes, but she was watching the pirates as well and holding her breath. If we played our cards really well . . .

I fixated on Alexander and raised my voice for Rynn's benefit. "Seriously? You actually believe he's giving you supercurses to finish taking out Lady Siyu and Mr. Kurosawa? Jesus, Alexander, if I'd known you were this lousy of a negotiator, I'd have kept working for you. He's screwing both of you—ow!" Odawaa jabbed me again with his gun. I glared. "You know, Odawaa—you're standing awful close. You might just be part of Cooper's magic zombie army as well—and you know that lightheadedness is from the vampire over there—"

The maddened fury filled Odawaa's face again, and he snarled. "For the last time, I do not believe in your zombies or vampires—or whatever nonsense Cooper has concocted."

"A little hypocritical, isn't it?"

He raised his gun to hit me again. "It makes no never mind what he believes or lies about. He pays our fee."

"That's enough, Odawaa," Cooper said, raising his voice. "I need her alive, otherwise there's a fourth one still out there who will start shooting." Then he yelled, "Isn't that right?" Cooper flashed me another smile. "Oh yeah, I know about him. Alexander was kind enough to tell me about the incubus."

I glared at Alexander. "Seriously? You really set your eyes on fucking the pooch this time, didn't you? You know the incubus has a cell phone. How much do you want to bet he's calling Mr. Kurosawa right now? Seems to me like your cursed artifacts are only good if they don't know. The vampire Grand Poobah isn't going to be real happy bout this. Especially when humans start vampire hunting next week—"

That got him. "Could you *please* muzzle the Owl?" he snapped, his calm demeanor vanishing.

Good. He *should* have his tail between his legs.

For the first time, Daphne spoke up. "The incubus was part of the deal, Cooper Hill," she said. I had to hand it to her, she had a hell of a voice. I don't know if I'd call it beautiful, but I couldn't not listen.

"In fact, if I recall, that was my only requirement, and as I hold the artifacts you require, I'd be more concerned with him than the human and her psychotic cat." She then arched a crimson eyebrow at me. "No offense."

"Almost forgot," Cooper said, pulling out a new cell phone. He dialed, waited for someone to answer, then offered it to her.

She took the phone and said "hello" in English before switching to supernatural. Who the fuck did Cooper know who spoke supernatural? *Whoever was pulling the strings.*

I don't know why—maybe partial hallucination—but for some reason, my brain started spinning, making connections where maybe there were none.

She handed the phone back to Cooper and nodded. "I stand corrected."

Damn it. I glanced around the cemetery again, hoping to catch some sign that Rynn was OK . . . Maybe that was why he hadn't done anything yet. If there was another supernatural involved, that changed the game . . .

And I sure as hell didn't want to wait for them to make an appearance.

Time to save ourselves.

I caught Captain crouching behind the tombstone and looked out towards the dark graveyard. I sure hoped Rynn was still out there watching . . . I'd have to time it real well, otherwise Captain wouldn't be the only one getting shot. I also had no illusions about how much longer Captain would hold out against vampire bait.

I focused back on Alexander. No illusions about Alexander having any feelings remotely resembling guilt either—but he did care about his own neck.

"You're going to start a goddamn zombie apocalypse, Alexander," I told him.

"She's raving," Cooper said. "Barely knows what she's talking about anymore, last stages of the curse."

"You know what, Cooper? Fuck you and the horse you rode in on."

He smiled and crouched down in front of me. Odawaa's grip on my hands tightened. "You want to know why you're still alive, Alix?"

"Because you traded me and my cat to the idiot vampire?"

Cooper laughed. "Because I still need a sacrifice for this whole thing to work," he said.

Sacrifice? I didn't remember anything about a live sacrifice from the inscriptions . . . just a lot of dead or dying bodies . . .

Shit.

I nodded my head at Odawaa. "Somehow I don't think this guy will take kindly to being skewered in some ancient ritual—and he does have a lot of guns."

He smiled. "You know me, I hate to risk anything. No, my sources say the sacrifice has to be real specific. Someone who's been mortally betrayed. And let's face it, as far as stacking my deck goes, you're about as betrayed as they get."

Mortally betrayed? That wasn't in the instructions—"Hey, Nadya, do you remember anything about betrayed sacrifices?"

She shook her head.

I wondered just how far off the temple script Cooper was going—and how much was courtesy of his supernatural benefactor, who'd known exactly what to bait Daphne and Alexander with. Come to think of it, that'd been the underlying theme of this entire disaster. Lady Siyu got the opportunity to make my life miserable, the IAA had me to go after as their thief, Alexander and the siren were being offered something that could take down their betters; hell, even me with the gold cuffs in Algiers. At some point we'd all been offered something we couldn't pass up . . .

"What were you offered, Cooper? Money? A promotion?"

He laughed and pushed me to my knees with one of his gloved hands. With the other he took the bronze sword and held it against my forearm, angling it carefully over the bowl. "Here's the thing, Alix. You were never any good at figuring out people's motivations. Mine are real simple. I'm ambitious, and I'm the best at what I do. No one has ever gotten supernatural magic to work—if I've got to do it through raising an army of zombies, so be it. And as far as being the best? You still breathing, even as a thief on the IAA's most wanted list, puts that in jeopardy. Tough, but them's the breaks." He winked. "On top of that, I want to see just how much the IAA will let me get away with."

I got a chance to see where everyone was as Cooper pushed my head onto the bench and held it down. Carpe and Nadya were still held by two of the pirates near the mausoleum wall, and the remaining two had their guns trained on Daphne and Alexander standing at the edge of the bridge—not that guns would do them any good.

Odawaa, deciding I was no longer a running risk now that I had a knife at my throat, stood between them and Cooper.

I checked Captain's tombstone, and for a second I wondered whether the gunshot had sent him running. I caught white fur skulking at the edge of the water. Captain crawled out onto the grass and gave himself a shake before crouching down out of Cooper's line of sight right behind me.

I looked at Captain and mouthed, "*Wait.*"

Cooper lined up the knife, and I felt the cursed bronze burn into my skin. Reflex made me jump back.

"Hold still," Cooper growled.

"Hey, Odawaa!" I yelled. "You might not believe in the supernatural— and to be honest, I don't blame you—and the whole denial thing seems to really be working in your favor. But that doesn't mean it isn't your problem."

Odawaa's smile was cruel and manic. "And why might that be?"

"My cat believes in vampires and is pretty sure one's standing behind you."

Odawaa frowned.

"You're in his way." I jerked my head around and nodded at Captain. "Now, Captain!"

He let out an ear-shattering howl and launched himself across the lawn. Odawaa didn't react fast enough. Captain's claws latched onto Odawaa's chest. He crawled up Odawaa's face in an attempt to scale him to get to Alexander.

Vampire pheromones will dull even the most trained reflexes. Odawaa screamed and batted at his face, letting the gun fall to his side.

Pandemonium ensued. Nadya used the distraction to judo-throw her pirate into the water, and Carpe . . . well, all of a sudden Carpe just wasn't in that spot. I caught him a few feet away, back on his laptop, crouched behind the mausoleum.

I shook my head. Elves.

Alexander and Daphne were backing away from Captain as he scaled down Odawaa's back. And me? I did something I'd wanted to do for about two years; I took the lapse to knee Cooper as hard as I could in the sweet spot, and when he doubled over, I connected my knee again, this time with his face. "That's for shooting my cat," I said. Cooper crumpled to the grass, not quite sure whether to grab his bleeding nose or between his legs.

My vision clouded with the exertion and wavered for a moment, like I was going to pass out. I shook it off and searched until I spotted Captain.

He was racing down the bridge after Alexander, who was battling Daphne, of all people, to get across—she not wanting to leave the artifacts, her one and only bargaining chip to take out Rynn.

Odawaa was recovering, his back towards me.

The light-headedness hit me again, and I forced myself to search for something, anything to hit him with and keep him down . . . Rope? No . . . Gun? No way in hell I could aim in my state. I spotted a rake leaning against the mausoleum wall. Must have been left by one of the gardeners . . .

I dove, then crawled for it, stumbling over the uneven lawn until it was in my hands.

Clutching the rake, I headed for Odawaa as fast as I could manage. I wound the rake up and made damn sure my aim lined up.

"Alix," I heard Nadya yell as a shot rang out.

I looked behind me but not before something slammed into the back of my legs, sweeping me over. I landed flat on my back.

Cooper stood over me, blood streaming down his face. "You know, just for once I'd love it if you could stick to the script."

"Hey Cooper, might have put a damper in your army." I rolled over onto my stomach and got my legs underneath me. Running was out, but I still had the rake and figured I could use it for balance—or, if I could muster the coordination, to hit Cooper with. The vampire pheromones had to be affecting him by now. He took another step forward, and I stumbled out of his way.

"Not so fast—I still need you," Cooper said. He tripped me and pushed me face-first into the ground. Something cold and metal burned against my forearm. I kicked, but it did no good, as Cooper drove his knee into my back. I felt the warm blood run down my arm into the stone bowl waiting in his gloved hand.

Shit, the bowl and the knife down—only the flint piece left. "So you've got a pocket supernatural?" I said, trying to distract him.

"The dragon's not the only one collecting archaeologists."

"What is it then? Vampire, demon?"

"Sorry, not part of my deal."

I snorted. "You never did play fair."

"And you were always really naïve—desperate too," he said.

"Desperate? Seriously?"

"Come on, look at you. Channel eighties action movies much?" He hauled me by my hair to a kneeling position.

I glanced down at my now ripped jeans and T-shirt. "I clean up just fine."

Cooper patted his heart. "It's not what's on the outside that counts, it's what's on the inside—and face it, your self-esteem sucks."

A small puddle of blood had gathered in the Neolithic bowl, the flint piece waiting beside it.

"Good thing I don't play fair anymore," I said.

I grabbed Cooper's knee and pulled with every ounce of strength I had left. It was enough. He fell backwards, and I lost no time crawling on top of him. "This is for screwing up my life and trying to turn me and my friends into zombies," I said, and delivered an elbow to his face, followed by a second and a third. On that last one, Cooper's eyes rolled back into his head and he passed out.

I rolled off him and almost passed out myself. I could hear fighting still going on around me. I needed the bronze sword. That was the only thing keeping me going. I felt my hands clasp around it. Now, stop Cooper's curse . . .

I searched for the bowl.

Shit.

In my scuffle with Cooper, the bowl had tipped and spilled my blood over the stonework. I watched, helpless to stop the blood trickle towards the flint piece.

Too little, too late.

I felt the ground shake as the shock waves of magic traveled out.

"Owl, tell me that wasn't the curse!" Nadya yelled.

I opened my mouth to say, *We're too late,* but any noise that came out was overshadowed by what sounded like hundreds of feet and hands banging underneath the ground and in the buildings around us. The deafening noise was coming from everywhere.

Maybe there was still something we could do . . . I didn't know, sound an evacuation? But who the hell besides the handful of supernaturals there would believe us?

Alexander screamed as Captain got a clawhold in the vampire's hand, and I ducked as a stray bullet hit the grass nearby. Being superstitious, the remaining pirates were unnerved by the banging, but still held it together. Odawaa, on the other hand, was curled in a ball by the mausoleum doorway.

His eyes fixated on me with pure hatred. "*You,*" he said, "are behind this madness."

Note: not Cooper, not the supernaturals, not himself for following Cooper—me. People love to blame me for all their problems.

There was a hiss that carried over the banging. A loud, vicious string of supernatural followed.

Daphne froze, and even Alexander—after un-attaching Captain from his hand and flinging him across the grass—stopped in his tracks.

Captain landed nearby, and I grabbed him by the scruff of the neck and ducked back under the bench.

I heard the telltale click of heels on the wooden bridge as a very disheveled Lady Siyu strode into the flashlight-lit area. Her shirt was uncharacteristically untucked, and her black hair hung in a thick braid down her back, a handful of loose strands sticking to her face. On closer inspection, I even thought the white buttons were off . . . Damn, Lady Siyu must have been in a hell of a state . . . she looked pissed too.

I narrowed my eyes at an object she was holding—a spear, maybe, but my vision sucked right now . . .

This time that voice I knew so well rang out in English, still managing to carry over the restless and soon to be walking dead. "As Mr. Kurosawa's representative, I order everyone to cease their activities—*now*."

Two of the pirates turned around and aimed their rifles at her. "Get on your knees," one of them said.

My eyes widened. Shit, that wasn't a spear—it was a double-barreled shotgun. Lady Siyu smiled as she shot the pirate who had spoken with barely a glance or hitch in her step. As the second pirate raised his gun, she shot him as well. The remaining two looked like they might run.

I started to crawl out. "Damn, I never, ever thought I'd say this—"

"*Sit*," Lady Siyu said as she strode across the bridge. Daphne and Alexander retreated a safe distance from her, but not far enough to earn her wrath. I felt arms wrap under mine and pull me out. Rynn. He gave me a quick nod but was more concerned with the color of my skin.

"You're still alive," I told him. "I was worried after what Cooper said—"

"I could say the same thing." I didn't miss the worry in his voice.

I thought I saw a plot of grass lift by one of the nearby headstones. If anything, the banging had intensified . . . "Ahh, Lady Siyu, we have a problem—" I started.

"I thought I told you to be silent," she said, and strode over to me and Rynn.

"But the curse—zombies," I said, nodding at the graveyard.

She glanced at the spilled bowl and blood-soaked flint, then surveyed the graveyard. She said "*seereet*" under her breath, then pulled a black velvet pouch out of her bag and began to shake a fine, cinnabar-colored powder over the bowl and flint, muttering in supernatural. The cinnabar singed as it touched the blood—my blood—and black smoke coiled into the air.

Where a second before there'd been hundreds of banging feet, now there was nothing. No army, no zombies. Just like that. I knew I should be happy the zombie army had been stopped in its tracks.

I pushed myself up to my knees as Rynn protested and tried to keep me down. "That was it?—shit!"

Lady Siyu placed a stiletto heel on my chest and pushed me over onto my back, then kept me pinned with her heel. She retrieved a glass vial from her purse, along with a handful of thicker, meaner-looking acupuncture pins.

"Whoa—just one sec," I said, and tried to wrench her foot off.

She shot me a look of death, her eyes now a pair of black slit pupils set in yellow. She pressed the heel harder into my chest, her forked tongue passing over her lips. "I will *not* warn you again; I am less than patient today for your incessant prattle. You will not like the alternative."

Rynn stayed nearby but only offered me an apologetic look, whereas Captain just backed the hell up.

"Turncoats," I said to both of them.

Lady Siyu showed me the two snakelike fangs that protruded over her bottom lip. I gulped and lay where I was as she dipped the handful of pins into the vial of black liquid. After examining the needles with her gold snake eyes, she barked out something in supernatural to Rynn.

"She needs the sword, Alix," he said. "And whatever the hell you do, don't stall." I nodded at the bronze sword beside me. Lady Siyu took it gingerly between her fingers and, with more enthusiasm than I thought entirely necessary, made a second slit down my forearm.

"Goddamn it—you could have warned me," I said, for both Rynn and Lady Siyu's benefit.

"*Be quiet*—I will not tell you again," she said, a hiss escaping between her teeth as she dipped each of the five needles in my blood that had collected on the sword . . . Oh no—I closed my eyes as she raised the first needle up and stuck it into my stomach, followed by the other four, one each in my arms and thighs.

I breathed in, then out, waiting for something—anything—to happen as Lady Siyu recited a string of musical-sounding supernatural. She removed more powder, white this time, from inside her bag, which she sprinkled over the acupuncture needles of death now sticking out of me. The powder curdled and hissed, giving off an acrid, incense-like smell.

"You need to give something up," Lady Siyu said.

I stared at her in confusion.

"In order for the anti-curse to work, you need to offer me something of value," she clarified.

"I've got a stockpile of Japanese Asuka-period pottery—one from the royal court of First Empress Suiko. You can have it," I said.

Lady Siyu isn't one for emotion—or, well, any expression really . . . except sneering. She's got no problem expressing that. Her face went blank for a moment as she watched the pins, then gave her head a slight shake. "That is an . . . interesting offer, but inadequate—"

"Inadequate? Do you have any idea how hard it is to come across those pieces?"

Lady Siyu hissed, her old, disdainful expression right back where it belonged. "Something you part with that easily clearly means nothing to you. The magic in the pins cannot be lied to so easily."

"Oh for—Who the hell made up these stupid rules?"

Lady Siyu leaned in close, her fangs extended, barely holding her human form now. I guess I just have that effect on supernaturals. "If you cause me to fail in Mr. Kurosawa's task, I will make your last moments on earth the most unbearable you could possibly imagine." To make the point, she dug her clawlike fingers into my side. I yelled as she hit my bruised ribs.

I was about to tell her she and her damned pins could have the pick of my collection—hell, all of it—but I was wracked with a fit of coughs.

I heard Rynn yell at me somewhere, and Lady Siyu grabbed both my shoulders and shook me. "Agree to give me your most treasured possession," she said.

Damn it . . . the Algerian cuffs, the ones they used to drag Cleopatra II and her brother in front of the new emperor. The first thing I ever excavated as a grad student. Not a hell of a lot I could do with them if I were dead . . .

Goddamn it, universe, why do you do this to me? I swear, every goddamn time . . .

"Swear it," Lady Siyu said.

I took as much of a breath as my burning lungs would let me . . . "Fine," I said as I reached up and grabbed her collar, pulling her in close. "You want my most valued treasure? You've got it—take your damn pick. Just get this curse the hell off me."

Lady Siyu and I both glanced at the pins. The metal began to glow hot white. I screamed as my skin seared.

Lady Siyu smiled. "That will apparently do," she said, then shook her head in an uncharacteristic show and added, "such a curious specimen of your species."

I'd have come up with something to say, but the pins began to glow a black red. It hurt—more than you could imagine—but I was too spent to do anything more than whimper. Captain rammed his nose in my face.

Everything hurt.

But almost as soon as it had happened, the pins flared white again, burning off the red stain.

I breathed. My lungs weren't on fire anymore . . . I sat up. "It worked," I said, looking at my hands—*really* looking at my hands, since it had been days since I'd been able to see straight.

I was fine. Lady Siyu had cured me . . .

I heard laughter coming from where Cooper was still lying in a heap. "I'll tell them it was you," he said between laughs. "Who do you think they'll believe?"

"Benji will say something." Benji might not be a hero, but he had a conscience. Besides, he wouldn't want someone like Cooper in charge of the rest of his life.

Cooper shook his head, still laughing. "Benji will play ball because that's what he does."

I should have hit him harder when I'd had the chance. Didn't change the fact that he was right, of course.

"Oh they won't believe Owl," Carpe said.

I turned to where he'd spent the fight, hiding behind the mausoleum with the laptop. Not even a scuff.

Lightweight.

Carpe spun his computer around for Cooper and me to see. "But I'm betting on them being real interested in this YouTube video. Has a ton of views already, and I only posted it a minute ago."

I watched the arrogance fade to disbelief, then shock as the video played out. Carpe had been live-streaming Cooper trying to sacrifice me on the bench, going on about zombies. Everything had been picked up in the audio, including Cooper talking about his supernatural ally.

Never, ever underestimate a hacker.

Cooper's eyes shot to me, then Carpe. In a surprising show of athleticism, he bolted up and ran for the bridge. He would have made it if Nadya hadn't clotheslined him.

Rynn caught him, and I'm pretty sure he dislocated Cooper's shoulder before connecting Cooper's face with his knee. Before Cooper could scramble back up and make another run for it, Rynn caught him by the back of his green cargo jacket. "New model, remember?" he said, and hit Cooper in the face.

Nadya kicked him hard in the kidney. "If you ever tell me I look good again, Cooper, I will do worse than Alix and Rynn combined."

Cooper stared at her, not believing that the woman previously known as the "superhot chick" amongst our archaeology cohorts had taken him out so easily.

"What do you want to do with him?" Rynn asked me, still holding Cooper's jacket.

"Knock him out until the IAA gets here. And get the damn lamp—"

A gunshot sounded. Rynn, Nadya, and I dove out of the way, leaving Cooper where he was.

Odawaa, his sanity looking worse for wear, kept the gun pointed at us as he motioned for Rynn to back up. The downfalls of fights in places with no cover; I was completely exposed, and so was Rynn.

"I need to recover my losses somehow," Odawaa said as he grabbed Cooper and began to drag him towards the SUV.

Rynn and I started to run after him as soon as the car started, but Carpe stopped us. "Owl!" he yelled. "You need to see this—now." He showed me his laptop.

A CNN bulletin from L.A.—Hollywood Boulevard, to be precise— was now playing. A news presenter was trying to broadcast what looked like a mob of people screaming and running for their lives behind him.

That wasn't what got my attention though . . . it was the line that scrawled across the bottom of the screen. *Zombie Apocalypse of 2014.*

Shit.

20

The Summer Zombie Invasion of Hollywood Drive

Well . . . That one's out of the bag.

I couldn't pull my eyes off Carpe's computer screen.

It was . . . well . . . surreal.

Not the zombies, mind you . . . just how prepared everyone was . . .

"We're not entirely sure yet if this is a hoax or an elaborate publicity stunt orchestrated by one of the local movie production companies," the newscaster said. "But one thing is for certain; locals are voicing their concern—"

I figured the newscaster would've said more, but he was forced to dive out of the way as two Humvees screeched by; their passengers held various weapons out the window, including baseball bats, a rifle, a handgun or two . . . and at least one chain saw. In the background I heard someone yell, "Everyone out of the way—zombie apocalypse—we know what to do!"

I watched a few more seconds of video play out as the Humvees knocked over a street sign and caused two cyclists to careen into a bus stop. I think there was a gunshot fired as well before the camera cut out.

Not one zombie had made an appearance on-screen—just panicking people.

OK . . . somehow I wasn't the least bit surprised. Where there's a will, a way, and a large conglomerate of people with semiautomatic weapons . . .

"I hate to say this, but this is kind of like that game Zombie Walkers—"

Nadya just stared at me in shock. "How stupid are you people?"

"Have you played our video games? We're practically conditioned for this stuff."

She said a few less-than-complimentary things in Russian while I frowned at the screen.

"That's Hollywood Boulevard—there's no way zombies got that far before Lady Siyu dropped them" . . . unless they'd started running. Not a comforting thought . . .

Carpe already had YouTube videos up on-screen. "I think the problem is worse than we initially thought."

He showed me a choice video highlighting a very fresh-looking zombie in a hospital gown. In fact, all the zombies in the image looked . . . well . . . fresh. It really wasn't doing much, just randomly changing direction as people ran and screamed around it, though it did lunge at someone who got too close. Well, at least Cooper had no ambition besides filling the streets with zombies—he hadn't told them to attack or chase or run.

I turned to Lady Siyu. "I thought you said you got rid of the zombies?"

She curled her lip. "I did," she said. "Every zombie here is no longer moving."

"Cooper's curse must have had a wider range than we thought," Rynn added.

She seemed to consider that. "I suppose, not knowing the effect of the multiple artifacts and the addition of your blood, that is possible."

I jerked back from the close-up on the screen as an arrow lodged into the hospital-gown-wearing zombie's forehead while the nearest neighboring zombie had its head smashed in as two guys rode by on bikes, one carrying a crossbow and the other a baseball bat. They traversed the crowd, picking off zombies.

"People are going to get killed," I said. If they hadn't already. "Any sign of the lamp?"

Everyone shook their heads. I noted there was no sign of either Daphne or Alexander. Amidst the gunfire they'd disappeared—without their artifacts, so at least for now their teeth were cut . . . figuratively speaking.

Well, at least I wasn't cursed anymore . . . "Damn it, we need to get that lamp off Cooper."

"He went with Odawaa in the jeep," Rynn said. "Lady Siyu, the elf, and I will deal with them."

I didn't argue. We didn't have a lot of time before the IAA was all over this place—and let's face it, Lady Siyu and Rynn were the best suited to handle the situation.

"We'll try to curtail the zombie hunters before anyone else gets killed," I said, and grabbed Captain's leash before heading off to the gates with Nadya.

"I believe you are forgetting your payment to the pins," Lady Siyu said.

There was the trace of a smile on her face, and she looked happier than she had any right to be. I stuffed Captain under my arm. "Yeah, well, it'll have to wait until I'm back in Seattle. You can have your pick of the treasure then—"

"The payment has already been decided on, and as you are carrying it with you, I see no reason to delay." Her smile widened, and I followed where she was looking.

Captain mewed at me, wanting to be let down.

My heart caught in my chest, and I tightened my grip around him. "No—there is no way I offered you up my cat—"

"You offered your most prized possession, which I attest you are currently holding. The pins do not lie," she said.

My prized possession meant treasure; Captain wasn't a possession, he was my damn cat. Besides, I wasn't convinced I could make him stay with anyone—even if I considered it, which I wasn't. "Over my dead body," I told her.

I think that's what she'd been waiting for. "I will be happy to arrange," she said, and took a step towards us.

Realizing something was up, Captain let out a cross between a mew and a growl.

Rynn stepped between us and grabbed my shoulders. "Alix, not now, it's not worth it," he said.

"I'm not giving that harpy my cat—"

Rynn turned to Lady Siyu. "I don't believe the cat will go willingly this evening, and there is the issue of Alexander and any other vampires in L.A. Can we agree to leave this matter until later?"

She inclined her head in agreement, but the smug expression didn't vanish as she headed towards the black convertible she'd come in.

"Rynn, under no circumstance am I handing over Captain to *her*."

"I don't think it will come to that, but now is not the time or place. We'll find something else, I promise."

I drew in a breath and let Captain down, still holding his leash for dear life. "I'm trusting you," I told him. How could I have been so stupid—it was Lady Siyu!

"I know," he said as he touched his head to my forehead, a heavy look on his face. "Alix, be careful."

I snorted softly. "You're the one going after the pirates and the zombie king. We're just going to try and persuade a few zombie apocalypse enthusiasts to stop . . . well, shooting." I pushed away, wanting to get Captain as far away from Lady Siyu as possible right now in case she changed her mind, but Rynn held me back.

"It's not the humans I'm worried about, it's the supernaturals who might be involved." He glanced to where Lady Siyu was pressing the horn in the black convertible. "Think. Out of all the convoluted things you've seen over the past week, does it make sense that Alexander and

Daphne were behind it? You said it yourself, they had no idea what they were orchestrating." He nodded around at the chaos around us. "And whoever is behind it is someone Lady Siyu, Mr. Kurosawa, and I can't pinpoint—and they don't want us to know what their game is yet." He looked around the cemetery, as if searching. "Despite the chaos, it feels like this was a test—probing, to see where the weak spots are."

"I'd be more concerned about you; you're the one chasing after the powerful artifacts with the Naga."

"Oh I plan on being careful," he said. He kissed me fast—without worrying about who the elf was looking at this time—and ran to join Lady Siyu and Carpe.

Captain with me, I joined Nadya in our jeep. "I don't know about you, but I'm ready to get this clusterfuck over with," I said.

"What is the plan when we reach the zombies?" she said, gunning the engine.

"Your guess is as good as mine, but I'm sure we'll figure something out."

—⁂—

Nadya and I peeled out of the cemetery. We didn't have far to go before we ran into the first batch of zombies. All we had to do was follow the screams.

"Now that we've found them, what the hell do we do with them?" Nadya said as she halted the car in front of a troop of ten or more zombies wearing nothing more than morgue tags.

"That depends—how stupid are these guys?"

In response, Nadya honked the horn three times and hit the floodlights.

The pack of hospital zombies turned away from their slower, screaming, and panicking prey in favor of us.

"Pretty stupid," she said.

I searched around the area. Paramount Pictures wasn't too far away—they had to have gates and buildings that could hold back a few zombies. "We'll lead them out of the way."

Nadya honked the horn again to make sure we kept their attention, and we started leading them towards the movie lot. Best-case scenario, we could get the bulk of them locked up. Once we got to breaking Cooper's damn spell, it'd be easier to spin it as a promotional prank— the IAA loved that stuff.

If we didn't figure out a way to break the spell? Well, worst-case scenario, the assholes at the IAA would eventually find the zombies . . . and they wouldn't be able to attack anyone in the meantime.

Apparently lights and horns were too delectable a temptation for the zombies to resist . . . not only did they take the bait, they picked up their pace too.

"Back up, back up," I yelled at Nadya, banging the top of the jeep as the first few zombies staggered within grabbing range.

"No backseat driving." Nadya threw it in reverse—not too fast, in case the zombies lost interest—and maneuvered into the Paramount lot.

There was a warehouse not too far away. When we got within running distance, I could jump out and open the doors—it looked like we might even be able to drive right through. Lead them in, then close the barn doors behind them, so to speak . . .

It was a good, clean plan. The kind of solution I'd brag about to Rynn the next time he accused me of being reckless.

If it hadn't been for the Humvee cruising by the lot, I think it would have worked.

It was the same guys from the video; a man, who looked like he'd be more at home on the beach, leaning out the front passenger window with a chain saw, and a woman in a camouflage baseball cap leaning out the back window, brandishing a sawed-off shotgun.

The Humvee stopped outside the main gates, and a few moments of silence passed as we sized each other up. Me and Nadya with our pack of zombies, and the zombie hunters with their guns and chain saws.

Yeah, there was only one way this was going to go . . .

"Zombies!" Chainsaw yelled as a battle cry.

A Molotov cocktail followed. Nadya and I ducked as the bottle exploded—spectacularly, to say the least—just short of our jeep, in the midst of the zombies.

Now, you might think this was a fantastic idea. Why not kill all the zombies using fire, then add a few bullets? That solves the problem, doesn't it?

The problem isn't killing the zombies; the problem is firearms and explosives in the average video gamers' hands are dangerous for everyone else around them.

The guy's aim was good. The Molotov cocktail burst over one zombie's head, and from there the fiery contents splashed out onto the rest of the pack, as well as some nearby plants. Those went up fast, the dry leaves acting as an accelerant, and in a matter of minutes the fire had engulfed the guardhouse and the front of Paramount in flames . . . On top of that, zombies now burning towards a second death strayed from the herd, running in every imaginable direction.

We'd only been a few feet away from the open storage trailer too.

Damn it.

A security guard burst out of another building after two flaming zombies crashed into his door. Yelling, the guard ran for the front gate, only slowing down as he caught sight of more flaming zombies setting anything and everything they collided with on fire.

"To your left!" Chainsaw yelled.

Camo hat in the back swung her ponytail and aimed her sawed-off shotgun at the guard, pulling the trigger.

The security guard never knew what hit him. One minute he was watching something out of a bizarre movie, the next . . . well, that was it.

It happened too fast for me to do anything except watch the disaster unfold.

"Son of a bitch, they just shot him," I said.

We both ducked as bullets ricocheted off the jeep. It was only a matter of time before they confused us for the walking dead as well.

Shotgun yelled, "You two been bitten? Come out so we can see you."

Oh for Christ's sake . . . I stuck my head up. "Fuck off, you stupid gamers. This is not a fucking zombie video game."

I ducked back down as they answered me with a shot. Who knew this many people were waiting for a zombie apocalypse in L.A.? Texas, Montana, sure, but L.A.?

Guess an unhealthy fear of home invasion will do that to you . . .

"Well, at least if they're shooting at the jeep, they aren't shooting other people at random," I said to Nadya.

"We need to work on your definition of bright side."

My phone rang. I checked the ID. What the hell did he want?

"Artemis? Bad timing," I yelled as another bullet struck the jeep.

"You're welcome. Been watching things on the news. Quite the Rome burning you have going on out there."

"Can't take all the credit," I said, peeking around the jeep.

"Hey, question . . . are you looking for two men, one brunette all-American, the other African with a number of very scary-looking guns strapped in various locations, possibly towing around a bunch of zombies? Because they're out front."

Fuck.

"I'll take that silence as a yes," he said.

"Thanks, Artemis, I'll get back to you," I said, and hung up. I dialed Rynn next. I swore as his voice mail picked up, then I stole another glance at the trigger-happy zombie hunters.

"Remind me not to play Zombie Walker when it comes out," I said to Nadya.

"Just remember you said that when the time comes."

Now what to do? "We need to split up," I said.

Nadya scowled at me. "Are you sure Lady Siyu lifted that curse? That's the worst idea you've had yet."

"Well, I'm open to suggestions. Otherwise Cooper might get away."

"He doesn't have the other artifacts."

"He only needs those to control the zombies. The lamp is enough to raise them and control the ones walking around here already."

"We both go then," Nadya said, and went for the jeep keys. I stopped her. I did not relish the idea of leaving these nut jobs unchecked.

"We'll flip a coin," I said. "Heads, we both go to Artemis's and look for Cooper, tails I go, you try to handle the Humvee zombie-hunting terrors."

"Deal," Nadya said.

I tossed a coin up in the air, catching it on the back of my hand. Damn, it felt good to have coordination back . . . "Tails," I said.

Nadya swore but didn't try to stop me when I held out my hands for the keys. She hopped out of the jeep . . .

One of these days in the very near future she was going to figure out I had a double-tailed coin . . . I didn't relish that talk, but hey, use the advantage you have.

Before gunning the jeep, I waited for Nadya to run for cover and made sure Captain was safely in his carrier in the backseat.

I didn't have to wait very long. No sooner was Nadya in the clear than she yelled, "Zombies, over here!" at the top of her lungs and booted it behind one of the studio buildings.

It had the desired effect, I'll give her that.

The zombie hunters forgot all about me and took off through the gate after her. I waited until I was sure Nadya was out of range before flooring it onto Santa Monica Boulevard.

I pulled out my phone. "Phone, get me to Artemis Bast's house," I told it. Hopefully I'd be able to reach Cooper and Odawaa before they managed to raise any more zombies and mayhem.

—m—

I turned down Artemis's street and parked in his driveway. No sign of Cooper and Odawaa's SUV, but that didn't mean they hadn't had the brains to hide it somewhere first.

I grabbed my gas mask out of my backpack before stepping out of the car. Somehow I figured that just because there was a zombie apocalypse didn't mean Artemis was going to cancel a party, and I'd had enough incense to last me a lifetime.

When I reached the front though there was a marked absence of . . . well . . . anyone. The door was cracked open, and when I peeked inside— *carefully*—the foyer lights were off and the genie bodyguards absent.

"What do you think, Captain?" I said.

He sniffed around the door before sliding past me on his leash. I followed, losing my gas mask. There was no party, and I don't know if it was lack of incense or the emptiness, but the front ballroom had lost its sheen.

No one was here.

"Got bored rounding up the dead coming to life out there, did you?" Artemis said, though it took me a second to find him.

I did a double take when I spotted him. Artemis Bast was sitting by himself, pouring what had to be a second, third, or fourth drink from a bottle of Jack Daniel's.

He had a spare tumbler beside him and offered it to me. When I hesitated, he added, "No need to worry, I don't bite—much."

As much as I would have loved a drink right about now, something about the situation made me shake my head again.

Artemis shrugged and poured himself another. "Suit yourself," he said, and downed the glass.

He picked up a remote and turned on the television mounted over his bar. Most people were running away from the city center, but there were the select few who were crashing towards it.

Artemis arched a blond eyebrow at me, in almost perfect mimicry of the expression Rynn made. "Apparently the police are asking people to stay indoors. No reason given yet except for civil disturbance."

"Funny that."

He inclined his head and finished off the tumbler of whisky. "IAA will have a hell of a time cleaning this mess up," he said.

Well, on the bright side, I hadn't actually been the one to start the first zombie war of L.A. Still, the way Artemis was watching me . . .

"You said Cooper was here."

He looked down at the glass before looking back up at me. "I lied," he said. "It's been known to happen."

Funny, he didn't seem real remorseful about that . . .

Captain's Spidey sense must have been up too, because he wound his tail around my legs and made a low, questioning growl as he sniffed the air.

"I'm guessing my cousin didn't elaborate on the more sordid details of my bad behavior." He swirled the bottle, his eyes not leaving mine now, but still the pale green.

Captain's hackles rose as he narrowed in on a closed door, stalking towards it as far as his leash would let him. It was the same door I'd stumbled down in a haze, the one that led towards the kitchen.

I frowned at Artemis. "What did you do?"

"*What did I do?*" he repeated, stressing each word carefully as he glanced up at the ceiling. "Let's say someone outside my usual circle of friends made me an offer I couldn't refuse."

I pulled out my phone and speed-dialed Rynn.

"Oh he won't be able to take your call—my new friend was quite adamant about keeping my cousin and Lady Siyu busy for a while."

I left a message anyway. "Rynn, cleanup on aisle six, otherwise known as your delinquent cousin." To Artemis, I said, "Who's your new friend?"

"Wouldn't you like to know?" he countered. "I'd be more concerned about the offer, to be perfectly honest."

I tracked Captain to where he was pushing at the door. Whatever was behind it wasn't a vampire, otherwise he'd be throwing himself at it.

Artemis didn't make any move to stop me, and still no glowing eyes. I pushed the door open just a crack.

There was a woman dressed in a purple dress reminiscent of the one Violet wore the night of the incense party. She turned, slowly.

Shit.

"Charity, right? See, I told you I'd get to stay here forever," she said in a dry imitation of Violet's happy-go-lucky voice.

What had been Violet—or was left of her—was now a wraithlike, dehydrated husk of herself, still wearing her bright makeup, her dress and hair hanging off her like clothing stuck on a Halloween skeleton . . .

I took a step back, shaking my head. "Violet, I am so . . . so . . ." What, sorry? Terrified? A mixture of the two? I took another step back into a broad chest, Artemis's burnt sandalwood and amber musk hitting me.

"Boo," he said in my ear.

I spun around. He loomed in the doorway over me, raising his bottle and pointing at Violet. "I suppose you'll be wanting an explanation," he said.

I wasn't sure which way to turn—Artemis or Violet. Captain wasn't sure either and settled on backing into my legs.

"I'll let you in on a little secret, Owl. I've been very, *very* bad."

21

Skeletons in the Closet

12:00 p.m., Artemis's house of horrors

"Rynn wouldn't approve," Artemis said, leaning in closer.

I ducked under his arm, and Captain and I retreated back into the ballroom. Captain, not sure what to make of Artemis and Violet, gave a confused bleat and hugged my legs.

Artemis's eyes blazed green—brighter than I'd ever seen Rynn's—but the pupils had corrupted to a shade of red.

Shit. I looked at the ground—had to avoid his eyes ... *Come on, Owl. You can handle an incubus* . . . a manic, sociopathic incubus who now collects ... well ... whatever I was supposed to call Violet.

Unfazed, Artemis closed the door on what had been Violet and slowly prowled after me, his head lowered. "I warned you to step out, Alix. Never good to get too mixed up with our kind," he said.

"What the hell did you do to her?" I checked over my shoulder for a window, door—anywhere to run away from Artemis.

He shrugged. "A legend when I was a child, bedtime stories about bad incubi and succubi who drained humans of their life. Wraiths is what you'd call them, I believe," he said, dodging around the table.

I picked up a bar chair and threw it at him. He danced out of its way.

"Rynn said incubi couldn't do any harm," I tried, searching for something to put between us.

"*Choose* not to is more accurate. And that?" he said, pointing back at where Violet had been. "That is something else entirely. Believe me, it was a surprise for me as well. I didn't believe him when he said he could give me this."

Yet another supernatural that had been tempted with something he couldn't refuse. I swallowed, pushing a bar table over as I fled Artemis's advance. "No offense, but your standards in women have really dropped."

He seemed to consider my statement before picking up the table with one hand, as if it weighed nothing at all. It was a copper-top number with a metal base—I'd had to work to push it over. It sure as hell wasn't something I'd ever seen Rynn do before.

From the expression on his face, it seemed to surprise Artemis too. "Hunh, what do you know? Wraith strength bonus. The wonders of my new benefactor never cease." And with that, he launched the table at me.

I dodged out of the way, dragging Captain with me by his harness.

"Depends what you're looking for, now, doesn't it?" He curled his lip. "And I've decided Violet does more for me this way than as a decoration."

I ducked around another bar table—I was fast running out of things to hide behind. Captain wound his way around my ankles, still trying to decide what to make of Artemis. "Captain, if there was a time to go ballistic and attack something, now is it," I whispered. It was no use, though. It was as if Artemis had short-circuited something in Captain's brain.

"Tell you what, let me and the cat go and I won't tell Rynn about Violet of the living dead."

He smiled, but it wasn't meant to reassure me. "How stupid do I look?"

"Seriously? Dude, no offense, but pretty stupid if you think Violet is a healthy expression of affection."

I caught the twitch in his mouth and flash of green before he lunged at me. *Shit, Owl, back up faster . . .* I knocked over another barstool to see if I could trip him up, then ducked around the last table left. I might as well have thrown pillows in his way for all the good it did.

"You know, Alix, I'm not one for cat and mouse. Comes from being a rock star for so long. You get used to getting exactly what you want when you want it."

"I thought you said you were on your cousin's side," I said. I'd run out of bar, but there was a TV area a few feet away. I bolted for it and scrambled over the couch, Captain jumping after me. Artemis didn't bother picking up the pace, continuing his prowl as if he had all the time in the world.

I checked over my shoulder. Artemis was blocking the main exit, but if I remembered correctly, there was a spiral staircase leading upstairs . . .

There was. All I had to do was reach it ahead of Artemis . . . a fall from the second floor wouldn't kill me, would it? Considering my choices were that or whatever Artemis had planned, I was going with fall.

"Now, look at it from my point of view," Artemis said, sounding closer than he should have been . . . like right by my ear.

I gasped as Artemis closed his hand over my mouth. In the moment I'd taken to eye escape routes, he'd closed the distance.

"That disaster a few months ago in Las Vegas did more damage than Rynn and the dragon are letting on," Artemis continued. "Other powerful supernaturals plan on taking advantage of the situation. I'm not one to jump sides at random, but they offered me something I couldn't refuse—" His eyes blared green again, and I turned away. "I think we both know I'm not one to resist temptation."

He grabbed my chin and forced me to look in his eyes. I shut mine tight.

"Rynn's taken an awful lot of things away from me over the years. Let's see how he likes me taking his toys away, shall we?" he said.

I did the only thing that came to mind: slammed my forehead right into his nose. Pain shot through my forehead, but the satisfying crunch of cartilage and yell from Artemis were worth it.

I kicked him off and dove under the glass coffee table, scrambling out as he jumped on top, cracking the glass.

"There's no escape," he called out. "It'll be easier if you just stop running and accept it."

Screw that. I kept running—the stairs weren't that far away.

"I mean it, Alix. I'm too used to instant gratification to give chase."

I hit the stairs running as a beer glass shattered across the banister. Another shattered a framed Kaliope concert poster. Captain bolted past me, taking three at a time.

I made it to the top; Artemis, for all his bluster, wasn't willing to break a sweat and took the steps in his own time. He was reckless and an ass, but he wasn't a total idiot . . .

"Come on," he said, "give in to temptation, just this once."

"Yeah, not tempted," I yelled down. Incubi were harmless, my ass. I was going to give Rynn a piece of my mind on what constituted harmless.

I took off down the hall. Now, to find a second-story window . . . I reached the first door and tried it. Locked.

"Come on now, think of it this way; how will you know you don't like it unless you try? Violet hasn't had any complaints."

Keep him talking, Alix, so you can gauge how far behind you he is. "What kind of idiot do I look like?"

"You *are* dating my cousin."

He must be at the top of the stairs now. I tried the second door. No, that one wouldn't work either.

"Here's the thing. They found me something I wanted more than staying in Rynn's good graces. I'm weak, Owl. Instant gratification is what I live for . . ."

No shit . . . Third door, and no escape there either. I was running out of doors.

"Oh come on now, I know you have a thing for incubi. How the hell else could you stomach Rynn for more than a week—Mr. Fucking Responsible?"

The fourth door opened. Captain darted in ahead of me. "Bing-Oh sweet Jesus, my luck can't be this bad."

The room in front of me was large—more living room than

bedroom, with two large curtained windows on the other side. Nothing between them and me except a collection of ten wraiths still dressed in their nightclubbing outfits . . . with maybe a stripper or three tossed in the mix.

As one, their attention shifted away from each other and the window and fixed on me and Captain.

Captain crept forward, sniffing a hand one of the wraiths stretched out to pet him with.

"Captain," I whispered, and made a grab for his harness. He danced out of my way. I swore and tried again. "Back away from the harem of wraiths, cat." As soon as I had him, I'd follow my own advice . . .

"I wouldn't be so hard on him. They have the same effect on me."

Shit. I turned into Artemis's chest. He grabbed hold of me—painfully, I might add—and half dragged, half towed me towards the nearest wraith, one dressed in a short gold dress eerily similar to the one I'd been wearing my first night here. Captain was still creeping around the wraiths, examining them with his nose, but never getting close enough for them to touch him.

Artemis stroked the wraith's cheek, and she closed her eyes and leaned in, in a twisted caricature of affection from the both of them.

I cringed and tried to shake his grip. "She looks like a corpse," I said.

He glanced down at me. "I figure I've broken a number of rules this time," he said offhandedly. "Though I've been promised Rynn won't be a problem this time. Not until we're done." His eyes glowed green. "Then he can see what it feels like to lose something."

I kicked him in the shin—hard—but it was no use. He only tightened his grip. I stopped struggling. At this rate I'd never get free. I needed time—either for Rynn and Lady Siyu to get their asses over here, or to get me and Captain some serious running room.

"What the hell did you do to them?" I said.

He trailed his thumb down the side of the wraith's cheek until he reached what was left of her lip. "I'd think that was obvious, dear," he said, green eyes back on me. "I've made them completely and utterly *mine*."

I swallowed and focused on the side of his face. "Somehow I don't think that's what they signed up for."

He tsked. "They don't know any different—lost in ecstasy." He breathed in deep, as if the air itself was intoxicating. "And the rush—there's nothing like it, and I've been around a long time." He turned his green eyes back on me before sweeping my legs out from underneath me. I landed hard on the floor, the wind knocked out of me. "Aren't you the least bit curious?" he said, straddling my chest.

I turned my eyes away fast before the incubus bullshit could take effect. *Come on, rein in that flight instinct that keeps you alive* . . . "Why? I mean *look* at them," I said. Bottles, bottles—there had to be an empty bottle or two around here somewhere. This was Artemis, for Christ's sake!

He breathed in deep again. "Rynn was right; I can't help myself from pushing the boundaries," he said, more to himself. "Look, Alix, I'm not a complete monster, but it's Rynn's turn to lose something he cares about."

"What the hell could he possibly have ever done to you?" If I could keep him talking and avoid looking straight in his eyes, maybe he'd give me another opening.

Artemis laughed. "Don't let Rynn fool you with the sympathetic incubus act. Deep down he's just as bad as the rest of us, and believe me, he's not above ripping the odd human throat out to prove a point. Hell, he's done it right in front of me." Artemis growled the last part as I tried to buck him off. It didn't work.

"I'll even give you a choice, which is a far sight more than he ever did for any human I knew. Either become one of my thralls, or die."

The girls started to gather around me, touching my hair and my jacket with their clawlike fingers. "Is this the new friend you brought us? I don't like her dress," one of them said.

"Not as pretty as the rest of us," the one who was touching my hair said.

OK, looks insulted by wraiths—new rock bottom for me.

"Now be nice, girls," Artemis added.

I spotted a bottle by the bed . . . "You want to know what I choose, Artemis?" I said, grabbing his shirt and pulling him close, careful to avoid the eyes. With my foot I rolled the bottle towards me.

He smiled. "Dying to know."

"I'd rather die than join your fan club." As fast as I could, I reached down for the bottle and slammed it into his face. He yelped—whether from surprise or pain, I didn't really care. It had the desired effect. He let the hell go.

"Come on, Captain," I said, sliding out from under him and bolting for the window. The wraiths got out of the way, and for once the cat listened.

I threw back the curtains. The windows were barred.

"We're in Hollywood, dear, what did you expect?" Artemis laughed, still recovering on the carpet from the blow to his head.

I tried to run around the wraiths, but I tripped and landed flat on my face. I glanced down at my feet. They were tied together with panty hose. The wraiths had tied my feet up with damn panty hose while I'd been pinned by Artemis . . .

"Told you they had their uses," Artemis said, pushing me over and pinning my chest with his knee. His eyes glowed green again. I cranked my head to the side, but too late. I felt the euphoria start to spread through me . . . It wouldn't be so bad to look at him? Would it?

Captain's distressed meow broke the hold Artemis was gaining over my mind. I tried to slide out, but Artemis just pinned me harder, forcing my face back where I couldn't help but look at him. For the second time I shut my eyes.

"Open them," he growled.

Part of me really wanted to, was begging me to. I spat, hopefully hitting his face. "Fuck off," I said.

I don't know what shocked me more—the fact that Artemis kissed me, hard, on the mouth, or that his lips burned. He broke it off, still holding my jaw in place.

I started to kick, not that I got anywhere. "At what point did you figure that was a good idea, because I'll tell you right now, your brain fucked it up—"

"Open. Your. Eyes," Artemis said, pronouncing each word like a command. That's just about the effect it had on me.

"Let go of me!" But even as the words left my mouth, I could feel something else creeping through the back of my mind, telling me it wouldn't be such a bad idea—come on, how long could I hold out? Really?

I yelled as Artemis pried my eyelids open with his fingers. I forced the alien thoughts down and struggled harder.

"I hate to do this, I really do, but I don't need to win you over. By the time I'm done with you, you'll love me more than life itself," he said.

"You don't seriously believe those things love you?" I said. I saw Captain creeping up behind Artemis. *Stall, Owl, stall . . .*

"Not really, but it's close enough. Better than the real thing if you consider the perks. And they'll never leave me."

I swore as Artemis straddled my chest, driving his knee into my throat while holding my chin in place with his free hand. I could barely breathe. Why the hell is it that every time I end up dealing with the supernatural, I get the shit kicked out of me? Anyone want to touch that one? Seriously?

The problem with being choked like this is it's damn near impossible not to open your eyes . . .

Artemis's eyes were glowing green, the pupils a dark red. "Time to make you love me," he said.

I started to tell Artemis to fuck off—the words formed in my mind, I started to say them . . . Nothing came out. My mind filled with—well, I won't say it was pleasant, just blank. No pain, no pleasure . . . not a damn thing . . .

I felt something alien reach in, twisting my memories, nothing was off limits—Rynn, Carpe, Nadya. It hurt like a son of a bitch, enough so it snapped me out of the haze and I got control of my voice back.

"Now, Captain!" I yelled as loud as I could manage.

Then it was as if every pleasurable moment in life was ripped to the surface of my mind all at once . . . and tumbled right back down.

Artemis screamed as he clawed at his own back. Captain was riding him as well as any vampire, his tail switching back and forth as he bit him.

Adrenaline helped clear the fog out of my head, and I scrambled out from under Artemis.

"Not so fast," he said, grabbing my foot and dragging me back across the floor. Then he grabbed Captain by the scruff of the neck and threw him at the wraiths.

"Son of a bitch, that's my cat—" I went for his knee, but he caught my ankle. "That emptiness in between the pain and elation?" Artemis snarled. "That's what we live in. We feed off emotion—attraction, lust . . . but love, that's the one we never get enough of. We're parasites, Alix, we don't love anything. We take it to fill the damn void of a pit left inside. It'll be Rynn feeding off yours until your dying breath—how is that for a raw deal? The wraiths? I've drained them dry of every drop of love they've ever had, but at least it's quick and honest, not pulled out over the years. Rynn has screwed you over more than I ever will. Think of it this way. I'm doing you a favor."

Somehow I got the distinct impression this had more to do with Artemis's baggage than any perks . . .

Once again that voice of surrender seeped back into my brain, stronger this time . . .

"Come on, Owl—just let go," Artemis urged, and forced my face to look at the mirrored closet. "Take a look, you're halfway there."

In the mirror was something akin to a wraith, with sunken eyes and graying skin . . .

It was me. Whatever Artemis had done, I looked more like one of the husks than my old self.

"See? I've already won," he growled.

I stared at my reflection a second longer. I had two choices; give in to an inevitable descent into wraithdom, or tell Artemis to take his warped harem and fuck off. I think we know by now which way I go.

I fought harder, kicked, screamed. I watched Captain get back up on his feet and shake his head as the wraiths surrounded him. "Captain! Run, you stupid cat," I managed. If he didn't move it now, one of the wraiths would get him.

Don't ask me how or why, but a single voice crept through the back of my mind, demanding my attention as Artemis pinned down my arms.

"You know, now would be a really awesome time to use that get out of jail free card."

Despite my situation, I snorted. Somehow I seriously doubted Hermes's get out of jail card would do dick all.

"Just saying . . ." Hermes's voice in my head continued. *"Unless that whole wraith thing is what you're going for. To each their own, I guess. Just seems real stupid is all."*

Oh what the hell, I was going to be dead anyways . . .

"I'm trading in my get out of jail free card, Hermes," I said. "Get me the fuck out of here!"

It all happened in a matter of seconds. Even though my eyes were closed, I saw white light blare in front of me, and my jacket pocket warmed against my skin. The scent of burning fabric hit my nose.

Artemis screamed—high-pitched and inhuman—and I felt him roll off me.

I opened my eyes. He'd retreated a few feet away, huddled in a ball. Hermes's card, now singed, fell out of the burned remnants of my coat pocket.

Son of a bitch, it'd worked . . .

Artemis lifted his hand to his face. It was covered in blood from a gaping hole in his chest caused by the flare. "Oh you've got to be fucking kidding me," he said. He threw his head back and laughed, not a sane one. "I cannot fucking believe he got involved. Can't trust fucking supernaturals anywhere." Then Artemis stopped laughing and collapsed back on the floor, his eyes closed.

All the wraiths still surrounding Captain fell in a heap, as if their strings had been cut.

I crawled over to the mirror and breathed a sigh of relief at my reflection. Back to normal. I wasn't a wraith.

Captain growled at Artemis's collapsed body but gave it and the wraiths a wide berth as he headed over to me. I gave him a quick once-over, which he protested. A few bruises from being thrown, but otherwise none the worse for wear.

My phone buzzed. It was Rynn. *There in two.*

I shook my head as I pushed myself up. I checked Artemis. Still unconscious, but I saw his chest move.

Yeah, not leaving him here—I didn't think he'd get up and walk away, but you never knew. Somehow superproximity to the wraiths didn't strike me as a good thing. I grabbed his foot and dragged him out of the room and down the hall. I didn't bother watching his head on the stairs. He deserved whatever headache/hangover he got, and then some . . . Captain rode him the whole way down. There were a few more holes in Artemis's shirt by the time his head hit the ballroom floor.

The main floor was a disaster . . . though oddly enough, the bar itself was still mostly intact, including the booze.

I dropped Artemis, leaned over the still-standing bar, and grabbed a Corona out of the fridge. I took a swig before grabbing a barstool, no lime required.

Next I checked in with Nadya. She'd managed to vamoose the Paramount lot before the IAA agents swooped in. Carpe's YouTube video had apparently garnered a lot of hits before it was mysteriously blocked. I didn't bother giving her the whole rundown, as I thought this was one of those occasions when one had to see to believe.

Rynn showed up first.

"The best part is upstairs, fourth door on the left," I said.

He took in the entirety of the ballroom and checked Artemis before sweeping the rest of the mansion and coming back to join me at the bar.

"Is he dead?" I asked in between sips as Rynn slid onto the barstool beside me.

Rynn shook his head. "Out of commission for a few weeks, but alive."

He nodded at the still-standing rows of alcohol. "I'm beginning to think you want all your fights to end in a bar," he said, then helped himself to a bottle, shaking his head.

Well, there were worse places to end up . . . "How the hell—"

"Don't ask me about the wraiths, Alix. For once I have absolutely no idea." He shook his head again, and I realized Rynn was about as shaken up as me. Artemis had said the wraiths were legend more than anything else.

What Artemis had said to me about Rynn came back, but I pushed it aside. I wasn't giving that much credit to a pissed-off incubus trying to turn me into a wraith. Besides, I may hate the majority of supernaturals—Artemis had climbed spectacularly high on that list— but out of all the people on the planet, Rynn was one of two, maybe three, if I ever forgave Carpe about the cargo plane, who cared about what happened to me.

That meant more to me than the whole wraith/Artemis disaster spread out before us.

Rynn flipped on the TV. More coverage of the zombie war still unfolding in the streets, though the zombies themselves were scarcer. I hoped to hell that was because Lady Siyu had managed to shut the curse off. . . .

I decided we'd both had enough serious supernatural bullshit for a while. "On a scale of one to ten, how mad are you at me for coming here on my own?" I asked.

It took him a moment to catch on. "Depends," he said carefully. "Carpe and Nadya said you destroyed all the pirates' records of dig sites. Tell me why."

I took another sip of my beer. "You're bringing that up now?"

He shrugged. "You asked me if I was mad. It's a valid question. Let's face it; you could have stolen them."

"Don't think I don't have copies," I said.

"Wouldn't dream of it."

"So what is the point?"

"The *point* is that when left to your own devices in a treasure room, you didn't act like a thief first—you did the right thing."

I mulled that one over in my head. "I'm still a thief, Rynn—"

At that he grabbed my chin and made a show of turning my face from side to side. Examining me. He leaned in close enough to kiss me and did.

"Debatable," he said when we broke off.

I let the kiss and what he'd said sink in while I finished off my beer.

"You still scare the shit out of me half the time," I said, and not just because of the supernatural thing.

"You're still a complete and utter train wreck—unless you'd like to argue the point, though I have to warn you the entire supernatural community is on my side." I didn't miss the trace of a smile. "Just give me a few more months," he added. "We'll see how much of a thief you still are."

I frowned at that. I don't like change. Rynn was change, working for Mr. Kurosawa was change . . . Then again, as hallucinated Captain had suggested, maybe reevaluating my life wasn't necessarily a bad thing. I shook that idea off before it dug any more roots into my brain than I was comfortable with.

Give credit where credit is due; Rynn knows when to drop a subject. He nodded back at Artemis's body.

"Care to explain how that hole in his chest happened?"

I gave him the short run of events and finished by pulling Hermes's now charred card from my pocket. I figured I'd keep it as a souvenir. I frowned as I noticed the gold letters had changed, and there was now a red void stamped on the card. *Score one for Owl not fucking up. Thank fucking God, cause I had twenty grand riding on this.*

I snorted and resisted the temptation to crumple the card as I forked it over to Rynn. He turned the now fragile piece of paper over in his hands before handing it back to me. Then he wrapped his arm around my waist and pulled me in, touching his head against my forehead.

"Alix, you may be the biggest train wreck I've ever known, but you're lucky as all hell."

Any minute now Nadya and Carpe would come crashing through, but somehow this toed the balance between enough and not too much between us—at least until we got this mess cleaned up and the hell out of Dodge.

You know, I try to stay away from the supernatural. I'm terrified of them, they hate humans, every time I run into them something goes horribly wrong . . . I mean, Alexander is still trying to kill me . . . probably Daphne now too . . .

I used to go by one rule; no supernatural jobs.

But then again, I don't do normal—or at least I sure as hell don't do it well—and out of the three people I call friends in the world, only one is human.

Oh screw it. What I need to do is make a rule about lying to myself.

I'm Alix Hiboux, supernatural antiquities thief for hire . . .

—⁓—

The door to Artemis's mansion slammed open, and the telltale click of expensive heels fell across the floor.

Lady Siyu. Shit.

She strode right up to me, carrying a bright red cat carrier over her shoulder. She held it out to me. "The cat, as per our agreement," she said.

Oh hell no. No way was I following through on this. I grabbed Captain from where he'd wound his way around my feet and clutched him to my chest. "Go to hell. It was a bad deal and you know it."

The corner of her lip curled up. "Yes, well, you are the expert at bad deals, aren't you? The cat. *Now*," she repeated.

I clutched Captain tighter under one arm while I reached back with the other and palmed a bottle. "Over my dead body," I said.

Her smile widened, showing a hint of fang. "My pleasure," she said, and took a step towards me.

"Alix, no!" Rynn added something to Lady Siyu in supernatural before pushing me behind the bar as she retreated to the doorway.

"Rynn, what the hell are you doing? I could have gotten the drop on her with the bottle," I said.

"You have to give her the cat," he said.

"Are you out of your mind? I am *not* giving Captain to that monster. He isn't some possession to be handed off."

"Believe me, I know. But you made an agreement with her."

"Yeah well, the agreement *sucks*."

He glanced over his shoulder to where Lady Siyu waited, watching us. "Please, I'm begging you. If you don't uphold your end of the bargain, there'll be nothing I can do. You, Captain, Nadya—everyone will die."

"So, what? Just give in and fork over Captain? Rynn, I can't do that to him!" Captain was more than just my cat. He'd saved my life more times than I could count, and he'd been my best friend for the past year. Hell, that cat was the last redeemable quality I had left! I couldn't just fork him over.

Rynn was looking worried now and hazarded another glance at Lady Siyu. He tightened his grip on my arms. "Please, I'm begging you to trust me. I swear to you, we'll get him back, but this isn't the way."

Trust him. He couldn't have started off with something easy, like falling back with my eyes closed?

Deep down I didn't think I could beat Lady Siyu in a fight. And Rynn was right; if I couldn't beat her, all running would accomplish was getting all of us dead. I was good at running, but I couldn't guarantee I was good enough to evade Mr. Kurosawa's reach—not if Nadya and Captain's lives were both on the line.

Son of a bitch. "I can't believe I'm doing this," I said to Rynn as I walked back over to where Lady Siyu waited.

I grabbed the red carrier from her hand and headed back to the bar. I held it open for Captain, and after a quick sniff he walked right in. I was starting to wish I hadn't trained him to do that. *Come on, Alix, do this fast, otherwise you won't be able to go through with it.* I zipped it up and pressed my face against the screen.

Sensing something was up, Captain let out a questioning meow.

"OK, I don't know how much of what I say you actually understand, but this is temporary, I promise."

Before I changed my mind and without sparing another look at Rynn, I walked back to Lady Siyu and handed her the carrier. Captain meowed again, this time more insistent. How the hell did I explain to my cat what was going on?

"It's temporary," I told her. "And if there's so much as a scratch on him—"

Rynn added something I didn't understand, but to be honest, I didn't care. Captain let out another distressed meow, and it was all I could do to keep staring at Lady Siyu's face.

She hefted the carrier over her shoulder. "Wouldn't dream of it," she said. Spinning on her heels, she headed back outside.

With my cat.

Figuring something was up now, Captain howled and began to attack the carrier door. "Captain, I'll get you back, I promise," I yelled. Yeah, I know cats don't speak English. I didn't care.

Rynn stopped me from following her outside. I think he knew I was close to breaking my bargain. "We'll get the cat back," he told me.

I didn't break away as Lady Siyu drove off with Captain. I just hoped to hell I'd put my trust in the right person this time—because if I hadn't, I didn't know if I'd be able to live with the price.

Epilogue

Crawling Out of the Woodwork

Two weeks later, early June, Seattle

I wound my way past the early weekend tourists out of Pike Place Market, red flames baseball cap pulled down and cargo jacket on. I fit right in. Damn, it was good to be back.

I'd been back at my apartment for a couple days now without Captain. It'd taken almost two weeks to recover from the curse, and Lady Siyu had refused to let me out of her sight. Trust me—neither of us had enjoyed a minute of it, but she takes her orders very seriously. Good thing Rynn had been there, because I'm pretty sure I would have hit her. If I never hallucinate again, it'll be too soon—that goes double for evil incubi and curses.

Man, if Mr. Kurosawa ever gives her the OK to kill me . . .

At least a long scratch on Lady Siyu's arm told me Captain had gotten a good swipe in, letting her know who was in charge. Lady Siyu might have my cat now, but she wasn't keeping him. Not if I could do anything about it.

On the way back home, I passed by a pub TV screen recapping what had been dubbed the "L.A. summer zombie fiasco of 2014," Cooper's face pictured in the upper left corner. At the next red light, I stopped to check my news feeds. Some people said it was an elaborate publicity hoax perpetrated by Zombie Walker, while others said it was a small-scale terrorist attack. There were two things everyone agreed upon though; a citywide dispersal of LSD and the involvement of former archaeologist Dr. Cooper Hill . . .

I shook my head and kept going. Same old IAA . . . at least they'd found Cooper where Rynn and Lady Siyu had left him. Lady Siyu had wanted to kill him, but Rynn had managed to convince her the IAA would do much worse. He was right—they would.

Though I have to admit, Cooper in Siberia brightened my day . . . and it being June, Seattle was having its brief run of sun. My week was looking up.

I lugged my groceries back into my building, restocking the fridge—with food, not beer. Rynn was arriving this afternoon. I'd spent the last three nights playing World Quest—true to their word, the game designers had left our characters intact. I'd been getting back at Carpe in my own way. I'd had an item in my inventory for a while—a pair of gloves called Black Friday. They let me pilfer from the loot piles before Carpe could see what was there. Byzantine had been bleeding him dry.

I won't pretend things were back to normal, but I think by now we've established I don't do normal. I'd settled on calling this downtime. Rynn was still working for Mr. Kurosawa, but they were looking for a replacement now. And Rynn was taking a step back from overseeing my projects, instead acting as a consultant. I think Rynn might have been happier about that than I was . . .

To be honest, I don't think I'm ever going to get used to the whole "relationship thing" . . . but maybe that's what makes it special? Who knows? I'm done with philosophizing about the ins and outs of the human mind for a few months—I'd leave that to Rynn's hobby and worry about pretending I'm a responsible adult in a mature adult relationship.

I don't think I'm fooling anyone, most of all Rynn.

Regardless, I'm not going to run, and Rynn will stay out of my work.

We've agreed to that much.

I give Rynn two days past my next job . . .

The only thing I hadn't talked to him about after the zombie fiasco was what Artemis had told me about Rynn and incubi in general. Not for the reasons you might think though. Oh I'd be lying if I said it wasn't wedged somewhere in the back of my head, but if I started listening to every crazy supernatural who shot their mouth off while they were trying to kill me, well, I'd go nuts . . . or take their advice and proverbially jump off a cliff.

Besides, it brought up things that went well and far past my comfort line in the sand.

As far as Cooper, Odawaa, and the lamp? It's a hell of a lot more boring than you'd think. Rynn and Lady Siyu eventually caught up to Cooper, took the lamp, and—at Rynn's insistence and against Lady Siyu's inclinations—left him tied up like a present for the IAA. Like the genie legends of old, as soon as the lamp changed hands, the magic animating the zombies was broken. The invasion was over. Odawaa got away—not surprising, considering he's a pirate. The more unsettling question was who the hell was pulling all the strings.

Someone had told Artemis how to make wraiths, a trick that had long been forgotten . . . for good reason. It drove the incubi and succubi nuts. Artemis included. The same someone was behind Cooper, and Alexander and Daphne as well.

I did my best not to think about it. If I could help it, I planned on staying the hell out of supernatural politics. Note I didn't say never—see? I'm learning.

The kitchen light was on when I opened the door to my condo. I could have sworn I'd turned it off.

"Rynn?" He'd texted me when his plane left a couple hours ago, but he shouldn't be here yet, should he?

My phone rang with the '80s video-game chime and snake hiss before I could consider it more. Damn it, my day had been looking up.

"Lady Siyu," I answered.

"I instructed you to call once a day."

Come on, big breath, Owl. She's in Las Vegas, she can't hurt you ... much.

"I did. I texted you this morning." Besides, the headaches left over from the curse had ebbed off, along with the dreams. I barely needed her help anymore. What I needed was my cat ...

"Clearly you do not grasp the difference between a phone call and a text. I suggest you familiarize yourself with those terms—the internet should prove useful."

Now she gets a sense of humor ... "My apologies, oh great Lady Siyu, for assuming a text would be adequate when you requested a phone call."

I dropped my groceries on the counter, headed to my kitchen window overlooking Seattle harbor, and grabbed a beer from my fridge.

"See that it does not happen again. I have sent a list of instructions for your recovery."

"Got it," I said. Basically a list of approved things for me to eat and not eat. Let's just say I was glad to be as far away from her as possible. Beer was not on the approved list.

"I took the liberty of having tea delivered to your residence," Lady Siyu continued.

I noticed the paper bag on my counter and opened it. Inside was a large glass tub of tea, along with other packets. "Found it," I said. More out of curiosity than anything else, I opened it up and took a whiff. "Jesus Christ, what the hell is in here?"

"You will drink that tea three times a day."

"Like hell I will. Have you smelled this?"

"I do not care what you do, or do not wish."

Goddamn it . . . just when you think you get away . . . "This must really kill you, being forced to keep me alive. I mean, does Mr. Kurosawa enjoy sticking the knife in and turning?"

"*Silence,*" Lady Siyu said. There was a brief pause on the other end, which I used to gulp my beer. "Unlike you, I possess not only your cat but honor—" she continued.

She had to rub it in.

"As such, until I deem you fit from your most recent self-inflicted disasters, I am charged with administering your care. You will make a full recovery as per my instructions from Mr. Kurosawa, which means you will follow my diet and drink the foul tea. Do I make myself clear?"

There was a threat in her voice I didn't like. Only Lady Siyu could turn being some kind of supernatural healer into a threat. "Or else what?" I asked.

There was that hiss—long and drawn out. "If for one moment I get the impression you have deviated from my instructions by even a fraction, I will have no choice but to travel to Seattle. You do not want me to have to travel to Seattle," she said, and hung up.

I stood there and stared at my phone. I'd worry about Lady Siyu when Rynn got here. He'd know how serious her threat was.

I headed to my office. I was still hoping I could find something in my collection Lady Siyu wanted more than Captain, though I hadn't had any luck so far . . .

I stopped in the doorway. Now, I know I hadn't left that open.

Shit.

Sitting in my office chair was the IAA woman with brown hair wrapped in a bun, who'd been tailing me in Egypt and shown up at Alexander's bar on the Sunset Strip. I took a step back and glanced at the kitchen . . . where the hell did Rynn say he'd ditched the knives? The not kitchen ones . . .

The woman stopped me though by raising and aiming a small black handgun. She was as bad as Nadya; the gun matched the suit.

I noticed my gold cuffs—Cleopatra II's, the ones I'd lifted in Algeria—sitting on her lap.

I frowned. I hate it when people touch my stuff.

"I'm just here to talk," she said, returning my cuffs and standing up, leaving the shadow caused by my office's artificial lighting and lack of windows. I take preservation of my artifacts seriously.

Yeah, IAA. Just here to talk. I took another step back. Damn it, I wished I had Captain here—or Rynn, or Nadya . . .

I swallowed. "You always bring firearms to friendly conversations?" I did my best to keep my voice civil as I checked the doorways. No shadows, and they hadn't bothered to kill the lights . . . apparently this was the only IAA suit here. I still had to stop myself from running for the front door. I would have if I hadn't thought there was a slight chance she'd shoot me.

She smiled at that. "Never hurts to be cautious. Where's the incubus?"

"Coming from the garage," I lied.

There was that smile again. "We can kill him, you know."

"Doubt that very much."

She smiled. "I can kill you."

I shrugged. "You're welcome to try, though in all fairness, two vampires, a crazy, power-mad incubus, and a pack of Somali pirates didn't manage it. My boss the dragon will be pretty pissed too." I noted the black comm piece. Someone above her pay grade would be listening in. "Go on, check with your bosses. I'm betting you aren't cleared to do anything more than talk to me."

Well, maybe rough me up, but nothing serious. Kidnapping was out. Again, angry dragon.

As I suspected, someone confirmed more or less what I'd said, and her smile faltered. OK, I was on better ground than I thought.

She switched tactics. "The incubus left the airport twenty minutes ago, though my operatives are tailing him."

Yeah, somehow I didn't think they were tailing Rynn as much as they would like to think they were. I'd be willing to put money on them being in for a surprise.

"And you are correct. Incubi are notoriously hard to kill—even when they're weakened like our reports indicate he is." Her eyes perked up with renewed interest as she regarded me.

Maybe supernatural wasn't above her pay grade.

"Is that why he's hanging out with you?" she asked. "We've been trying to figure that one out. Never ceases to amaze me how far off psych exams can be. Never pegged you for someone to fall in with an incubus, but then, one never can tell. We never figured you for someone to go rogue."

"What do you want?" I said, pronouncing each and every syllable so she got the idea I wasn't interested.

She pulled out a folder and placed it on my coffee table, one that Alexander's vampires had trashed with knives and I hadn't yet had a chance to fix.

"You're a very difficult woman to find, Ms. Hiboux. If it hadn't been for your escapades through Bali last year, we would never have picked your trail back up." She looked up at me. "Lucky us."

I wracked my brain. I'd covered my tracks well—I know I had. Hell, Carpe had even said I'd covered my tracks . . .

On top of the file was the one thing I hadn't counted on. A printed cell-phone snapshot of me getting off a flight in Bali as my alter ego, Charity.

"How?" I said, holding up the photo.

"Oh it took us a while to piece everything together. That's why I wasn't here two months ago. You're very good."

Not fucking good enough apparently . . .

"We want to hire you," she said, and pushed the file towards me.

I snorted. "Go to hell." Like hell I was working for them. I'd be better off having them ship me off to Siberia and throwing me in a jail cell. At least there was a chance I'd escape from Siberia. Working for them? That'd be like letting a cancer keep growing.

My refusal didn't bother her one bit. In fact, she smiled. "We thought you might have that sort of response, which is why I have leverage to negotiate."

She pulled a file out of a black leather briefcase and handed it to me. It was a professional folder, expensive and leather-bound. Inside was a contract.

"It is perfectly legal," she said. "I suggest you have your current employer vet it so you can be assured how serious we are."

"What is it?"

"A very detailed and complex legal document."

"The short version. For the disgraced and retracted archaeology thief in the room, please."

"It is a contract exonerating you from any wrongdoing during your research tenure and in any of your activities since then. It also includes a provision to accept your thesis, as well as award your degree and admission back to the IAA ranks." She paused to let that sink in. "It also gives you the choice of several project sites, fully funded. The Ephesus site you applied for during your last year is listed there as well."

The contract felt hot in my hand—and not some remnant from the curse but because the IAA didn't make deals like this, regardless of whether they were in the wrong.

This was blood money.

On top of that, I didn't for a second believe they had any intention of keeping their word.

I glanced back up at the agent. "You can walk yourself the hell out of my apartment before I throw you out."

"Don't you even want to hear what the job is first?"

"No, you already know too much about me, and I already know too much about you." I tossed the contract back on the table. "And you forget; I know you guys don't keep your word. I signed one of these two years ago."

Her smile faltered at that. "That contract was unfortunately never recorded by Dr. Hill and was missing until quite recently. We regret any inconvenience that might have caused you and as a result are waiving responsibility for your activities over the past two years. Of which there are many."

I pointed down the hallway. "Right now I want you out of my apartment," I said. The woman smiled and stepped by me, gun still out but no longer aimed. "I'll just leave this with you, shall I? In case you change your mind."

There was a threat veiled in there. "Just remember, lady, I've got more problems with supernaturals than I can handle. You barely rate a sweat."

The smirk was back but not nearly as pronounced as before. "That's right, you do have a habit of pissing off . . . well, everyone."

I watched her until she reached my door, then she slowly turned on her heels. "Aren't you even curious what we want?"

I shook my head. "No."

"World Quest," she said.

I shrugged, trying to convey nonchalance. "Open the computer and log on. Can I have my IAA pardon now?"

"Not the game," she said. "The IAA wants you to find the developers." And with that, she let herself out.

Shit. I locked the door behind her and ran a program that swept my place for bugs before picking up the file and opening it.

Two hazy head shots that looked vaguely like the developers' characters, a list of IP addresses of last known locations . . .

I had no interest in finding these guys. The IAA could take their shiny get out of jail free card and stick it back through their black hearts. I knew from experience their deals weren't worth the paper they were written on.

I'd have tossed the file in with the rest of the garbage except for the note at the bottom. "Oh you got to be fucking kidding me . . ."

They weren't just contacting me. If it had just been me, I'd have had no problem ignoring it.

They'd opened up a bounty on the World Quest developers.

Acknowledgments

Thanks go out to my husband, Steve, and my friends, Leanne Tremblay, Tristan Brand, and Mary Gilbert, who read each and every chapter. I don't know if I would have finished the book without their feedback and encouragement.

I also have to thank my agent, Carolyn Forde, who picked my manuscript out of the slush pile; Alison Clarke and Adam Wilson, who both saw something in Owl; and my editor, Sean Mackiewicz, for his keen eye and hard work. There are many other people who have mentored and encouraged me in my writing career over the past few years, but this space is small. Thank you all!

Finally, there is one nonhuman without whom this book would never have been written, and that is my cat, Captain Flash, on whom the character Captain is absolutely based.

About the Author

Kristi is a scientist and science fiction/fantasy writer who resides in Vancouver, Canada, with her spousal unit, Steve, and two cats named Captain Flash and Alaska. She received her BSc and MSc in Molecular Biology and Biochemistry from Simon Fraser University, and her PhD in Zoology from the University of British Columbia. Kristi writes what she loves—adventure-heavy stories featuring strong, savvy female protagonists.